Corporal Jack

Corporal Jack

MARJORIE QUARTON

COLLINS
8 Grafton Street, London W1
1987

AUTHOR'S NOTE

This is a book about a famous regiment and a real dog. Jack, the regiment mascot until its disbandment, was discovered wounded in a German trench at Festubert on April 12th 1917. The military actions in the book are fact and I have used contemporary letters, diaries and trench maps as well as the official regimental history.

The characters, except the historical characters, are fictitious and resemblance to anyone living or dead is accidental. Events other than battles are fiction as are most of Jack's adventures, although I was told as a child that he was 'both promoted and decorated'.

Many thanks to the people who have helped me in my research for the book.

William Collins Sons & Co. Ltd
London · Glasgow · Sydney · Auckland
Toronto · Johannesburg

Permission to quote from 'Fruit Gathering'
by Rabindranath Tagore is gratefully received
from Macmillan Publishers

BRITISH LIBRARY CATALOGUING IN PUBLICATION DATA

Quarton, Marjorie
Corporal Jack.
I. Title
823'.914[F]   PR6067.U3/

ISBN 0-00-223069-0

Photoset in Linotron Meridian by
Rowland Phototypesetting Ltd
Bury St Edmunds, Suffolk

Made and printed in Great Britain
by Robert Hartnoll (1985) Ltd., Bodmin, Cornwall

Festubert, April 12th, 1917

The spring night was clear and cold. The snow had stopped falling an hour ago; the wind had dropped, and it was starting to freeze. There was muddy snow in the bottom of the trench, and clean snow on top of the sandbagged parapet. Beyond the parapet lay the terrifying unknown. As always in snow, it was not quite dark. What light there was glimmered ghostily – somehow more threatening than utter blackness.

There was tension in the air – a feeling of expectancy. Jack pressed companionably against Kurt's leg in its high, clumsy boot. A dog needed human company in such a place.

Jack looked up doubtfully at Kurt's familiar figure; friend of a thousand days' shooting, snaring and trapping of game in the Baltic forests of their home. With Kurt beside him, Jack almost persuaded himself that he must be safe, although this freezing, slushy ditch did not feel like a safe place. Kurt will protect me from danger, thought Jack.

Kurt was trembling from head to foot. Perhaps he was cold. His ill-fitting grey uniform smelled, as Kurt did himself, of sauerkraut and sausage – a homely, interesting smell. He wore a little round cap with a band of Prussian blue on his cropped, sandy head.

As well as the familiar scents of food, sweat and beer, Jack's sensitive nose picked up more disquieting signals. He smelled fear and steel and filth and blood and death. Why, oh why were they there? Gritty snow stung his paws. He raised one, examined it, and licked it like a cat; then his thoughts returned to Kurt, alone and in danger. There were others in the trench, but Kurt and Jack stood apart, at the top of the ten concrete steps which led down to the young Baron's dugout.

What seemed like sinister silence to the men huddled in the trench was a medley of sounds to Jack's sharper hearing. Down in the dugout, he could hear the murmur of old Helmuth's voice as he helped Hansel to get ready for bed. A sentry changed places with another; in the distance a horse moved restively. Jack could hear the breathing of the nearest group of soldiers and see the mist of their breath. Faint creaks and rustlings were on all sides. Somebody stifled a sneeze.

Suddenly, close by, a nightingale sang. Kurt started violently. Until now, Jack had tried to believe that Kurt was not afraid. Now, there was no denying that fear – fear which was close to panic. What evil fate had brought them to France? Jack must hide his own fears now. He must reassure Kurt, whose long bony wrist and workworn hand were just visible in the gloom.

Kurt was terrified. He was only seventeen, the same age as the century. He had been moved up to the support trench half an hour before, and had been separated from his master, the young Baron, Hansel von Hessel. With one sweaty hand, he convulsively gripped his rifle, the other hand fondled Jack's smooth black head. Kurt's mouth, usually half open, quivered over clenched teeth.

Jack pushed his nose into the boy's damp palm. It was many years since he had thought of his mother, but now a picture came to his mind. Jack remembered the stable where he had been born, and his mother, Lottie, a present fit for a king.

Autumn 1909

CHAPTER ONE

King Edward VII was in a bad temper. Sourly, he glanced at the streaming window panes and edged his armchair nearer to the fire. His private study was warm, even stuffy, but he shivered. He felt horrible. His head ached, his stomach ached, his chest felt raw from his last bout of coughing. He reached for his cordial, gulped half, grimaced, swallowed the rest. Wiping his beard, he glared at Sir John Hawk, his secretary.

'I tell you, I can't remember a thing about it. Get rid of the man. No – give him some tea or beer – whatever you like. Come back in half an hour.'

The King leaned back and shut his eyes as the door closed behind Sir John. Asleep at his feet, Caesar, his fox-terrier, whined and twitched, hunting imaginary rabbits in his dreams. He pushed the dog gently with his foot to quieten him. God, he felt ill! He couldn't for the life of him remember inviting Baron Heinrich von Hessel to Balmoral for a week's shooting; he must have been mad. Yet there must have been an invitation, dates must have been discussed, arrangements made. For here was the Baron at Sandringham, at the beginning of the shooting season, his great bulk almost filling a cab, a satisfied smile on his usually impassive face. Behind, two more cabs carried a retinue of servants, a lame schoolboy, a smaller boy and a mountain of luggage. Yet another cab carried a small armoury of sporting guns and equipment. Why, in Heaven's name, had he asked them to come?

The Baron was a relation. All of Kaiser William's cousins were relations. Had to be – the Kaiser was the King's nephew, and one of Queen Victoria's many grandchildren. The King had never really sorted them all out. There were scores of foreign relations – German, Russian, Greek – he found the pedigrees of his racehorses more interesting. Winning the Derby with Minoru had been the one bright spot in a dismal year.

Ah yes, he remembered now. It had been during his first and last state visit to Germany in January. The King had been advised against travelling by his doctors, and had refused to take their advice. A mistake. He'd had bronchitis and had quarrelled with his nephew. Everything had gone wrong. The reception committee had met the wrong train, he'd had a frightening fit of choking at dinner, his uniform had been too tight.

There had been a dreadful banquet, with endless speeches, at Potsdam, followed by a visit to a sporting estate miles from anywhere, buried in pine forests. Stralsund, was it? Practically in Poland anyway. The shooting party had been caught in a blizzard, and they had all stayed overnight in Baron von Hessel's enormous and rather beautiful house. Yes, of course. He also had an enormous and rather beautiful wife. Six feet tall in her brocade dancing slippers, her piled-up auburn hair added another eight or nine inches. Eloise. Yes. There had been some brats about, he seemed to remember, two boys and a plump schoolgirl with flaxen plaits. The girl had a pretty little English governess, Miss Briggs.

Surely he'd suggested that the whole family should come, not the males alone. Oh yes, he remembered now. The party collected in front of the huge creeper-covered, many-gabled mansion, himself in expansive mood. The Baroness had the best cook in East Prussia, and the Baron the best cellar. What a dinner it had been! And he and Eloise von Hessel, seated at the end of the great gleaming table, fully twenty feet away from the Baron at the other end, had talked about boating on the Thames. This German Juno, this Valkyrie, wasn't at all what she appeared to be. She had been born in Surrey. Amazing.

'Why, I am more German than you are, Baroness. I've played many a hand of whist with Reggie Entwistle.'

'I am German now. A genuine *Hausfrau.*'

Clear green eyes met opaque blue. The butler poured more wine.

The next morning, the King extended a warm invitation to his host and hostess to visit England later in the year. It was rapturously accepted. The Baron, an important man in his own area, was no end of a snob, and expressed his thanks in a wordy, complicated speech. Finally, overwhelmed, as he said, with joyful gratitude, he presented his royal guest with a valuable retriever bitch named Lottie.

This sort of thing was one of the hazards of kingship – receiving unwanted presents at every turn. Whatever one's feelings of revulsion or embarrassment, one must pretend delight, while graciously accepting the offering. State visits were the worst, but even on a private holiday in Scotland he had managed to return home with enough tartan material to kilt a Highland brigade, and a portrait of himself and his Queen carried out in needlework by orphans.

The dog would at least be useful. Large, heavily built and handsome (like the Baroness), Lottie was highly intelligent and perfectly trained. The King had noticed and admired her. Unwise to admire other people's property – he'd found that out years ago.

The easiest way out of his social obligations towards the Prussian Baron and his entourage was to plead illness, and despatch the lot of them to Scotland for the whole of their stay. Perhaps the Duke of Buccleugh would put them up. He'd been obliging about the rude and troublesome Crown Prince. His home was almost as grand as Balmoral, and much warmer.

He rang the bell. The Duke must be asked immediately.

'Kindly send Sir John Hawk to me.'

Baron Heinrich von Hessel was unused to being snubbed. He, cousin and friend of the Kaiser, holder of the coveted Order of the Black Eagle, had been sent off to Scotland to stay with some Duke unknown to him. Intolerable! He had been publicly humiliated. He did not accept his royal cousin's plea of ill-health, neither did he believe that Eloise's letter had gone astray.

How glad he was that he had not allowed Eloise to accompany him! Unbending in matters of protocol, she was even quicker than the Baron to suspect an affront. The King would not have slighted *her* with impunity, that he knew.

The Baron, transferred at Sandringham from his cab to a royal Daimler, continued to rage and fume throughout the day-long drive up to Scotland. When he arrived, he sulked and gloomed, and made the long-suffering Duke of Buccleugh heartily sorry for agreeing to put him and his valet up overnight. The rest of the entourage had travelled north by train, and the Baron would join them at Balmoral. He was only slightly mollified by the promise of a two-day shoot on the royal estates.

Next day, the Baron bowed the stiffest of farewells to his host, and departed for Balmoral. Circumstances demanded that he share his car with his valet, Helmuth Müller. Never before had he been forced to drive with a servant other than a coachman or a chauffeur. Disgusting! The drive passed in total silence.

The Baron's temper improved when he reached Balmoral. The rest of the party, who had not stayed with the Duke, were there before him, the accommodation was suitably grand, and the servants treated him with the respect he considered to be his due.

He was pleased to note that the retriever bitch that he had presented to His Majesty looked well. She had produced seven puppies by the very best of the King's famous black retrievers. He understood that four of the whelps had died young. That was regrettable, as was the insolent manner of the elderly retainer who had charge of the dogs. However, one must be magnanimous; one must not blame Cousin Edward for the carelessness of a gamekeeper. The Baron had many times regretted his generous impulse; it had been madness parting with Lottie. He should have kept her to carry on her line. For the Baron, the management of his estates came a poor second to his sport.

The bitch recognized him with evident pleasure. She too had always treated the Baron with deference.

*

Unknown to her late master, Lottie had sinned. Her sin, however, was fashionable in the Edwardian era. Lottie had been seduced; but that was not how Hamish McKenzie, retired gamekeeper, had put it.

Hamish had been both angry and worried. He might easily be blamed for Lottie's slip-up. She had been sent by train to Sandringham to be mated with Shot, the best retriever in the kennel. On her return, Hamish had locked her in a stable with a zinc-lined door, and pocketed the key. You couldn't trust the new stable-lad an inch; Hamish meant to make sure that Lottie didn't get out. There was a little window high up in the wall, but she was far too heavy to scramble up there. He had considered blocking it up and decided not to bother. It was higher than his head.

The following morning, Hamish had taken Lottie her food as usual, and found two shame-faced dogs waiting for him, apologetically wagging their tails. Hamish had grabbed Roy, the shepherd's dog, hauled him through the door, and would certainly have kicked him if he had been more active, or the dog less so. For a time he had cursed his misfortune, and cursed Lottie, now placidly eating porridge. He had resolved to tell nobody. Perhaps the bitch would breed to the arranged mating – it was more than probable, he told himself; if not, why, Roy was the cleverest working collie in the area. If he hadn't been clever, he wouldn't have got through that wee window.

Lottie's puppies gave the show away completely. Four of the seven had white rings round their necks – nobody but Hamish ever saw *them*. One puppy had white toes on both hind paws, the other two were black all over. Perhaps their muzzles were a little more pointed than Lottie's, their ears set rather higher, their coats less dense and close. Hard to say at that age.

Hamish had worked at Balmoral, first as keeper, then as odd job man, for more than sixty years, so he felt entitled to a little peace in the afternoons. Once praised by Prince Albert, he had a secure position for life, and had long ago become a Character with a capital C. All the royal visitors declared that he was a dear old man, and pressed shillings and even florins into his knotted, leathery hands. The other servants thought he was an expensive old nuisance; idle, bad tempered, and collecting tips others had earned.

Guests usually walked round the gardens before luncheon, then round the stables. After that, they were seen no more until next day. In any case, visitors nowadays were rare.

Hamish considered the jobs he still had to do. None was vital. No one would be any the wiser if he knocked off as soon as he'd fed the bitch and her remaining three puppies. He was preparing food for them in the sculleries, when his name was called by Baird, who had succeeded him as keeper. Hamish grunted, without moving. Long service gave him the right to be rude, he considered. Anyway, what was Baird doing here? The King was down at Sandringham; no shooting guests were expected.

'I've found a use for you at last,' said Baird, who gave as good as he got when it came to rudeness. He hated Hamish. 'There's two German lads here, dukes or earls or some such thing. You're to keep them amused for a couple of hours while their Dad sleeps off his lunch. They're coming now.'

Hamish glowered at Baird, sucking his toothless gums. 'Amused? How?' he asked.

'Don't ask me. Show 'em the dogs. Tell 'em some funny stories.'

Baird walked off, chuckling to himself, as the housekeeper led Axel and Hansel von Hessel into the yard. As she withdrew, both turned and bowed stiffly.

'Many thanks, *gnädige Frau*,' said Axel as he bowed.

'Come wi' me,' snapped Hamish, as the boys turned to him. 'I'll show ye the dogs,' . . . for two hours, he added under his breath.

'Kindly lead the way, Ancient One,' said Axel. The boys followed Hamish's bent back and stick-thin gaitered legs as, indignation in every line, he led the way across the yard.

Jack was the puppy in the middle, his usual place. The three of them were growing fast, and Lottie, her milk supply drying up rapidly, was tired of them. Hearing footsteps outside, she jumped up, grumbling at them, scattering the three fat bodies, velvet coated and soot black. At once, all three dashed at her, and, rearing up on their hind legs and kneading with their paws, began to suck again. Lottie growled. She turned the nearest puppy onto his back, and snarled in his face. '*Leave me, greedy one, else will I bite thee!*' He picked himself up and all three backed off.

Jack was the first of the puppies to notice the little group watching them over the half-door of the loose-box which was his world. Old Hamish and two strange boys. The taller boy had one leg in irons. His thin, sallow face was marked with pain. Axel was fifteen – a bitter disillusioned fifteen. To be born a cripple and heir to the von Hessel estates! It was a crime, no less.

His brother Hansel was a sturdy, fair-skinned small boy, dressed in a miniature Norfolk jacket, shooting breeches, stockings and brogues. He looked up at Hamish, then ducked his head in a jerky little bow.

'Is it permitted that we enter, Ancient One?'

'Not so much of your "Ancient One", my lad. Aye, ye can go in.' Hamish flicked his fingers, and Lottie came to him, grinning and swishing her tail.

'Is not a litter of only three a small family for a retriever?' asked Axel. 'For you must know that, when in my father's possession, she brought forth no less than ten whelps.'

'Aye, she'd mair,' Hamish answered tersely. This was dangerous ground.

'What has become of them?'

'Drooned.' The finality of the old man's tone silenced both boys, much as they would have liked an explanation. Their English, they had been told, was perfect, so what strange word was this? Perhaps the Ancient One was speaking in the Gaelic tongue.

Hansel was only nine years old. For a moment, he almost forgot the formal manners taught him by his father and tutors. He had been going to pick up Scot, the friendly one, but drew back in time.

'Is it permitted that I pick up one of the whelps, honoured sir?'

'You're a strange laddie and no mistake. Aye, play wi' them if ye like, but dinna touch the bitch.' Hamish fastened Lottie to a chain in the corner. Mac, the shy one, sheltered behind her. His eyes, still milky blue, watched curiously from a safe position. Jack, the thoughtful one, stood squarely in the middle of the stable, his head on one side, sizing up the visitors. He took a tentative step towards Hansel.

'See! He likes me!' Sunday manners forgotten, Hansel spoke in his native language. He scooped the puppy up in his arms, cuddling the broad black head under his chin, caressing the soft skin, still loose and folded, the strong little paws with their needle claws.

'What silky ears! And his toes, see? They are snow white.'

Axel spoke severely in English. 'Hansel, do not fondle the dog; you are not a woman. And recall that it is not courteous to speak German in the presence of those who do not comprehend it.'

Hamish wished the boys would go away. He was sick and tired of them. He should have been enjoying a pipe, followed by a good sleep. Why should he be expected to keep these outlandish boys amused?

'Reckon you could take home the little 'un with the white on his paws,' he said. 'The other two might pass.'

Hansel had ignored Axel's rebuke, he was still cuddling Jack. He looked up, hardly able to believe his ears. 'A thousand thanks, honoured sir,' he said, clicking his heels as well as he could for straw. 'I will inform my father of your generosity.'

Autumn gales raged over the North Sea, and Jack was sick. He was only eight weeks old, and loneliness almost made him forget how ill he felt. After a few hours, his natural optimism and strong constitution came to his rescue. He sized up his new situation, and decided it wasn't too bad.

Axel and Hansel were sharing a cabin, and Jack had been provided with a kennel small enough to fit under a bunk. Hansel had left the door of it open, and Jack emerged warily. At once, Hansel picked him up. Jack stiffened his legs, and twisted his head sideways. A cuddle was all very well, but enough was enough. Besides he still felt queasy and his bladder was full.

Jack had reservations about Hansel. He felt the natural affinity of one young creature for another, but there was something here that wasn't quite right. His unformed puppy mind could respond to warm natural affection, but there was a desperation about Hansel that made him uneasy and suspicious.

Jack knew only the uncomplicated love of his mother. The wish for her offspring to excel and be manly had no place in Lottie's scale of values. She fed her brood, cleaned them up, kept them warm, and would have risked her life for them without a second thought. Then, when their teeth and claws began to bruise her teats, and their appetites seemed to be insatiable, she made it perfectly clear that she had had enough of them. In the meantime, she exacted obedience.

Hansel's mother, the statuesque Eloise, had withdrawn all tenderness from him as soon as he could toddle.

'You are not a baby now, you must learn to be a man,' she had said when he cried.

Jack struggled and flailed, twisting his head about. He was being held too tightly. Disappointed, Hansel set him down. Jack squatted, and a fair sized pool appeared and trickled away under the bunk as the ship tilted. He had known he should not foul the little kennel – had known about keeping his bed clean since he was three weeks old. Vomiting one could not help.

'Filthy little creature!' Hansel stuffed him back into the kennel and banged the door.

'Call Klaus,' said Axel indifferently. Klaus was the boys' personal servant.

Jack retreated as far as possible from the mesh-covered door of the kennel. It appeared that he had done wrong. He wondered where he should relieve himself in future. Still wondering, he fell asleep.

Baron Heinrich von Hessel had the traditional Prussian fondness for all things military. He would have liked to have been a full-time soldier, but the size of his estates prevented this. Hansel was earmarked for the army, ruthlessly drilled and subjected to a Spartan regime. From six years old, he had a cold bath each day, dry bread to eat and, to sleep in, a carpetless room as cheerless as a prison cell. Poor Axel, lame and sickly, would inherit the land, Hansel would perhaps some day fight for the glory of the Fatherland.

Hansel had the makings of a good horseman. He had courage, good hands and a secure seat. He needed all three. He never rode a pony, but started his riding lessons on one of his father's weight-carrying Hanoverians. Hansel's short legs hardly reached below the saddleflaps, but he delighted his father by coolly picking up the reins, and asking not for a neckstrap but for a whip. He was to pay dearly for this early display of confidence, and it was surprising that his nerve for riding wasn't permanently broken.

With his fair hair cropped close, and wearing a replica Hussar uniform, correct in detail down to the last button, Hansel was always mounted on a horse too strong for him. As he became able to handle each mount in turn, he would be forbidden to ride it in future, and he would be obliged to start all over again on some unruly beast a size larger. He was drilled daily, either by his father or by his tutor, a retired cavalryman with no teaching qualifications.

Hansel's heart belonged to his sister's governess, Miss Briggs. His mother was just as stern an advocate of cold baths and dry bread as his father. She was also kept busy running the household where the servants outnumbered the served by five to one.

Every afternoon, Miss Briggs drove out in the pony carriage with blonde, pig-tailed Ilse, while Hansel, if he could escape from his tutor, pretended to be a cavalry escort. It would have been a better game if he could have controlled his horse. It would suddenly bound forward, and career ahead of the carriage, startling the pony, and making his beloved Edith Briggs laugh at him. That he couldn't bear.

Trained from babyhood to be proud, Hansel would have been annoyed to learn that Miss Briggs was sorry for him. She thought it a sad pity that a nice ordinary boy was certain to be turned into a younger version of his insufferable father.

*

Edith Briggs, pinning on her hat in front of the damp-spotted mirror in her bedroom, smiled at her own reflection. Her pale face and white blouse stood out in the sombre little bedroom, tucked away in a corner of the Baron's dark and draughty mansion.

The outside was so charming, thought Edith, stabbing another hatpin into place. All those funny little dormer windows, and the ivy-covered watchtower just like something out of Grimms' Fairy Tales. But her bedroom was hateful, impossible to like. It was cold, dark, musty-smelling, and crammed with heavy oak furniture. Oh, how it made her long for the Rectory at Wynter St Mary's, and the white-painted room she'd shared with her sisters Lena and Audrey for so many years.

She slung her plain navy jacket over her arm and, gloves and purse in one hand and her long skirt caught up with the other, she hurried downstairs, feet echoing on the uncarpeted treads. The vast gloomy hall bristled with the heads of animals large and small which had fallen to the Baron's gun. He had travelled all over the world, and his favourite trophy, the head of a mammoth bison, hung above the door.

At the foot of the stairs, Jack was waiting. Naturally obedient, he knew he must stay downstairs, but he stood up panting, his little tail wagging so hard that it swung his hindquarters from side to side. The lady tutor, beloved by the good, the gracious Hansel, was late. Almost, he had supposed there was to be no drive today. Hansel's sister Ilse following, pallid and heavy-footed on the stairs, he ignored.

'Ready for your drive, Jack?' Edith, like Hansel, always picked him up on sight. 'You darling.' She kissed the top of his head and he wriggled, trying to lick her face. Clasping him in her arms and talking to him all the time, she went out under the sardonic gaze of the bison, a maid following with rugs, parasol and a dropped glove.

Edith looked forward to her afternoon drive all day. True, Ilse came with her, but Ilse was as silent as the pony. The little four-wheeled carriage was old and comfortable, and in it one could get away from the ever-present servants for a while and relax. She must be careful not to relax too much, or the

Baroness might find out and object. It was almost impossible to believe that this alarming woman was English born. She always spoke German to Edith, and spoke English to Ilse, whose slow brain worked only in German.

Edith was right to be cautious. Already, Eloise was wondering whether an older woman would not have made a more suitable governess for her daughter. Neither Eloise nor Ilse could imagine why Miss Briggs should wish to take Hansel's new puppy out in the carriage with her. They supposed it must be a harmless eccentricity to do with being English. Eloise had long ago pulled up her English roots.

Edith lifted Jack into the carriage where he sat on her foot, the groom stood aside, and they trotted away down the sandy road, between fields of rye. After a mile or so, the rye gave way to groves of silver birches, mantled with mistletoe, then they passed by scrubby copses where pigs rootled. Further on still, the sandy road disappeared under a carpet of pine needles as they entered the forests which stretched for miles.

Edith leaned back against the dusty cushions, reins held slackly, gazing at the vista of slender trunks bordering the road until they seemed to meet in the distance. On each side they rose, rank on rank, straight and tall, and without undergrowth. Oh, how different from the friendly Devonshire lanes, red-earthed and sunk deeply between flowery banks. For a moment, she closed her eyes, trying to imagine herself back in the pony trap at home. She would be driving fat old Trixie, half listening to her father's gentle monologue. Then back to the Rectory for tea with her mother and all her sisters squashed round the table. Freda was married now, but Olive, Violet, Audrey, Vera and Lena were all still at home, schooldays over, and with precious little to do. Few parishes were so well provided with free female help for Sunday school teaching and the running of charitable events.

The sisters considered Edith wildly adventurous when she advertised for a teaching post abroad, and indeed she'd hoped for something nearer home herself. She was dreadfully home-sick in Prussia.

'All those German princes, darling,' said her mother vaguely.

'And they're related to our own dear King too. Poor soul – they say he's far from well.'

So Edith, her youngest, put up her long light brown hair (it was soft and slippery and kept falling down again), lengthened her skirts from ankle to ground length, and went by train to London, where she survived being interviewed by Eloise. After this, the journey to Germany was a minor undertaking, and she felt grown-up and confident as she walked under the bison's head into that echoing hall for the first time. Slim and pale, she had a fragile prettiness which enchanted Hansel straight away. The rest of the family decided she needed feeding up. She also, they said, needed fresh air, hence the daily drives.

The pony's hoofs made no sound, Ilse made no sound, Jack was asleep. Far away behind them, a harsh voice barked orders. Hansel was being drilled. Poor Hansel, thought Edith, I hope he gets off soon; he might catch us up. She drove slowly, but nothing was seen of Hansel until they reached home. Then, as the groom took the pony's head, he came trotting up, accompanied by the Baron. Oh dear, Edith loathed the Baron. She supposed he was quite handsome in a florid way, but she found his squarish head and fat neck only slightly less repulsive than his personality.

Heinrich von Hessel was one of those men who honestly believe themselves to be irresistible to all women. He assumed that the governess, being apparently normal, must be in love with him. Poor thing. If, on the other hand, she was not in love with him, she must be as cold as ice and singularly lacking in judgement. He was rather sorry for her – pretty young thing, breaking her heart over the unattainable. Unattainable mainly because, selfish and aggressive as he was, the Baron was far too frightened of Eloise to put a foot out of line. When Eloise was angry – he preferred not to think about it. His manner towards Miss Briggs was heavily bantering. He also had a habit of twirling his moustache, which he wore waxed and turned up in imitation of the Kaiser. Edith would have preferred the curt tones he reserved for Hansel.

The Baron dismounted, and gallantly assisted Edith to descend from the carriage. She, perfectly aware of his

thoughts, blushed crimson with annoyance. Horrible man!
The Baron put down the blush to unrequited love. Edith
gathered her skirts in one hand; the Baron steadied her other
elbow. 'So, *Fräulein*,' he said, 'you have returned from your
drive.'

There is no answer to such a remark. Edith murmured, 'Yes,
Baron,' and stooped to restrain Jack from getting under the
horse's feet. Hansel climbed down from his over-large and
difficult mount, and Jack went to him. At present, he was
nobody's puppy. Already he had a good dog's natural desire
to be owned and trained by somebody, so he wasn't altogether
happy. Was he Hansel's dog? He wasn't sure.

Edith had a way of fondling his ears, kissing his head, then
drawing away. 'No, you darling puppy,' she would say. 'Go
away, I'm getting too fond of you.' Dogs don't ration their
affection – Jack didn't understand.

'Make the most of him, *Fräulein*.' The Baron laughed loudly
as though somebody had made a joke. 'A few short months,
and the puppy is no longer a pet. He becomes a dog, and must
be trained to find birds and to retrieve.'

'He's going to be small for a retriever, isn't he?' Edith had
thought for some time that King Edward's retrievers must be
different from other people's.

'Small?' The Baron bent down, and looked closely at Jack.
'Ach! It is a crossbred – a mongrel. See those white hairs, that
tail? It shall be shot!'

Jack wagged the offending tail, hoping to please. He seemed
to have done something wrong again.

Hansel knew to his cost that his father never spoke idly and
would bear no argument. He stood in mute despair.

Edith, all her homesickness and tension suddenly coming
to the boil, dropped to her knees on the gravel, catching hold
of Jack with shaking hands. 'No, no . . .' she managed to say,
and burst into tears.

Ah Youth! Curious the way that love for her employer could
affect an otherwise sane young woman. 'It is only a dog,
Fräulein. It does not merit tears, alive or dead.'

Edith cried harder. Her shoulders shook. Unstable. She must
be dismissed.

'Please, Papa . . .'

'Silence, Hansel. *Fräulein*, rather than distress you further, I will give the dog to my head forester.' The Baron mounted, and sat scowling on his horse, Hansel beside him, biting his lip. Ilse, who had all this time been sitting silently in the carriage, climbed out and walked into the house, without giving her weeping governess a glance.

Edith blew her nose. She knew that the Baron, whatever his faults, was a man of his word. She hoped the head forester would appreciate Jack. The puppy looked so intelligent. Tearfully, she stammered her thanks.

Jack stood perplexed. The emotions in the air were as plain to him as the things he could see and hear. He sensed misery, anger, hope – the air was thick with emotion. He had a feeling that Miss Briggs was going to hug and kiss him again. He was taken by surprise when, obeying a barked order from the Baron, a gardener left the border he was digging, picked him up, and took him away to the stables.

The next day, the head forester collected Jack, and carried him away to his cottage in the heart of the pine forests.

CHAPTER TWO

The head forester rode a thickset cob on his rounds. When he was not on its back, it was tied, ready saddled and bridled, just outside the door of the thatched house in the heart of the pine forest.

The head forester's name was Johann. He had little to do with the felling of trees, was more like an English head keeper, as his principal work was to see that no poachers interfered with the game. He also waged a running battle with thieves who stole firewood, and was responsible for keeping the roads clear of fallen trees.

The woods stretched unbroken for twenty miles, and were ten miles wide in places. Johann was a heavy man, and the cob bore the brunt of his work. It had developed a sort of shuffling run, neither walk nor trot, fairly comfortable to a rider who had never heard of the English custom of rising to the trot.

Jack, in a satchel on Johann's back, was not at all comfortable. 'Oh, sir, I am upside down. My paws are higher than my head. I cannot remain in one position. I fear I may soil your excellent bag. Please pause and allow me to right myself.'

'Peace. Do not whine.' Johann nudged the bag with his elbow. The cob shuffled on. Jack, head downwards in a corner of the bag, sneezed as he found some feathers from long-dead pigeons.

The satchel was intended for Johann's spare clothes when he had to stay overnight in one of the forester's huts on the estate. As it happened, he was a shameless and successful poacher, and the bag had never held anything except small game until now. Not that Johann had any objection to big game; he had a large family, all of whom liked venison. The Baron, God grant him long life, always gave him several days' warning when he was planning a shoot.

When Johann reached his home with Jack in the satchel, he threw him down, bag and all, saying, 'See, Kurt, here is a playmate for you.' Kurt knelt down and unbuckled the straps. What could it be that wriggled so? His eyes and Jack's met. It was love at first sight.

Fat Marthe stood in the cottage doorway, her youngest on her hip. Red-haired and weather-beaten, she looked older than her years, aged by poverty and too many babies. Her lined face softened as Kurt's doltish features broke into a smile of great sweetness. She knew how lonely the child was, isolated by his simple mind. He was supposed to attend the village school but did not; learning was beyond him. For all that, Kurt was far from being an idiot. He could do simple sums in his head, and make himself useful about the place. Marthe's ever-growing family had edged Kurt, the eldest, out of his place in the back room, where now four children slept in the truckle bed. Kurt slept on the old sagging couch near the kitchen stove, and spent his days in the woods unless Marthe needed him at home.

'Look, husband, the dumb creatures all know what a good boy our Kurt is. They know more than the schoolmasters.' For Jack, looking into the round eyes, saw straight through to the kind, honest nature behind. He nestled against Kurt in delight.

Later, when they were in bed, Marthe voiced her doubts. 'Why didst thou accept the dog? We cannot afford to keep a pet. Already there are nine mouths to feed. It had been wiser to have given it to somebody else.'

'What, woman, and anger the Baron? Am I mad? Also the puppy came from England they tell me, as did the Frau Baronin. Wouldst thou have me anger the Frau Baronin?'

Both shuddered at the bare idea.

'Anyway,' said Johann, 'the child needs a companion. He

is learning how to trap and snare, and a hunting dog will be
of use in getting meat for the pot.'

'Meat for the pot? If that dog was likely to be of any use,
would it have been given to us? I think not . . . leave me be,
Johann, did I not say we already have too many mouths to
feed?'

But Johann didn't believe in heeding his wife's protests.

Jack slept at Kurt's feet. He had eaten a little broth made from
barley, and the crusts from Kurt's hunk of rye bread. Plainly,
food was scarce. But what is food when one has found
a friend? They had sat in the dark in an outhouse, and Kurt
had told him about himself. A pity he did not appear to understand Jack's language. One had thought him not far removed
from one's own kind. Ah well, one could not have everything.

Kurt knew Jack's name. That was surprising. They curled
up together on a pile of old sacks as Kurt talked softly on.

'I know thy name – it is Jack. The beautiful Fräulein called
thee Jack. I heard her when she had picked a bunch of weeds
and thou sattest on them in the carriage. She had to pick some
more. That was funny, eh Jack?' Kurt laughed loudly, and
Jack stretched his jaws, going 'oo-ow-oo' and wagging his tail.
They talked for hours.

Child and puppy together became boy and dog, and brought
home so much small game that the family was seldom hungry.
Johann thought to take Jack for himself, but the dog refused
to go with him.

Jack was leading a happy and fulfilled life. He found game,
retrieved and did all that a good gundog should do. Yet, in the
back of his consciousness, there was something else. A vision
of white woolly creatures, bunched in the open, and himself
racing round them, bringing them to Kurt. And Kurt would
catch one and kill it, and they would dine like kings. There
was something wrong with the dream. These things are too
difficult for me to understand, thought Jack, but the vision
persisted.

So months passed, and years. Jack grew into a handsome
dog, and Kurt into a great maypole of a lad, all hands and feet.

Jack called him friend, never master. Their standing in the household was roughly the same.

Jack did not see Miss Briggs again. Once, the Baron visited the village in his cumbersome, old-fashioned carriage, accompanied by the Frau Baronin. Jack and Kurt concealed themselves behind some sacks of potatoes in the shed, and peeped through a knothole in the wooden wall.

The Baron's hectoring voice rang out, as Johann stood humbly, cap in hand. Meanwhile, Marthe nervously answered the Frau Baronin's questions; her children, scrubbed and silent behind her, the baby in her arms.

Kurt's eye was applied to the knothole. 'That is the Frau Baronin, Jack. Even her husband fears her anger. Only see for thyself, but do not be seen, or we will both be beaten.'

Jack squinted through the hole, and was in time to see the Baroness being assisted into the carriage by Johann. Jack tried to tell Kurt that he was already familiar with the red-haired lady. Had she not spoken sharply to Miss Briggs? He was as anxious as Kurt not to be noticed.

Eloise, Baroness von Hessel, had returned to her native England only once since her marriage. A spoiled beauty with too much money and a violent temper, she had felt cooped up in her father's Elizabethan manor house beside the river in Weybridge.

When the infatuated Baron had likened her to a beautiful tigress pacing in a gilded cage, she had seen nothing even slightly incongruous in the comparison. She had expected, even courted opposition to her proposed marriage, and indulged in a fearful and unnecessary scene with her parents. They had nothing against the florid young German except his foreign accent, they said; they would have been happy to spread themselves and give their only daughter an expensive London wedding. By the time they had recovered from her attack and were ready to discuss dates, Eloise had gone to Berlin, taking only her maid, so the wedding took place in Germany.

Once married, Eloise had to invent drama where none

existed. She severed all relations with her parents and friends, and it was only at her husband's insistence that she engaged an English governess for Ilse, and had her sons taught guide-book English by their tutors. Eloise herself spoke fluent German, and when King Edward dined at the house, the Baron realized he hadn't heard his wife talking English for years.

Hansel shuddered when he remembered the occasion of his grandparents' death.

Sir Reginald and Lady Entwistle were a formal pair, known only to a favoured few as Melia and Poor Reggie. Amelia was extremely stout, tall and broad, upholstered from shoulder to ankle. She weighed fourteen stone. Reginald, who could barely see over her massive shoulder when they danced, was the prototype of the little man on the seaside picture postcards – bald, pot-bellied, knock-kneed. Like the little man, he had a talent for doing the wrong thing. Nobody knew how he had earned his knighthood. 'Services to the Nation,' said the citation.

When Amelia fell overboard at a boating party, she sank like a stone, and Sir Reginald gallantly dived in after her. As he was a non-swimmer and she was weighted down with bulky skirts and petticoats, both were drowned.

This was in 1913, when relations between England and Germany were beginning to be strained. The Baron, cousin both to Kaiser Wilhelm and to George V, had vowed he would never visit England again after King Edward's insulting behaviour.

Eloise, sweeping up Hansel, Ilse and Edith Briggs in her turbulent wake, descended on Weybridge like a whirlwind. Brushing aside the remaining English relations, she flung herself into organizing the joint funeral, and a memorial service in Westminster Abbey. Perhaps remorse or even guilt had something to do with it, but Eloise showed no sign of regret. All she wanted was the maximum pomp due, she felt, to the in-laws of a great man.

They stayed with Aunt Agatha, who had been one of Queen Alexandra's ladies-in-waiting. The poor lady was horrified at Eloise's apparently total lack of concern for her parents' fate. Magnificent in black ostrich feathers, black veil and black furs, her hair like a blazing bonfire, Eloise attracted as much attention as she could have wished. Hansel never failed to cringe when he remembered the evening that followed at Wellington Court, one of the stateliest homes in England, where, at the invitation of the Earl of Wiltshire, the party assembled for dinner.

Before the meal, Edith Briggs paraded Ilse and Hansel in the drawing-room, and accepted a glass of madeira. Hansel, awkward in clothes he was outgrowing, stared at her in adoration. From her soft puffed-out hair to her small, arched feet she was perfect. Her plain, long-sleeved brown velvet dress in Hansel's eyes made the other ladies' finery look vulgar. Ilse, whose thick flaxen plait was tightly bound about her broad pale face, was unsuitably swathed in white, with frills and black bows.

Then came the nightmare. Eloise started a discussion with Lord Haslemere, who had been invited especially because his wife was German born. He and the two ladies talked for a while, apparently in agreement, sipping their wine. Hansel could relax and watch Edith, shyly answering the questions of their host's son. Jealousy gnawed. He became aware of his mother's voice raised.

'You are English, completely English. Why? Why have you rejected your homeland and withdrawn your allegiance?'

'Really Baroness, you go too far. It's time we changed the subject.' Lady Haslemere gave her husband a look imploring help. 'I know your part of Germany only through the work of a novelist,' she continued bravely, when no help came. 'I suppose you've read *Elizabeth and her German Garden*?'

'I consider the woman and her work alike trivial. The Kaiser . . .'

'I think we should keep the Kaiser out of the conversation,' observed Lord Haslemere mildly.

Eloise tossed off her glass of wine and accepted another. 'Ah! So you think our ruler should be ignored. Swept under the carpet. Let me tell you, he might easily have been at Sandringham, and your George of the House of Gwelf in Berlin. The merest accident.' She turned with renewed anger on poor Lady Haslemere.

'Your King – your husband's King, I should say, has more than once been mistaken for Tsar Nicholas of Russia. The family likeness is astonishing. Our Kaiser is a finer-looking man than either, but if he wore a beard, even you would see the resemblance.'

'I won't listen to any more of this rubbish!' Lady Haslemere, red-faced, moved away as Eloise allowed her glass to be refilled.

'Hansel, have you noticed the pictures?' Oh, blessed Edith! 'This is the first Countess of Wiltshire, painted by Gains-borough. My goodness, what a hat!'

Eloise's voice easily rose above the others. She was speaking to Sir Michael Daniels now.

'Do you realize,' she demanded, 'that when our Kaiser was born, a new verse was added to your National Anthem?'

Hansel clenched his fists. The outrageous hat of the first Countess of Wiltshire swam and blurred before his eyes. Would she? Oh, dear God, surely not . . .

Eloise drained her glass and set it down with care. She took a step back, and took a deep breath which made the fringes of jet beads sway on her black satin bosom, catching the light. Having gained the attention of the whole room, she threw back her head and began to sing in a fine contralto:

> 'Hail, the auspicious morn,
> To Prussia's throne is born
> A noble heir.
> May he . . .'

'Dinner is served,' announced the butler.

A guest standing near Hansel murmured to his companion, 'Appalling woman that. Pretty terrifying, even when she isn't in her cups.'

'Awful, isn't she? Brightens up a dull party, though. Get behind me if you're frightened.'

'Frightened? I feel she might throw me across her saddle and gallop off to Valhalla with me.'

Both laughed. Hansel felt sick. He almost wept openly with relief when the housekeeper shepherded him, Edith Briggs and Ilse upstairs for a supper of shepherd's pie and rice pudding.

The rest of his stay in England, mercifully brief, was forgotten, overshadowed by the shame and embarrassment of that evening.

Ever since that mortifying occasion, Hansel had tried to put England out of his mind. Or rather, his thoughts of it were confined to Devonshire, the home of his dear Miss Briggs. England to Hansel was a West Country paradise of green meadows and lazy afternoons. Edith was lonely, and her tales of her home were biased. Hansel imagined that it never froze or snowed there, and that nobody was poor or unhappy. His mother had again put England out of her mind, so there was nobody to disillusion him.

Edith Briggs returned to England as soon as war seemed to her to be inevitable. She parted from her employers with profound relief, from Ilse with indifference and from Hansel with regret. Perhaps it was all for the best. If the Baron had known of Hansel's hopeless devotion for his daughter's governess . . . Edith shuddered. Even she was not supposed to know, but Hansel had not yet learned to hide his feelings.

Edith said goodbye to Hansel under Eloise's eye, and cut short his unhappy stammerings with a cheerful assurance that they were bound to meet again some day.

Hansel was left in a state of misery and confusion. The few months that passed between Edith's departure and the outbreak of war were the loneliest of his life; then the Baron left for the front and Hansel's unhappiness was greater still. Eloise spoke often of England's weakness – decadent, she said. That insignificant little Miss Briggs – typical. Then came the news that the Baron was dead.

Russia was so much nearer than the Western Front, everyone had expected the Baron to stay at home and defend his estate, but no. He had galloped off with his beloved cavalry to some godforsaken spot in Flanders. Wearing the conspicuous uniform of an officer of the famous Death's Head Hussars, he had been killed within a week.

The Baron's body was brought home at extreme inconvenience and colossal expense, to be buried in the family vaults. His personal guard of men drawn from the estate, rather like the original British Yeomanry, came too, also his valet, Helmuth. Almost all were suffering from fever – a fever, bred in the Belgian lowlands, to which the Prussians had little resistance.

The sickly Axel lived only a month to enjoy the title of Baron von Hessel, and fourteen-year-old Hansel succeeded him.

Immediately, Eloise, acting as a sort of regent, took charge. She rounded up the Baron's guard who had slipped quietly back to their farms, and turned them over to a warlike neighbour who was training a corps to wage war on the Eastern Front. She assumed sole command of the estate, dismissed the steward who had been feathering his own nest for years, and stepped up Hansel's instruction in the warlike arts.

Hansel had feared and disliked his father more and more as time passed, his mother had done her best to kill his affection for her, and Axel's constant pain made him a spiteful and querulous companion, whose death made little difference to Hansel. He wore his black armband with the rest, but he could not mourn. It was the loss of Edith that he felt. Secretly, he thought his father and brother were better gone. Hansel felt sure he would be a better landgrave than either.

'You will be a soldier like your father,' stated Eloise.

Was he not to look after the estates then? He loved riding round the farms, inspecting the crops and livestock, even more than hunting with his deerhounds. The Baron's harsh methods had paid off Hansel rode well: and was already a good shot with his light rifle.

Whenever he was indoors and could avoid his family and tutor, he studied English from Ilse's schoolbooks and, in particular, the works of Byron, Tennyson and Elizabeth Barrett Browning. Nourished on this heady diet, he wrote a number of sonnets to Miss Briggs. That was the title of the collection – 'Sonnets to Miss Briggs'. Even in German, Hansel was a bad poet. In English, he made 'be with' rhyme with 'Edith'. Robert Browning could have done no worse.

It was inevitable that Eloise should find out. The fact that Edith was far away in Devonshire made no difference. She raged at Hansel, calling him traitor, fool, false to his father's memory. The Baron in amorous moments had called her his Brünnhilde. Certainly there was something Wagnerian about her size, her wrath, and the amount of noise she made as she stormed at the trembling Hansel. Nobody could have guessed that this was the daughter of Melia and Poor Reggie Entwistle, hurling German abuse at her son.

Sulkily, Hansel mounted his horse, and rode away through the woods where the first frosts were yellowing the edges of the silver birch leaves. Allowing his horse to walk on a slack rein, he gazed up at the slender branches for inspiration, trying to compose fresh lines to Miss Briggs. Cruel fate . . . Born too late . . . Jealous hate . . .

If Hansel had not been engrossed in trying to find a rhyme for enchantress, he would have seen Kurt and Jack, and certainly wouldn't have fallen off. He hadn't fallen off a horse for years. The horse, well fed, well bred, and knowing perfectly well that Hansel's mind was on other things, seized the opportunity to bounce him off, a thing it had tried to do before without success. A lanky, rough-haired lad sat skinning a rabbit, his dog beside him. Hansel landed neatly on his head in the middle of the road.

The horse whipped round and galloped home.

Hansel, knocked senseless, lay still for a moment, then rolled onto his stomach and painfully pushed himself up on all fours. Kurt stood up, dropping the rabbit, and gaped with his mouth open. He was a great gangling youth with the voice of a man and the eyes of a child.

Jack looked from one to the other uncertainly. With some idea of fetching help, he set off along the track which led to Kurt's home, not far away. Then the sheepdog half of his ancestry asserted itself, and he ran back to round up the two boys, his imaginary flock. He crouched behind them on the path, tongue out, looking helpful and encouraging. What should he do if the noble Hansel were to attack his Kurt? But no, Hansel was in no shape to attack anybody. He stood up, staggered and nearly fell again. Kurt caught him in his arms and supported him, and the two boys lurched like drunks to the head forester's house.

Jack had thought that life held no greater happiness than to go rabbiting with Kurt, to spend all the hours of daylight with him, and sleep at his feet at night. But now, in the first half of the war, came a truly miraculous interlude. The young Baron, the excellent, the infallible Baron Hansel von Hessel, was graciously pleased to call Kurt his friend. He bore no malice for the bump on his head, and taught Kurt how to handle a gun. (Kurt managed not to confess that he had been shooting the baronial game for two years already.)

Hansel asked that Kurt might be allowed to share his instruction in the use of the sabre, the pistol and the rifle. Jack always went with Kurt to the plain where this took place. He would lie, proudly guarding the boys' coats until it was time to go home. When game was shot by either boy, Hansel was often generous enough to present Kurt with the kill. On several occasions, the young Baron spoke kindly to Jack – words of praise and admiration. Jack was suitably honoured by the attention, but Kurt had his heart.

Kurt grew taller. His ill-fitting clothes left his wrists and ankles bare. His voice grew even gruffer than before. His mind remained childlike. Hansel grew away from him mentally, began to chafe at his simple outlook. Hansel's divided loyalties and his forebodings creased his forehead, and made his young face gaunt and troubled. At seventeen, Kurt needed to shave, but Hansel's fair skin was as smooth as a girl's.

At the head forester's cottage, where now there were twelve mouths to feed, the family fared reasonably well.

Kurt and Jack had evolved between them an efficient if unsporting method of shooting the small deer which abounded in the forest. With no Baron to shoot them, and with Hansel absent more and more with his sergeant-major tutor, the wild creatures had multiplied.

Kurt would go at sunrise to a place where he thought deer might be grazing. He was seldom wrong about that. Then he would whisper, 'Bring them to me, Jack.' And Jack, instead of drawing the wood as a good retriever should, would set off in a long circling cast, half a mile or more, before turning in towards the spot where he scented the deer feeding. As he slipped quietly along, the vision of white woolly animals hovered disturbingly on the edge of his mind. Certainly he had never seen a deer that grew wool.

Once in position, he would start to draw the wood towards Kurt, until the sound of shots told him he had been successful. The family ate venison every day, and Jack grew quite fat.

Hansel, guilty because of his neglected friendship with Kurt, was horrified when he heard that the boy was to go to the front with him. He even overcame his lifelong habit of not arguing with Eloise.

'Mother, he is not fit to go. He cannot read or write.'

'He need not read or write. He can shoot, you tell me.'

'He is a better shot than I am, but his mind . . .'

'It will not be necessary for him to think.'

It would soon be over. Everybody said so. The British were cracking, their morale destroyed. The battle of the Somme had broken the English nerve. Men out there were going crazy every day. There was mass desertion. One had only to read the papers. Soon the British would be on the run, seeking the best terms they could. There was no need to worry.

That spring, the spring of 1917, was late in coming. The winter, known afterwards as the 'turnip winter', had been hard and long. They were lucky to have their pigs, rye, turnips and potatoes. Others weren't so lucky.

Early in April, Eloise packed both boys off to the front, just like that.

War. Hansel had been trained for it from the age of eight. His father had impressed on him that a soldier's life was the only one. Time not spent fighting was best employed in sport – the killing of animals and birds rather than men. It kept one's hand in. Hansel had obediently learned to fight, in spite of his sneaking wish to farm the estates; a wish he daren't have owned to. But fighting was one thing, war was another, surely. War with England. His English mother was certain of a German victory. What of her relations? It would be for their own good. Ilse never expressed any opinions at all.

But Edith? War against Edith? Hansel remembered all the little things she had told him about her home and family in Devonshire. It sounded a carefree life, free from the restrictions which had hedged him in all his life. Hansel didn't want to go to war with England.

Helmuth, the old valet in whose arms Baron Heinrich had died at Mons, was long past the age for military service. He was well over sixty. Now he volunteered to look after Hansel, who had never in his life looked after himself.

Hansel took his two horses with him, and fully expected to take his deerhounds. At the last moment, he discovered that they wouldn't be allowed to travel on the overcrowded train. So he filled in a form for Jack Shultz (Schultz was Kurt's surname) and, in the general chaos, got away with it and took Jack instead.

Kurt was overjoyed. He had dreaded parting with Jack more than the dimly understood hazards of war.

It was Easter 1917. All was confusion. Nobody knew for certain what was happening. Easter fell on April 8th, and a cloudless morning was followed by a violent blizzard. Everybody knew that much. Huddled in a French town hall, stiff with cold and weariness, they passed the word round that there had been – was now – a battle for the town of Arras. That was where they were going, wherever it might be. Nobody knew which side had launched the attack, or what had been the outcome.

The village was well to the east of the firing line. Although damaged earlier in the war, the French civilians had not left it. They had nowhere to go. Troops, retiring to rest camps, straggled through the streets, grey-faced, unshaven, exhausted. The horses of Hansel's troop jingled past them, going the other way, to quarters west of the village. Hansel's two were particularly fine; great shining bays, Hanoverian crossed with English thoroughbred. They had travelled in more comfort than their master.

On the Wednesday after Easter, the men were moved from the village to a château a few miles away. They were lined up in rows in front of the building and counted. 'Like so many sheep,' muttered Hansel disgustedly, hunching his shoulders and trying to see where Kurt was. The men from the von Hessel estate were at the back, and Hansel, the most junior officer cadet present, was ignored by everyone except one youth who asked his name.

'Von Hessel. Baron Hansel von Hessel,' answered Hansel proudly.

'Hansel? I thought it was Gretel,' laughed the other boy, turning away.

Tears of rage and exhaustion blinded Hansel. A tremendous roaring, followed by a succession of explosions about a mile away drowned his angry retort. The men crowded closer together as the noise died away, leaving the sky to the right stained red. Distant unearthly shrieks could be heard, confused shouts, lesser bangs and the rattle of bullets; then silence.

'I didn't think men *could* scream like that!' Hansel, sweat running into his eyes in spite of the cold, turned to old Helmuth who carried both their packs.

'Not men, horses. Those were bombs.'

Hansel digested this, and decided that Helmuth's mind must be unhinged by fear. They were miles behind the front line. 'Are we going to freeze here all night?' he grumbled.

'Silence, cub.' A young Prussian lieutenant, pale as death, and dressed like Hansel for riding, not marching, led the new draft of young officers through the great doors of the château.

'We were to have had four weeks training here,' he said when they were inside. 'Now it appears we will not have even four minutes. Sleep if you can. We are going up to the reserve trenches in two hours.'

Trenches? Baron Hansel von Hessel in a trench? The man must be raving mad.

Kurt stretched out his tired body on the straw in the stable. He wasn't used to dealing with more than one emotion at a time. At present he was hungry, and hunger was consuming him. Cold, fear and fatigue were all overshadowed by his hunger. He had a piece of sausage, but superstitiously was saving it up, rather like carrying a Pfennig so as never to be without money.

He laid his head on his pack and tried to sleep, but in vain.

If Kurt does these strange things, they must be right, thought Jack, but why have we not eaten?

Some time later a soldier came out to the stable with a great metal pan full of soup. This he ladled into the men's mess tins. It was poor stuff with lumps of fat and pieces of cabbage floating in it. Jack watched Kurt, noisily drinking it, and his stomach rumbled sadly. 'I too am fond of soup,' said Jack, but he knew quite well that Kurt could not pick up the messages he sent him.

'Have you any food for my dog?' asked Kurt, when a second pan of soup arrived.

'Your dog? That's a good one. The meat in your soup might well be dog if this war lasts a few months more. We've been out here almost three years. Now they send children and dogs.' The soldier spat on the straw and went out.

When Kurt had left home, his mother had wrapped quite a large piece of sausage in oiled silk and told him to keep it in case of dire need.

'Is your need dire, Jack?' asked Kurt.

Jack smiled, drawing down his ears and licking his lips. 'I do not know what you mean, my friend. I know only that I am very hungry.'

Kurt unwrapped the sausage and, with his hunting knife, cut off several small pieces and fed them to Jack, one by one. He rewrapped what was left, and put it back in his inside pocket. Its warm, homely smell helped him to sleep. Jack curled up in the crook of Kurt's knees. He ran his tongue round his mouth, savouring the last of the sausage. He fell asleep.

'A raid! An enemy raid! Bestir yourselves! Quickly, you mis-begotten Pomeranian clods – Out!'

When Jack had curled up to sleep, the distant rumbling that he'd noticed as soon as they'd left the train had helped to soothe him. It was less disturbing than the silence. He didn't know what it was, and, after three days' slow, uncomfortable travel, he didn't care. Presumably it was normal in this part of the world, as nobody seemed disturbed by it. He jumped up, alert in a moment. The rumbling had stopped. Kurt was propped on an elbow, rubbing his eyes. All around men were scrambling to their feet, struggling into their packs, blundering into one another in the dark, grumbling, swearing in a variety of country dialects.

'Silence!' roared the Sergeant who had woken them. 'Do you want the enemy to hear you in Béthune? *Ach Gott!* What have I done to be saddled with a rabble of infant swineherds from the Baltic? You should have been left for the Russians.'

As he spoke he shone a torch this way and that, while two very young officers at the stable door waited to lead the untidy column who presently stumbled out of the yard into the road, adjusting their packs, rubbing their eyes.

Jack kept very close to Kurt. Nobody had said anything about him. He might have been left behind, tied up even. How, then, could he have protected Kurt from the Enemy? How, in any case, could he protect Kurt if the Enemy had a gun and had already been woken up? He padded alongside the sleepy, untidy procession, conscious of Kurt's large feet moving beside him. Marching was not the word. Jack couldn't see much, but he would have known Kurt's feet anywhere. Beautiful big knobbly feet with welts on the soles. Only last week, he had watched Kurt trimming his toenails with that same knife he had used for the sausage. Kurt was indeed skilful. Few could have trimmed so close, yet shed no blood.

The road was covered with dirty snow, pitted with holes full of slush, and strewn with stones as large as a man's fist. In one place a crater was bridged with planks which rocked as they crossed. The going became rougher as they went on, and finally they reached a place where the road was completely blocked by a great fallen elm, wreathed with barbed wire, every gap filled with sandbags.

They turned aside and crossed a ploughed field, boots crunching on the rime. On the right, they were partly concealed by the remains of a hedge; much farther away, some dark heaps of stone and brick were just visible.

'That is Festubert. Or was,' murmured one of the two young officers at the head of the column. 'My father was killed fighting for those piles of bricks, two years ago. Now, they say, hundreds of British are living in the cellars. I do not believe it.'

'Nor I. Here is the trench at last.'

A ditch crossed their path. It was a roughly dug narrow trench with snow on its edges and cat-ice on the water at the bottom.

In single file now, they slid down into the ditch, and shuffled along for a hundred yards or so until a bigger trench crossed their ditch at right angles. It was deserted.

'Are we safe here?' a boy's voice asked. An older man answered kindly, 'Safe enough for a while. Both sides have burial parties out.'

They spread out along the empty section of trench. It was fortified with sandbags, but there was no wire, as it was not in the front line. That was about two hundred yards further forward. It was wide enough for men to pass easily, and steps led down into dugouts here and there. Jack pricked his ears. Surely that was Helmuth's voice. He was out of sight in a dugout.

'See, Baron. Here is light at the flick of a switch! Your bed made up, table, easy chair, chest for your clothes. You might imagine yourself at home, might you not?'

'Hold your tongue, you old fool,' said Hansel.

Jack had made an interesting discovery. A young man, quite dead. He had been moved to the back of the trench, and a rifle with fixed bayonet had been stuck into the earth, both to show where he was, and to prevent him from rolling into the path of the men.

He had been shot through the head.

Plainly, this was the work of the Enemy. The man was little older than Hansel or Kurt. Men were not shot for being gun-shy or vicious – Jack knew that. He wasn't sure whether very old men were shot when they were of no further use. Baron Heinrich's hunting dog, König, had been shot for being old. He had no other fault. Johann had done it. And Eloise's saluki had been shot because he had a sore which would not heal. Jack examined the dead man carefully. He appeared to have been perfectly healthy. Kurt had not noticed him.

The confusion had died down. Kurt leaned against a concrete support. The steps down to the dugout were concrete too, and the dugout was proof against anything except a direct hit.

Jack pushed his nose hard into Kurt's limp, calloused hand. Nose and hand alike were cold and moist. What a disgrace, thought Jack, that Kurt's coat was so thin. The young Baron wore a greatcoat which reached almost to his spurred heels, although he had no need of it, warm in the underground chamber which was far more luxurious than the bedroom of Kurt's parents. Jack could hear Helmuth's nannyish tones as he tried to coax Hansel, who was young enough to have been his grandson, out of his fit of sulks.

A few flares traced green and yellow paths in the night sky over to the west. Kurt clutched Jack's muzzle and whispered something. Jack pulled away, licked Kurt's hand in apology. Kurt was trembling; it was very cold.

Jack had an overcoat. He could have done without it. How unfair that Kurt should shiver, while Jack was snug in field grey alpaca, bordered with Prussian blue. On one side, a Prussian eagle glowered in gold, on the other was the insignia of the Baron's household. Jack wore a more valued article round his neck. The collar had been beautifully made by Kurt, from softest leather, tooled with his name. JACK.

Silence. Darkness. A rat hurried by. Rats were not the concern of the Gracious One's personal guard. Still, one could not help one's hackles rising. The rat observed Jack, and quickened its pace.

In the east, a pale glimmer appeared, reflected pinkly on the snow. Gradually, it deepened to a glow. Soon it would be dawn. A star shell curved into the air, hung for a moment over no man's land and floated slowly down, shimmering, dazzlingly white, beautiful beyond words. A lovely, harmless firework. Kurt wiped his nose on his sleeve, and watched, sniffing. He craned his head to see better – began to relax. At his side, Jack too raised his head, puzzled by the sudden brightness.

'Keep your head down, boy, if you value it.' The sergeant spoke fast, in a thick, unfamiliar dialect. He was walking past with an officer who seemed just to have arrived from the rear.

Kurt lowered his head and listened, understanding little, as the sergeant went on speaking to the officer. He sounded tired and exasperated.

'We cannot support an attack, sir. These schoolboys and pensioners could not support a house of cards – they have had no training at all. Some Pomeranian madwoman sent them from her estate, and they were directed here by mistake in the confusion yesterday. At best they can be employed for guard duty, and for the filling of sandbags and repairing of wire. The men in the firing trench are all that remain after yesterday's attack. All the trained men are already in the front line, not more than twenty all told, exhausted and unfed. We need . . .'

'Yes, yes. You are telling me what I already know. If your support troops are as useless as you say, send some of them out to draw enemy fire. By such means two days ago, our guns eliminated an enemy battery.' The rest of the officer's words were lost to Kurt as the two men edged past the dead soldier, now faintly visible, lying with crossed hands, his head pillowed on his haversack.

Kurt's eyes followed the pair in alarm as they moved away, the outline of the officer's spiked helmet clearly to be seen, long coats flapping, boots smashing through the cat-ice to the mud underneath.

Kurt sidled down the highest of the dugout steps, Jack, like a dark shadow, close to his side. 'Come Jack, we will go down here. We value our heads, thou and I.'

As they went down the steps, Hansel's voice came clearly from below. 'Silence, Helmuth. I need no nursemaid to tell me if I may take off my breeches.'

'Take them off, Excellency, if you wish.' Helmuth's patience had snapped at last. 'If you prefer to fight the English in your shirt tails, that is your affair.'

Hansel's voice rose angrily. 'Insolence! My father would have had you court-martialled!'

'Your father, may he rest in peace, was a man. You are a spoiled child. Have me court-martialled then, but be prepared for the mockery of your elders when I give evidence.'

'Go away! Get out! Send Kurt to me.'

He is angry, thought Kurt.

He is afraid, thought Jack.

Helmuth emerged without a word. He looked old, tired and defeated. He shouldered past Kurt, who nervously took his place.

The dugout was a complete little room, lighted by an electric bulb. The ceiling was low, the walls made of concrete, with railway sleepers set upright at intervals to help support the heavy concrete roof. There were two chairs, a table with a wine bottle and a glass, and a vase of artificial roses. Pictures of the German royal family were tacked to the wall, and Hansel's greatcoat hung on a nail. On one of the chairs was a new pigskin dressing-case, gold mounted and initialled. Hansel sat on the camp bed, sulkily pulling on his breeches.

'Come in, Kurt. Don't stand gaping. You look like a fish.'

Kurt shut his mouth. Tears filled his eyes. He said nothing. Once more, he felt Jack offer the comfort of a cold nose, pressed into his hand.

Jack feared that Kurt was about to weep aloud, and that if he did, the Gracious One also would weep. A scene one would prefer not to witness. Jack hung back unhappily. 'Come, my friend, let us leave this place.'

'I've decided to lie down in my clothes for a while – I badly need some sleep. Go back up the steps; see if you can find out what is happening. Helmuth forgets I am not a child. He was rude – impertinent. I was obliged to send him away.' Hansel spoke huskily, the bad-tempered edge gone from his voice. 'You may leave Jack down here with me,' he went on. 'He will be in the way in the trench.'

Kurt gave Hansel a desperate look, hesitating in the doorway. Without Jack, he would be, if possible, more frightened than he was already.

Hansel, fastening his breeches, kept his eyes down. He fumbled with the buttons, trying to keep his hands steady.

Kurt's shaking fingers fondled Jack's ear. 'Sit, Jack,' he whispered. Jack sat. 'Stay.' Kurt retreated slowly up the steps, with backward glances.

He disappeared from view.

Jack was eight years old and had been thoroughly trained.

Obedience was ingrained in his nature. Never, since he was a puppy, had he disobeyed Kurt. Not once. He sat with his back to Hansel, listening with pricked ears.

'Here, Jack, come over here.' Hansel clicked his fingers. He who had hurt old Helmuth. He who had made Kurt weep.

Jack stood up, turned his head and looked straight at Hansel. He walked to the nearest railway sleeper, cocked his leg against it, and trotted back up the steps.

CHAPTER THREE

Sergeant Talbot, Royal Artillery, took off his mittens, tucked them into his belt and blew into his cracked palms to warm them. He'd always been a martyr to chilblains. At the moment, they occupied most of his attention, even though he could sense, and indeed shared, the unease of the crew of number four gun. It was beginning to get light, and for almost an hour the crews had been waiting for orders: waiting in the shelter pits and dugouts where the melted snow had turned to icy slush.

During the night, the limbers had brought up fresh supplies of eighteen-pound shells, their six-horse teams and drivers frighteningly visible against the snowy landscape. Something was afoot.

The battery hadn't recovered from its terrible hammering on Tuesday. Sergeant Talbot glanced lovingly at number four, the only gun of the six still in action when the order came to cease fire.

The gunners worked 'blind'. Major Graham, their forward officer, had been far ahead, hidden in the corner of a ruined barn. They hadn't seen when a shell carried away half the barn, and the Major with it. Their Battery Commander killed —but the crews hadn't known that at the time, only that the field telephone had gone dead just as they had found their range.

Lieutenant Foster, the Gun Position Officer, passing on messages from the Forward Officer in his dugout, had emerged, shouting for a man to go forward, repair the wire and take Major Graham's place if necessary. Until the wire was mended, the guns had to stop firing. An attack was in progress, and the gunners couldn't see their target two miles away. If their sights were a fraction to right or left of their aiming point, if their range was shortened or lengthened, the shells could well fall on their own troops. They had waited by their guns, frustrated.

That was when the German guns had raised their sights, and homed in with terrifying accuracy on the battery.

The crew of number five had been killed to a man while, by some freak of blast, the gun remained unharmed. Thank God the telephone was working again – Sergeant-Major Simpson came running, giving orders breathlessly as he came to a slithering halt.

Number two had been put out of action without firing a shot. Number one fired . . . number three . . . four . . . six . . .

A pause while the gunners had adjusted to new angles and ranges in response to a string of bellowed orders. Six men had been killed instantly as a shell exploded under the muzzle of number two. Number one had been hit, and keeled over on her side as the crew jumped for safety and, hardly pausing, ran to man number five.

Number three fired . . . number four . . . number six. Two men sprawling, others drag them out of the way. 'Get back, Sanders, knock up some reinforcements – Who? Anybody. Hurry.'

Then Philips had left his post on number six. Philips of all people. Most of the time, Sergeant Talbot managed not to think about Philips. 'Poor sod,' he muttered to himself. Men were groaning, crying out – you took no notice – hadn't time. Be glad it wasn't you . . . forget everything but the job in hand. Bung in a shell, slam the breech shut, jerk the firing lever; snow on the ground, sweat in your eyes, your feet numb. Smell of lyddite and hot iron and blood. Made you feel sick.

'Number three's jammed, sir.' The man had sounded relieved. Conditions had grown if possible worse when the crews were patched up with unskilled men – officers' grooms, servants, orderlies – anyone who could lift a shell and do as he was told. Fear made them clumsy; their hands shook; they slipped and stumbled and swore.

Number four gun fired . . . number six . . . Seconds later,
stretcher-bearers were running to number six, where three
men lay wounded and the gun stood idle with damaged sights.
Number four fired . . .

Now, two days late, the gunners who had survived were
still jumpy and irritable, snapping edgily at one another. The
wounded were gone, the dead buried. Number one gun was
right way up and ready for action. Philips – no use thinking
about him. Number two and number five were serviceable
again. Fresh supplies of shells were waiting beside them.

Sergeant Talbot came from industrial Lancashire. This level
landscape, with its slag heaps and factory chimneys made him
feel homesick. No wonder the Frenchies didn't like smashing
it up. Sergeant Frewen from the New Forest had felt the same
about the Somme last year, he remembered. But Frewen was
dead. Like Philips. Funny about Philips really. Such a quiet
bloke. Liked a bit of fishing better than anything, Philips did.
And a good cool-headed gunner. The last man you'd expect
to go crazy in the middle of a barrage. Crazy! He hadn't half!
You couldn't blame young Foster for shooting him – nothing
else to be done, was there? Sergeant Talbot shivered, and
turned to curse a man who had bumped against him.

Their position was so damned flat. The tottering factory wall
was sure to fall down before long, and there they'd be, set up
like so many Aunt Sallys. Gunshields weren't any good – not
against shrap. It came down on you, not at you. You felt naked
with nothing but a camouflage net between you and Jerry's
shrap.

Too quiet by half this morning. Soon be light. The Jerries
might be trying their latest trick again – getting crafty, old
Jerry. He'd deserted his front-line trenches on Monday, drawn
the Frenchies in, outflanked them, and enfiladed their positions with machine-gun fire. Now it looked as if he might be
trying it on us. No use wasting shells on empty trenches,
smashing them up when the Royal Dublin Fusiliers were going
in.

Are we going to sit here until we bloody well freeze solid?

Sergeant Talbot put his mittens on again. He was pleased
when the new Battery Commander arrived in the half light

with orders. The officer vanished in the direction of the obser-
vation post – or what was left of it – and the guns were trained
on a target. Sergeant-Major Simpson yelled through his mega-
phone and the guns began to fire. One round, shorten the
range a little, two more rounds. Cease fire. Only three rounds!
Not worth getting up for, standing to for hours on end. Three
flaming rounds! Sergeant Talbot breathed on his swollen
fingers. There was no response from Jerry's guns – that was
something.

Half an hour later, the Forward Officer appeared, looking
as if he'd never heard of snipers, swinging his binoculars.
'Going to snow,' he said.

'Any other news, sir?' Lieutenant Foster tried to sound
casual without much success.

'Those Germans are surrendering. They looked a job lot
from where I was. First shell landed slap in their support
trench, and one of the next batch blew a gap in their barbed
wire. I don't think we've done them much harm. Might be a
trap, I suppose. The Dublins are occupying the trench now.'
He wandered off in the direction of the clump of trees which
hid the horse lines, swinging his glasses and humming 'Tipper-
ary' very much out of tune.

At first, Jack thought the Noise must have killed him. It was
possible, he was sure – such a dreadful sound could certainly
kill. I think, therefore I live, thought Jack. But there is no light
. . . no air . . . I am crushed.

His paws were at work already, digging wildly at the cold
lumpy earth. No thought of Kurt – survival comes first. Dig –
and push the earth aside, trying not to breathe it in. Dig in
panic with bursting lungs, dizzy and choking – this is the
end. Suddenly earth slides aside and pebbles fall. The fearful
pressure has gone.

Jack's head emerged from the mound of clay, then his
frantic paws. The noise hit him like a sledgehammer. It was
something like that which had so nearly killed him, but further
away. He paused, blinking, shaking his head so that his ears
flapped; then hauled himself to the surface hampered by the
heavy jacket whose straps dragged at his chest. He rubbed his

eye with the inside of a foreleg. It felt gritty but he could see.
I have been wounded, thought Jack. My side is hurt. There
is blood. He shook himself violently and sneezed. *Kurt!* My
friend – where is he? Memory was coming back. Before the
Noise, he had been trying to comfort Kurt by licking his hand.
Kurt had been weeping, and was sniffing, wiping his eyes on
his wrist. They were standing together, near the Gracious
One's underground bedroom. Now there was a great hole as
deep as a well where the bedroom had been. Planks and rocks
were tumbled together with bags split open and spilling sand
at the bottom of it. Jack turned away, puzzled. He looked the
other way. There was old Helmuth, climbing out of the trench
with half a dozen others. They held up a white tablecloth and
shouted 'Kamerad!' Kurt was not among them.

Jack was alone. Without doubt, Kurt was buried. The dog's
sober sensible nature was shaken to its foundations. Never in
his life had he been alone. For a wild moment, he wanted to
run – anywhere – round in circles perhaps; to howl, to bark.
Anything rather than admit to himself that Kurt was beneath
that mound of earth, and that he, Jack, must try to rescue his
friend; must return to that living grave.

Fusilier O'Hara, short, grizzled and bow-legged, peered into
the gaping crater where Hansel's dugout had been. Proof
against anything except a direct hit. Wasn't that a suitcase
down there, among the busted sandbags? Queer the way some
things missed getting smashed up. It looked a nice little case
with goldy corners on it. It could stay there.

The Second Battalion Royal Dublin Fusiliers, the Old Toughs
as they were called, had been slow to occupy the support
trench. There had been uncannily few men in the front line,
a mixture of boys and old men, all falling over one another to
give themselves up. A handful who looked more like regular
soldiers had surrendered as well. They seemed to have no food
and no ammunition, and shuffled off apathetically with their
captors. Then another batch of lads and grandfathers had come
swarming out of the support trench, their white flag so large,
it kept flopping down on their heads. Fearing a trap, the
Dublins advanced cautiously, using the communication

trenches, ready to lob a grenade ahead at the first sign of opposition.

'Come here, will you, and take a look at this,' Fusilier O'Hara shouted without turning his head.

'What've you found now, Willie? You'll get killed hunting for bloody souvenirs.' Corporal Eugene Boyle joined him, picking his way over the debris.

'You're the souvenir hunter, not me, Corporal. There's a fine case in that crater if you feel like climbing down for it. Solid gold.'

'Go on out of that – solid gold! Did you call me over to look at a dog? Bad luck to you.'

'What's he after, I wonder.'

'Digging for bones,' said Boyle sardonically. 'There's no shortage around here.'

'He has a coat on him. The Jerries must have had a great regard for him. It's all blood, look. He's hurted.'

'You'll get shot, standing up there, watching an old dog digging a hole. He's after rats. Have sense.' Boyle moved off.

Willie O'Hara had a black dog at home. A clever creature of uncertain ancestry, called Tip. He was a devil for finding useful bits and pieces on their walks – brought him a mouth-organ once. And he loved swimming off Dollymount Strand, fetching in bits of driftwood. Willie tried not to think about home and Alice and the young ones. He went down on his knees.

'Hey boy! What're you after then? – Oh Mother of God!' For Jack, his breath coming in great heaving gasps, had un-covered the side of Kurt's head – and the head moved.

Willie reached down to grab Jack's collar, but the back-ward snarl and clash of teeth made him change his mind. An interested circle of men began to collect as Jack, gently now, pushed the soil aside and licked mud from Kurt's cheek. 'My dear friend, I am here at thy side. Lie still so that I may assist thee.'

'It's only a young lad,' said someone. 'Catch the dog, Willie, till we get him out.'

Jack cried out in fear and grief as he felt suffocating cloth drop over his head, then Willie's firm grip on his collar. Willie understood dogs, and he quickly slipped a noose of string round Jack's nose, pulled it tight and tied it behind his ears. 'We'll keep him,' he said. 'He's the very same as Tip at home.'

He held the dog firmly, as three of the soldiers uncovered Kurt's head and shoulders and brushed the earth from his face.

'He's smothered.'

'He is not, he only got a crack on the poll. He's coming out of it.'

Kurt moved his head again slightly. Muttered.

'What's he saying?'

'Wants his mother, poor lad. Shame, isn't it?'

Jack almost pulled Willie O'Hara off his feet. He had got his wind back. 'Release me, fools. Can you not see that my friend needs me?'

'Let him see the dog, lads.'

'Jack,' said Kurt clearly.

'My friend, I am so sorry. I have been wounded myself, otherwise without doubt I should have reached thee more quickly. Farewell, my friend.'

The blue eyes opened, focused on Jack for a moment, then glazed. 'Might as well cover him up again,' said Corporal Boyle.

Jack had lost a good deal of blood. He was weak and dazed, and once more alone. He allowed himself to be picked up by the enemy soldier with the kind voice, and carried away.

Jack's whole life had been spent helping with the organized killing of wild creatures – hare, buck, wildfowl. He was familiar with death; so familiar that he attached no importance to bodies. König, the old Baron's hunting dog, had known the precise moment when von Hessel had died, hundreds of miles distant. His howls of despair had kept the other dogs awake. But the faithful hound stretched on his master's grave until he starved was a creature outside Jack's understanding.

Jack's friend had gone. The corpse was simply a dead thing, with a good piece of sausage going to waste in its pocket.

One certainty shone clear in Jack's mind, easing his pain and misery. Kurt had understood his last message perfectly, and had replied, *'Farewell, my dear friend,'* in Jack's own language.

Captain Tom Daly twisted a candle firmly into the neck of an empty whiskey bottle and lighted it. Although two other candles were alight and it was morning, the cellar was a place of inky shadows and deep gloom. His servant Mick McCoy was preparing food in an adjoining room.

Tom unscrewed the cap of his silver fountain pen, looking at it fondly as he did so. On it was engraved, 'T.W.D. from C.L.S. 10.8.1916.'

'Darlingest One,' [wrote Tom]. 'It's quiet again here, after a busy morning, so I snatch this moment to write. What are you doing today I wonder? Are you out riding Split-the-Wind, or playing the piano, or writing to me, perhaps? Out here, it's still snowing on and off, but somehow I can't imagine you in the snow. When I think about you (most of the time), it's summer at Shane Place and you are playing tennis with me, laughing, and with your hair all over the place, and sending ball after ball smack into the net. Oh darling, I love you so much, although you don't play tennis very well! I remember those happy days, and try to forget the goodbyes at Kingsbridge. I hope you do too.

'Celia, I'm shocked at myself. I find I don't care much any more about anything except you. My strongest emotion is disgust, varied by fright if there's any shooting and apathy if there isn't. Three years. That first autumn we countrymen used to feel dreadfully guilty about flattening the standing corn. We minded. When we heard good news, which wasn't often, we were simply thrilled. Can't remember if I told you a story about the Royal Irish after Mons. An officer and a trumpeter rallied the troops with a toy drum and a tin whistle when they were ready to drop. The Royal Irish fired the first British shots of the war, you know. Things like that don't seem to happen any more, or if they do, we're too cold and tired to care. What a dismal letter! Sorry.

'Another thing I remember that first year, was coming across the remains of a French company, lying about in the corn in their blue tunics and funny red trousers. "The many men so beautiful, and they all dead did lie —". It seemed unreal at the time. The colours have gone now. Everything is brown or grey or khaki. Thank God we seem to be winning at last, but we don't talk about "Having a go at the Huns" any more.

'Here comes McCoy looking hard-done-by as usual. I'll finish this later . . .'

'Yes, McCoy?'

'You're wanted, sir.' McCoy had slipped in unheard, an irritating trick — made you jump.

'The men in the back trench, the Jerry support like, they're fighting over a dog, sir.'

'A dog? How ridiculous. Whose dog?'

'A Jerry dog like. He's wounded, sir. That O'Hara wants to keep him like. Corporal Boyle's for shooting him. They're fighting like tinkers, sir.'

'Very well, I'll go. I'll be back in a few minutes. See if you can organize something to eat, will you?'

Why the hell couldn't young Fetherston manage without sending for him? God alone knew how he would react in a real emergency. Tom saw that it had started to snow again. He pulled on his balaclava, turned his greatcoat collar up, and looked out. He was going to be pretty conspicuous. He knew damn well McCoy hadn't been across. He probably picked up the information from somebody coming back. Better wear a tin hat. He took it off its peg and crammed it over the woolly helmet. Crossly he set off, dodging through the ruins of Festubert.

Half a mile and a quarter of an hour later, Tom dropped into what had been the German support trench, where supposedly a dozen men were employed moving sandbags from the front to the back, and digging firing steps on what was now the front. Of course, the dugouts were all on the wrong side now, but they were beauties, deep and strong.

There was Lieutenant Fetherston without his habitual grin. The fight seemed to be over. O'Hara was sitting on a packing case with a black dog stretched across his knees. Its head, legs and tail were filthy, its body comparatively clean. Over its ribs was a deep gash, oozing blood.

'He's living, sir. If we get the cut stitched, he could come all right.'

Tom bit his lip. He liked dogs, and hated having to shoot one. This was the third casualty in a week. 'Sorry, O'Hara, I'm afraid he's done for. Put him down there will you, and I'll finish him off.'

Willie O'Hara was a decent chap, but really this was too much. Instead of obeying, he stood there, obstinately holding the dog in his arms.

'I said put it down.'

The dog raised its bedraggled head and looked straight at Tom. Its muzzle was tied with a piece of string. There was something about its eyes . . . O'Hara still hadn't moved.

Tom returned his revolver to his belt. 'Poor fellow. Perhaps he isn't as badly hurt as I thought at first.'

O'Hara spoke eagerly. 'Sergeant Rourke was down at the dressing station having his hand fixed, sir. He said there was nobody there hardly. He said they were cold down there for the want of a job. Will we take him down?'

Tom laughed. He liked Willie O'Hara who reminded him of the groom at Shane Place. 'Right you are. You carry him, and I'll come and see fair play.' They set off for the dressing station, and at once an argument broke out behind them.

'It's mine. It's a souvenir.'

'It belongs to the dog.'

'The dog's dying. It's mine. I'm keeping it.'

Tom looked round at the two angry soldiers. 'Let's see the souvenir, Corporal.'

The other man said eagerly, 'It's the dog's tunic, sir. He'll want it to keep him warm.'

Corporal Boyle sullenly held out a muddy, bloody piece of cloth.

'Not much of a souvenir – you're welcome to it. No, wait a minute, what's this?' Gold braid had caught Tom's eye. 'It's a coronet – a Prussian eagle, Fetherston, look at this. Tell you what, Corporal, you have it washed so we can see it properly,

I'll get details of the crest, and you can have your souvenir to keep. It must belong to one of the Prussian bigwigs. It might tell us who was in that dugout.'

'Corporal Boyle gave me this dressing case he found,' said Charles Fetherston, with slight ironic emphasis. 'Gold corners, initials, everything. Locked, of course. Shall I take it back?'

'Yes, do.' Tom turned to Boyle. 'Some day, one of your souvenirs will blow up, and serve you right,' he said pleasantly. He raised his voice and added in sudden impatience, 'I don't want any more squabbling here. Get back to your posts.' As the men bent to their work, Tom followed O'Hara in the direction of the first aid post.

Lying across Willie O'Hara's knees in the trench, Jack had wanted to die, but the will to live had begun to assert itself in spite of everything.

These alien soldiers were fighting among themselves, who could tell why, their voices rising and falling. Should they not have been speaking English, the language of the beautiful Miss Briggs? Their tongue was not like hers.

The small man with kind hands, upon whose knees Jack lay, had removed the field-grey monogrammed coat with care. 'Easy, now, boy.' He had lifted the sodden cloth gently away from the wound. He had examined the place that bled with stubby fingers. It was painful, but not beyond bearing. One could not cry out with one's nose tied, in any case. Jack had shut his eyes, worn out.

Some sort of upheaval had brought Jack back to reality with a start. The soldier who held him was now standing up. Boots were approaching; alien boots, not made of leather, but of a substance which smelled strongly. He had been unable to place the smell, but a memory flashed through his mind of Baron Heinrich's automobile. Tyres, that's what it was. Look higher. Breeches, shabby but of good cut, under an open khaki greatcoat. Mittened hands – one had held a small gun, such as the noble Hansel had used for target practice.

Jack had gazed up at a face which, in other circumstances, would have pleased him. The eyes, as blue as Kurt's, had an expression of annoyance, the nose was straight, the mouth sensitive, beneath a tidy brown moustache. The eyes had looked forth from a woollen hood with a basin-like metal hat on top of it. In spite of this strange attire, the man had not appeared ridiculous. The enemy soldier with the kind hands had been ordered to lay Jack down, so that the hooded one might shoot him. That was plain enough.

One has but a single language, and humans do not understand it. Except Kurt − a little, at the end . . .

'Must I too be shot? I have harmed nobody; my wound is not mortal. May I not be made a prisoner of war?'

Jack had looked into the blue eyes without hope, then shut his own. He had not been laid on the ground. No shot had come. They had talked together for a while, the soldier and his superior − he that carried the small gun, then Jack had been carried away somewhere and set down on a hard surface. Then he had lost consciousness.

Jack came to with painful suddenness. He was in a small building, somewhat like the cottage of Johann and Marthe. He had been laid on a kitchen table, a rough affair of planks, covered by a sheet. Overhead, a brilliant light dazzled him, and gave out a hissing sound. Strange. There was a strong, peculiar, but not unpleasant smell. Soldiers held him, while brown liquid which burned was poured into his wound. He whined, thrashing his legs, and a voice spoke.

'I told you he'd need more gas − give me that pad. All right, old man − have you fixed up in a jiffy.'

The smell grew stronger, and it seemed to Jack that he floated above the table where an injured dog lay unconscious, watching without pain as a khaki-coated person put nine stitches in the wound. Feeling returned as he was lifted clear of the table, and a piece of lint wrapped right round him, and after that a bandage − round and round. The man with the gun spoke his name.

'There's a name worked on his collar − Jack − funny name for a German dog. The collar's beautifully made, isn't it? I'll bet they thought a lot of this chap.' He opened a pocket-knife, and carefully cut Jack's string muzzle.

'Careful, sir, he'll bite you.'

'Not a bit of it. You won't bite me, Jack, will you? Try him with a drink of water.'

This person spoke more nearly in the fashion of Miss Briggs. Also, he had intelligence. Water! Jack could not remember his last drink. His dry mouth and throat troubled him as much as his gashed side. The water had a strange taste, but what of that? He drank it all.

'. . . Well, Celia, I'm back in my cellar again, plus one wounded and shell-shocked dog. You can imagine how I stared when McCoy called me out to settle a quarrel about a dog! The poor fellow's master was buried by a shell blast, and "Jack" was busy digging him out. The German was dead, and one of the men managed to muzzle "Jack", who had a nasty cut on his side, and was in no mood to fraternize with the enemy, I can tell you. He's a sort of small black retriever, a mongrel, I daresay, but he has a beautiful head. Major Lambe, who is an absolutely top-notch surgeon in peacetime, stitched him up.

'Extraordinary thing is, the dog was wearing a coat – a sort of crested livery, and he must have belonged to somebody important.

'I must finish this, and get back to work. Darling, I shut my eyes and I can see your face, carefree and happy, always smiling. Are you the tiniest bit of a flirt? No, of course you're not. You are the light of my life, the only reason . . .'

'Yes, McCoy, what is it?'

'The suitcase, sir, I have it cleaned up like.' He set it on the table, and Tom impatiently snatched away the three thin sheets of paper he'd been writing on.

'It's a nice little case,' Tom said. 'Locked, of course. It seems rather a pity to break the lock.'

'A bit of wire, sir. It'd be easy opened; I could do it for you like, no bother.'

'Could you, McCoy? I expect you could. Very well. Get it open.'

'. . . Another interruption. I must watch the unspeakable McCoy pick the lock of a little dressing-case the men found in the captured trench. It may have papers in it, and McC. isn't above pinching a gold-mounted toothpick if he gets the chance!

Blessings,

your own
Tom.'

'There now, sir, it's opened and the lock hardly scratched at all.'

'Thanks. Get that meal ready, soon as you can. Mr Fetherston should be in by now.'

McCoy gave Tom a sour glance, muttered 'Yes, sir,' and slid out of the cellar, silent in his rubber boots.

Tom put his letter in his tunic pocket, and drew the case towards him. Pigskin, gold mounted, initialled H. J. W. H. von H. I'd suppress those initials, he thought, not emboss them in gold. Inside, gold-backed brushes, comb, jars . . . the damn thing was worth a fortune. The man must have been mad, bringing it out here. A solid gold cigar box caught Tom's eye. He took it out, startled at its weight. All this must be sent back to base where it could be locked up. He noticed a morocco-bound notebook which had been under the box, and picked it up. It was rubbed, and the pencil which fitted down its back was chewed at the end. Perhaps this was something important. He opened the book. A page of German script, clearly written in a childish hand. Tom knew just enough schoolboy German to make it out.

July 1st 1914

"Today is my Feast. I am fourteen years old. My father is making ready for the war which is coming, and Miss Briggs has already returned to her home.

This book is for Miss Briggs
SONNETS
by
Hansel von Hessel."

Tom whistled. Von Hessel, eh? Must be pretty closely related to the Kaiser. He turned over the pages, and saw with relief that the German script gave way to English copperplate.

> 'I would give all I own to be with
> The Fair One whose first name is Edith . . .'

Tom smiled, not unkindly, and glanced through the pages. The book was full.

> 'Ah, sweeter, far sweeter than Heaven,
> To dwell with fair Edith in Devon . . .'

Poor boy – he was still almost three months short of his seventeenth birthday! Tom buttoned the book into his pocket, and didn't mention it to Fetherston, who bounced in at that moment, bringing an unnecessary amount of snow with him, and demanding food.

'How's the dog?' he asked, as he sat down.

'I'm not sure,' said Tom, looking at Jack's inert body, just visible in the shadows. 'He's breathing, and seems warm enough. Lambe didn't know how much chloroform to give him. First he didn't get enough, and started to come round too soon. Then I suppose we gave him too much. Poor old Jack.'

'Are we going to keep him then?'

'If he lives. The men want him to be a regimental mascot. They had a tame tiger in India – they loved that.'

'If you ask me, that dog should be put out of its misery.' McCoy spoke just loud enough to be heard as he brought in a bowl of hot stew.

'We didn't ask you,' Tom snapped. He ate a little stew, and pushed it away. 'Sorry, Charles,' he said to Fetherston, 'I'm in a vile temper. Can't seem to help it. Ah well, we'll be relieved tonight, if the Argylls make it. Then we'll go to Paris on the razzle, perhaps.'

'Really?' said Fetherston, eagerly. 'How ripping!'

Tom gave him a look of annoyance. 'No, not really,' he said coldly. 'And you'd better get yourself cleaned up as soon as you've finished eating. The C. O. said he'd be along soon.'

He took his hardly tasted stew over to Jack, and knelt beside him. 'Want some dinner, Jack? Nice bit of horse?'

Fetherston's maddening grin had disappeared. 'Horse? It isn't actually horse, is it?'

'Actually a nice bay mare – sorry, Charles, I was pulling your leg. It's genuine British fourteen-year-old cow, I promise.'

Baffled, Fetherston went through into the room which was his and another lieutenant's sleeping quarters. Tom saw him go with relief. Young Charles Fetherston had been out only a week, and his unrelieved cheerfulness was altogether too much of a good thing.

Jack lay stretched out on his good side, the right. His stitches throbbed, but he didn't turn his head to bite at the bandage. Kurt is dead, he thought, and I am prisoner of war. I am indeed fortunate not to be dead also. The person whose boots smell like tyres is merciful.

The younger man, whom Jack's rescuer addressed as Charles, had returned from the inner room, and was seated on a wooden box, laughing and talking. His laugh was loud and foolish. Although the moustached one called this Charles 'Mr Fetherston' when speaking to the dishonest servant, it appeared that he who laughed was also an officer.

Jack had accepted some gravy from the stew, and another drink of the curious water. With a slight groan, he settled himself more comfortably into the nest of cloth, which might be an ancient velvet curtain. It smelled of long-dead bats. Even so had smelled the little shed where he and Kurt . . .

'What's up, old fellow? What are you whining about? Ribs hurting you, eh?' Tom Daly bent down, resting his hand for a moment on Jack's head. 'Eh, Jack, old lad?'

'No, my enemy, not my ribs. It is my heart that aches.' But Tom, like Kurt, was incapable of picking up the messages Jack sent him.

Jack felt a sense of shame. He should not have called his deliverer 'enemy', but if not that, then how to address him? Friend? Never! Master? No, not yet; perhaps not ever. Who could tell? It is good to call someone master, because a dog without a master is like a cart without a horse or a bird without wings.

Jack, wakeful now, looked closely at the two men, and his puzzlement grew. What kind of men are these, who are soldiers and officers, and go into battle wearing soft collars and neckties? Slovenly amateurs! thought Jack with a spurt of anger, as he remembered Kurt's bare sunburned throat, and Hansel's chokingly high-braided collar.

The laughing man wore no boots. His legs were wrapped with strips of cloth, closely resembling those worn by Prussian peasants when they go to work in their turnip fields. They too bind their legs with cloth against the cold. Boots cost many marks. They are not for daily toil.

And this older man, he who had been prepared to share his food with a dog, was of superior rank to the laughing one. A captain. But although he wore three stars on his shoulder, he still wore his helmet of wool. An officer should wear a helmet of patent leather or of brass, spiked, or perhaps plumed. His eyes should gleam with eagerness to join the fray, his cheeks should bear the scars of other fights, his spurs should clank on his tall shining boots. One such might be master, but could never be friend. Neither would he concern himself with a dog. One could not envisage such a person offering one the remains of his food.

Jack gave up trying to understand. He closed his eyes. Ah, Kurt, Kurt my friend. Why did you have to travel so far and so painfully to die so soon?

CHAPTER FOUR

Jack lay hour after hour in the damp, gloomy cellar room. The officer with three stars on his shoulder, addressed by the laughing one as Daly, spoke often to Jack. He did not speak in mockery as to a defeated foe, but in the tones of one who addresses a wounded comrade.

When no officer was present, the servant, McCoy, busied himself sweeping and tidying the room. This person, who smelled like one who did not change his underwear sufficiently often, ignored Jack. He resented his instructions to keep the dog's water bowl replenished, although he dared not disobey.

One day, as he bent down to perform this task, Jack, disturbed from feverish half-sleep, started up, trying to rise. This he could do. He could, given time, scramble to his feet and walk stiffly outside in order to relieve himself, but sudden movement was painful. He made a strangled sound, half yelp, half whine.

'Ah, you'd go for me would you, Fritz, you stinking hoor?' McCoy's army boot shot out, striking Jack on the hindquarters. He slammed down the drinking bowl and marched out, followed by Jack's angry snarl.

'Evil-smelling, lying servant! You who examine the letters of the Herr Hauptmann and fawn and thieve! My late master would have had you whipped. Not for two days would you have been kept by His Excellency. Scoundrel!'

Thereafter, Jack never failed to growl at McCoy's approach, and several times he would have been left thirsty but for the consideration of the officer, Daly.

Jack had no knowledge of the passage of time, as his fever came and went, and little daylight reached the corner where he lay. Perhaps three days had passed, perhaps four, before his fever subsided. The same day, Captain Daly entered the room with his tunic off, and his sleeves rolled up. He carried a bowl of warm water, which he placed on the floor. Jack lay still as death, but he watched every movement.

'Sorry about this, old boy.' In a flash he twisted a tape around Jack's muzzle, just as the other soldier had done. Jack clawed at it to no avail. The captain was busy with sharp scissors, cutting away the bandage and cloth that bound Jack's body, until the blood-soaked dressing was reached. This he soaked off with warm water, uttering senseless remarks the while.

'Steady the Buffs,' he said. 'That's it. Now then!' A curious language, English. One had considered oneself familiar with it. The wound was clean, and Captain Daly did not replace the bandage. He applied a fresh lint pad, and fastened it in place with pink strips of material which adhered firmly to Jack's fur. Tom pulled off the muzzle, keeping clear of Jack's teeth. 'I think you and I would be friends if you could forget your German master,' he said.

'Sir, we can never be friends. I thank you nonetheless.'

Tom lacked something to do. There was no word of an advance, one could not go out without being fired at, and the orders were, not to return fire. The four officers played bridge, wrote letters and read. Tom's last two letters from Celia were rubbed almost through at the creases.

'Every morning,' she wrote, 'when I look out of my bedroom window, I remember the first time we met, when I did just that, and there you were. Walking up the drive in uniform, carrying your little suitcase. I remember how you looked up and waved, and I went tearing down to meet you. Do you remember?'

Of course he remembered. As if he could forget. There'd been a muddle about trains, and he'd walked to Shane Place from the station. It had been his first leave since the war started, and he'd spent the first week of it in Dublin, where his mother had been living. The family place, Liscullen, had been let to Tom's uncle on the death of his father, many years earlier. Tom's visits there were brief and rare; he didn't like to seem interfering, or to be impatient for Uncle Fred to retire.

Unattached and personable, Tom had found himself in demand in Dublin. Fresh from the horrors of the Western Front, he had tried to get them out of his mind as he squired pretty girls to balls, theatres and the fashionable poetry readings. Tom would have been horrified if he could have heard these young ladies discussing him. They had decided that his life must have been blighted by an unhappy romance. How else could he have escaped marriage for so long? They hadn't been far from the truth. Tom liked the company of women as much as anyone, but his only serious affair had done much to shake his faith in women in general. The lovely Judith, whom he had met in India, had had a stony heart and a calculating brain. Tom had found this out in time, but even now, his memories of Judith made the Dublin girls seem insipid. Was he turning into a cynical old bachelor? Tom had wondered.

Tom had visited Shane Place because his cousin, Michael St John, missing since Mons, had been engaged to Laura Shane. Tom had been the last to see Michael – had seen him pitch head first into a shellhole. Tom had returned to look for him, but had not found any trace of him. By Michael's bed, Tom had found a letter addressed to Laura, and had decided to deliver it in person. He knew and liked Laura, but remembered Celia as an overgrown schoolgirl, handing round cakes at tea.

Celia at just seventeen was as tall as Tom himself, just over five feet ten. Her hair hung loose down her back, a sign that she had not yet 'come out'. It was held back by tortoiseshell combs and tied with ribbon. Her white blouse and ankle-skimming serge skirt had been school uniform, but she had left Miss Condell's establishment a month earlier.

Celia's warmth and lack of artifice had captivated Tom. Her unconcealed admiration would have flattered almost anyone. And her beauty had stopped him in his tracks, even while discretion warned – too young – keep off.

Celia had run across the gravel to meet him. 'Captain Daly? I'm Laura's sister Celia. Do you remember me? Oh I do hope you've brought her some news – I can't bear to see her so miserable.' She had held out her hand unselfconsciously. What a refreshing change!

'How do you do, Celia. I'm sorry, I haven't any good news for your sister. I've brought a letter Michael left, and I can tell her a few things she might like to know, but that's all. I'm afraid I'm frightfully early.'

'Never mind, we haven't had breakfast yet. I'll tell Bridget to fry more eggs.' With a sudden reversion to childhood, Celia had dashed into the house.

Tom had been going to stay overnight, but the visit stretched to three days. Celia, who was motherless, had much more freedom than most young girls of her time: Tom had played tennis with her on the mossy court where the balls hardly bounced and the net was full of holes. Celia had played with great enthusiasm and no skill, so they had spent a good deal of time searching for lost balls among the rhododendrons where her slapdash swipes had sent them. At times Tom had almost forgotten the war. They had laughed and run and shouted as if he too had been seventeen.

Tom had kissed Celia the day he left, all good resolutions forgotten. They had run to shelter from a shower under the giant copper beach whose falling leaves did nothing to improve the tennis court. It was a gentle kiss, Celia's first, Tom was sure. He hadn't wanted to frighten her or to spoil their friendship. Some day, he thought, if I survive this war, I'll ask her to marry me. Celia's response had both delighted Tom and alarmed him. She had thrown her arms round his neck, and returned the kiss rapturously. 'Oh Tom, I love you.'

'Love's a big word,' said Tom, releasing Celia breathlessly.

'But I do love you. Darling Tom, I really do. Don't you love me? I thought you did.'

'Yes, I love you too, Celia.' (Good God, what had he said?) True, he *did* love what he knew of her. He had kissed her again. Celia's immaturity would be outgrown in another year or two, and what a glorious woman she would be then. Anyway, he was sick and tired of sophistication.

Celia had assumed that a kiss amounted to an engagement, as it did in all the popular romances. Tom had felt more and more uneasy.

'You mustn't promise to spend the rest of your life with someone you've only known three days. You might change your mind tomorrow when I've gone, or something might happen to me. Besides, your father would say I was cradle-snatching – I'm almost thirty!'

'Oh, but I *want* to be cradle-snatched,' Celia had said eagerly. '*Please* can't we be engaged?'

'Not just yet, you ridiculous darling.'

'Will you write to me? Proper love-letters? *Please.*'

'Yes I will, and you must write to me. That would be grand. Something to look forward to . . .'

So they'd written to each other, putting down on paper, in spite of the censors, far more than they would have said aloud.

Tom's next leave had been almost two years later, and he had survived the Somme campaign. He had again been slightly wounded, but was more damaged in mind than in body. He felt that his youth had gone forever.

It had seemed an age since his first goodbye to Celia at Ballinasloe station, when he'd watched her tear-stained face recede, and had waved until it was out of sight. Three days – what could they really know of one another? Even so, Tom had been sure that Celia was the only girl for him.

On his return, she seemed hardly to have changed at all. A very young eighteen.

Celia's uninhibited and touching devotion had been just what Tom had needed. She made him laugh. She bought him presents – a fountain pen, a book of poems. Together, they'd chosen an engagement ring, and talked hopefully of the future.

One day, just before Tom had left, they had been sitting at the foot of the copper beech. 'There's something about you I can't put into words,' Tom had murmured. 'You remind me of beautiful, simple country things – wildflowers and young saplings and songbirds.'

'And spring lambs and home-made bread?'

'Yes, those too – I'm serious.' He had laid his head on her lap.

Celia had traced his features with a finger. 'I love your forehead, such a nice square shape, and the way your hair grows – why, you've got some white hairs! I even love this –' she touched the scar on his jaw. 'I know it's a bullet wound, but won't you tell me how it happened? Don't you want to?'

'No. Not really.'

'I wish you'd tell me more about the fighting; I feel shut out. Do you carry your sword?'

'Not now. We did in 1914. We were supposed to hold them high when we led an attack.'

'Like Henry the fifth at Agincourt?'

'Not in the least, and they're no use against guns. Please, sweetheart, don't let's talk about it.' He'd been worried by Celia's new fondness for propaganda magazines, and her willingness to believe anything, however absurd, about the Germans. He had been sure, though, that he could influence her – she was still so young.

Thinking about Celia made Tom smile, and as he read and re-read her letters, the lines round his mouth relaxed. He shut his eyes in an effort to banish the damp, squalid cellar with its guttering candles and its sour smell. He tried hard to recall her, sun-dappled under the copper beech; sweet and impulsive, and as warm as life itself. Lovely Celia! Delicious, delightful, delectable! What is she doing now? he wondered.

There had been a time when Celia Shane could sleep dreamlessly for ten hours at a stretch. How was it done? she wondered. The bedroom she shared with Laura, directly over the front door, was comfortable and bright, catching the morning sun. The room had been first nursery, then schoolroom. It still had white-painted furniture and two narrow white iron beds with crocheted counterpanes. A moth-eaten golliwog lolled on the window seat. There were a few signs of broadening interests and growing up – the gramophone, scattered records, prints by Arthur Rackham on the walls. Silver evening slippers lay on the floor, and powder bowls and scent-sprays cluttered the dressing-table.

Celia crept out of bed. Laura was asleep, her short fine hair spread over the pillow, an arm thrown above her head. Lord, how thin she was! Celia cautiously drew back a curtain, careful not to let the light fall on her sister's face. It streamed in, callously, she thought, like an overbright hospital nurse. 'How do we feel this morning?'

Irritable, was the answer. Irritable and restless. Gently, Celia raised the window higher, and propped it on a pair of wrought iron tongs. The sashcord was broken.

Below and to the right, she saw her father, Maurice Shane, coming through the side door, out into the dewy May morning. He never, or hardly ever used the front door, a pretentious affair with an ornate knocker and a bell which didn't work.

Celia smiled a little. Maurice's stealthy exit and furtive backward glances suggested an unsuccessful burglar rather than the owner of Shane Place. (He didn't look like a successful anything, thought his daughter.) He was a tall thin man, fiftyish; his narrow shoulders stooped in a frayed jacket. His tweed breeches and his stockings, like the coat, were all of the same indeterminate fawn colour as his wispy hair. He crammed a shapeless fawn tweed hat onto his head as he came out.

Celia held her breath as he soundlessly closed the door. He must have oiled the hinges since yesterday. If he woke Aunt Lily, she'd go to her window and call down to ask him where he was going. Did he know it was only half past five? Why was he up – couldn't he sleep? And Maurice would mutter something and run. The poor love never stood up to his aunt. He'd been going on early morning walks ever since Mummy died, ten years ago, so Laura said. Celia had only lately begun to understand the continuing pain which Daddy had allowed to fill his life, just as Mummy's presence had filled it when they were children.

Maurice was odd man out anyway. Grandpapa, the old General, had made Shane Place over to him years ago, but only, apparently, on paper. Celia was aware that her father existed in a personal cocoon of unhappiness, sandwiched between two generations. He shared his house with his father and aunt, as well as with Celia and Laura. The things he enjoyed doing were simple – walking, fishing in the river Suck, following the East Galway Hunt at a respectful distance. He was a poor horseman. It was lucky his tastes weren't expensive. Castle Shane, the vast ivyed ruin which overshadowed Shane Place and darkened its back rooms, had been the family home until Grandmama rebelled. Then the General had spent all that he had and much that he hadn't on building the great flat-faced Victorian mansion, whose Corinthian pillared portico was just a little bit lop-sided. The farm wasn't good enough or the General's pension big enough to build a house like that, let alone keep it up. So it wasn't kept up, especially after Grandmama died.

Celia didn't resent her father's neglected education, because she couldn't imagine him any different. That was how Daddy was, and she accepted his amazing ignorance and his Galway brogue. When he spoke to his workmen, he talked exactly as they did – kitchen, the girls called it. To his father and aunt, he talked drawing-room. Laura and Celia could talk kitchen too, in spite of the efforts of an English governess and Aunt Lily, but they could shed their accents at will, and did so now, most of the time.

Celia hid behind the curtain as Maurice turned his head to look back at the house. He always did this at the same point, whether to make sure Aunt Lily wasn't watching or to admire his home wasn't clear.

Years of living at Shane Place had made Celia oblivious to its ugliness, even when the bright pink roses bloomed on the bright yellow stucco. She knew Maurice loved the place, and thought it quite proper that he should devote his life to it, now that his main reason for living had gone.

'Go back to bed, Celia, it's not six o'clock.'

Celia started. 'Thought you were dead to the world. I can't sleep.'

'Neither can I. I've been watching you for ages. What were you staring at so intently?'

'Only Daddy, creeping out as if he'd stolen the spoons. Aunt Lily didn't hear him – he's oiled the hinges.' Celia left the window, and came to sit on Laura's bed. She tucked up her cold feet under her long white nightie, a demure garment with pintucks and pearl buttons, and a frill round the neck. Her hair, thick and glossy, the colour of a bay horse, hung in a heavy plait to her waist.

Laura sat up in bed, dragged at her eiderdown. 'Move your bottom, idiot; put this round you – you'll freeze.'

'How you boss me about, don't you? It must be inherited from Grandpapa.' Celia obediently put the quilt round her shoulders. Suddenly, she twisted round to face Laura and burst out, 'Couldn't you possibly get me into the V.A.D.s, Laura? I'm much bigger and stronger than you are, and I did come out top in my first aid classes.'

'No, Celia, I couldn't, and a good job too. Nineteen's far too young. If you did get in you wouldn't be allowed to go to France with me, and you can't want to spend the rest of the war rolling bandages in Ballinasloe.' Laura added with a half laugh, 'I couldn't wait for my twenty-third birthday, and now I sometimes wish I could back out. I'm rather frightened. Training at Beach House was a baptism of fire. So many men, so few helpers, so few beds. And I know how much harder it will be in France.'

'I can't imagine you being frightened of anything,' said Celia. 'The thing is,' she went on, twisting the end of her plait round her finger, 'I don't know how I'm going to bear staying here without you. Nothing to do, only Daddy to talk to, and he doesn't listen. You can't count Grandpapa, he's as deaf as an adder, and as for Aunt Lily . . .'

'Did you say anything to Daddy about working in Woolwich Arsenal? Mind you, I don't suppose he'd let you go.'

Celia twitched the quilt round her indignantly. 'Yes I did, and he damn well laughed at me. Said I'd have to cut my hair or I'd get nits in it. As if I cared.' She jumped up and rummaged in a drawer, dumping the contents on the floor. She emerged with a magazine: *T. P.'s Journal of Great Deeds of the Great War*. 'There's a bit in here, addressed to "Our Women", listen. "Every girl who goes to work in a munition factory is bringing the end of the war a little bit nearer. Every gun, every shell, every bullet and cartridge case brings victory closer. Have *you* got somebody out there? What would *he* think if he knew you could help but would not?"'

'Does Tom want you to go to Woolwich?' enquired Laura. 'I wouldn't have thought so. And there's bombing, you know – it's riskier than nursing.'

'Tom's like Daddy. I don't think he took it seriously. His letters are all about picnics and playing tennis. He thinks of me as still seventeen. Oh Laura, I don't know what I should do.' She dropped the magazine, and crept into the narrow bed beside Laura. She was tall, still a little plump, although her puppyfat was disappearing. Her skin was creamy fair, soft and satiny. She had never done a day's work of any sort in her life.

Laura moved over to make room for her sister. Celia had dark shadows under her eyes. Such eyes! Huge and grey, long-lashed and wide set. Celia could have modelled for a picture postcard any day. Lovely little nose, and intelligence to save her looks from being insipid. It was a strong face, for all its young roundness, and happy, with a funny little wedge-shaped chin, whose deep dimple was almost a cleft. A real head-turner, Celia. Laura had never been pretty, even before she fell off Split-the-Wind and broke her nose.

Laura picked up *T.P.'s Journal*, and idly turned the pages. '*You* must join your King's Army, and learn to sing God Save the King *with a gun in your hands*! . . . Women and Warriors . . . Cross of Iron or Cross of Wood . . . The Flame of Victory from the Ashes of Defeat . . . A Mother's Love.'

She turned to the readers' letters. Here was one from a vicar who was also a tool-turner for munitions of war. She made a face, laid it aside, and put her arms round Celia. Shutting her eyes, Laura sent up a fervent prayer for Tom Daly's safety. It hadn't worked for Michael, but what else could you do? She clenched her hands and squeezed her eyes shut, concentrating fiercely. Celia was saying something.

'Tom seems happier than he was; his last three letters are full of a dog he's got hold of. It was a German dog they captured, and the battalion is going to have it for a mascot. What does a mascot *do*, do you know? The poor thing was hurt, and Tom goes on about it rather. You know how much he loves animals. I try to take an interest, but I'm not mad about dogs, and if I were, I'd hate to think of one in the trenches.'

'Imagine taking a dog out there,' said Laura. 'Trust the Germans to do such a beastly thing. Worse than the poor horses.'

'They say horses like a battle. The Bible says they do. He says among the trumpets, "Ha ha", according to Job.'

'That's silly,' said Laura. 'I don't suppose horses like being hurt any more than people do, and think how the smell of blood terrifies them. I hope they'll soon be able to use tanks and motor-lorries for everything and do without horses. Michael thought that would happen one day.'

She brought out the name defiantly, and Celia didn't answer. Michael was almost certainly dead, although still officially missing, believed dead. Laura had lived through a hell of uncertainty and vain hope for three years now. She had aged ten years in the space of three, while Celia agonized over Tom, Michael's cousin. Both girls wore engagement rings.

Celia was falling asleep, a soft heavy weight leaning against Laura. Poor darling. She had led the most sheltered life it was possible to imagine. Laura had visited relations abroad, but the war had stopped all that. Neither did Celia share her sister's passion for horses which led to foxhunting and, in turn, hunt balls.

Celia was the one to take her mother's place, arranging flowers, shopping, ordering meals. Aunt Lily seldom left her stuffy room, the General lived in the prison of his deafness, Maurice in the prison of his sorrow. They didn't deserve to have a lovely affectionate girl to keep house for them, thought Laura angrily. Soon, Laura would be in France. How could Celia manage on her own? She was sensitive, and worry was making her jumpy. What would she do in a hospital? Or in a factory?

Celia suddenly raised her head. 'What's the time? I'm getting up. Laura, do you honestly think I'm too young to go with you? If I faked a birth certificate?'

'Oh, Celia, it's not only age. You'd get involved. Every wounded man would be Tom; you'd tear yourself to pieces. You're far too emotional.'

Celia sprang out of bed. Tears spurted from her eyes, her voice shook. 'I'm not emotional, I'm not! You treat me like a baby!'

Furiously, she abandoned her nightie, grabbed her clothes, threw them on at top speed. 'Oh heavens, I forgot to wash.'

She dragged her blouse off again and rushed to the washstand, hiding her tears with a spongeful of cold water. 'Sorry,' she muttered.

Laura swung her legs out of bed. 'Listen,' she said earnestly. 'You wouldn't be nursing. You'd be sweeping and dusting, collecting filthy dressings and emptying pos. No soothing fevered brows. Why, we're hardly allowed to speak to the patients.' She picked up Celia's scattered belongings from the floor, and stuffed them into an overfull drawer. 'You'll have to be tidier if you live in digs,' she said. 'I'm going for a ride before breakfast.'

'Hang on, I want to read you a bit of this letter of Tom's.' Celia flattened out the thin sheets, almost like tissue paper, and read aloud.

'"You ask me what it's like here, and there's no answer. I don't know what it's 'like'. I could tell you all sorts of things – funny, horrible, touching, but you still wouldn't know what it's like, because it's outside my experience as well as yours – I'm sorry, I can't explain.

'"The men have a rougher time than we do, but we have the crushing responsibility. They are amazingly cheerful, especially since Jack arrived. If anything happened to that dog, the whole battalion would mourn him. He rather grudgingly accepts a man called O'Hara and myself, going fairly willingly with either of us, but I have never once seen him wag his tail. The puzzlement and desperate sadness in his eyes . . ."

'You see, Laura, he goes on and on about this dog, hardly mentions the Germans at all, doesn't seem to hate them like we do, and he pretends he's frightened all the time. I can't understand it.'

'I'm sure he's frightened. So would I be. Or you.'

'That's different. Tom's never afraid. Then he says here, "I say to myself, 'Be strong and of good courage.' It helps." That's the Bible again.'

'Celia darling, any sane man out there would be frightened, and Tom's as sane as anyone I know. I don't mean just afraid of being . . . hurt, he'd be frightened of seeming cowardly to the men. Nobody must know how he really feels, and it must be a dreadful strain. Finding the dog would help to take his mind off the horrors, and he doesn't want you to know about the ghastly things he's seen.'

As Celia said nothing, Laura went on, 'Tom's brave, we both know that. To be brave you have to defeat your fear by willpower. You hear of people who are afraid of nothing. They have strong nerves, rather than courage. When a person like that cracks up, his nerve goes and he has nothing to put in its place. Old Mr Conroy lost his nerve for hunting years ago, but he still keeps on riding over the stone walls. That's brave. His horses know, though,' she added reflectively.

'Yes, I see that, but there's so much that I don't understand.' Celia put the letter away. 'There was a big battle at Easter, and he called it "Rather a noisy show" and said his feet were cold – in every sense. That was all. Never a word about killing Germans. Well, I've made up my mind. I'm going to Woolwich, whatever Daddy says, and I hope I help to kill hundreds.

'I'm going to meet Daddy coming back from his walk.' She rushed out of the room, pulling the door to behind her, and catching the tail of her skirt in it. There was a rending sound.

'Not only is nineteen too young, but you behave more like fourteen. No, I won't mend your skirt – mend it yourself.'

Slight and small in her shabby riding habit, Laura hurried down the back stairs and out to the stableyard. All this emotion! She couldn't stand any more. Her own emotions seemed to have boiled dry. After so much strain, she was no longer a slave to them. That made them no easier to bear in others. She needed to get back to work. Thank God, tomorrow she would be on her way to France.

Maurice Shane, returning from a leisurely inspection of his rocky, sheep-nibbled domain, noticed Laura in the distance, riding the old mare. Split-the-Wind had been brilliant once; only her age had saved her from being requisitioned. Laura was off tomorrow, wasn't she? thought Maurice vaguely. And here was Celia, tousled and flushed, running to meet him. She had enough of her mother's looks to hurt, but she'd never be in the same street as Rose.

'Good morning, Celia.' He kissed her, and released her

quickly, as she flinched. How could he know that the smell of tweed, tobacco and shaving-cream was an almost unbearable reminder of Tom.

'Daddy darling.' She was over effusive to make up for the flinch. 'How nice your old jacket smells. I love the smell of tobacco.'

'Look, you've torn your skirt. Better not let Auntie see that, she'll eat you.'

'I won't. I'll change. Listen Daddy. Dear, kind, sweet Daddy, please don't laugh at me. *Please* say I can go and work at Woolwich Arsenal. I've got to do something to help Tom, and every gun, every bullet brings victory a little closer. Please.'

Maurice took Celia's hand, palm up, and turned it over. Shapely, white, soft, with dimpled knuckles and a smallish emerald on the fourth finger. 'I don't think you'd be able for the work, childie. You can go if you're set on going, but I think you won't be long away.'

He half expected Celia to throw her arms round him and hug him, as she so often did. He felt guilty because her embrace meant so little, merely touching the raw nerve which was all he had left of Rose.

Celia didn't hug him. A delighted thank you, and then she became businesslike. 'There's a form for you to sign because I'm under twenty-one. After that it's easy. And I won't come whining home because the work's too hard. Oh! I am so happy!' she cried suddenly. 'Happier than I've been since Tom's leave.' She put her arm through Maurice's, and they went through the side door together, under the curious stare of Aunt Lily in curl-papers and winceyette.

'Good. Good,' said Maurice, his mind elsewhere. Already, he'd almost forgotten why Celia was so happy. He'd miss the pretty creature about the place. Ah well, she'd soon be back.

CHAPTER FIVE

The front line in a battlefield is no place for a wounded dog, but neither can he be passed back to a Casualty Clearing Station for a decision about his future. Jack convalesced in comfort if not in luxury at the Company Command Post in the ruins of Festubert.

He kept quiet and troubled nobody, watching and listening in silence as officers came and went, talked, studied maps, sometimes argued. The post was underground, in an old basement kitchen, and led out, up half a dozen steps, onto a small paved courtyard, its wall smashed down to three or four feet high. Here there was a well, and although the pump was broken, the water was sweet and could be drawn up in buckets. Fallen tiles and bricks had been tidied into heaps, and spring grass sprouted between the flagstones. Jack examined every corner with care, and learned far more about Festubert and its last occupants than the alien soldiers would ever know.

Many things troubled Jack. He was uneasy about calling these soldiers 'alien'. He no longer thought of them as enemies, but neither did he make friends.

My captors use me well, he thought, as he sat in a shaft of sunlight, warming himself. Herr Hauptmann Daly is good hearted and a gentleman. One would be happy to serve such a man. Surely a person endowed with so many virtues would not knowingly have helped to kill my friend Kurt. Jack was certain he would not.

Last night had been made horrible by the sound of shells not far away. Jack's nerves had quivered at the noise of the bursts. He would not stay outside alone when they were near.

If one must be obliterated, let it be in the company of one's comrades, whoever they might be.

Jack had understood from the preparations going on that they were going to leave this place soon. Let it be very soon.

Tom Daly came to the cellar door and called softly, 'Jack!'

'I come sir, but slowly, because I am not yet well, and also because you are not Kurt.'

Tom clicked his fingers invitingly. 'I'll bet you could walk faster than that if I'd brought you some grub.'

Jack followed Tom down the steps, and through to the inner room. He suppressed an involuntary twitching of the hairs at the end of his tail as he recognized Willie O'Hara – he of the kind hands, to whom he owed his life. Jack sent a message of welcome and profound thanks to O'Hara. It was couched in formal terms. One must not become too friendly, but he kept his tail still with an effort.

O'Hara's smell, composed of sweat, beer and Woodbines, was as different from Tom's as Kurt's familiar scent had been unlike Hansel's. Like Kurt and Hansel, the two men spoke the same words, but differently. How much there was to learn in this strange world.

O'Hara grinned widely when he saw Jack. 'Didn't I tell you, sir, he's as right as ninepence, and not a week since you were for shooting him.'

'Most people would have shot him without argument,' said Tom. 'Yes, poor old Jack has you to thank for that – I only hope he keeps out of more trouble. I sent for you because I knew he'd remember you and we could get these stitches out without upsetting him more than we need.'

Since Jack had unwillingly submitted to having his bandages and dressings taken off two days before, the wound had healed, the hair starting to grow furrily round the neat knots of the stitches.

'Now then, Jack old boy, O'Hara will hold you so you don't bite my ear off, while I snip these stitches.' Tom's curved nail-scissors clicked through the catgut nine times and he drew the stitches out by their knots.

'Keep still, Jack; good boy.'

'I am your prisoner, sir. It is right and fitting that I

should submit. You are treating me with kindness which I did
not expect.'

'I hear you've volunteered to come with us tonight, O'Hara,'
said Tom as he pulled out the last stitch.

'I have, sir, and ten more of the lads that was in the Cuinchy
raid with you as well.'

'Well done. I couldn't have better men. Report to me and
Mr Fetherston at ten o'clock.'

Charles Fetherston still found life on the Western Front a
tremendous lark, a marvellous scrap. Tom wondered how he
managed it. Had he no imagination at all? Fetherston's loud
laugh grated on Tom's over-stretched nerves, his slang infuriated, his funny stories weren't funny. Tom caught himself
wanting to swear at Fetherston twenty times a day. So far,
he'd managed to remember the boy's youth and inexperience,
and desist; but so far, they hadn't been in action together.
These fresh lads hadn't had their egos deflated by long spells
of tongue-lashing from sergeant-majors. Tom remembered his
own introduction to the regular army and shuddered.

Reading the papers at this time, Tom was surprised to find
little mention of the part of the Dubs in the battle of Arras. A
raid which had cost fourteen lives was described as a brief
skirmish. Tom scowled at the report. He had led the raid, and
seen two of his closest friends blown to pieces. Tom's coolness
and daring had been noted by his seniors.

Three times, Jack had seen Tom return exhausted to the
cellar room. Once with a hand torn and bleeding, once limping
in a boot split from knee to heel, always hollow-eyed and
tense. Jack could not yet read all Tom's thoughts – he could
read Kurt's like a book – but he got the gist of them. The dull
feeling that the next time would be the last time, that there
would be one close shave too many.

There had been a big raid for prisoners just before Jack's
arrival, involving both 'C' and 'D' companies, led by Tom and
by Major Jim Harper. Both officers had escaped death by a
hair's-breadth. Jim Harper had made a feeble attempt to joke.
'Thought I'd be harping in Heaven tonight.'

Fetherston's maddening laugh rang out. 'I wish I'd been asked to go,' he said.

'So do I,' said Tom. 'Instead of me.'

'I bet you don't mean that. I bet you wouldn't have missed it for anything.'

Tom shut his teeth hard and grimaced at Jim. The poor deluded blighter meant no harm. Why bother to curse him? He was much too young and not very bright, that was all.

Young Charles was going to get his chance tonight, thought Tom. He was brave enough. Too brave, from lack of experience. He was just the sort to get himself killed, and a good N.C.O. killed as well, trying to save him. 'I'll have to keep an eye on the stupid sod,' muttered Tom, spreading out a map on the table and studying it.

Today, the unceasing gunfire was distant enough to be no more than a solid wall of sound in which separate explosions were lost. There was none of the swish-crash of the near one, or the shriek-whoosh-crash of the not quite so near. Shellfire not only killed and mutilated, it terrified. One cowered, waiting to be hit, unable to hit back. Tom dragged his mind back to the map, flattening out the creases, and frowned at it. Why had the last raid failed? In a sense, it hadn't been a total disaster. They'd captured a number of prisoners, including a senior officer. But he'd been killed along with two of the Dubs as they were dragging him back across no man's land. Later, two men had risked their lives bringing in his body, only to find that he had no papers of importance on him.

Machine-gun fire had come from an unexpected quarter with horrifying results, and Tom was damned if he knew how or when the Boche had moved up those Maxims. Machine-guns were much more deadly than heavy artillery, but much less feared. Given a chance, infantry could deal with them.

Stop thinking about shells and concentrate on the map, Tom told himself. He moved aside some of the papers on the cluttered table, and drew the oil-lamp nearer. He spread out today's map beside the old one. It was waterproof, greyish-white. 'Secret', was printed in red in the top left-hand corner. The Allied positions were shown in blue, the German in red. It was a trench map like hundreds of others: fresh ones were issued every week, while the old ones were covered with pencilled corrections as they went out of date.

Tonight's raid would be an attempt to knock out two machine-guns. Tom was glad it wasn't another prisoner hunt. They had too many already, and could ill spare the men to guard them, or food to feed them until they could be shifted.

The main objectives on the maps were distinguished by their colours; blue for the first, then black, then green, and finally red. There were just two objectives tonight, marked by pencilled crosses with dotted red rings round them. A row of red crosses indicated German barbed wire.

Tom read his instructions again. The C.O. had been over earlier. He was confident that the guns could be knocked out, he said.

'It may cost us some valuable men,' Tom had said. And the C.O. had answered briskly, 'In a successful raid on this scale, we must accept that some lives are almost bound to be lost. Think of the lives that the action will save.'

That's Field Marshal's talk, thought Tom bitterly. Guns may be lost, a field kitchen has been lost, lives are bound to be lost. A polite way of saying, men will die in agony.

The rickety door creaked open, and Major Harper joined Tom at the table, along with Greer and of course Fetherston, full of beans as usual, blast him.

'See what you make of that, Harper. I think there could well be another gun, behind that ridge to the right.' Tom sat down, putting his hand to his forehead. 'My brain isn't functioning at the moment,' he said. 'Got a rotten headache.'

Jack came out of the corner where he had been lying, moved eighteen inches nearer to Tom, and lay down again.

Jim Harper glanced worriedly at the younger man. It was too soon after the last raid for Tom to lead another, and this time Jim wouldn't be going into action alongside him, fewer men were involved. If Tom didn't stop volunteering for this sort of thing, he'd soon be dead. He was getting the look, familiar to the veterans, of a soldier who had endured too much.

'Why don't you turn in for a couple of hours, Daly?' Jim

asked. 'I'll give you a shout about six. You don't look as if you've slept.'

'I haven't much. All right, I will.'

Stretched on his camp bed, Tom tried in vain to sleep. At last, he lit a candle and felt in his pocket for Celia's latest letter to re-read. There was no point in going over and over the coming raid in his mind. If he could deflect his thoughts, perhaps he might drop off for an hour or two.

Instead of the letter, Tom found Hansel's notebook. He opened it at random.

> As all alone I sadly wander
> I see fair Edith passing by.
> She clasps a puppy to her bosom,
> Ah! Happy Hansel, were it I.

Hansel's writing was improving with practice, Tom noted, as he turned the pages.

> I fain would join my Edith fair
> At the ancient manse where she was born.
> Methinks I see her playing there
> With siblings six upon the lawn.

Siblings six, good lord. Oh well, his English isn't too good. Perhaps he thinks they're more puppies.

Tom put the poems away carefully. Not for anything would be have shown them to his friends.

Tom blew the candle out and turned onto his side. He shut his eyes and tried to think of Ireland and Celia, but the coming raid filled his mind.

He worried about the last of the snow. It was a moonless night. Success would depend on surprise and total darkness, and there was no snow left within fifty yards of the trench. There, it had turned to dirty slush, but in the middle of no man's land there were still a few patches of white. These must be avoided at all costs. Had he mentioned this to Fetherston? He wasn't sure. Then memories of the Cuinchy raids came flooding back to torment Tom. Travers, McHubert . . . 'Stop that,' he said aloud.

Tonight, there would be no guns to back them up, and no way of letting anyone know if they were in trouble. Flares would draw German fire faster than they would bring support. To off-set the danger, there was something about a night raid which stirred the blood. Tom supposed it was the cloak and dagger stuff, the secrecy and the silence, the blacked faces and, of course, the double rum ration. No work for rifles tonight. They would carry hatchets and knives, as well as wire-cutters and grenades.

In 1914, most of them had thought that throwing a grenade into a dugout was an unsporting thing to do. Not any more.

Tom's jaw had been grazed by a sniper's bullet in 1914, when he'd been in France only a week. He hadn't had time to be frightened. It had been the first of a dozen close shaves; the closest and the least alarming.

On leave at Shane Place for the first time, the wound had still been very noticeable.

At dinner, Tom had sat beside the old General, who had asked about the straight red scar along his jawbone.

'Knifewound?'

'No sir, a bullet.'

'A what?'

'A bullet,' said Tom, loudly and embarrassed.

'What are you saying? Speak up man.'

Aunt Lily on Tom's far side came to his rescue. 'It was a bullet, Gerald,' she murmured in her thin reedy voice. For some reason, the General could often hear Aunt Lily – if he wanted to.

'Are the Germans as dreadful as they say?' Aunt Lily asked Tom. 'I believe they say the only good German is a dead German.'

The General heard this. 'The only good dead German is Beethoven,' he stated. 'And he was Dutch.'

'Surely –' protested Aunt Lily.

'Ludwig van Beethoven. Von, German. Van, Dutch. Now then, young man, you were telling me about that knifewound of yours –'

An awful meal. Tom tried again to think about Celia. He wished she wasn't going into munitions. He wished . . .

'Will you permit me to enter, sir?'

Tom got up and opened the door. 'Hallo Jack, thought I heard you. Be quiet like a good fellow. I want some sleep.'

Jack lay down and slept.

Tom dozed for a time, and woke with a start as someone banged on his door and shouted. Jack sat up and growled. Time to get up. Time to go to the trench which would be their jumping off point. Time to brief Fetherston. Tom would shut Jack in the coalshed at the foot of the cellar steps, with a sack to lie on. He'd been left there before. Tom didn't want to trust him to McCoy; their dislike was mutual.

Before he left his room, Tom dashed off a note to Celia. Then, as he always did before going into action, he murmured a prayer. His own personal talisman, this one; he felt that, if he forgot it, he would certainly be killed. He had found it in a book of poems Celia had given him, and he had learned it by heart.

'Let me not pray to be sheltered from dangers but to be fearless in facing them.

Let me not beg for the stilling of my pain but for the heart to conquer it.

Let me not look for allies in life's battlefield but to my own strength.

Let me not crave in anxious fear to be saved but hope for the patience to win my freedom.

Grant me that I may not be a coward, feeling your mercy in my success alone; but let me find the grasp of your hand in my failure.'

As he quietly spoke the last words, Tom felt Jack's steadfast gaze fixed on his face. Almost as if the dog was trying to tell him something.

'Do not leave me here with alien soldiers
But take me with you.
You are afraid and I too am afraid
So take me with you.
Do not allow the servant with the lying tongue to touch me;
Take me with you.
Sir, I am but a dog, and I do not like to be alone –
Please take me wherever you are going.'

'Jack, old man, what ever is the matter? Don't look so wretched, let's see you wag that tail of yours. Come along, we'll find you some dinner.'

It was perfectly dark.
'It's frightfully dark, isn't it? Absolutely pitch.'
'Fetherston if you say another word, I'll break your bloody neck, I swear I will.'
'Sorry, sir.'
Tom couldn't see but could imagine the boy's shocked face. Charles Fetherston was a pest, a liability.
'Don't leave my side until we are in contact with the enemy; don't get cut off from your own men, keep quiet, and get back as fast as you can afterwards. Got that?'
'Yes, sir.'
'I hope you have. Twenty men are depending on you –' (God help them, he thought.) 'You must try to see to it that you bring twenty back. If we don't knock out those guns, we don't, but we can't afford to lose good men. Got that?'
Not waiting for an answer, Tom turned to his own party with final instructions. No whistle signalled this sort of attack – a quietly spoken, 'Come on, lads.'
'Good hunting, sir,' whispered irrepressible Charles.

Once he was clear of the trench, Tom's nerve steadied, as it always did. His greatest fear now was of losing his way in the dark. However well prepared, these night operations could be an indescribable muddle, and you could never be sure of anything. Unexpected obstacles seemed to rise up out of the dark; wire which surely should be further to the left, loomed up, twined round you, had to be cut. Be quick! They seemed to Tom to be making more noise than a herd of elephants. Where the hell was Fetherston? He must be ahead.
They almost stumbled into a German gun emplacement, and pandemonium broke out. The Maxims opened fire, and there were more of them than Tom had bargained for. They fought blind, gunflashes and bursting grenades their only light. Cries in the dark, thudding feet, a sudden loud scream. One

of the guns captured, its crew killed, another destroyed. As Tom rallied his party to return, he fell over a body. The dead could wait. Vaguely, he wondered who it was.

The Germans were blazing away with everything they had now, and Very lights illuminated Tom's company as they retreated.

The man wasn't dead after all; Tom heard a faint cry, 'Help!'

Fetherston. It *would* be, thought Tom unfairly. 'Get back to the trench, men, fast as you can. You there, help me with this wounded man.'

Willie O'Hara's voice answered, 'It's the Lieutenant. He has great courage, that one – pelting grenades like snowballs.' They stooped together to lift him, and carried him back, their boots sliding in the slippery mud, both expecting every second to be their last as the rifle bullets whipped by. They lowered their burden carefully over the parapet, and hastily jumped down themselves.

Tom bent over Fetherston, and saw that he was dead.

'Those Jerries can see in the dark like cats,' remarked O'Hara, as they moved the body out of the way into an unused sap. 'Going for them at night's like pouring boiling water into a wasps' nest when the water isn't boiling. Mr Fetherston ran straight at the guns like a madman, and two of the lads after him. They must've got killed as well. I didn't hear tell of them since.'

Tom didn't answer, he was sick at heart. He wished the night's work was over. Thank God the Germans had quietened down for the time being. There'd be reprisals, but the Seaforths would have to deal with those. Now, everyone must be checked, then he must write his report. Tomorrow there'd be telegrams going off to the next of kin, and he'd have to write to Fetherston's mother. She'd lost her other son at Gallipoli. What a bloody waste.

'Are you hurt, Daly?' It was Jim Harper.

'No, I was lucky, didn't get a scratch. Fetherston's dead, though, and at least two men. We've knocked out the guns all right, but there was no chance of capturing them. 'Tom went on to describe the action, marking the map as he talked.

It was another hour before he could make his way back to the command post in the cellar.

Tom was sitting on his camp bed, dazed with weariness, when he remembered he'd left Jack shut up in the coalshed. The dog had seemed miserable when he left him, and had whined and yelped. Tom had shouted 'Shut up!' and forgotten about him. With a sigh, Tom got up and made his way along the dark passage to the shed. There was no doubt that Jack was pleased to see him, coming to him willingly, padding along the passage at his heels, and finally lying down beside the bed.

'Jack dog, war's a beastly business. Poor old Charles has gone.'

'I know that, my captain, you have carried his body in your arms. Do not distress yourself; like me, you did not admire him.'

'I wish I knew what you were thinking, boy. Do you think we're all mad? I sometimes wonder myself.' Tom reached out a hand, and gently scratched Jack's ear. There was a faint thump. One could not always prevent oneself from wagging one's tail. Possibly there was no harm in it. The tail thumped twice more.

The next night, the second battalion moved to the Doncaster huts at Locre. The first hour was spent edging as quietly as possible along communication trenches. The trenches were only about a yard wide, damaged in places, and ankle deep in muddy water. The last of the unseasonable snow had melted, and left slimy mud and surface water behind. Jack, paddling along at Tom's heels, had forgotten his fears of the night before. He was more comfortable now that his stitches were out, and he had breakfasted on bread and jam, and dined on broken biscuit into which somebody had slopped some beer. He had also drunk a dish of cold tea. He approved strongly of these rations.

Further back, they turned into a broad, undamaged trench, which had been built as a rear of defence. Here, Tom flattened himself against the side, as a column of Seaforth Highlanders went by, moving up to the front line.

Jack hopped up onto a firestep to watch yet another marvel: grown men, soldiers, wearing skirts. Astonishing. Petticoated they might be, but they looked every bit as tough as the Dubs. Jack had learned that the second battalion was known as the 'Old Toughs'.

They met another party of Highlanders later on, after they had left the trenches, and taken to the lanes. They were swinging along in the first light of a chilly spring morning, filling the narrow lane as they marched at ease in columns of four. Scots and Irish exchanged greetings as they passed, the Dubs making way for the relieving troops. The Seaforths marched with their rifles slung, thumbs in the slings – some of them were singing.

Perhaps they do not know where they are going, thought Jack. Perhaps they imagine that they are going home. What a terrible enlightenment awaits them. Perhaps Captain Tom will warn them. Yes, Tom was showing a map to one of the officers. But the officer did not turn back. He spoke to the leaders of the column, and they resumed their march.

While Tom had been talking to the Scottish major, a party had brought horses for Tom and Jim Harper. They mounted, and rode forward together, talking; Jack was forgotten.

Jack had followed Tom for hours. He was very tired, and his wound itched. He dropped back, searching the passing column, until he saw Willie O'Hara; marching on the outside, he was pleased to note.

'Hallo Jack. Didn't know you was one of us. Thought you was an officer. Thought you'd be riding a bloody horse.'

'Do not mock me, soldier. I must make my way as best I can. I am no longer a prisoner, I run free. Are you not gratified that I choose your company?'

'He has a proud way with him, that old dog,' Willie remarked to his neighbour. 'You'd think he was doing us a favour by coming with us.'

'If I catch him with his German gob in my mess tin, the bugger'll never know what hit him,' was the unsympathetic answer.

They were still within range of the German guns when they stopped for a meal in a ruined village. Not one house was standing, but the French had returned, and were busy in he fields and gardens. In the distance, an old man was ploughing a battle-scarred field with a horse and a mule, while a party of elderly people and children were attempting to fill up the yawning craters in the village street. Dead animals, garbage and broken bricks formed the foundations, which were topped up with planks, sandbags and stones. Lastly, the least able-bodied of the work force filled the cracks from buckets of rubble.

Most of the soldiers stretched themselves out on the damp grass for a few minutes' rest. The sun had risen, and men and horses alike steamed in its warmth. Corporal Eugene Boyle off-loaded his equipment onto the floor, beside the counter of a ruined estaminet. Weighed down with souvenirs, he grumbled long and profanely about the heat.

'What did you do with Jack's tunic?' asked O'Hara, tucking into the pork and beans in his mess tin.

'It got lost back there.' Boyle stacked his belongings carefully and sat down on them.

'I suppose it did.' O'Hara's voice implied total disbelief, Jack noted. 'He'll need another for parades and that. The Argylls' goat has a tartan plaid, so he has.'

'I do not wish to wear an alien uniform. I am not a goat. Neither am I a man. I can go naked without appearing ridiculous.'

'Bless the dog! What's he bristling about now? We'll get some cloth and make him some fine tunics. Wasn't I apprenticed to a tailor myself?'

Willie shared his rations with Jack, for the second time. And what rations! Pigmeat, and vegetables in a delicious gravy. White bread and a piece of some kind of sweetmeat. A pity there was not more. Kurt had lived on black bread, with cabbage stew every second day, when no game was to be had. Sausage had been a rare treat.

'Many thanks, Herr Wilhelm, I am much obliged to you.'

At Locre the following day, Jack was formally enlisted a private in the second battalion, and given the freedom of the sergeants' mess. He received a thin steel chain to wear below his old collar, with an identity disc. Pte JACK 87611 R.D.F. The number was Willie O'Hara's in reverse.

The men's time was filled by drill, instruction in the use of the Lewis gun, and organized games to keep them fit. In their spare time they played cards, smoked, wrote letters and slept. Tom Daly had gone off on some course, O'Hara wasn't sure what. The word was that the battalion was being rested before taking part in the much-talked-of attack on the Messines Ridge.

'Fattening us up for the butcher,' said Fusilier Pat O'Shea.

'Less of that talk,' said Corporal Boyle sharply. 'You know what you get for spreading alarm and despondency.'

Jack's battledress tunic was ready. It was a khaki coat, bearing the insignia of the regiment – a brass 'D' and 'F', joined by the emblem of the grenade. This was the badge worn by the rank and file. The coat was comfortable, though much too warm, and was neatly fastened by two brass hooks across the chest. Webbing straps with brightly polished brass buckles held it in place. Wearing it, Jack felt pleased with his appearance. He wished Captain Tom were there to admire.

A few days later, fresh troops from England arrived at Locre, and the Dubs were moved ten miles further back, to a small town which was more or less intact, and where, for the French, everything seemed to be business as usual. Tom was waiting to join them there.

The Dubs marched into the town led by Willie O'Hara with Jack walking proudly beside him on a burnished chain. Right down the main street they went. Ah, if Captain Tom could but see me now, thought Jack.

There he was! Coming to meet them. They halted in the square, and Willie stood stiffly to attention. How gladly would Jack have run to meet his captain, but he was restrained by the chain. His tail swished to and fro, and he leaned against his collar, tongue out, begging to be noticed. Formal words passed between Captain Tom and Lieutenant Greer, there was much saluting, yes sirs and no sirs. Would his turn never come? Not long since, he had refused to hurry when his captain called him to his side, now he was punished. His ears drooped, and his tail. He drooped all over.

'Jack does you credit, O'Hara, I've never seen such a change in a dog. It was time we had a mascot.'

'Thank you, sir.'

And with those secondhand words Jack had to be content.

The house where Tom, Jim Harper, Lieutenant Greer and the young man who had taken Fetherston's place were billeted, was small but comfortable. For the first time in months, Tom knew the luxury of roof, doors, and windows with glass in them. There was a bathroom with taps, and water in the taps. Tom, like the others, spent hours soaking off the grime which felt as if it was crusted into his skin. Dressed in a clean uniform and with a good meal inside him, he relaxed in a comfortable chair with a glass of whiskey in his hand. He grinned at Jim Harper, and raised his glass.

'The mail, sir.' McCoy slid into the room, placed the package beside Major Harper and disappeared as silently as he had come.

Tom started violently, slopping his drink. 'Blast that man! Can't we hang a bell round his neck?'

'Good idea, Daly, I've a feeling he eavesdrops.'

They settled down to read their letters, Jim's from his wife, Tom's from Celia (three of them), and the two younger men's from their mothers.

'Celia's started work in Woolwich Arsenal. I hoped she'd given up that idea.'

'Hm?' Jim was still reading his own mail.

'Think of the thousands of wasted shells,' Tom went on. 'And I sometimes think the Lewis gunners blaze away for practice. Hundreds of young girls are risking their lives in the factories, and do the gunners ever give them a thought?'

'I doubt it,' said Jim, folding his letter with a sigh. 'Celia must have changed since I met her. I remember her as a typical dutiful daughter, keeping house for widowed father. Face like an angel though.'

'She still looks like an angel, even in that hideous uniform – Look at this photograph. She says she can't think of any other way of killing Huns, bless her bloodthirsty little heart. I hope to God the Zepps keep off.'

Jim put away his letter. He liked Daly a lot; he searched his mind for something to take Tom's mind off Celia.

'What's happened to your dog? I haven't noticed him about. Thought you'd have him here with us.'

Tom's face relaxed at once. 'He's not my dog – I wish he were. Now that he's Private Jack, regimental mascot, he lives with the men. He's having the time of his life. The men simply love him, they're sure he brings them luck. You'll see him tomorrow when we go out after rabbits. O'Hara's bringing him across. We think he may have been trained to retrieve.' He put his letters away, and turned his attention to the packet of newspapers sent by his mother.

Tom was half dozing over the letters to the editor in *The Times*, when one of them caught his attention. He sat up and read it again.

'That's extraordinary,' he said aloud.

'What is?'

'Sorry, Harper, nothing really. It's too complicated to explain. I expect I'm wrong anyway.' He read it again.

'Sir,

In a recent edition of a popular national journal, I read with dismay a letter from a Vicar who is also a tool-turner in a factory making munitions of war.

Whatever we personally may think about the ghastly struggle now taking place, this is surely not a fitting occupation for a man of God. The obvious course for a Clergyman who feels he is not doing enough for his country, is to apply for the post of Army Chaplain. If it is not possible for him to leave his parish, there is still much that he can do. He can offer practical as well as Spiritual aid to bereaved families, and to wounded or shell-shocked members of the armed forces.

Our duty to our neighbour must not be obscured by our natural feelings at this terrible time, neither let us give way to vindictive hatred towards the entire German race. I am not ashamed to say that the youngest of my seven daughters held a post as governess to a German

family immediately before the outbreak of war. Although
not everyone she met was congenial, there were some to
whom she was sorry to say goodbye, especially among
the young people.

   The sooner this conflict for civilization is won, the
better; but let us not lose our sense of fitness, or our
Christian charity.

Yours, etc.

(Revd)Arnold Briggs
The Rectory
Wynter St Mary's
Devonshire.'

Tom was willing to bet that the Reverend Briggs's seventh
daughter was called Edith, the object of Hansel von Hessel's
devotion. It had to be the same girl.

Tom drew his chair up to the table, and wrote,

'Dear Mr Briggs,

   I was interested to read your letter in *The Times* of April
12th, and agree absolutely with your sentiments.

   I have in my possession some papers which may be of
interest to a member of your family. If the daughter you
refer to is called "Edith", she must be the person for
whom the papers were intended.

   Perhaps you would be good enough to write, or ask
your daughter to write to me at this address . . .'

He finished off his letter, and addressed it to the Devonshire
Rectory. Only when he had posted it did he remember that
Edith Briggs's young admirer had started his work on his
fourteenth birthday, about the time that Edith had left Germany. Not a shared romance then, but the boy was dead, and
Miss Briggs would be stony-hearted not to be touched by his
efforts. They must be sent to her or destroyed.

   Tom had destroyed his own poem to Celia before the Cuinchy raid.

CHAPTER SIX

The warm spring sun shone down, and there was a holiday atmosphere in the village of Dernier the following morning. The battalion was due to return to the front line soon, but nobody mentioned this.

Jack breakfasted on porridge, sardines, fried bread and his favourite cold tea. Glorious. Tentatively, he extended a paw, and placed it on Willie O'Hara's boot.

'Have you a little more gruel to spare, comrade? Another crust? Perhaps even, another of the beautiful little fishes?'

Willie cuffed him affectionately. 'Get away, you greedy old devil. Look at him, Pat. You'd never guess he was the same dog we picked up a month ago, would you?'

Pat O'Shea wiped his greasy plate with a piece of bread, was about to put it in his mouth, but changed his mind and held it out to Jack who accepted it politely. Pat was Willie's friend. Jack did not accept titbits from every hand that offered them. Food was plentiful and good in this wealthy part of France; the only scarcity was of young men. The Dubs were having a wonderful time.

Like many other units in the regiment, the original 'D' Company had all come from the same area. Willie O'Hara and his companions came from a poor part of Dublin, north of the Liffey, and had been recruited all together after a boxing match. At the time they had badly paid jobs or none at all, and the army offered a regular wage, however miserly, and adequate food. Certainly, loyalty to King and country had very little to do with it, especially as they had volunteered in peace time.

Traditionally, Irishmen had fought for Britain, notably in the Peninsular War a hundred years earlier. Like the Duke of Wellington, Lord Kitchener had been born in Ireland, and the 'Old Toughs' were among the famous first hundred thousand to answer Kitchener's call for a million men. They formed part of the tenth infantry brigade, fourth division, and were intensely proud of the fact.

A shilling a day was less than some of them had been earning in Dublin, but they didn't have to buy food, clothes or cigarettes out of their pay. Most of them had been unmarried when they joined up.

In May 1917, only six men of the original 'D' Company were left, of which Johnnie Duggan was a sergeant and Eugene Boyle a corporal.

All members of the same platoon, they kept together whenever they could, a closely knit little unit within a vast structure. They had become efficient professionals, careful, brave and steady. Men like these were beyond price. If one of them volunteered to take part in a raid, they all did, and all of them admired and respected Tom Daly.

Unlike the enlisted men, most of the officers of the battalion came from outside Dublin. This was because so many had joined up straight from university, and had been with the Officer Training Corps at Trinity College Dublin. They came from all over the country. Tom was from Co. Galway, Jim Harper from Co. Carlow, the Colonel from Co. Meath. Charles Fetherston's home had been near Tom's.

Breakfast over, most of the men lighted up Woodbines and sat back in their chairs talking, or merely relaxing. They had a rare few minutes to themselves before the Sergeant-Major came round. Then there would be drill and instruction, or bayonet practice or P.T., and some of them would have to take their turn at fatigue duty. This could mean peeling potatoes or cleaning latrines, or simply tidying up.

Willie O'Hara searched in his pack, and brought out a grey flannel army issue shirt, with one sleeve and most of its tin buttons missing. He opened his hussif, a small folding case containing mending equipment and scissors, and set to work.

He cut off the remaining sleeve in one piece with the

shoulder of the shirt and studied it critically. Then he cut off
the cuff, along with the lower sleeve to just above the elbow.

'Making Jack a shirt?' enquired Pat O'Shea. Willie's peacetime apprenticeship to a tailor already meant that he mended
and patched and sewed on buttons for the whole platoon.
Since Jack's arrival, Willie had 'found' various garments and
cut them up for the dog's use. His grey army blanket was a
cut down version of Willie's own, his khaki tunic was made
from the skirts of a discarded overcoat; his wet weather tunic
was lined with grey flannel shirting.

'I'm making him a respirator.' Willie went down on his
knees, and fitted the shoulder part of the shirt over Jack's
head, so that his nose was inside the upper sleeve.

'My friend, I will endure much from one to whom I
owe my life, but I do not care for this game. I cannot see out,
and also, this shirt has been worn by one recently dead. I do
not like it.'

'Keep still, you old fool. Don't be clawing at that. It might
save your life yet. There now, I'll take it off.'

'I am obliged to you. That is better.'

Jack retreated under the table, more annoyed than he had
yet been with his friend. Willie was marking two circles on
the grey material with a piece of chalk. These he cut out with
the scissors.

'Come out of that, Jack, a minute. Here boy.'

'I do not wish – do not drag me by my collar, friend. I
value my collar. Leave me in peace, I say!'

'If you growl at me, you hoor, I won't bother making you
a respirator at all. Now, how's that?'

Shouts of laughter arose. Jack's furious eyes now glared
through the circles cut in the shirtsleeve. Willie pulled it off,
and Jack dived out of reach.

'Leave me be, I say. I have breakfasted well; now kindly
allow me to digest my meal. No more childish games, I beg.'

'A bit of mica in the eyeholes, and elastic round the neck.
A right job.' Willie was busy with the scissors again. 'Then I'll
tighten the sleeve up to fit his nose, and put a filter pad in it,
the same as our own.'

As he snipped and stitched, the other men got bored with

Jack's respirator, and fell to discussing the latest cookhouse rumours.

Rumours were everywhere this morning. Jack was strongly aware of some sort of undercurrent, and he tried hard to identify it. Curiosity was here certainly, and doubt, mixed with a kind of excitement which was of the head not the body. Anxiety is here, but it is not my concern, he thought. No doubt he would discover the reason for it in time.

Most of the rumours were correct, for once. The C.O. had been transferred to a newly formed battalion. Major Harper had been promoted in his place. The men hoped that Tom Daly would have been promoted too, but he had been bypassed. An older captain, Basil Shine, from another battalion had been promoted to the rank of major in Jim Harper's place.

'Who in hell wants Shine?' an angry voice rose above the others. 'Captain Daly junior to Shine – Jesus!'

'What kind of a man is he?' asked a newcomer.

'Whiskey-swilling skirt-chaser,' was the succinct reply.

'I'd follow Captain Daly into hell, so I would,' said Willie O'Hara simply. There were murmurs of agreement.

Every one of them knew that Tom was feeling the strain, and was fighting his own private battle with fear, fatigue and misery. Every one of them knew that Tom's superiors had noticed too, and were deliberately avoiding giving him yet more responsibility. Everyone knew, but nobody mentioned it.

Jack lay under the table, his anger forgotten, digesting his superb breakfast. He was sleepy and contented. Kurt was dead, but he had found a new friend. Not as dear as Kurt, but a friend nonetheless. In some way Jack could not define, Tom meant more to him than his new friend Willie, but his captain's duties kept them apart. This, thought Jack, was as it should be.

There was a scraping of chairs as Willie and Pat O'Shea got to their feet. Jack came out from under the table, stretching each hind leg in turn. He yawned, and gave a slight belch.

'Wake up, Jack, we have a job for you this morning.' Willie grinned at the other men, still sitting smoking round the table. 'See you later, lads,' he said. 'Mind you listen to the

Sergeant-Major. We'll expect you to know how to put your rifles together by the time we get back.'

Laughing at the chorus of vile abuse which greeted this, he and Pat left the house with Jack at their heels.

Jim Harper had already taken over command of the battalion, and had left for headquarters. This was a cruel blow for Tom, who had been with him right through the war.

Major Basil Shine had arrived early at the officers' billet, and had gone straight to bed. Nothing had been seen of him since. Two subalterns had arrived with him, and were hanging about uncertainly.

These changes were unsettling, but they were over-shadowed by more sinister rumours about the state of the French army. Their frightful losses at Béthune, early in the battle of Arras, had brought their casualty list to three million, and reports of mutiny had been coming in ever since. The French generals spoke of 'collective indiscipline' in their com-muniqués. This euphemism compared to the familiar – 'retir-ing according to plan' which could mean anything from a strategic withdrawal to a rout.

So far, the French generals had managed to delude their government, even while military policemen were being beaten unconscious and left hanging from lamp-posts by their feet. It was said that there were only two loyal divisions between the enemy lines and Paris. Fortunately, the Germans knew nothing of this state of affairs, but it was causing acute anxiety to the Allied Command.

The Dubs would be leaving Dernier in forty-eight hours, or Tom would have called off this morning's shoot.

Willie O'Hara and Pat O'Shea arrived at Tom's billet as McCoy gave a final polish to Tom's shotgun, then raised it to squint down the gleaming barrels. 'Brought the German dog, have you,' he said, not looking at them.

'Irish dog,' Willie answered calmly. It would be easy to start a row and have the whole thing called off. That was what the bastard wanted, he thought. He said, 'Jack's an Irish dog now, and he's the mascot of this battalion – yours and mine, Mick McCoy.'

McCoy clicked the breech of the gun shut, and transferred his gaze to Jack. 'Guten Tag, Herr Johann,' he said, pronouncing it 'Gutten Tag her Joe Hann'. Jack lifted his lip, disclosing faultless teeth. 'Savage brute. Pity he didn't get a bayonet in his guts.' McCoy backed towards the door.

'We won't cry if you get one in yours,' said Willie, his voice rising in spite of himself. 'But *you* won't get hurt – you're always hiding when . . .'

Tom Daly appeared in the doorway, and there was silence. Jack was fully expecting his comrade Willie to attack the cowardly servant who had once kicked him. Had kicked him when he was lying in his corner too ill to retaliate. Jack chose the exact spot where he would bite – on the thigh. He doubted whether his teeth would penetrate the leggings of cloth.

Jack was disappointed when Captain Tom took the gun away from McCoy and gestured to the other two men to follow him into the house. He gave no sign of having heard the quarrel.

The scene in the living-room was a familiar one – a group of officers, studying a map. Tom brought Willie to the table.

'Look here, O'Hara; this is the wood. We stand here, while you and O'Shea bush-beat from here . . . to here. I've got a spare gun for you, but don't fire over poor old Jack. We'd better find out if he'll retrieve first.'

'Yes sir.'

'My captain, not only will I bring you anything you shoot, provided it is not beyond my strength; but also I will surprise you by bringing hares and small deer within range of your weapon.'

'Hallo, boy. You look pleased with life today. Let's get this jacket off him, he must be far too hot.'

A man of extraordinary discernment, thought Jack, straining to convey his appreciation to Captain Tom. If one could only speak!

At the table, Jack recognized with distaste Lieutenant Tony Greer, a stocky ginger-haired young man who had taken part in the battle when Jack had been imprisoned in the coalshed. This young man could not have enough of battles, possibly because, as yet, little harm had come to him. He was coming shooting this morning, but was not listening to Captain Tom. He was gazing about him, his eyes very wide open as he walked about the room, restlessly smoking.

It must feel strange thought Jack, to have no hackles to raise, no hair along one's backbone to bristle, no tail to hold stiffly in the air when one wishes to fight. This young man seemed always to be seeking a fight. Jack fancied that his red moustache bristled unduly, and he showed his teeth when he talked.

Tony Greer stubbed out his third cigarette since breakfast. 'I'm looking forward to this,' he said to Tom. 'If we can't shoot Huns, rabbits will have to do. Help us to keep our eye in.' He added proudly, 'I know I personally accounted for three Boches the other night.'

Tom faced Greer, his back to Willie and Pat. His voice was low and shook with anger. 'For Christ's sake leave it alone,' he said. 'We're resting, aren't we? It's the first time some of us have had a sound roof over our heads for nearly a year. Be a good chap, and shut up about the Boche for a bit.'

Greer shut up. Sulkily, he fingered his purple and white M.C. ribbon. He'd been told off by Tom before, but not in front of the men. That was when he suggested that the troops should be told before an attack that they would have to share their rations with any prisoners they might take. Apparently there were no soft spots in Tony Greer's make-up, and he prided himself on his rock-like nerve.

'Greer'll finish up a general,' Tom had said to Jim Harper.

'He'll finish up a dead lieutenant,' Jim had answered.

Jack felt real happiness spread through him like a warm glow as he walked between his captain and his comrade. This was life. The madness and the killing of men must have ceased, for a hunt for game was promised. This was one's true vocation.

The wood, untouched by war, was beautiful in the spring sunlight. Sturdy young oaks and larches covered a gentle slope with a clear stream at its foot. Bracken grew among the trees, and spring flowers on the banks of the stream. The larches, coming into leaf, were clothed with a mist of tender green; squirrels chattered in the branches.

The officers spread out in a line along the bank of the stream, while Willie and Pat set off round the wood in opposite directions. Willie followed a track into the wood, Jack at his heels. Soon a shot echoed through the trees and Tom's voice called, 'Go seek, Jack. Go seek.'

The words were wrong, but one was not a fool. Jack pushed his way through the bracken and found the warm body of a rabbit at once. He didn't know the Queensberry Rules for retrievers, so he took it firmly in his jaws and broke its neck. A precaution in case it was merely stunned. Then he carried it joyfully to Tom, and dropped it on his foot.

'Perhaps his mouth is a little hard,' admitted Tom, picking up the mangled corpse and patting Jack's delighted head. The others laughed, with the exception of Tony Greer, who paced up and down, smoking.

'Did I not do well, my captain? Am I not a fine retriever? Now that the fighting is ended, we will have some rare sport, will we not?'

The wood covered about twenty acres, and Tom told Willie which way to go, pointing to the right with a swing of his arm. Jack knew this sign well. Kurt had taught it to him. He set off right-handed round the wood as fast as his legs would carry him.

'Jack! What on earth? Come back, lad!' But Jack ignored Tom. He would give Captain Tom a fine surprise. As he raced round the wood, a vision returned to him for the first time in many months. White woolly creatures would be feeding, and they would see Jack and run into a flock, and Jack would crouch and creep, and bring them to Captain Tom, and his captain would shoot them all.

There were no white woolly creatures, but seven or eight small deer grazing in a clearing were startled when Jack came panting up. He was totally unfit for his duties, he thought. He must train seriously. The deer fled.

Back at the other side of the wood there was a crashing sound; the deer broke cover and raced away.

'If I'd known there were deer, I'd have brought a rifle,' said Tom to Tony Greer, who turned his wild eyes toward him without answering. A moment later, a cock pheasant rocketed up. 'Yours,' said Tom, lowering his gun. 'Why didn't you fire?' he said in surprise, as Greer made no move.

'It's May – you can't shoot a pheasant in May. It's the close season.' Greer sounded horrified.

'Words fail me,' said Tom.

Later on, the party assembled in a sunny clearing, where they sat on fallen logs smoking, or sprawled on the ground. The game retrieved by Jack was stowed in a sack. 'You can have this rabbit for yourself, Jack,' said Tom. 'It looks as if it had been run over by a tank.'

'My captain, you are too good. This one was not quite dead, so it is possible that I may have crushed it slightly.'

Even Kurt had never given him a whole rabbit, all to himself.

Tom lay back on the damp grass. The light streaming through the slender branches hurt his eyes, and he pulled his cap forward to shield them. I wonder what Celia's doing at this moment, he thought. I wonder when I shall see her again.

At that moment, Celia was striding up and down the narrow platform at Ballinasloe Station, in such a mood of elation that she couldn't keep still. Laura was buying a newspaper, while their father hovered vaguely in the background.

When the train clanked into the station, Laura kissed Maurice soberly on the corner of his sad, light brown moustache, and followed the porter to a corner seat in a first-class carriage. 'Goodbye, Father, I'll write soon. Take care of yourself,' she said. Having seated herself, she didn't look out.

Celia hugged her father violently. 'Goodbye, Daddy darling, goodbye . . . goodbye . . .' She was still waving her white hanky from the window after he had receded from sight.

Celia plumped down on the buttoned plush seat, spreading her skirt so as not to crease it. She beamed across at Laura. 'I'll be earning thirty-five shillings a week – think of it!' she cried.

'You'll earn it,' said Laura, grimly.

'Oh, that's just sour grapes, because your work's voluntary. V.A.D. Voluntary Aid Detachment. I think it should stand for Very Asinine Decision.'

'Why, Celia, only yesterday you were begging me to get you

in too. You know quite well that most of us wouldn't be earning anyway; we'd be living at home and getting a dress allowance. We don't belong to the working class.'

'I wish we did. I hadn't realized I could earn all that.'

'Don't be so silly. The work's highly paid because it's dangerous, necessary and normally done by men. As soon as the men come back from the war, the girls will be sent home.'

Laura opened her newspaper, crackling it impatiently. She had started her sketchy training as soon as Michael was posted missing, with one end in view. In France, she might find him, or someone who had seen him — alive or dead.

Laura was wearing uniform. The ugly black bonnet tied on with strings made Celia giggle. 'Take it off. You look like a mouse peeping out of a coal-scuttle.'

'Can't. You wait till you see your nice mob cap.'

Laura's travelling cloak reached almost to the ground. Her ankle-length dress revealed a modest few inches of thick black woollen stocking, and serviceable black laced shoes. She wore a short scarlet cape, with the pink Alexandra rose between the shoulder blades.

'V.A.D.,' repeated Celia, still giggling. 'Very Awful Dress.'

'Some of the soldiers say it stands for "Victim Always Dies",' said Laura. 'I know it looks like fancy dress, and it's anything but practical; still, women managed to nurse in the Boer War in this sort of get-up. I'm sure it was designed to keep the patients at arm's length.' She extended a woolly ankle, and studied it distastefully. 'Fraternizing is strictly forbidden, and who'd want to flirt with a girl in an outfit like this? The real nurses' uniforms are most becoming.'

Celia sprang to her feet, and set her jaunty green hat straight in the mirror which was flanked by views of Connemara. She tidied the escaping wisps of hair, studied the effect, and sat down again. 'How lovely for you to be going off at once to join in the war, while I have all these formalities to go through. I do wish I'd started sooner.'

'Oh, Celia, I wish you'd stop bouncing about. We shan't reach London until this time tomorrow. The Arsenal will probably still be there. Calm down.' Laura returned to her paper.

Celia rubbed the steam off the window and stared down at the broad Shannon as the train crossed it at Athlone. Then her native Connacht was left behind. She sat back and tried to doze, but it was impossible. So she took Tom's latest letter out of her bag. It was a fat letter, five pages. The one before had been a note scribbled in pencil, saying only that he loved and missed her, and prayed that they would meet again soon.

A long letter was a sure sign that the battalion was out of the front line. Short passionate notes were written in trenches, dugouts, cellars – they meant an imminent action. But the battle would be over long before the letter arrived. And if Tom were killed, she would get four or five more letters after hearing of his death.

This letter was bitter and happy by turns. She had read it this morning, but without having time to do more than skim through it. It was bitter because Tom's leave was postponed, and happy because of the reason. This was that Tom had been sent on a course which he was finding interesting. Security prevented him from describing it.

'I do so miss . . .' Celia smiled as she turned the page '. . . Jack, who is . . .' That wretched dog! There was a whole page about him. She glanced down it. '. . . Well darling, you must be getting bored with Jack' (I am). 'So I won't mention him again this time. Perhaps I'll bring him home with me some day . . .' (You'd better not.) 'My precious, I'm so worried by your final decision to go into munitions. You've no idea of the danger. The Germans are improving their aircraft all the time, and a single bomb could wreak such ghastly havoc. I hate to think of you there. However, as you've made your mind up, I can only admire your courage, and pray for your safety.

'I forgot to mention that Jack, who may be a trained gundog . . .' Celia skipped '. . . all my love, my own sweetheart, from your devoted Tom.'

Both Celia and Laura had visited relations in England several times. They were familiar with the short sea journey in the small hours from Kingstown to Holyhead, the sleepy transfer to the London express, and the hours in the sleeping car on the train. Celia loved every minute of the journey, and was out on the platform at Euston the moment the train stopped. She wore a long green skirt, whose matching jacket reached to her knees, and was cut in the fashionable military style, with tabbed pockets and an unnecessary number of buttons. Underneath was a pale grey lawn blouse and on her head a small green hat with a greeny-black cock's feather.

As usual, offers of help came from every male in sight, porters and passengers alike, and Laura, getting her valise down from the rack, drily reflected what an undeserved advantage good looks gave to a woman.

The taxi-driver looked dubious when Celia asked him to take them to Halifax Street. The lodgings had been recommended as being within walking distance of Woolwich Arsenal. The district looked extremely seedy, and many windows were boarded up or mended with chicken-wire and talc. The Zeppelin raid in November had left its mark.

Nothing could damp Celia's spirits, and she arrived at her digs ready to like everybody and everything. She and Laura followed Mrs Parker the landlady up three flights of stairs, Laura with a sinking heart. Celia's room was tiny, shabby and dark. Admittedly it was clean – Mrs Parker had boasted that you could eat off the floor. The mud-coloured lino was as clean as it could be made.

'How lovely! The little bed's just like ours at home.' Celia pulled off her hat and flopped down on the white painted iron bedstead. It even had a white crocheted counterpane. Over the bed, hung a sampler with the words, THOU SEEST ME worked in threatening purple.

Celia would be the only lodger at Mrs Parker's with a room to herself. Never having been at boarding school, the idea of sharing a room, unless with Laura, was repugnant to her. There were twenty girls staying in the house already, four and five to a room. Celia's was little more than a cupboard – the price of privacy. She left her bags there, and went with Laura, first to a restaurant for lunch, then to Victoria station, where they were to part.

London was full of men in uniform, the restaurant was packed with them. The men who had come from areas where the fighting was heavy were easily recognized. Their eyes gave them away, even when their lips smiled.

Laura's spirits rose slightly as she waited for her train, but she felt as if she were abandoning a child to its fate when she kissed Celia goodbye. Half a dozen other V.A.D.s had joined her, and they crowded onto the train and were carried away.

Celia called after her, 'I'll be right as rain – don't worry.' She took a taxi back to her lodgings where taxis were seldom seen, and her euphoria lasted right through to the next day.

Celia had a letter of introduction to a Mr Jennings, but she never met him. She went to the office as instructed, and waited there all day. The room was crammed with girls and women. Every ten minutes or so, one would be called and would disappear through an inner door. Morning turned to afternoon, and still there were more than twenty girls waiting, sitting on benches. Celia noticed that most had brought sandwiches. She was dreadfully hungry. At four o'clock, a tall woman opened the door, said, 'That will be all today, thank *you*; ten o'clock tomorrow. Thank *you*. Good afternoon.'

Celia started back to Mrs Parker's, hungry and disappointed. The Admiral Lord Nelson looked cosy, but of course one couldn't go into a public house. She hurried down the road, her nose assailed by a powerful smell of boiling fat. The café had a stove in the window, with sausages frying in a pan. It didn't look at all the sort of place her family would approve. She was hungry. She went in.

Celia was waiting at the factory gates when they opened at eight o'clock next morning. The girls were coming off night shift, and she had to remind herself not to stare so rudely. She knew she would be working twelve-hour shifts, and here came hundreds of girls who had just completed their twelve hours. They stumbled along in ragged groups, their caps awry, with damp strands of hair escaping from them, hanging in wisps down their dirty faces. Milling about like cattle at a market, they made their way to the building where they could wash, and exchange caps and overalls for hats and coats. It was a fine morning, and the sun shone cruelly on their weary faces. Some of them had skin stained yellow – the 'canaries'

Celia had heard of. Their job was to pack shells. Other girls wore bright red hats marked F.M. She discovered later that this stood for fulminate of mercury and that the girls' work was particularly dangerous.

Today, Celia ignored the door marked 'Enquiries'. She marched straight through the gates as soon as they opened to let the night shift out. She made for a door marked 'Office', knocked, and walked into a small ante room. Here, an armed sentry stopped her, and ordered her out. Nobody had ever ordered Celia anywhere. Disconcerted, she returned to 'Enquiries'. She had nearly two hours to wait before the first name was called. She stopped the tall woman who had dismissed them the day before, as she swept through, her arms full of papers.

'Excuse me, I have a letter of introduction to Mr Jennings.'

'Have you indeed? Who are you?'

'Celia Shane. I —'

'Wait your turn. You will be called.'

The morning was almost over when Celia's name was called. The room was quite full of young women. They chattered together, giving Celia curious glances. Evidently she had broken a fundamental rule by accosting the tall woman.

Near her, a quarrel broke out, and abuse such as Celia had never heard startled her. Bitch! Cow! Whore! And a number of words she didn't know. She wondered if they would be in her dictionary. The girls began to scream and pull one another's hair, and were separated by their friends.

When Celia's name was called she found the tall woman sitting behind a desk in the inner room taking the particulars of three other girls. 'We'd like to work together please, Miss Robinson,' said the boldest.

Miss Robinson looked them up and down. 'Willing to work with the yellow powder?' she demanded.

'Don't mind,' said the spokesman.

'No, Miss,' said the other two together.

Miss Robinson took off her spectacles and glared at them. They cowered.

'Have either of you got relations at the front?' she asked, in a dangerously gentle voice.

'Yes, Miss.' Both girls began to list brothers, sweethearts, uncles.

Miss Robinson cut them short. Addressing the elder of the two, she said quietly, 'Two brothers, you say. Your uncle and your future husband. Do you know, have you any idea, what they are going through – for you?'

'Sort of,' muttered the girl, looking down. The other began to sniff.

'Sort of. And you tell me that you are unwilling to get your hands discoloured at work which will shorten their ordeal and bring them home sooner? You surprise me.'

All three girls, one sobbing noisily, agreed to work with the yellow powder.

Celia waited impatiently for her turn. 'I am Celia Shane from Shane Place, Ballinasloe, Co. Galway,' she said. 'I'm willing to work with the yellow powder.'

'Very likely.' Miss Robinson wrote down the name and address. 'Age?'

'Nineteen.'

'H'm. Have you a letter from your parent or guardian?'

Celia produced the letter addressed to the invisible Mr Jennings. It also contained a doctor's certificate. Laura had heard of the semi-public 'medicals'. Celia was glad she would be spared that humiliation, thanks to her sister's foresight.

'Go to the main office at 7.30 tomorrow morning. Show the sentry this chit. Day shift. Machine shop 3.'

'Thank you. Shall I be filling shells?'

'No. Cartridge cases. Punch operator. Next.'

For twelve hours a day, six days a week, Celia stood in a long row of girls, endlessly pulling down a lever. Each pull punched a hole in a cartridge case. Sometimes one of the machines stuck. There would be pathetic cries for 'Johnny!' Sometimes there was a ten-minute break and a mad rush for canteen or lavatory. There wasn't time for both. The canteen food was plentiful and bad. Celia ate it without tasting it.

The first day was a nightmare.

The second day was worse. Celia set her teeth and worked on.

After that, she learned how to husband her energy. She grew used to the racket that battered her ears all day. She grew used to the heat and the smell. She rediscovered how to sleep dreamlessly for ten hours at a stretch. She grew used to seeing girls faint at their machines.

She never grew used to their language.

CHAPTER SEVEN

Tom couldn't settle down to enjoy the comfort of a good billet in the village of Dernier. He slept badly, ate badly, and was perpetually irritated by the men's petty dishonesties and their constant swearing. When he had first joined up, he had felt disquieted; now it was just another pinprick. He often had to remind himself of his affection for these men, victims of circumstance like himself. Naturally, there were good characters and bad among them, just as there were among the officers, but the good outweighed the bad. Cheerfulness and loyalty within the battalion more than offset a bit of pilfering and a lot of foul language.

Celia regularly sent a war magazine to Tom. Tom regularly passed it on to Tony Greer after a quick look through its inflammatory pages. He'd lost patience with this paper since reading the statement, 'With each successive action, the soldier's confidence increases, fuelled by patriotism and devotion to duty.'

This had struck Tom as such utter rubbish that he merely riffled through the remaining pages in case his own unit was mentioned, then passed the paper across.

'Here you are, Greer. According to this chap, "The British Tommy is a simple soul, whose honesty and plain goodness are deservedly world famous."' Tom pushed back his chair. 'I'd better go down to the square; the men are due to leave in twenty minutes.'

'Need you go? Won't the N.C.O.s see to it?'

'I needn't go but I will.' Tom didn't care for Greer, preferring the men's company. With each day that passed, Tony Greer became more eager to get into action, and more abrasive to

Tom's tattered nerves. He liked the two new subalterns,
Bowles and Bellamy, pleasant, ordinary young men. Dick
Bellamy, the younger of the two, looked as though he should
be still at school; Brian Bowles was a tall, awkward twenty-
year-old, with a slight stammer. Tom was sorry for the pair.
They hung about together, obviously unhappy at having sudden responsibility without adequate training. However, both
were plainly so much in awe of Tom that he found it hard to
make friends with them.

Only the troops were going to camp at Arras that morning,
in charge of Sergeant-Major Thompson. They were to rest
there for a fortnight, then move on to Clare Camp for a week's
specialized training. Tom Daly and Tony Greer were going
straight to Clare Camp, for a longer spell of training.

Not all the battalion was in action at any one time; the
lessons of the Somme had been well learned. A battalion
reduced by half – perhaps with no officers left – was desperately difficult to patch up and re-form. Bringing in strange
officers from other units had a demoralizing effect on the
troops. So what was called a 'cadre' or skeleton battalion was
held in reserve.

The cadre of the second battalion, Royal Dublin Fusiliers,
was to remain in Dernier, with Major Basil Shine in command.

Tom walked along the village street, and heard the men before
he turned the corner into the square. Like most Irish soldiers,
one of their favourite profanities was 'whore', pronounced
'hoor'. This epithet was used as noun, verb or adjective, and
might be applied to anything from the weather to the Colonel,
regardless of gender.

Tom heard someone ask, 'Are you taking that black hoor of
yours up the line, Willie?' and looked up and down the road
in bewilderment until he saw Jack. The dog was lying beside
Willie O'Hara asleep, his head resting on his crossed forepaws.
Poor old Jack, thought Tom. Ah well, I expect I'm a hoor too,
when I'm out of earshot.

The men were in holiday spirits after their long overdue
rest. The day before, the whole division had held a horse show,
and Tom had won the jumping competition on a remount

which he named Split-the-Wind after Laura Shane's old mare. Every military vehicle and turn-out available had entered, and every animal, including the mules.

Tom saw Willie O'Hara's small bow-legged frame, almost submerged with bags and bundles. 'You seem to be carrying more than your share, O'Hara,' he said.

'Yes, sir, I have Jack's kit to carry as well as my own.'

'Oh? And what does Jack's kit consist of?'

'Bedroll, spare uniform, hairbrush, towel, louse-powder, respirator, canteen, water-bottle, emergency rations, sir.'

'Good lord! I didn't realize how much equipment one dog would need. How did you get hold of a respirator for him?"

'I made it, sir,' said Willie. 'I put it on him every so often to get him get used to it. He tried to claw it off at first. Wouldn't it be a terrible thing if he got gassed after all he went through?' He searched in Jack's kitbag, which Tom noticed had the dog's number painted on it like the troops', and produced a new satchel. Jack, recognizing it, got behind Tom.

'I permit my friend to play this game because he seems to wish it. It is not my choice, my captain.'

Willie proudly showed Tom the neat grey flannel gas-mask, with mica eye-pieces, and a gauze pad in the nose-piece. Jack reluctantly allowed him to fit it over his head, and to tuck the end under his collar.

'Well done – I'm impressed,' said Tom. 'There's one thing though, you'll have to look sharper than that. You can't possibly get your own respirator or in less than three seconds, and it's taken you about fifteen to do Jack's. Don't forget what the instructors tell us. "In a gas attack there are two sorts of soldier – the quick and the dead."'

'I'll practice, sir, when I get the time. Never fear but Jack will be safe from the gas, whatever about myself.'

'You must put your own mask on first, O'Hara. That's an order.'

'Yes, sir,' said O'Hara, unwillingly.

It had been drizzling, and Jack was wearing his waterproof jacket, fashioned from one of the capes the men wore and hated. The jacket, like his cloth one, was decorated with brass regimental badges and a gold wound-stripe. He also wore the red, white and blue watered silk ribbon of the Mons Star.

'He shouldn't be wearing that ribbon, you know,' Tom tried to sound more severe than he felt. 'He wasn't at Mons, and it might be resented by men who were.'

'I'm sorry, sir, but we don't know for sure if he was at Mons or not. Maybe he was. And if he was fighting for the Jerries, he wasn't to know he was in the wrong.'

'Very well, O'Hara, he can keep his ribbon as far as I'm concerned, but don't give him the D.S.O., will you? The Colonel might object.'

Willie looked shocked. 'He isn't entitled to a D.S.O. A D.C.M. maybe, but he couldn't have a D.S.O. unless he was promoted.'

A fleet of red double-decker buses came into sight, one heading for the Strand and two others for the Elephant and Castle, if their signs were to be believed. They pulled up, and the men gathered up their belongings. Corporal Boyle sneered at Willie, who was shouldering Jack's pack; 'You've forgotten his bandolier and binoculars.'

Crammed with men, the buses roared away into the morning mist in the direction of Arras. Tom watched them go, then he walked back to the village, his head lowered, his hands clasped behind him. A mood of the blackest depression filled him. Those men were all so familiar to him, and during the last fortnight, he'd got to know them as individuals even better. The strength of the oldest platoon in the battalion was less than forty men now. He must stop thinking of them as individuals, or life would be unbearable. The battalion, the company, the platoon, the section even; but never Willie and Pat and Denis and Mick.

Specialized training at Clare Camp, he thought. He'd be with them there. Jack would have to be left behind. Then the great spring offensive would begin. The mines would explode, the whole Messines Ridge would burst apart, and the army would advance – the deadlock broken. This was what the High Command seemed to expect. And when the attack came, the battalion would be up there in front again, and 'D' Company, especially the original six who rashly called themselves the

Indestructables. Seven, thought Tom, not six. I should have counted Jack. He's done more for morale than a victory.

As Tom crossed the square, he saw Lieutenant Foster, an Irishman from Letterkenny, pacing up and down. Foster was a gunner, and Tom knew him slightly. Foster's attitude – head low, hands behind him, was exactly the same as Tom's. Each, noticing the other's bearing, straightened his shoulders and raised his head. They stopped to talk.

'Going to Arras today, Daly?'

'No, but I'll be going there shortly. We've just got a major from another battalion, and I have to go through some papers with him today. You look a bit down in the mouth, Foster. Anything wrong?'

'No – well, yes, there is; but I can't talk about it.'

Tom's quick sympathetic look was automatic, but Foster didn't meet his eyes. His own eyes, large and brown, flickered restlessly in his pale face. A nerve twitched steadily at the corner of one of them, and the dark smudges below them told of sleepless nights. Foster. Wasn't he a crack shot? Didn't he win a cup for the best shot of the year at O.T.C.? Tom thought.

'Come and have a drink,' he said. 'My major seems to be sleeping off last night's binge.'

'A coffee please, I'm not a drinking man.'

'I'd prefer coffee myself. My billet smells like a distillery. If anything could put a chap off whiskey, it would be the smell of it before breakfast.' Tom led the way into a stuffy little estaminet where only the grey-haired proprietress was about, and ordered two coffees. Foster took off his cap, smoothed his already smooth hair. He stood about nervously, turning his cap in his hands until Tom had seated himself on a wooden bench.

They drank their coffee in silence, then Foster ordered two more. He brought them to the table himself, and sat down sideways, not facing Tom. He stared at the open iron stove as if he were talking to it.

'I shot a man, back in April,' he said.

'That's not a crime,' Tom said encouragingly. 'At least, here and now it isn't. I know there are times when . . .' His voice trailed away as certain memories rushed back. Speaking more firmly he said, 'It can't be helped, Foster. That's what we're here for – like it or not.' To himself he added, You gunners shoot men all the time. Difference is, you don't see the mess you make close up. 'Sorry Foster, what did you say?'

'You don't understand. He was one of ours. Chap called Philips. I liked him.'

'An accident?'

'No. He went berserk.' Foster told his story almost in a whisper, with long pauses between sentences.

'There'd been an aeroplane over our gunpits earlier, and he spotted us. The Boche heavies got our range and knocked hell out of us. They were using H.E. shells and they put five out of six guns out of action. Two of the crews were literally blown to bits, and some of the men had such wounds . . .' He shook his head and shut his eyes.

'Go on,' said Tom briskly. 'Try not to dwell on that – we all go through it. Tell me about Philips.' A matter-of-fact tone was essential if Foster wasn't to break down completely. Tom held out his cigarette case, but Foster shook his head.

'There wasn't anything we could do,' he said. 'We had to sit it out and keep firing as long as we'd anything to fire with. Philips left his gun. He screamed and swore, and hit out at a man who tried to hold him. Then he grabbed Walton's pistol. Walton was dead – we'd had no time to move him. So I shot Philips. I shot him dead, God forgive me.'

Foster put his head in his hands; Tom thought he was crying.

'Only thing you could do,' Tom said. 'Rotten luck it had to be you, but somebody had to. You couldn't try to reason with an armed madman in the middle of a show. He'd have shot you, or somebody else.'

Silence. Foster's shoulders shook.

'Listen, Foster, it had to be done. Lucky you had the guts to do it. Think of the damage *he* could have done! I'll tell you a story about myself. Come on, drink that coffee – it'll do you good.

'In nearly three years, I suppose I've killed a few Germans, well I know I must have done, but I've never shot a man in cold blood. I'm not sure that I could. I'll tell you about a time when I should have shot somebody and didn't. You don't remember the Christmas truce? 1914?'

'Before my time,' muttered Foster. He blew his nose.

Tom sat back, not looking at the other man, crossed his legs and drew deeply on his cigarette. 'It was incredible,' he said. 'The powers that be on both sides took damn good care that it didn't happen again. Of course you've heard about it, how we met in no man's land, sang carols and exchanged souvenirs. Well, I'd been hit by a sniper just after I came out to France. Look – you can see the scar, here, on my jaw.'

'That was a near one.' Foster's voice was almost inaudible. He gulped coffee.

'Too near to be funny,' said Tom. 'I thought at the time that it was a hell of a lucky shot. I could just see the blighter up a tree, miles away. Didn't think he'd bother to waste bullets on me, and he damn near got me.' Tom fingered his jaw. 'Anyway, there we all were on Christmas Day, fraternizing like nobody's business, when a nice looking chap, fair-haired, about my age, came across to talk to me. We found we had a lot in common. My German's pretty basic, but his English was perfect. He was a countryman like me; his family had been breeding horses for generations, importing thoroughbreds from England. Sigmund – that was his name – thought the world of these horses and was tremendously knowledgeable about them.

'Sigmund showed me a photograph of his wife and their little boy, and I told him a bit about my girl and showed him her snapshot. Then he pointed to this scar of mine and said, "I gave you that. I am glad that I did not kill you."

'I couldn't believe it. Then he showed me his rifle. It had telescopic sights, the first I'd ever seen. We talked for ages, and forgot we were supposed to be enemies, trying to kill each other. He signed his name in my diary, and gave me a pocket calendar as a memento.'

Foster had upset some coffee. He was scrubbing at it with a piece of paper which was dissolving into damp shreds. He said, 'Go on.'

'It was months later,' said Tom, 'just before the spring offensive got going – we were all a bit on edge, I suppose. I went off on my own to have a look round Shell Trap Farm.

We'd been told it was deserted, but I'd a feeling it wasn't. Off
I went – bloody stupid, actually, I wouldn't do it now – and I
met Sigmund face to face round the corner of the farm house.
He'd had the same idea. Sigmund was as surprised as I was,
and I could tell he recognized me too, but neither of us spoke.
We looked at each other, and went back the way we'd come,
both of us . . . If he'd shot me it would have been my own
fault; if I'd shot him, I'd have felt like a murderer for doing
my job. I do know what you're going through, but I'd advise
you to concentrate on being glad your chap didn't shoot you
first.'

Again, Tom held out his cigarette case and this time Foster
took one and lit it with hands that shook only slightly. 'Bloody
snipers,' he said.

Tom talked on, watching the younger man and speaking
casually. 'Have you noticed that the chap up a tree trying to
shoot you is a bloody sniper, but if you climb a tree yourself
and bag a German officer, you're a bloody fine marksman,
and probably wear a badge on your sleeve to prove it.'

Foster's cigarette had gone out. He raised a reddened face
as Tom struck a match. Tom turned away to order more coffee.

'Thanks, Daly. You're quite right. Our marksmen think no
end of themselves. Trained by a big game hunter. Some of
them mark up their kill with notches on their rifle-butts.' He
drained his cup. 'You must think me an utter fool. Thanks for
the coffee and the story. Perhaps Philips will stop haunting
me now. I only needed to talk to someone.'

'Of course you did. But surely your own lot who saw it
happen didn't hold it against you?'

'No. They patted me on the back. Praised my presence of
mind – that sort of thing. Made it worse.' Foster stood up,
pulled down his tunic and put on his cap. 'I must be off,' he
said. 'We're moving today.' They left the estaminet, and Tom
watched the young man walk away up the narrow street,
feeling profound sympathy for him. Philips's death wasn't the
sole cause of Foster's state of mind. It was the last straw to a
young mind already full of fear, horror and guilt. Lucky Foster
isn't an infantryman, Tom thought. He'd soon crack.

As Tom walked back to his billet, a sluttish, middle-aged

woman stopped him and asked for a cigarette. She had made
pathetic attempts to make herself look younger, but without
success. In spite of Major Shine's stories, this was the only
woman Tom had seen him with. The attractive young women
of Dernier were either closely guarded by their mothers, or
attached themselves to the younger men. Tom, who had been
approached by more than one, was by no means blind to their
charms, but each in turn was mentally compared with Celia
and found wanting. Tom gave half a dozen cigarettes to the
drunken old trollop that Shine always referred to as La Juliette,
and shook her off with some difficulty.

When Tom reached the house where he was billeted, McCoy
was tidying up, while Major Shine wrote at a table, his
shoulders hunched. He looked up, puffy-eyed. Although perfectly tidy, and with his black hair well slicked down, Basil
Shine always seemed somehow tousled, Tom thought,
especially in the mornings. He was one of those men who
look as though they need a shave, even when they've just
had one. His moustache and eyebrows were very black, his
teeth very white.

'There you are, Daly. I'm seeing double this morning – some
night, eh?'

'So I heard. I turned in early myself.'

'By God it was. It'll be a long time before Dernier forgets
the Dubs.' Shine shook his head, rubbed his eyes and stowed
his papers in an attaché case. 'You know, Daly, you overdo
the devotion to duty. I'm told you're a damned good officer,
but enough's enough. Relax a bit. Enjoy yourself while you've
got the chance. Get yourself a girl – two girls – they're most
obliging round here, the mam'selles.'

'I've got a girl at home,' Tom answered shortly. He disliked
Shine too much to want to discuss Celia with him. None of
the pretty French girls could hold a candle to her, he thought,
and La Juliette was cheap and grubby by any standards. Tom
wasn't anxious to hear any more highly coloured accounts of
Basil Shine's adventures in pursuit of the 'mam'selles'. Having
listened unwillingly more than once in the mess, where there
was no escape, he had decided that his new superior was a
liar. Tom was a natural respecter of seniority, and he was

disconcerted and worried by having to obey a man he despised.

The mail was in. As Major Shine seemed to be in no hurry to see his reports, Tom took Celia's letter to his room. Written the day before she left Ireland, it was full of her impatience to start work, and Tom found himself remembering Fetherston's eagerness to 'get at the Huns'.

Celia's large looped writing covered sheet after sheet. 'I wish I could put on a uniform and carry a rifle,' she wrote. 'I might be a funny looking soldier, but I'd be a very fierce one.'

Even as he smiled at her words, Tom wondered guiltily whether, in that uncertain future when he hoped they would be married, he could match her enthusiasms. She made him feel old.

He smiled again over the loving sentences at the end of the letter. There was a postscript. 'Next time you write, darling, *please* let's have more Tom and less Jack. It's *Tom* I love. C.'

Tom folded the letter and put it away thoughtfully. This morning, he had sent Celia an account of the shooting party with Jack as retriever, and yesterday . . . There were at least three letters on their way to her with anecdotes about Jack in them. Some men, Tom knew, wrote about their hardships, described their privations, their dangers, and the aftermath of battle. He had censored many such letters himself. What a pity. He had enjoyed telling Celia little stories about Jack.

The bell tent was large enough to hold fifteen men, but it was conical and lacking in headroom. Only in the centre of it could a man stand upright. There were dozens of these tents in the camp outside Arras, as well as smaller rectangular ones, and huts made of planks and corrugated iron, known as elephants.

Jack hadn't liked living in the tent. It had no corners, and he was afraid of being stepped on when he was asleep. Willie O'Hara, understanding Jack as always, had made him a neat kennel just outside the tent. It was constructed from ammunition boxes, with a floor, and a low sill to keep the rain out. Jack was tied up at night with a light chain which was clipped onto a 'picket screw'. This was a stake used for supporting barbed wire entanglements. It looked like a giant corkscrew and could be twisted into the ground in silence.

Jack didn't mind being tied up. It helped him to feel that he belonged to somebody who would mind if he were to stray away. He missed Captain Tom, but no doubt there was an excellent reason for his absence. He dozed as the long light evening wore on. The memory of his supper (hot bully beef, a fried egg and cold tea) lingered pleasantly, while his sixth sense was trying to tell him something else. They were going to move again; he knew the signs. Perhaps tomorrow they would ride again in a high scarlet house on wheels. On the whole, Jack thought, he preferred to walk. But it was not the feeling of impending departure that bothered him. There was something worrying Willie.

His friend Willie was downhearted. Why should this be? It was something to do with Jack — something unpleasant.

Jack slept soundly on his grey army blanket. If he didn't exactly sleep through such disturbances as bugle calls, neither did he allow them to worry him. He was becoming accustomed to army life. Also, he was no longer young. He was no un-trained puppy, plunging on the end of a hated chain. He was of mature years, awaiting his captain in patient sobriety.

Voices. Footsteps. Captain Tom was coming! Jack shot out of his kennel, the chain rattling out behind him until it brought him up with a jolt. That was foolish — the exact length of the chain was known to him — he had hurt his neck. But what of that?

'I am here, my captain! Over here by this beautiful bedroom of wood, constructed by my friend. Can you not see me?'

'Hallo, if it isn't Jack! This is Jack, the battalion's mascot, sir.' Captain Tom patted Jack's head, rubbed behind his ears — rapture! The man Tom had called 'sir' was white-haired, short and solemn, heavily moustached. His uniform was trimmed with rows of medal ribbons and much shining brass. He carried a small stick under his arm. He said, 'Ah yes. I believe you mentioned him earlier.' He did not smile, but Jack detected mockery in his tone. It was plain that this old person held a position of great responsibility. Even Major Jim called him 'sir' speaking with deference. For Major Jim was there too, friend of Captain Tom and always kind to Jack. He said, 'How are you then? Eh, boy, eh? Eh, Jack old lad?'

Possibly there was some meaning in these phrases which escaped one not from the same country. Major Jim was wearing the sort of boots that Jack approved of, tall and well polished; immaculate breeches and his best tunic. In some indefinable way, Major Jim had changed. Captain Tom too was wearing leather field boots and spurs. That was more befitting an officer.

The white-haired one departed with two attendant officers. Captain Tom stared after them. 'General Plumer himself,' he said. 'Things are hotting up, Harper.' He unfastened the dog-chain, and Jack capered round him.

'My captain, I am beside myself with joy. To-morrow we will go hunting perhaps, and I will fetch you fine rabbits. How I shall snap their necks! What happy times lie ahead.'

Tom turned to Jim with a wry smile. 'I can't get used to you being C.O. Bloody nuisance. I was going to ask you to look after Jack while we're away. I don't want to take him to the camp, still less the front, and he and McCoy hate one another's guts.'

Jack stopped capering. Where was it that he might not go? Why was he to be left behind? If Willie and Captain Tom were both going away, it would take a stout chain to prevent Jack from following them. He pressed himself against Captain Tom's leg. Surely, surely, some at least of his thoughts must reach a brain so much superior to his own.

Then another officer, addressed by Major Jim as Shine, but unknown to Jack, joined the little group outside the tent. Tall and heavily built, this man, Jack knew at once, was not deserving of love and respect. His scent was somehow wrong. The whiskey scent was familiar and not unpleasant, but there was nothing else . . .

'So this is Jack, the famous mascot. Taking him up to camp, are you?'

'I may. I'd prefer not to.' Plainly, Captain Tom disliked this man. He added 'sir' after an interval which was a fraction too long.

'He can stay with me,' said the person named Shine, 'as

long as he behaves himself.' He grinned, showing teeth as white as Jack's own.

As the party moved away, Tom paused to tie Jack up. He checked that his collar was not too tight, and examined Jack's new identity discs. In place of the old grey disc, each man now wore two, a green and a red. Jack's, issued with the rest, dangled from a thin chain, one above the other. Tom looked down at Jack, biting his lip. 'No, damn it, I won't take him,' he said, apparently to himself. 'He doesn't deserve that.'

'I implore you, my captain.'

'Goodbye for the present, old man.' Tom walked away. Jack crept into his kennel. He heard the voice of his friend Willie, and a mention of food, but he remained where he was.

'I will follow Captain Tom and my comrade Willie. I will not stay with that new person. It will be easy to evade him, for first he will become intoxicated, and then he will go in search of a woman and I will be forgotten. I hope his servant is careless.'

Jack was perfectly correct in his summing up of Major Basil Shine. He had been unpopular in his previous battalion, and there was at the time a shortage of senior officers in the Dublins. Shine had been 'promoted out of the way', and was what the men called a 'bush in the gap'. He tied Jack to a table leg with a leather lead and forgot about him. Jack chewed through the lead with two swift, hard bites. Then he lay down, and waited for the careless servant, Dan Casey, to leave the door open.

Nobody missed him until Casey discovered the remains of the lead dangling from the table leg more than twelve hours later.

The battalion had left the camp at nightfall, Jack decided as he sniffed the air. He could not isolate the scents of individuals in the powerful army-on-the-move smell, but he knew the smell of his own unit intimately. He set off, trotting steadily, keeping in the shadows thrown by the waning moon. It was just after midnight, and in this lunatic world he lived in, a lonely dog might easily be shot. There was no hurry. He would

overtake the battalion. His friend Willie had corns. Jack had
heard him grumbling about them as he greased his marching
boots.

Jack trotted sedately, mile after mile. The road was the usual
pavé, cratered and broken in places. Jack kept to the side and
the softer going on the grass where long lines of poplar trees
had once stood. Some had been shattered by shellfire, some
cut, hundreds still remained. The scent he was following was
as plain to him as a brightly lighted street would have been to
a person. It grew steadily plainer; Jack was catching up. As
the first light of dawn streaked the sky to his right with pink,
he paused to drink brackish water from a stagnant pond at
the roadside. He was approaching a cross-roads, the scent lay
straight ahead.

As Jack finished his drink, he heard noises approaching
along the right-hand road; the sound of many animals, ve-
hicles and a multitude of men on the road. In the distance, he
could see horses and riders coming in the half light. He retreated to the darkest shadows beside the pond and waited
and watched.

Jack had marched into Arras beside Willie O'Hara, to the
strains of the regimental band playing 'St Patrick's Day in the
Morning', the men swinging along, refreshed by their rest.
This must be a defeated army, thought Jack. He did not know
that it was a division returning from the front line, moving
during the short June night, before the German aircraft got
busy.

Jack inhaled the rank smell of horses' sweat as he watched
a passing forest of legs, followed by heavy wheels. The guns
on their limbers were rumbling by, the men astride the gun
horses slumped forward, seeming to ride in their sleep. A
white bandage round a horse's dark neck showed up for a
moment and was gone. The horses plodded past, heads low,
then came mules, laden, men at their heads. Then – ah, food!
Another sort of smell altogether, delicious stew. But there was
no stew for Jack. The smell came from the cumbersome field
kitchens trundling along behind the guns. Carts came next, a
whole convoy of supply wagons, some drawn by horses, some
by mules.

Jack pricked his ears as a long, long column of soldiers shuffled by, four abreast. Their helmets were tilted at odd angles, many limped.

Young officers with no heavy packs to carry, and N.C.O.s, marching alongside at intervals, tried in vain to keep the shambling cavalcade in step. Beyond the reek of sweat and filth, Jack could discern the more subtle odour of exhaustion and misery. The men made little sound. Their boots thudded softly on the dirt road. There were subdued creaks and clinks, sometimes a cough. The procession seemed endless.

Bringing up the rear, a handful of mounted officers, round-shouldered and slack-reined, might almost have been asleep. One swayed in his saddle, and another rode alongside and spoke softly to him. The man's head jerked up and he rode on. By the time all had passed, the sun was up.

Jack stayed where he was until he was sure that all was quiet again, then he crossed the road and picked up the scent he'd been following on the other side. A large wood lay beside him not much damaged and he kept to the trees, his paws cushioned by moss, his mind full of questions that nobody could answer for him. Let them wait until he had found his friends again.

Jack knew he was nearing his destination. He sniffed the air, turned to the right and made his way through the trees. When they thinned out, he trotted through grass which was almost hay. Here, the flotsam of war was all about him. Broken wheels, thousands of empty tins, planks, lengths of battered corrugated iron, a wagon smashed to pieces, horses' bones, coils of rusty wire. Jack picked his way distastefully.

Beyond, he came to a place of many white crosses. Most were marked with a name and a number, others bore the inscription, 'Known only unto God'. To Jack they were mean-ingless obstacles, planted all over a humpy field.

There was wire round the camp, but it was not hard to penetrate. It served to mark the perimeter and keep would-be deserters in rather than to keep dogs out. Sentries patrolled the wire. Jack kept out of sight but not, apparently, out of earshot.

'Halt! Who goes there?'

Jack crouched, perfectly still while the man stared straight at the clump of tall grass which concealed him. Somebody inside the wire shouted, 'What's up, Charlie? Having a parley voo with the rabbits?' The sentry didn't answer. He stared at Jack's hiding place for a heart-stopping minute. For the second time in two months, a loaded gun was pointed straight at Jack. 'Seeing ghosts, chum?' enquired the same scornful voice. The sentry resumed his march. Jack was taking no chances. He chose the place where he would enter, where a tent offered immediate cover, waited for his opportunity like someone crossing a busy street, then flew like an arrow across the well-trodden path and under the wire.

Tom was sharing a small oblong tent with Tony Greer, whose thirst for battle was as keen as ever. 'Sharpening up his knife and fork,' Tom had overheard Pat O'Shea say to another fusilier. Greer, whose undoubted courage was fuelled by his firm belief in his own luck holding, slept like a child in his camp bed. His sandy eyelashes and freckles stood out against the pallor of his skin as he slept. We've all spent too long underground, thought Tom. We're like celery, life in trenches blanches us.

For some reason, he found Tony Greer's peaceful slumber infuriating. What's the matter with me? I never used to be bad tempered. Sleep was impossible, especially now that dawn was breaking. It was five in the morning. He reached for his pencil and notepad, and scribbled a letter to Celia. At first, the letter followed the well-worn pattern of unfulfilled love and separation, anticipation of leave and memories of the last one. He began to write, 'We've left Jack behind,' and scratched it out. Some of his irritation spilled over onto the pages.

'What sort of letters do you want, darling? Must I write about blood and gangrene and rotting corpses? I don't want to do that. Writing to my sweet girl is escape from all that, and I thank God that you will never know the half of it.

'Yes, we get dirty and tired. Of course we do. What makes you think we aren't afraid? Most of us are at one time or another. In the front line, only a fool is never afraid.

'I hate to think of you in danger – I've heard of munitions

workers blowing themselves up when fatigue made them careless. Be careful, my dearest love, and don't, whatever you do, volunteer for extra work.

'Why may I not remember you in your white dress? You are wearing it in the picture I carry everywhere . . .'

Tom began to feel sleepy. He tucked the pad under his pillow, and arranged his body so as to avoid the worst lumps in the thin mattress. There was a sentry outside; Tom could hear his boots marching away . . . marching back . . . marching away . . . Lying on his back, he fell asleep.

Tom woke with a yell of fear. He was being attacked. An enormous German, armed to the teeth, had leaped on top of him and was about to throttle him.

'My captain, it is I, your dog. Have no fear – I have travelled so many miles! Are you not pleased to see me?'

'It's all right, Greer, go back to sleep. It's only Jack. God knows how he found his way here – frightened me to death. Get *down*, Jack.' The sentry appeared at the tent flap. 'Anything wrong, sir?'

'Nothing, no thanks to you. Didn't you see the dog? Where were you looking? All right, carry on; Jack can stay here.'

Sitting on the edge of his bed, Tom looked across at Greer. Incredibly, he'd gone back to sleep already.

'Jack, you black devil, you gave me a dreadful fright. My heart's still turning somersaults.'

Jack, sitting chastened on the ground, offered a paw. 'Pray forgive me, my captain. It was unintentional. I was overcome with joy, and was unable to restrain myself.'

Tom crept back under the blanket, and took the paw in his hand. 'What are you trying to tell me, old lad? You're sorry? Don't worry. I'm not angry with you. I might have known better than to leave you with Shine. Lie down now, go to sleep.'

Jack did as he was told. But he was very hungry.

CHAPTER EIGHT

The smallest unit in the battalion was the platoon section, and the smallest man in his section was Willie O'Hara. He was a bandy-legged five feet four. Corporal Eugene Boyle, senior man in this section, was unusually tall and well built considering his back-street upbringing and hungry childhood. Whether this was due to his talent for scrounging, or whether want had developed the talent no one knew. Eugene towered above his fellows; in peacetime, it was likely that he would run to fat and develop a beer belly. His nickname was Euge.

Euge had little interest in the expected breakthrough at Messines, aside from probable pickings afterwards. He was an efficient corporal, but would rise no higher.

He went with the rest of Tom Daly's company to look at the scale model of the scene of the attack, and stood with the others on the wooden gallery which surrounded the tennis court sized model of the Messines Ridge. He listened obediently to lectures, but his mind couldn't absorb all the details. He kept his gun oiled, harried the other men of the section, and thanked God that he wasn't a sapper.

Under the vital Messines Ridge, which overlooked Allied positions, nineteen mines, containing over a million pounds of high explosive, were waiting. This was General Sir Herbert Plumer's stratagem. Now it was about to be put to the test.

The salient had been held for two years by the second army which Plumer commanded, although most of it could be enfiladed by German guns, or even fired into from the rear. The ridge had to be taken, but a conventional assault over the exposed ground, uphill towards Wytschaete and Messines, could not possibly succeed.

So, two years earlier, in 1915, the sappers had started their mining operation, while the second army hung on doggedly to the salient.

The men of the second army lived more or less permanently under fire, entrenching themselves more firmly, building up their defences, and doing nothing to provoke an attack.

The mining had succeeded by its very audacity. How could shafts be sunk a hundred feet through the saturated subsoil to the blue clay beneath? Railways had to be built to bring up the heavy machinery that was needed, and the supplies for hundreds of workers. The shafts had been sunk in secrecy, and gigantic charges laid under the German front line. Incredibly, the preparations were mistaken for the normal build up for a new offensive.

Meanwhile, a hundred feet underground, the pumps worked incessantly, while thousands of men lived in subterranean tunnels like moles, never coming to the surface. They ate, slept and worked in the brilliantly lighted galleries, where night and day were indistinguishable, and the damp air was as cold as death. Often, they advanced only a few feet in a day; some of the tunnels were almost a mile long.

Although the telephone kept contact with the surface at the mouths of the shafts, the only way of knowing what the Germans were doing was by using human 'listeners'. The unnatural conditions affected the health and mind of the sappers, whose nerves were constantly at full stretch. Hardly anybody could stand the strain of staying underground for more than two months without breaking down either mentally or physically. At any time a mine could be detonated accidentally, or they might be discovered. In either case, they would be killed, or trapped a hundred feet down.

The tunnels had all been given names – the Newcastle Shaft, the Brisbane, the Perth. The Berlin Sap would in time, said the men, reach Berlin.

Four days were left before the mines were due to go up, and the tension was growing every hour. For more than a week already, at the camp, the noise of the preliminary bombardment had been deafening. The artillery had been battering Wytschaete at the highest point of the ridge for a

fortnight. Now gas was being sent over too, in order to keep
the Germans awake and constantly on the look-out for an
attack. Uncertainty and waiting, the two great enemies of
morale had taken their toll on both sides.

All day long, parties of men of all ranks studied the model.
All day long, senior N.C.O.s took it in turns to explain the
details. Euge was too good a soldier not to try to understand.
The sheer size of the operation baffled him. Like everybody
else, he expected it to be crucial – an end to the long deadlock.

Two things were bothering Euge, and neither was the battle
of Messines. One was the loss of his pickelhaube. This was a
German officer's ceremonial spiked helmet, and Euge had
been carrying it everywhere for more than two months. Now
some bastard had won it. This loss upset Euge more than any
single incident since the Somme. He got no sympathy at all
from the other men. 'When he found it, there was a head in
it,' they said. 'Jerry came back from hell and won it off him
when he was on the scrounge.'

The other thing on the Corporal's mind was the re-forming
of the platoon. When they'd been resting at Arras, it had
consisted of four sections of nine men each. When Lance
Corporal O'Toole was wounded, he wasn't replaced. The platoon was re-formed into three sections of twelve men each.
The sections now had to specialize; one was composed of
Lewis gunners, one of bombers, one of riflemen. Euge was a
Lewis gunner, and so were three of his old section. Either
there would be a reshuffle, or Willie O'Hara and Pat O'Shea
must train as Lewis gunners too.

'I might work the belt, I suppose,' Pat O'Shea sounded
doubtful.

'I'm not touching any Lewis gun – they're dangerous old
things,' said Willie stoutly. Only when he found he would
have to leave the section if he stuck to his rifle and bayonet,
did he relent. 'I'll carry the ammo,' he said to Pat. 'More than
that I won't do.'

The section shared a bell-tent at Clare Camp and outside it,
a geranium was flowering in a pot. Euge refused to take an
interest in this plant, in spite of constant reference to watering

it, pruning it and taking cuttings from it. He said, reasonably enough, that it wasn't worth while to start a garden, and ignored it. In the end someone had to call his attention to the beauty of the flower-pot. The geranium was growing in the missing pickelhaube, securely planted by its spike.

To avoid Euge's wrath, Willie went across to the camp kitchens to see how Jack was faring. This in spite of orders to leave Jack alone, as his presence might take the men's minds off the job in hand. Jack had been handed over to the camp cooks, and was chained to the wheel of a supply wagon. He was morosely sitting under the wagon, sheltering from a shower.

Willie's excuse for visiting the kitchens was trumped up and slender; he spent only a few moments with Jack.

'Why do you not release me, my comrade?'

'Aren't you fine and happy here with all the food you're getting? You won't want to come back to us at all.' Willie nervously glanced over his shoulder, then bent and patted Jack, whispering, 'We'll have a fine time when this bloody show's over, won't we?' He added, 'Get down, you old bastard with your muddy paws, you'll destroy my tunic,' but his voice didn't change. Jack knew that Willie would always sound and be exactly the same.

'Please release me, my friend. I beg you to.'

'I wish I could let you off the chain and take you back with me, lad, but I can't. I'll be back.' Willie held Jack's nose in his hand, and grinned at the dog. Then he left him.

One of Willie's old friends worked in the kitchens. 'Beer soup?' he said. 'For the dog? Christ, man, you must be raving!'

'I am not. Half beer, half milk, and beat an egg up in it. He likes cold tea as well.' Willie fled back to the place where he should have been all the time. He hadn't been missed.

Jack had beer soup for lunch.

The camp was vast. Thousands upon thousands of soldiers were gathered there, and groups of senior officers strolled about, preoccupied. In the warm summer evenings, they relaxed, smoking and chatting, sometimes playing cards in the open as long as it was light enough.

Beyond the camp, thousands of bivouacs covered the plain

on both sides of the road. Horses, each tethered with picket ropes by a headcollar and a hind leg, stamped and fidgeted. The whole area seethed with unrest and excitement.

Colonel Jim Harper arrived at the camp the day after Jack. Leaving his car, he asked where Tom Daly might be found. Tom was inspecting 'D' Company. Jim strolled across, but kept out of sight until the inspection was over. He noted that Tom looked happier. His colour had improved, and he seemed less on edge. The men too looked better. They had smartened themselves up, and the look of indifference and fatalism had faded from the faces of the veterans. Jim went to meet Tom who was returning to his tent, whistling 'They'll never believe me' under his breath.

'Hullo Daly – I've a bone to pick with you!'

'Oh, hullo Harper – sir. Nothing wrong, is there?'

'There is – very wrong. You deserve to be shot at dawn, you and your wretched dog.'

'I thought Jack did well to follow us here. I hope he may stay, now that he's here.'

'It's not that. I find that among my duties as your C.O., I have to fetch and carry for your dog. Next time he runs away, he can carry his own pack or do without it.' Jack's kitbag lay on the floor, along with his respirator. 'I got a signal,' said Jim, 'to stop at Arras on my way here from G.H.Q. I did, and a man came running out with this –' he touched Jack's property with his foot. 'My driver's comment was that it was lucky we hadn't gone another ten miles and had to go back for it. Not that I blame Jack for running away from Shine.'

Tom laughed. 'I assure you, I had nothing to do with the signal. I'm glad you brought the stuff. As we're only in reserve, the men are determined to bring Jack up to the ridge, and he may well need that gas-mask. You can smell our own gas from here.'

When Tom rejoined Tony Greer, he was poring over a table-top version of the scale model outside. There was a wide smile on his lips – he might have been a little boy playing with toy soldiers.

Tom retreated and stood outside, pulling down his cap to shield his eyes from the sun. Like everybody else, he looked forward to the detonating of the mines as a short cut to victory, as a saving of Allied lives, as a satisfactory outcome to a fantastic feat of engineering. But Greer was different. He liked the idea of Germans being blown up. He got actual pleasure from the thought of thousands of men meeting a horrible death, or being maimed and mutilated. To Tony Greer, the 'Huns' and the 'Boches' were subhuman barbarians to be destroyed. He enjoyed killing them to the point of being frustrated if someone forestalled him.

Tom had seen him sighting and aligning his rifle on a distant figure back near Béthune. There had been a sharp crack away to the left, and the figure spun and fell. Greer lowered his rifle, his face scarlet with mortification. 'That one was *mine*,' he had said.

Tom remembered the cock pheasant Greer had refused to shoot in May.

Jack knew that something, probably something unpleasant, was going to occur shortly. It was June 6th, warm and sunny. The bombardment continued unabated day and night. One could grow accustomed even to that.

It was early evening, and large bodies of men were leaving the camp, perhaps as many as a thousand at a time. Willie O'Hara came up at a trot, and – oh joy! unfastened Jack's chain. A further concourse of men was gathering, getting ready to leave.

'Look at 'em, Jack, look at the Irish! We're all in together this time. Ulster, Munster, our own Leinster, and Connaught. Hurry up now, aren't you a villain – no kit, and your paws all mud.'

'I do not understand you. Why are you proud? What is pleasing you so much? Let me run free, my friend.'

One wasted much effort trying to convey meaning to one's comrades. Sometimes they appeared to understand a little – not now. Willie, holding Jack's chain short, hurried the dog to the group of large tents which housed the battalion. The men were lined up in front of the tents, in full marching order. Carrying their packs and equipment, they assumed strange shapes like giant hunchbacks in the twilight. Willie, Jack at his side, joined their platoon. 'Sorry, Corp, I was quick as I could.'

'Get into line, get on with it,' snarled Euge.

Pat O'Shea was carrying Jack's kitbag, and his place as usual was by Willie's side. He also carried parts of a machine-gun, and he and Willie quietly shared out their load. The young officer with the red hair, who loved to kill, was addressing the platoon. His voice was raised in excitement. He was like a dog trained to bait wild boars, thought Jack. Without fear and very dangerous. Jack could smell his rage and hate.

Captain Tom appeared, calling to McCoy to hurry with the packing up. 'Well Jack,' he said absently as he passed. One might perhaps count it a greeting.

'My captain, I am enchanted to see you. I am going into action with my comrades. Observe my position at the head of the company.'

Captain Tom ignored this courteous greeting. He waited, foot tapping, until the red-haired madman had ceased to speak, then called him aside.

'Take it easy, Greer,' he said, too low for any but a dog's sharp ears to overhear. 'You're not leading the Charge of the Light Brigade. We won't be in action for twenty-four hours unless something goes badly wrong. I should save the heroics for when your platoon's going over the top.'

The red-haired one seemed as unaware of Captain Tom's meaning as humans were of Jack's. He said, 'Yes sir,' a meaningless formula. He wished to get to grips with his enemy; to take him by the throat and choke the life out of him.

The sun had set, but the heat was more oppressive than ever. Then great black clouds rushed up the western sky, and in a few minutes it was almost dark. Lightning flashed, but the thunder was drowned by the roar of the guns.

'Let us go to the tents, my friend, it is going to rain.' Jack nudged Willie's knee with his nose. Willie took no notice. It grew suddenly quite dark. The rain poured straight down, soaking everybody in a minute. Pools of water spread about their feet, the dust turned to thin grey mud. The order to move was given.

As the company marched away in a deluge of rain, Jack

wondered why they could not have waited. The torrents that sluiced down on their heads would soon cease. Such cloudbursts were always of short duration. Tomorrow, doubtless, the sun would shine once more.

'I don't know what to do about Greer; I think he's off his head,' said Tom to Jim Harper. 'I've heard him literally grinding his teeth.' They were sheltering in a hut, watching the Inniskillings march out of the camp, followed by the Royal Irish Rifles.

'You seem to be unlucky with your lieutenants. Last time it was Fetherston.'

'Fetherston was young and stupid. We were both sure he'd be killed in his first engagement, and he was. Got Treacy and McDonnell killed too, following him. No, this one's different. He isn't normal.'

'Are any of us normal, Daly? After all this time, I doubt it.'

'It isn't strain or shock. He hasn't been in many actions and he has no nerves. He got an M.C. in his first action, and his only slight wound in the raid when Fetherston was killed. He had to have a couple of stitches in his head. It looked like a simple cut from a splinter, but perhaps his brain was affected. He's been much worse since then.'

'I shouldn't let it worry you too much.' Jim had to shout above the noise of seventy tanks starting up. 'He's not frightened, that's the main thing.'

It took five hours to march to the assembly trenches, where the battalion took up its position in the reserve line. Ahead were the supports, and ahead of those the assault trenches, crammed with troops. Beyond them lay no man's land, where white jumping-off tapes had been laid the night before. The whole area was overlooked by Wytschaete, and Tom wondered how on earth it had been possible to mine the ridge, to build roads and railways, and to dig a network of trenches under fire.

It was two a.m., and planes were flying low up and down the German lines to drown the noise of the tanks moving up to assault positions. It had stopped raining, and a white mist was rising from the sun-warmed ground. The army waited in silence. Behind and ahead of them, the guns fired incessantly.

It's going to be beastly thick with gas, thought Tom. He found Greer and reminded him, 'You must go forward steadily without rushing. The craters will be colossal, and the edges will cave in easily. The important thing for us, is not to bypass any pockets of resistance – if there are any.'

'I hope there are.'

Tom hesitated. What more could he say to this fire-eater? He decided that there was nothing. He turned away to speak to the men of 'D' Company. There was Willie O'Hara with something in his hand. Jack's respirator. 'O'Hara! Have you forgotten what I told you?'

'No, sir.' Willie guiltily stowed the gas-mask away. His own was still in its satchel.

Greer's eyes gleamed in the darkness. 'Forty-five minutes to go, sir. What do you suggest we do?'

'I suggest we go back to the command post and get McCoy to organize a cup of tea.'

Captain Tom was a good and humane person, thought Jack. He would not permit his dog to be wrapped in a bad smelling hood of flannel. A pity he had been too preoccupied to spend a few moments in conversation.

The noise of the guns was fearful, battering Jack's ears. Some dogs there were, he thought, in Germany, wolf-like, whose ears stood erect. Ears of this sort would suffer even more than one's own. How thoughtful of a not always kind providence to arrange large ears that turned downward for Jack. The noise beat upon him unbearably. He whined and laid his head against Willie's thigh.

Many of the men came and gave Jack a stroke or a pat. They were convinced that he brought luck, and that touching him would preserve them from death. The German guns had stopped firing, so presumably the din was halved, but it did not seem like it. Jack and Willie entered a small dugout, and waited. Willie ate a sandwich and gave one to Jack. Beautiful tinned beef! Almost as good as home-made sausage.

The gunfire stopped. Jack's ears still rang, but now there was no sound at all. 'Ten minutes,' murmured somebody. A memory surfaced which Jack would have preferred to remain buried. Silence and waiting and doubt. And suddenly the song of a nightingale: they were singing now, in the distant woods. The men came out from the dugouts, and crowded to the front of the trench, raising themselves to look over the edge.

'I don't know about this – poor bastards,' said one.

'Better them than us,' answered two or three.

'One minute,' said the same voice as before.

Jack stood up on his hind legs, front paws against the side of the trench. What was all this about?

The ground, no longer solid, began to rock and heave; earth and pebbles rained down the side of the trench. 'I will not be buried alive once again!' Jack scrambled over the parapet as Willie grabbed his collar and hauled him back. Everywhere ahead huge terrifying fountains of fire arose, and pillars of dense black smoke. The earth was convulsed, rent apart from beneath. Running figures were outlined against the red. This happened in a long moment of total silence. Then came the sound. Willie pulled Jack to him, and held the dog's head tight against his side.

'You're all right, Jack – oh Jesus Christ, look at that! All right old fellow, I've got you.' For Jack was trying very hard to get away. The world was ending. The gates of hell had opened and they would all be swallowed up. No doubt some of them deserved to die, but not Jack – not Willie or Captain Tom. Jack cried out and struggled. His friend Willie carried him in his arms to the dugout, talking to him, reassuring him. He staggered under Jack's weight. Rude gibes were made by other soldiers.

'Put the child to bed, Willie; we want you out here.'

'Sing him to sleep.'

'Give him a dummy.'

In the dugout were boxes of Lewis gun ammunition. Willie placed one of them on top of another. Jack was grateful to be able to conceal himself behind them. 'Thank you, my friend. I will remain here; I have been very much frightened.' Was it possible that the world had not ended after all? The guns were firing again, assaulting the ears and the mind.

'Stay, Jack. Lie down there. Don't run off, will you? I'll come back for you.' The dugout was illuminated with flickering red light from outside. Willie's face loomed pink in the lurid glow. 'It's not fit for a dog to be out,' he said, and chuckled as if he were jesting. Even friends were incomprehensible at times.

It was past nine in the morning when the second battalion moved up to the jumping-off point. Tony Greer had been violently excited by the exploding of the nineteen mines. He had actual difficulty in restraining himself from leaving his position and running after the advance troops. Now when he and his platoon were to go forward over the cratered ground, heavy with gas, 'mopping up', he found that he could hardly speak to his men. He unclenched his teeth painfully. 'Give 'em hell, lads,' he managed to say.

'They've had hell already,' somebody muttered.

'What? Who spoke? Take his name, Corporal.' Sentimental fool, he thought. Milksop! Old woman! 'Come on, let 'em have it!'

The men clambered out of the trench wearing their respirators, and Greer was obliged to put his on as well. There was little noise – a splutter of machine-gun fire from the direction of Wytschaete, a dog howling somewhere. That bloody mascot! A dense fog of dust mixed with the remains of poison gas hung over the battlefield. The assault troops had used compasses to help guide them round the huge craters. The landscape was unrecognizable.

Blast this gas-mask, thought Greer. He would have liked to have rushed forward as at bayonet practice, bawling 'Aargh! Urr! Grrr!' A respirator stopped that sort of thing most effectively.

Some of the Inniskillings were coming back across the cratered ridge, shepherding a dozen prisoners. The Germans staggered along with blank faces.

There was some resistance in Wytschaete itself. Although shelled and mined to pieces, there was still some cover for light field guns, and these had been firing on the advancing British tanks. Most of the tanks were out of action, and the Dublins used the smoking hulks for cover as they advanced.

The fog thickened – dust, gas, whatever it was. Hot and stifling. Greer was wearing a private soldier's tunic, obeying orders. A lieutenant's life expectation was very short. He hadn't yet seen anybody to shoot. He carried a rifle and two grenades, and there were a hundred rounds in his bandolier. He'd show 'em! Only let a German try to stop him!

One did.

Greer twisted sideways as his leg crumpled. He fired wildly into the murk, emptying his magazine. Then he hurled his two grenades and felt for his revolver. Stretcher-bearers, running to help him, retreated until he appeared to have run out of ammunition. Then someone approached him cautiously from behind.

'You've got a Blighty one all right, sir.'

Greer was glad of his gas-mask. Without it, the silly devils would see his tears and think he was crying from pain or fear. They were tears of disappointment.

Tom trudged across the open space, licking the back of his hand. Blood was oozing from a dirty cut. He felt inside his tunic for his field dressing, and, using his teeth, bandaged his hand as he walked. He stopped to stick a safety-pin in the bandage, and looked about him.

All day the battalion, along with the rest of the forty-eighth brigade, had been consolidating its position. The German resistance died only out by two in the afternoon.

Confused by the fog, many men had been separated from their units, and got lost. Tom, having checked that the company wasn't split up, had been back to the casualty clearing station to visit Tony Greer who was due to be moved back to base. Greer was lying with a shattered leg on a stretcher. A blue cross marked on his cheek showed that he had been given morphia by the stretcher-bearers. He was out cold. Tom didn't delay. He left a message for Greer and went forward again.

Greer had said, 'We'll have a marvellous scrap out there.' Tom wondered whether he'd had the chance to work off any of his pent up violence before he was hit.

The battalion had met surprisingly determined resistance that morning. However, the men had moved up the newly built road known as Watling Street and occupied the strongly

fortified Usnagh Trench. Temporary headquarters had been
established in a house in a deserted hamlet. Seven men of the
battalion had been killed and twenty-four wounded, including
Tony Greer.

Tom had left the cratered area with relief. He looked across
at Hill 60 through his glasses. Those German strongpoints had
stood up to weeks of shelling; now they were in ruins. The
long banks of barbed wire had disappeared, or dangled out of
sight into the huge fissures. There were hunks of blue clay as
big as small houses lying about.

Beyond the craters lay the signs of defeat and hasty departure. As well as bodies heaps of every kind of German equipment remained, although the Allied troops had been helping themselves to anything they could carry all day; weapons, ammunition, rolls of wire, stretchers and rations. Burial
parties were getting to work, and the wounded had been
moved.

'D' Company had dug itself in on the right of the position.
Willie O'Hara was on guard duty, and Tom walked over to
talk to him.

'Are your lot all right, O'Hara?'

Willie knew that 'your lot' meant not the platoon but the
six Indestructibles – and Jack, of course.

'Yes, sir, all alive and kicking – only for myself.'

'What's the matter with you, then?'

'Something in me eye.' One of Willie's eyes was swollen
and bloodshot.

'Have you seen the M.O.?'

'No sir. If I'm sent down the line, can I take Jack?'

So that was it. Probably there was a speck of metal in the
eye. It looked pretty nasty.

'I'll take him myself. He can stay at H.Q. until you get back.
You must have that eye seen to.' Tom shouted to Corporal
Boyle, who had just dodged past, heavily loaded. 'Put someone
on guard in O'Hara's place. He's to see the M.O. as soon as
possible. Who's in charge in Mr Greer's place?'

'Sergeant Duggan, sir.'

'Send him here, will you? O'Hara, you can go and fetch
Jack.'

'I will, sir. He's below in a dugout. He was howling something awful when I had to leave him.' Willie darted away.

Jack was pleased to see his friend, and noticed with concern that his eye was damaged. He came out of his lair with reluctance. 'I am comfortable here, may I not remain?'

Willie clipped on his lead. 'Come on now. Captain's going to mind you himself, aren't you the lucky one?' Jack had already been moved twice from trench to trench as the line advanced, each time by a different soldier. It was extremely unsettling. Willie hurried with him across the desolate wasteland where gas still hung about.

Jack observed and wondered. Truth to tell, he was still unnerved, and started in alarm when machine-gun fire rattled in the distance. The artillery was silent. Jack tried to ignore the frightening sights and smells, and concentrate instead on his friend.

'Got me in the eye, lad,' Willie was saying. 'Drove me goggles straight in, it did. Only for the goggles, I was blinded.' His hand went to the puffy lid. 'I'd've been straight off to the M.O. only for yourself. Who says you haven't got a friend?'

'I did not say so. I have called you friend for many weeks.'

'You could tell some stories if you could talk, couldn't you now?'

Jack liked the way that Willie chatted to him as long as there was none to hear. He went on chatting; apparently the grisly reminders of the morning's events bothered him little. 'Wait till you see old Euge,' he was saying. 'He has two fine pairs of field-glasses and three Lügers. He's hardly able to stand up under the load.'

The battalion was assembled in an open space. Some familiar faces were missing. The field dressing station was in the support trench where Jack had been sheltering earlier. He had seen the red-haired one carried in, and had later seen his captain go by on his way to visit him. Jack had stayed where he was, torn between a desire to make his presence known to Captain Tom, and fear of being taken up to the front line. Prudence had prevailed.

Major Jim, who was now, Jack understood, commanding
the battalion, was talking to the men. Captain Tom was with
them, and Willie unclipped Jack's chain. The dog looked up
at him enquiringly.

'Off you go, Jack. I have to get the old eye fixed.'

A few minutes later, Jim and Tom were walking back to
headquarters, Jack padding happily at their heels. The old
brick farm with its low-pitched tiled roof was comfortable; the
owners must have left within the last few days.

Jack had fresh vegetable soup, chicken and cream cake
for supper. Whatever McCoy's shortcomings, he was a good
contriver and an excellent cook.

The house, not far from the ruins of Messines, was sheltered
by what remained of the once beautiful woods where, not so
many hours before, nightingales had been singing. The birds
were silent now, the ground cratered, the tall oaks and larches
shattered or uprooted. It was now a wasteland which could
be penetrated only by tanks.

Ahead, the advance troops had reached Oostaverne, their
objective. The Dublins had three days to dig in, and set up
communications with other regiments in the area. There was
some shelling from German guns, but it seemed that the
enemy were only playing for time while their heavy artillery
was moved back.

Besides Greer, a major had been wounded, and a second
lieutenant killed in the advance. This threw extra work onto
Tom and the two young lieutenants who, apart from the
Colonel, were now the only officers with the battalion.

Tom wrote far into the night while Jack snored at his
feet. By day, Tom was always busy. Jim Harper now had no
adjutant, so the work was shared by Tom and Lieutenant
Bowles. As soon as the younger man was familiar with his
duties, Tom would hand over to him. In the meantime, he
was tired and cross.

Where Tom went, Jack followed. He had recovered his
nerve, and the sound of the guns didn't make him flinch. He
was with his captain, and all would be well.

They left the village, and moved slowly forwards, supporting
the advance troops, stopping at night in different ruined ham-

lets – Flêtre, Westoutre, and the larger Sylvester Capell. There they established headquarters in a strong undamaged house late at night, and, tired after a long day, they went to bed. The lower part of the house consisted of two large rooms, with an attic bedroom above. The owners, luckier than others, must have had time to plan their departure. Only a heavy dresser, the cooking stove and dining table remained. McCoy erected camp beds for Jim Harper, Tom and the two lieutenants in what had been the parlour, and one for himself in the kitchen. Jack lay in his accustomed place by Tom's bed.

Lieutenants Bowles and Bellamy tumbled into bed, and were asleep a minute later. Tom and Jim enjoyed the luxury of a thorough wash in hot water, heated in a giant cauldron on the kitchen range. They took turns with the hip-bath, and Tom, towel slung round his neck, was stepping out of it, when Jack came out of the shadows, and placed both front paws on the rim.

'Down, Jack. You'll upset the bloody thing.'

'My captain, I too enjoy a bath. My fur is choked with dust. I smell.'

'Shall we bath him, Harper? He does niff rather.'

True, the water was no longer clean, nor very hot, but what bliss, what glory was this. To sit in warm suds and be scrubbed by one's colonel and one's captain, both of whom laughed and joked, enjoying the task. Captain Tom rubbed him dry with a damp and filthy towel, while the excellent Colonel Jim emptied the bath and mopped the floor. They both made childish jokes about mopping-up operations. They did not sleep in shirts, these British. No, when they felt sufficiently secure from attack, they wore cotton suits for sleeping, patterned with stripes.

The two men got into bed, and Jack lay down beside Tom, trying to imagine the late Baron Heinrich von Hessel in a striped cotton sleeping suit. He failed. Lulled by distant gunfire, he fell asleep.

Jack woke abruptly, his hackles rising. Before he could wonder what could have roused him, there came the shriek and crash of a shell, uncomfortably near. Both the young lieutenants rolled out of their beds, and ran outside. Jim muttered, 'Curse 'em,' and burrowed further under his blanket. Tom sat up in bed, with one of his meaningless statements.

'Five point nine,' he said.

'My captain it was a shell, was it not?'

It was early dawn, scarcely light. As Jack looked up, he saw the wall which divided the two rooms crumble and topple. Of a sudden, they were in a half-house, the other half a pile of rubble almost hidden by clouds of smoke and dust. The shriek and crash came together, drowning the sound of falling stones. Jack's ears were deafened, so it seemed to him that the walls fell silently; the bricks and tiles not rattling and clattering, but falling without sound, like snow. His hearing returned to the harmless-sounding tinkle of breaking glass.

Tom was half way out of bed and Jack half way into it when the ceiling tilted and slid. Tom yelled, 'Jim!' but could not help. He pressed back against the only standing wall, the one by the bed, and Jack, terrified, stood up on the mattress, his paws against his captain's shoulders, pushing his head under Tom's arm. Laths and slabs of plaster thumped down all over the room, followed by slithering tiles. The wall still stood, windowless and doorless.

Jack and Tom, as white as ghosts from plaster dust, were unhurt. Tom held Jack clear of the bed which was crushed by an oak beam. Jim's bed was covered with glass and debris, but as Tom climbed over the remains of his own bed, to go and help him, Jim sat up, his head bleeding. The blood ran down his face and soaked his pyjamas.

'Are you hurt, sir?' Second Lieutenant Bellamy peered through the glassless window frame at his C.O.

'Lord no, not a bit. The roof's fallen on me, that's all. Thanks,' he added to Tom, who was lifting boards off the bed. Both choked and gasped.

'Give me a hand, you two. You can look for your trousers when we've got the Colonel out,' Tom said. 'The rest of the house could come down any minute. Seen McCoy?'

Brian Bowles silently pointed. Where the other room had been was a gaping hole, a broken bedstead half in, half out of it. He went and looked down. 'Nothing,' he said. 'The blast must have completely destroyed him.'

Tom and Bowles half dragged, half carried Jim outside, and sat him down well away from the drunkenly leaning wall. Jim looked down with surprise at his blood-soaked pyjama jacket. 'Oddly enough,' he said, 'I can't feel a thing.' He keeled over, unconscious.

Willie O'Hara had a tiny sliver of steel embedded in the white of his eye. The M.O. showed the splinter to him. 'Almost invisible,' he said, 'but left where it was it could have blinded you. Come back to me tomorrow.' So Willie was detained at the casualty clearing station for two days, a wad of cotton-wool over his eye, although he was itching to get back to the battalion and to Jack. When at last he was allowed to rejoin his company, Euge, a lover of bad news, told him that H.Q. was shelled to pieces.

'The Colonel is nearly killed,' he said. 'Captain Daly was buried alive − so was your old dog, Willie − and the two subs escaped by a hair's breadth.'

'Where was Mick McCoy?' Willie sat down suddenly on a box, his inflamed eye glaring from his livid face.

'Killed in bed.'

'Captain Daly −?'

'I think he's alive. It was a holy miracle.'

'And Jack?'

'I don't know about the dog. A fatigue's gone to clear up.'

It was over two hours before Willie got first-hand news. He feared the worst, as Captain O'Dowd, who was not of their unit, ordered 'D' Company to prepare to move.

When the fatigue party returned, Pat O'Shea was among them, and like the others white from head to foot with plaster dust.

'How's the eye, Willie?'

'It's right enough. Are they all killed?'

'Don't fret yourself, man. The Colonel has concussion and a few cuts from glass. He's gone to hospital. Captain Daly has cuts and a bad foot. He walked on a nail. He's still up there. The others are fine. Not a bother on them.'

'What about Jack; what happened to Jack?'

'When I saw him last, he was eating three lots of scrambled eggs. The officers didn't fancy them on account of a bit of plaster among them. Made me wish I was a dog myself.'

CHAPTER NINE

Jack slept badly for weeks. He had evil dreams which caused him to thrash his legs as he attempted to flee from an unimaginable horror. He whined and yelped.

The house where they were staying now was more primitive than the one which had been shelled. The tiled roof sagged, the walls, once white, dripped dampness, the boarded-up windows made the tiny rooms even darker and more depressing. Captain Tom had to share the larger of the two rooms with Major Basil Shine – he who had tied Jack up and forgotten him. This obnoxious person was snoring loudly. Captain Tom had moved his bed as far away as the size of the room permitted. Jack could sense his profound irritation.

Some days had passed. Jack was not sure how many. There had been no more battles; instead there had been changes.

Major Shine was doing Major Jim's work, and Jack knew that this displeased Captain Tom.

Lieutenant Brian Bowles had a third star added to his shoulder-strap, and Jack heard him ordering Captain Tom's company about. Captain Tom had lost his uniform when the last house was shelled, and a new one had arrived for him. He was annoyed because the sleeves were too long. On the shoulders, instead of the familiar stars, were bronze crowns. This appeared not to be a mistake. Captain Tom was now Major Tom.

Jack drowsed, and woke shivering and moaning. His captain – no, major – no, let us settle for master, reached out from his bed to smooth Jack's head. When Jack fell asleep once more, the hand still rested on his head.

*

Tom wasn't particularly happy either. He was now virtually commanding the battalion, but was still obliged to defer to Basil Shine. It was grand to be promoted, to get a major's pay and perks, but Tom was doing a colonel's job. Shine was going back to England, it was rumoured. Unfair that incompetence could get a man a safe billet and a soft job for the duration. Thank God, thought Tom, Jim Harper was recovering and would soon be back. In the meantime, Tom and Shine had to share a room. Inevitably they quarrelled.

Tom had slept fitfully, thanks to Shine's snores, Jack's nightmares, and his own longing for Celia. He was determined that, on his next leave, he would persuade her to marry him at once.

In the morning, Tom got up first as he always did. Shine was an untidy dresser, a messy washer, and his inventions about his sexual exploits were getting on Tom's nerves. Shine and the revolting Juliette were well matched, thought Tom, eyeing the other man who lay, mouth open, sprawled on his back. He'd been drunk again last night.

Tom was almost dressed before Shine rolled, yawning, out of bed. He pulled off his pyjama jacket, and prepared to shave. This was a tricky operation, the mirror being tiny, and the water in the bowl scarcely warm. Shine yawned again, cavernously, and scratched the mat of black hair on his chest.

What a battered tomcat of a man he is, thought Tom, impatiently knotting his tie.

Shine pulled faces as he shaved. 'You should get acquainted with La Juliette,' he said. 'She'd do you good. Hot stuff.'

Tom shouldered into his tunic and quickly buttoned it. 'I'll be going,' he said. He'd given up listening to Shine long ago. As he reached for the door handle he heard Shine mutter. Tom didn't catch the words, but was sure of their meaning. Suddenly, he was infuriated. Thank God they were now of equal rank and he could answer the older man back.

'You're setting a rotten example to young Bowles and Bellamy,' he said. 'What must they think? And you might at least be more selective.'

'Celibate life doesn't suit me.' Basil Shine grimaced and scraped.

'It doesn't suit me either, but I can survive without that filthy old tart.'

'You're a prig, and I bet you've had no experience. I'm happily married myself. Five children – that I know of.'

'You'll catch some disgusting disease from your French floosies.' Tom, really angry now, itched to hit the other man. 'Your marriage won't be so "happy" then.' Jack, grumbling in his throat, came and stood beside his master. 'Quiet, Jack. What about Harper, then? I daresay he's as virile as you. He manages to keep away from the women out here, and he hasn't had home leave for a year or more.'

Shine, wet towel in hand, spun round. 'Oh for Christ's sake! What have you got in your veins, weak tea? Get out!'

'I'm going . . . sir. I've no wish to stay.' Trembling with anger, and furious with himself for being drawn into this stupid conversation, Tom left the house with Jack at his heels. Later he instructed Kerr, the new servant, to move his bed into the other room.

No smallest trace had been found of McCoy after the shelling of the house at Sylvester Capell. It seemed unlikely that he had stayed in bed after the first blast. Perhaps he had deserted, or gone out at night and been taken prisoner. 'Jerry's welcome to him,' said the men. His successor, Fusilier Kerr, had been a cook before he volunteered for the army. He was pleasant and, unlike McCoy, trustworthy and honest, but his cooking was a disaster. Given suitable ingredients, a stove in working order, fuel, and plenty of pots and pans, he was a far better cook than McCoy. Unfortunately, he needed too much time. He was quite unable to conjure up quick, tasty meals, even in quiet conditions in a sound house. In the front line, he would be useless.

'I suppose you couldn't shorten these sleeves for me, Kerr.' Tom stretched out an arm, the fingertips just visible.

'No sir. Never used a needle in my life. Willie O'Hara now, he's a tailor, *and* he can knock up a meal out of nothing at all.'

So Willie O'Hara became an officers' servant, to the delight of everyone concerned except Pat O'Shea. Jack was in seventh heaven.

*

As the cloudless June days passed, it seemed as if the spring offensive had stopped for good. There was no follow up after the battle of Messines, no breakthrough. The rumour was that the delay was due to arguments in high places; the failure of Lloyd George, the British Prime Minister, and Lord Haig to agree, and a reshuffling of generals and armies. The French army still hadn't recovered from the April mutinies.

The newspapers spoke of approaching victory for the Allies, and a speedy end to the war. In England, the production of guns and ammunition was speeded up, as more and more women went to work in the munition factories.

Celia threw her paper aside. 'I'm too tired to read,' she said. 'Half of it's rubbish anyway.'

Celia's family would hardly have recognized her. She had gone to Woolwich a healthy eleven stone, two months earlier; now she was down to eight and a half. She had cut her hair short, and her rosy complexion had paled. Thanks to her bone structure, she was still striking, but over-long hours on her feet at the machines and lack of proper food were beginning to tell.

Accounts of the battle of Messines and the explosion of the nineteen mines took up most of the paper. Celia had read the casualty list as usual – no mention of Tom, thank God.

Lizzie Watson, ex-parlourmaid, a cheerful Londoner who worked beside Celia at the Arsenal, picked up the paper and smoothed it out.

'Terrible battle seemingly,' said Lizzie. 'Was your bloke's lot in it?'

'Yes, lots of Irish regiments were. Tom won't write about the fighting though, he never does. Let's go to bed. I'm worn out, aren't you?'

'Not so bad, but then I'm used to long hours. Been working since I was twelve, eight years ago. Come on then.'

They trailed up the three flights of stairs to bed. They were on day-shift, so it was about 9 p.m. The two girls now shared a room. Celia had tired of privacy.

Lying in their lumpy beds, they listened to an air-raid warning without much interest. They heard the droning of a few machines, and a desultory clatter from the guns close by. None of the girls used the shelters. They had come to value their sleep more than their safety.

'What's he like, your bloke?' asked Lizzie. She now talked to Celia on almost equal terms, but rather than use her christian name, as she had been asked to do, she stuck to 'you'.

Celia thought for a moment before answering. How far away Tom seemed – in every sense. Marriage seemed far away too. 'Tom's much too good for me,' she said. 'He's straight and fair in everything; so honest and decent – lord! I'm making him sound like a pompous prig. He's not – he's wonderful company. He's just, oh I don't know . . .'

'He sounds like a proper gentleman,' said Lizzie.

'He's that all right. You've summed him up. Yes Lizzie, I'm very lucky.'

'What's he look like then? Is he handsome, as well as all the rest? He looks ever so handsome in his photo – shame it isn't coloured.'

'Oh yes.' Celia was on surer ground. 'He is handsome. Not terribly tall, but broad shouldered, with strong blue eyes that look straight at you, and a thin nose, and brown hair that he brushes straight back, but a bit sometimes falls over his forehead. He has a nice mouth too.'

'Aren't you lucky. What colour's the moustache?'

'Darkish brown, darker than his hair. He always has it like that, just down to his lip. Grandpapa's gets in the soup – I hope Tom never lets his grow long. I think Arnold's *very* good-looking,' Celia added kindly.

'Do you? I don't,' Lizzie answered bluntly. 'I count my blessings though. If he hadn't a limp, he'd be out there instead of here in Woolwich. Wonder if he'll ever get round to proposing.'

The 'all clear' sounded, and both girls were asleep in minutes.

Celia had lost count of the days. She was finding the work easier, but incredibly boring. The machines were designed to be operated by 'Females. Standard size, height 5'4".' Girls of less than standard size stood on planks. Celia wished she could have a pit to stand in. She always had to stoop slightly or bend her knees. As she endlessly pulled the lever, she encouraged herself by repeating softly, 'Every shell, every bullet, every cartridge case brings the end of the war a little bit closer.'

One day in early summer, the workers were assembled, and lectured by a thin, elderly man in uniform, with a patch over one eye, and one arm in a sling. They never discovered who he was. 'Nelson's bleeding ghost,' whispered Lizzie. His message was simple; output must be doubled, due to industrial disputes in other parts of the country. Extra workers were being taken on, but dozens had left, through illness or inability to stand the strain.

'I ask you,' shouted the thin man, 'to volunteer for double shift. If twenty girls work tomorrow night as well as tomorrow, no machine will be idle at any time. If they do not, twenty machines will stand idle for twelve hours. Unthinkable. Will the volunteers please put up their hands.'

Celia's hand shot up. Nobody else's. She looked in surprise at Lizzie beside her. Lizzie sullenly put up a hand. She would do anything – almost – for Miss Shane, but really . . .

The thin man resumed his harangue, and got his twenty volunteers eventually, but after day shift most of them pleaded sudden illness or fainting fits. Only Celia and faithful Lizzie returned to the machine shop after an hour's rest.

Eighteen extra workers had been recruited during the day. They were girls who, for some reason, had missed a shift earlier. No machine stood idle.

The sirens wailed soon after midnight. They could just be heard above the racket of the machines. Celia and Lizzie exchanged glances. There were shelters, of course. After a warning, any worker could go to them. However they all knew what the effect of a bomb on the Arsenal would be, and felt it would be better to be blown up than roasted in the ovens that the shelters would become.

Normally, they couldn't hear aeroplane engines above the noise, but tonight the roar was sudden and overwhelming. The sound of the guns was drowned by it, the building shook. The conveyor belts kept moving by, and the girls worked on. There were eight explosions, each louder than the last. A piece of shrapnel about as big as a football plunged through the glass roof and embedded itself in the concrete floor. Glass rained down in the centre of the building. The eighty girls at the machines, forty each side, were unhurt. Some of them screamed hysterically, others began singing music hall songs. The machines stopped, and the elderly women who worked in the canteen handed round cups of tea.

After a few minutes, the machines started again and work was resumed, while two boys trundled in a barrow to collect the broken glass. The piece of shrapnel, which bore an unnerving resemblance to a human head crudely carved in metal, was saved for a souvenir.

The 'all clear' sounded over two hours later. Bombs had been falling in the distance, and the shed was open to the sky. A team of men rigged up a tarpaulin over the hole. No more bombs fell near Woolwich that night.

At 8 a.m., Celia and Lizzie headed for the washrooms, sticky-eyed, and with feet which ached unbearably. They had a ten-minute walk to their digs, and both had to be back at their machines in twelve hours time. The grime which covered their caps, overalls and skin was slightly greasy, and only hard scrubbing with carbolic soap would get it off. Celia scoured her face like a saucepan. She was too tired to worry about the effect on her skin.

They threw their caps and overalls into the laundry bin, put on hats and coats, and walked out into the yard. The day shift, using a different gate, was already at work.

Blinking in the bright sunlight, the two girls stumbled past solemn groups of people, many of them in uniform, talking quietly, their faces shocked. Their talk was of the big raid – how close the nearest bomb had been to the ammunition stores, how many had been killed or were missing, which streets had copped it.

'I hope they're exaggerating,' said Celia. 'People generally do.'

They reached the corner of Halifax Street, and were halted by two policemen. 'Sorry, ladies. Street's closed.'

'But we live here.'

'Hang on a moment then. What number?'

'Twenty-seven.'

The policemen exchanged glances. 'Afraid twenty-seven's gone,' said one. 'You were lucky to be out. Half the street's gone.'

'But – but, there were twenty girls sleeping there, and Mrs Parker.' Celia's head swam; she mustn't faint. Lizzie began to cry, and one of the policemen put his arm round her shoulders while he pointed out the school. The doors stood open, and he told her to go there for help.

The other policeman put his hand on Celia's arm to steady her.

Sobbing quietly, Lizzie obediently headed for the school, but Celia hung back, staring down the street.

'Sorry Miss, afraid there's nobody saved at number twenty-seven.' Celia pulled her arm free and ran down the street, avoiding piles of rubble, tripping over bricks. She felt numb and light-headed. Greasy smoke filled the air, making her cough. Water from a burst main gushed from a hole in the ground and poured down the gutter. Gangs of men were digging and searching in the wrecked houses. There were two ambulances drawn up outside number twenty-seven, surrounded by silent crowds. 'This can't be happening,' Celia told herself senselessly.

Number twenty-seven had indeed copped it. There was nothing but a pile of bricks and slates where it had stood. The houses each side were also ruined: their walls crumbling, their roofs gone.

The baker's shop across the street had escaped, but the houses each side of it had collapsed. Sheeted stretchers lay on the pavement.

The baker's wife knew Celia and Lizzie. She was watching, white faced, as the covered stretchers were slotted into the ambulances. 'You!' she cried. 'I felt sure you was gone with the rest, dearie. Oh, those poor girls, and another twelve of them killed in the house next door.' Her face was streaked with tears, and Celia sat down in the dust and cried too; dry sobs which hurt and did no good.

Towards the end of June, the week-old English newspapers had been full of the biggest air-raid ever staged. Tom had read in alarm how London had been attacked, in direct reprisal it seemed for the mining of the Messines Ridge. 162 people had been killed, and almost 500 were injured or missing. The neighbourhood of Woolwich Arsenal had borne the brunt of the raid.

Celia had written on the morning before the raid. She said, 'I'm going to disobey you, darling. I'm on duty tonight as well as today. We were all asked if we'd volunteer for double shift, and I thought, what a splendid thing if everybody did. However, only Lizzie and I put out names down. I'm writing at 7 a.m., just off to work . . .'

Tom waited anxiously for another letter, and it came. Celia was alive, thank God. It was so heavily censored that very few words remained, and no reference to the air-raid. The day that this framework of a letter arrived, Tom got orders, granting him leave in England. His leave had twice been cancelled at short notice, and he felt less elation than he had expected. Somehow, the idea had lost much of its power to thrill.

As Tom wrote, 'Darling, I'm over the moon! I can't wait to see you again,' he knew that the clichés weren't true, just as surely as he knew that Celia would reply in almost the same terms. He had a disconcerting feeling that he was writing to an imaginary woman in an unreal world. *This* was real – *that* was not. It was high time he went home.

There was another letter for Tom in the same post. It was from Edith Briggs. 'I was a governess in Germany until 1914,' she wrote, 'so I must indeed be the person your papers were intended for, although I have no idea what they can be.

'I am not at home at present, as I volunteered for war work in London. You may write to me at the above address.'

Tom glanced at the top of the note, and saw that the address was in Camberwell. Wasn't that somewhere near Woolwich? He wasn't sure. Knitting his brows, he resumed his letter to Celia.

Jim Harper had returned from hospital with a slight halt in his speech. His concussion was worse than it had seemed at first. He willingly released Tom. 'Get off as soon as you can,' he said. 'It's long overdue. Remember me to Celia. Going home?'

'Galway? No, my leave's too short, and Mother's just remarried. I'm delighted, as she was dreadfully lonely, but my new stepfather isn't greatly concerned with my welfare. To tell the truth, we haven't anything in common, so I won't intrude. I'll see Celia in London.'

'Tell her that I've met her sister,' said Jim. 'She's at the base hospital. Great girl, Laura – got guts.'

The battalion was stationed west of Ypres, living in huts. Willie O'Hara had settled into his job, and Tom's clothes had never been so well cared for. His sleeves were shortened, his buttons shone. Jack was as sleek as a seal.

'Goodbye O'Hara,' said Tom. 'I hope there won't be any action while I'm away. Good luck to you.' Tom was catching a train that evening; a car arrived to pick him up and Willie put his valise and greatcoat into it.

'Goodbye sir. Never fear but Jack and myself will be here to welcome you back. Shake hands with the Major, Jack.'

Both Willie and Jack were proud of this simple trick. Tom held the offered paw for a second while Jack stared wretchedly at him.

'You know, O'Hara, that dog has the most speaking eyes I've ever seen. Goodbye, Jack old man. I hate leaving you behind.'

'Farewell, my master. I had thought I was to have travelled with you, but in this life, one does not get all one hopes for.'

'Poor old Jack. Cheer up, I'll soon be back.'

Jack and Willie watched the car as it bumped away down the pot-holed dirt road. Soon it was hidden by a cloud of dust.

'Courage, my friend. Our master has promised to return. Let us not repine.'

'Come lad, back to work. No rest for the wicked. The Major needs leave if ever a man did.' Willie stumped along muttering, half to himself, half to Jack. 'I heard that Shine giving out to him, so I did. The nerve of him! Bloody old ram, good for nothing. Wanted steak yesterday. Steak's what he'll get today.'

They reached their hut, and Willie set about preparing Basil

Shine's meal. He cut a thick slice of beef from a joint which had provided both Basil and Tom with a savoury casserole the day before. Willie put the beef into a pan of furiously boiling water on the oil stove, and added plenty of salt and half a turnip.

'Let him edge his teeth on that.' Willie watched the meat with satisfaction as it turned grey and curled up. He put the lid on the pot, and began to tidy the hut. Jack shook himself hard, and whitish dust powdered the floor. He sneezed.

'Ah, Jack, you're all dust. Come here will you.' Willie set to work on the dog's close black coat, using a bodybrush labelled 'R. A. Depôt. Arras. Not to be taken away.' Jack loved being brushed, and arched his back against the soft bristles. Even better was the grooming with a velvet pad intended for removing horsehairs from uniforms, which followed.

Willie looked him over proudly. 'Now you're fit for inspection. Shake hands, Jack – that's right. Now die for the Dubs.' Jack looked uncertain. He sat down.

'No, boy. Get down altogether. Lie. Die. It's nearly the same.'

'You are mistaken, my friend.' Jack lay down, and Willie rolled him on to his side. 'Head down, that's the finest. Good lad.'

Two more attempts were enough. Jack dropped flat at the first word, and was rewarded with trimmings from the meat toughening in the pot.

'It'll be a handy way of getting him down under fire,' thought Willie, as he sliced onions into the saucepan.

Pat O'Shea pushed through the door, carrying buckets. 'Here's your spring water and your spuds, Willie. What's wrong with Jack, is he sick?'

'I have just mastered a new and difficult feat.' Jack got up.

'Die for the Dubs, Jack,' ordered Willie.

Jack flopped down at once.

'Clever fellow.' Jack jumped up eagerly for his reward.

Pat said, 'Die for the Kaiser, Jack.'

Jack flopped.

'It's your voice, Pat. He didn't hear.'

'Go on with you, Willie. He's still a Jerry.'

'Ah, go to hell.' Willie laughed. 'Jack's as Irish as bacon and cabbage.' He fondled the dog's head. 'The Major's gone. By the look on his face, he'll be meeting his girl. He'll have a fine welcome waiting for him in London.'

CHAPTER TEN

Victoria station was full of walking wounded. Most of these men were casualties from Wytschaete and Messines who had been detained in France, waiting for transport while stretcher cases were sent home. Men with limbs in plaster or bandaged heads were everywhere, but their faces were alight as they were reunited with wives, families and sweethearts. Even the women who wept smiled through their tears.

Where was Celia? wondered Tom. She was on night duty at Woolwich, but had wired that she would meet his train. He pictured her tearing along the platform to meet him, as she had in Ireland, her face glowing. His eyes passed over a tall thin woman who was hurrying towards him.

'Tom! Oh Tom, it *is* you.'

'Celia – my darling!'

As he kissed her, Tom understood why he had not recognized Celia. Where were the plump curves, the laughing face, the mass of unruly hair? This was no exuberant and warm young creature, but a tired woman, hollow-cheeked and pale. He could feel her shoulder-blades and the bones of her spine as he held her close. The face, on a level with his own, had a closed and wary look. She wore a black velvet tam o' shanter, and as he kissed her again, it fell off, showing hair cut almost as short as a boy's. She still looked beautiful, but her grey eyes were sunken, and she wore limp, colourless clothes.

'Tom dearest, didn't you recognize me?'

'For a moment. Forgive me, but you've changed – except for this.' He touched the deep dimple in her chin. 'Dimple on chin – devil within,' he teased.

Celia smiled mechanically, and took Tom's arm. He led her to a bench where bandaged men waited, and the constraint grew.

'Tell me about the big air-raid, darling,' said Tom. 'Were the bombs near you?'

'I can't talk about it. I'm sorry.'

'Poor love, I do know the feeling.'

'How was the journey?' asked Celia.

Tom felt close to panic; he had no small-talk ready.

'Not too bad. Look, Celia, let's go and get something to eat. I haven't eaten for ages, and what about you? When did you last eat? You're so thin.'

'I think I had some breakfast.'

'You think! Well, you're definitely going to have some lunch. Where would you like to go?'

'I don't know. I eat in the canteen.'

They ate in the station restaurant and made conversation. They walked in Regent's Park, in silence.

They sat on a bench. The sun shone and pigeons cooed round their feet. Tom put his arm round Celia. 'What is it?' he asked gently. 'Are you simply tired out? Are you hurt because I didn't recognize you? You haven't met another man, have you? No, you'd have told me.'

'No, it isn't that.'

'What then? I still love you, darling, and want us to be married. You haven't changed your mind, have you?'

'Oh Tom, I don't know. I think the raid unhinged me a little.'

'Please tell me about it. The censors cut out most of your letter.'

'We kept on working. If they'd got the Arsenal, shelters wouldn't have saved us. A great chunk of shrapnel came through the glass roof. But that wasn't the worst thing, nobody was hurt.'

There was a long pause. 'Go on,' said Tom. 'Tell me.'

'Most of Halifax Street has gone. It's gone,' she said again, and her blank face reminded him of the German prisoners coming back from the Messines Ridge. 'All the girls in my digs were killed. There's only Lizzie and me left. All the girls in the houses each side were killed, or buried and frightfully hurt. They were too tired to go to the shelters . . . too tired. They were being dug out when Lizzie and I came off night shift. They were lying in the street, on stretchers.'

'My poor sweetheart, what a dreadful experience for you.' Tom tried to pull her closer.

Celia looked straight ahead. 'Tom, all those girls were my friends. I know I used to complain because they fought and swore, but it didn't *really* matter. We had the sort of comradeship *you've* described to me. So many wore a black armband for someone they'd lost, but they never grumbled except about little things. Oh God.' Celia turned and stared at Tom, and her expression frightened him. 'I wish I were a man,' she said.

'I'm damn glad you're not. Celia, my dear; dearest darling girl, it's happened and you've been through hell, but it's over. I do know how you feel, believe me. I was the only officer left alive after one of the Somme battles – sixty men left out of a fine battalion. I kept saying to myself, nothing matters any more, nothing can ever be so bad again. I dream about seeing my friends killed. Your letters used to make me feel better, keep me sane.' He hesitated, searching for the right words. 'We love each other, try to concentrate on that. Put these ghastly experiences behind you, and I'll try to do the same with mine. We can be strong together, and neither of us must let ourselves be haunted.' Tom managed to get both arms round her, and pulled her head down on his shoulder. She neither protested nor responded.

'Sweetheart, I've got eight days. Time to get a special licence. Will you marry me before I go back? Would your father agree?'

'I expect so, but please let's wait. Please Tom, I'm in such a muddle I don't know what to do.'

'You're working yourself to death, darling. Let's get married, and have a few days together at least. Where are you staying now?'

'Lizzie and I are lodging over a baker's shop; it's clean and cheap. It's in Halifax Street, but on the other side. Nearly opposite our old digs.'

'Would you – would you stay with me – in a hotel?'

'As your wife?'

'Yes, until I can make you my wife, and that'll be soon. Will you?'

'I'm sorry, Tom. I don't think I want to. A fortnight ago I'd have said yes. I'm sorry.'

'Let me see if I can make you change your mind.'

Celia burst into tears.

Tom offered a large, clean white handkerchief, and wished he were back in Flanders. He understood clearly now that he did not love this stranger called Celia. And she did not love him, thank God. He'd had a feeling of relief when she'd said no. He was truly sorry for the girl crying so bitterly in his arms. He was also sorry for himself.

'Cheer up. Dry your eyes. Let's forget about the war and our own troubles for a few hours. Would you like to go to a show tonight, or are you too tired? How long have you got off work?'

'I've got three days' compassionate leave. I'd like to go to a show with you. Thank you, Tom.'

He took her to see *The Gondoliers* and held her hand. It was thin and hard. For the first time since his arrival, she relaxed just a little.

Tom took Celia back to her lodgings in one of the few taxis. He was aghast when he saw the desolation. The baker's shop stood alone; for safety, the remains of the neighbouring houses had been demolished. All the way down the street were piles of rubble and jagged walls. The street had been cleared, but barriers kept pedestrians off the pavements.

'I thought I'd left this sort of thing behind,' Tom said. He led Celia round the barrier in front of the shop, and looked up at the boarded windows. 'I can't leave you here,' he said. 'Please come and stay with me. Please, darling.'

'No, Tom. Please not.' Celia fumbled for her key and opened the door. Voices could be heard inside, and the warm smell of baking bread gushed out. 'Have you still got that dog?' she asked, her voice once again bright and artificial.

'Jack? Yes, he's still around. You asked me not to write about him.'

'I know. I used to think from the way you wrote that he was more important to you than winning this beastly war. I felt you were playing at soldiers.'

'We weren't playing,' said Tom quietly.

'Tom —'

'Don't you bring no men in here,' shouted a Cockney female voice.

'Goodnight, Tom.'

'Goodnight, Celia.'

They kissed like social acquaintances.

Both slept badly; Tom at his club, Celia in the attic she was sharing with Lizzie.

Tom felt cruel disappointment and confusion. He was reluctant to let Celia go, but could he learn to love this stranger, teach her to love him? Perhaps, but it would take time, and there was no time. Anyway, nothing could bring back the lost Celia. His heart and body ached for her. He buried his head in his pillow and groaned.

Tom woke with a headache. He was breakfasting late and trying to concentrate on the *Morning Post* when he was called to the telephone.

'Tom, I want to apologize for last night. Truly I don't mean to spoil your leave.'

'Don't apologize, Celia. I think I understand.'

'I've been so worried. You came to London specially for me, and I've messed everything up. Do you know anyone else here . . . ?' Her voice trailed off.

'No, I don't know another soul.'

'Could we — would you mind if we — just spent some time together, as friends?'

'I don't understand.'

'I'd like to be with you for the three days I've got off work, but no war talk, no love talk, no tears.'

'We can try it. Where are you?'

'Green's Hotel foyer.'

'Next *door*? I'll be round at once.'

Celia had dusted her nose with powder and fluffed out her hair, but she wore the same floppy black beret, and when Tom gave her a friendly kiss, it fell off. He picked it up. 'Why do you wear that thing all the time?'

'None of my hats were any good. They were all meant to be pinned on top of a lot of hair. Anyway, I lost all my things in the raid.'

'Of course. What an almighty fool I am; I never thought of that. Let me buy you some clothes.'

'No thank you. I've replaced what I needed, and I borrowed the tam from Lizzie.' She glanced down at the same cheap grey cotton dress she had been wearing the day before.

'I'll buy you a hat. You can't walk round London in a hat which falls off every time anyone kisses you.'

Celia giggled; a ghost of the old chuckle which could turn Tom's heart over a lifetime ago. 'You shouldn't.' But she allowed him to take her to a modiste and choose her a close-fitting light green straw. The hats in the shop were all close-fitting. Most London girls were cutting their hair.

Celia put on the hat, and they went to a restaurant and lunched on rabbit pie. Food shortages came as a surprise to Tom after a year's absence. They talked about trivial things, enjoying one another's company. They lingered over cups of terrible coffee. Celia twisted the emerald on her middle finger round and round.

'You're being very sweet,' she said in a low voice. 'I was afraid you wouldn't want to see me again, and I would have hated that.' She took off the ring.

'No, Celia, keep it. There's nobody else I would want to have it. Wear it whenever you like.' He'd noticed that she no longer wore it on her engagement finger.

She held up her left hand. 'My fingers have got so thin, it wouldn't stay on properly. Tom, you must take it – I couldn't wear it now.'

Tom took the ring, put it inside Celia's right hand, and folded her fingers round it. 'Keep it. Consider it a present from an old friend. I bought it for you – it's yours – oh, for God's sake, don't cry!'

'I'm not crying, well, not much. I promise I won't howl and sob.'

'That's my good girl. And I think we should wait a little

before we say goodbye for good. We can't both have changed so much in a year, can we?'

Celia gave a tearful gulp. 'No, surely not.'

'Have you finished that coffee? Right then, let's go for a walk.'

'Tom, before we go, I want to say that I didn't mean that you were playing at soldiers. I know you weren't.'

'I think you read too many of these wretched war magazines. They give the impression that we spend all our time fighting at the front, but you know, it's not really like that. We spend a lot of time in towns and rest camps, trying to amuse ourselves, and there's often precious little to do. It's such a damnably unnatural way of life, it leads to bickering, petty jealousy, that sort of thing. Finding Jack was marvellous luck, but he's not the only pet in the regiment. The men will tame anything that's tameable. They had a jackdaw for months, and what an almighty fuss there was when it disappeared. Pets remind us of normal life. Most of us have a dog at home.'

'I think I understand.'

'You're a goose if you don't. Come on, you know London better than I do. Where are we going for our walk?'

It was late afternoon. Tom and Celia stood together at the end of Halifax Street. They'd come because Celia wanted Tom to meet Lizzie who was on night shift. She'd just be getting up.

Lorries were still carting away bricks and rubble. Groups of men hacked and dug and shovelled in clouds of dust. Where ruins had been cleared away, there were guard-rails round open basements.

A notice board pointed to a large red-brick house at the end of the street: REST HOSPICE. Enquire within.

'Are they looking after casualties there?' asked Tom.

'No, it's for bombed-out people with nowhere to go. Old people and children mostly. Those women playing with the children are voluntary workers. The children have lost their mothers, and their fathers are at the front.'

The building had been a school, and there was a small playground beside it, in which children of all ages were playing games. The voluntary helpers ran amongst them, blowing whistles and organizing a game of postman's knock. Hampered by their long skirts, the older women romped self-consciously.

Three of the younger helpers stopped, breathless and laughing, near Tom. He noticed how alike they were. Slight, fair-haired and trimly built, two of them were thirtyish, the other rather younger. All had bobbed hair and were bareheaded. Their faces were bright pink from their exertions. Had Tom but known it, he was looking at Audrey, Lena and Edith Briggs.

'Lizzie's sick,' said the baker's wife, holding the door a few inches open. She was regretting having taken the two girls in. 'She's in bed. Doctor's been, and he says it's the water. She's not to have visitors.'

'Oh but I must see Lizzie,' cried Celia. 'Let me in please, Mrs Hawkins.'

'She's asleep now. Doctor said not to wake her. He's given her something.' Mrs Hawkins firmly shut the door.

'Let's come back later,' suggested Tom. 'I don't like the look of your landlady.'

'Lizzie must have forgotten to boil the water,' said Celia, as they went back down the wrecked street. 'We've all been warned that it may be contaminated.'

'Good God! Celia, you *must* leave this place.'

'I'd rather not.'

'Let me at least take you to tea at Gunter's,' said Tom. 'Then we can go back and see Lizzie.'

At Gunter's, conversation lagged. We used not to need to talk, Tom thought. Searching for a safe subject, he said: 'I take *Fruit Gathering* everywhere with me. There's a sort of prayer in it that I've learned by heart. I say it when things look like getting rough.'

'Most prayers are soppy,' said Celia. 'All wrong for a soldier. More like a cry for help.'

'Perhaps sometimes we all need to cry for help.' Tom ate a piece of cake. She's still very young, he told himself.

Celia hadn't eaten anything. She pushed her ice-cream round her plate. When she looked up, she was so pale that her face had a bluish tinge. 'I feel faint,' she whispered, and to Tom's horror, she slid from view, down under the long white linen tablecloth.

'Diphtheria,' said the doctor at St Martin's, where Tom had installed Celia in a private room. 'Not good, I'm afraid. She's basically a strong healthy girl, but suffering from overwork and malnutrition.'

'Should I send for Miss Shane's father?' asked Tom. 'He lives in the west of Ireland, so it would take him twenty-four hours to get here.'

'Certainly, yes, I should inform the next of kin.'

Tom sent off a wire to Maurice Shane. Then he collected Celia's belongings from her digs, where Mrs Hawkins told him that Lizzie too had gone to hospital, the Woolwich Infirmary.

The next day, Celia was not allowed visitors and was described as 'critical'. Tom telephoned the Woolwich Infirmary. Lizzie had died.

He spent the rest of his leave staying at his club and close to Celia. When her father visited the ward, she failed to recognize him. He and Tom shared a miserable dinner.

'She would go. I couldn't stop her. She would go,' Maurice kept repeating.

'Mr Shane, I should tell you that Celia and I have broken off our engagement. We found we'd both changed so much in the past year, that we are different people. I'm still very fond of her of course, and hope with all my heart she'll be all right.'

'She's like her mother, lovely girl, goes her own way. Lovely girl, Rose was. Went her own way. Dead now.'

Tom realized that Maurice Shane was rather drunk. During the evening he drank a good deal more. Tom put him to bed, and then went back to his club where he sat until late wondering what to do about Celia.

Laura was in France and there wasn't another sensible relation who could be sent for. Maurice had managed to tell him that much.

Tom would soon have to go back to the front, and doubtless, Maurice would go back to Ireland. He had proved to be useless anyway.

The following morning early, Tom rang St Martin's and was told that Celia, although still on the danger list, had passed the crisis in the night, and now stood a fifty-fifty chance of complete recovery. Suddenly, the telephone cut off, in mid sentence. Tom searched his pockets for more change and found a small book; Hansel's poems, and inside it, Edith Briggs's letter with the address in Camberwell. Edith Briggs! Could she possibly help? It was worth trying. An hour later, Tom was paying off a taxi outside a tall terrace house.

Mrs Dixon, a neat shabby woman, was obviously impressed by Tom's good looks and major's uniform. 'Miss Briggs — which one do you want? I have three,' she said, as if offering merchandise.

'Miss Edith Briggs.'

'Ah, that's the youngest lady. They're still in their room. They work at the refuge all day. Step in here, sir, and I'll call her for you.'

Tom stepped into the stuffy little parlour. He waited. He had never read right through Hansel's poems, they had seemed too private. But now, while he waited for Hansel's beloved to appear, he opened the book near the end. A title caught his eye:

EDITH: SAVIOUR OF INNOCENT JACK.

The verses were carefully written, and Tom read them, half amused, half pitying. The last one read:

> Father, pause! Do not hurt
> My Edith weeping.
> Spare Jack — send him to Kurt
> For safer keeping.

At the bottom, Hansel had noted, 'My best poem, I think, but for Her I will do better and better. N.B. There is no rhyme for enchantress.'

Tom's idea of Edith was coloured by Hansel's rose-tinted spectacles. She was fair, sweet, blest. Forever desirable; forever unattainable.

*

'Major Daly? I don't think I know – oh yes! He's the man who
wrote to Father from France. I sent him a note after we came
here. I told you about him.' Edith rapidly brushed her hair
and buttoned up her best blouse. It was grey silk, with a
fashionable 'artist's bow' at the neck.

'Don't get excited,' said Lena. 'Majors are usually quite old,
and he's sure to be married.'

'If he's too old for me, one of you shall have him – draw
lots.' Edith made a face at her sisters, and hurried down to the
parlour.

The man sitting by the table rose and introduced himself.
Thirty? Thirty-two? No more, thought Edith, and he doesn't
look married. She liked his eyes with the crinkles at the corners,
and his firm mouth. They shook hands. His was cool. You
could trust him, she thought, and his head is a good shape
with neat close-set ears. She blushed.

'Mrs Dixon will bring a cup of tea if you like,' she said.

'No thank you. Not unless you'd like some yourself. We've
met before, Miss Briggs, or rather, I've seen you. At the rest
hospice, playing with the children.'

'I work there. It's rather exhausting, but tremendously
worth while. Before that my sisters and I had been knitting
socks non-stop for two years. I pity any poor soldier who had
to wear those socks on the march. Our first efforts were
dreadful.' She was chattering, she knew. Major Daly would
think she was a bore. 'We'll be at the hospice for as long as it
takes to find accommodation for the children. Several more
weeks, I expect.'

'I've come to give you this little book, and to ask rather a
big favour of you,' said Tom.

Edith took Hansel's book and opened it. She blushed crimson – why couldn't she outgrow that schoolgirl habit? 'I'd no
idea. Poor Hansel, is he dead?'

'Yes. I found the book in his dressing-case. No one else has
ever seen it.'

'Thank you for that.' Edith looked down at the book in her
hands, hiding her burning face. 'He was only a schoolboy,'
she said. 'His father was a conceited brute and his mother was
quite crazy. There was a daughter, Ilse. She was my pupil, and

so dull and stupid I wanted to shake her. She wrote to me from Switzerland not long ago, saying she'd run away because her mother was planning to poison both of them if Germany was beaten. I gather the mother is drinking too much. The Baron had a famous cellar, and the Baroness is drinking her way through it.'

Tom laughed. 'What a story. There's one thing I'm curious about. I admit that I've read some of the boy's verses. One of them was about a dog called Jack. Do you remember him?'

'Indeed I do. He was the most adorable retriever puppy. Hansel brought him from England, and he used to go out with me in the pony carriage. He was so clever and well behaved, full of character. The Baron got it into his head that Jack was a mongrel, and was going to have him shot. I'm afraid I broke down and made a fool of myself, but it did achieve something. Instead of being shot, Jack was taken away from Hansel and given to the head forester's son, a dim-witted lad called Kurt. I wonder what happened to Jack.'

Tom told her; she listened enthralled. 'What possessed them to take a dog out to the front? Did Kurt live? The poor boy, what a shame. Jack must be seven or eight now, perhaps more.'

'He's getting a little grey about the muzzle, but he's fit for anything. What an extraordinary coincidence, meeting you like this, Miss Briggs, and finding that you knew Jack. I owe that dog a lot. When we found him, he was trying to dig out the German boy although he'd been quite badly hurt himself. I was in bad shape myself at the time. Many of my best friends had been killed, and I was in danger of losing my nerve. Then I started to watch Jack and how he battled to adapt to us and our way of life, although he couldn't possibly have really understood what was going on. His courage is amazing, and I thought, if a dog can survive, surely I can. He helped to keep me sane. Does that sound totally idiotic?'

Edith was thinking how animation made him downright handsome. 'No, not a bit,' she said.

'Do you know Byron's epitaph to his dog Bosun?'

'I've heard it,' said Edith, 'I can't remember it exactly.'

'"Beauty without vanity, strength without insolence, courage without ferocity, and all the virtues of man without his vices." In case I make him sound too saintly,' Tom added smiling, 'I think Jack is a trifle vain, and more than a trifle greedy.'

'I wish you'd brought him with you. But what was the favour you were going to ask?'

'It's something I'm reluctant to ask a stranger, but I don't know a soul in London. A girl I know – we used to be engaged – was working in munitions. She's ill in St Martin's hospital with diphtheria, and still not out of the wood. You mustn't visit her, of course – it's frightfully catching. But could you possibly enquire by telephone every day to find out if there's anything she needs, until she's on the mend? I'd be everlastingly grateful. Could you do that?'

'Why of course I will.'

'Thank you, I was sure you would.' He put some money on the table. 'That's for the telephone and to buy her fruit or flowers, or anything you think suitable. "From Tom" is all you need put on the card.'

'Nice things are scarce now. It isn't easy to buy treats for an invalid,' said Edith doubtfully.

'I know, but please do your best.'

'I will. And I'll let you know how she's getting on.'

That night, Tom took Edith, Audrey and Lena Briggs to see *Chou Chin Chow*. He bought flowers for all three. Two days later he was back in Flanders.

Tom walked from the makeshift railway along the road in the direction of the camp. There should have been a car to meet him, but he didn't feel like waiting for it. He was sure to meet it on the way. He passed two mine craters, and their size shocked him all over again. The road had been rebuilt to pass between them. They were known as Etna and Vesuvius, and each was fifty yards wide and a hundred feet deep. He walked on. What had happened to the blasted car?

Tom's journey had been a miserable one. He told himself sternly that he'd been in love with a dream, not a person, but it didn't help much. And Celia was still very ill.

Tom's mind rejected the sick embittered girl lying in hospital, while the desirable, impulsive creature he'd loved haunted him. How could someone who was now such a stranger to him still claim a large slice of his heart, Tom wondered.

Edith hadn't touched his emotions. He'd been disappointed to find her no more than pretty, Hansel having led him to expect a raving beauty, but she was pleasant and kind hearted. He'd liked her. Oh, but who could replace Celia, the old Celia? Tom had left England not greatly caring if he were killed or not. Oh God! How he would miss Celia's letters. Still there was no sign of the car. He walked on.

In the distance, Tom saw a small black object. Jack! He whistled shrilly, and waited as Jack galloped full tilt towards him. Tom set down his valise, dropped on one knee, and Jack rushed into his arms. Fleetingly, unworthily, Tom compared his greeting with Celia's.

'My master, you have returned, and all will now be well.'

'Easy, lad, easy. Don't lick my face off. It's grand to see you.'

'I was aware, from the preparations made by my friend Willie, that you would return today. I have awaited you for many hours.'

Tom straightened up, and he and Jack walked on together.

'My master, why are you sad? What more can you want when I, your dog, am here to comfort you?'

'Jack, I feel bloody miserable, and you've no idea, have you? Well, here's the car at last.'

But the car was already occupied; Basil Shine sat in the back. It slowed, but Shine must have given the driver an order, as he speeded up again and drove on in the direction of the railway.

Tom stared after the retreating car. Shine! He should have left hours ago! He certainly wouldn't catch a train tonight. The thought of Shine waiting twelve hours for a train cheered Tom up immensely.

He and Jack had walked another mile before the car returned and picked them both up. Jack sat on the floor, and offered a dusty paw. 'My master I have good news. The man who snores, he of the gross appetites, has gone for good. He has taken all his possessions.'

'Now what's bothering you, Jack? Silly old dog.' Tom absently shook the paw.

Jack had been missing all day. Willie O'Hara was worried sick. What'll the Major say when he comes back and Jack's gone? he thought. He packed Major Shine's gear automatically and took it across the camp to the waiting car.

The driver held the door open, and Shine climbed in.

'Goodbye, sir,' said Willie.

'Goodbye, O'Hara. Be good, eh?'

'Yes, sir. Have a nice trip, sir. Sorry to see you go, sir.'

As the car pulled away, Willie saluted as smartly as his build would allow. As he walked back, he put his head into the hut where Pat O'Shea and others of his old platoon were cleaning their equipment.

'Basil big-balls is gone, thanks be to God,' he said.

'Thanks be to God,' echoed his friends piously.

CHAPTER ELEVEN

Battalion headquarters at St Lawrence Camp, west of Ypres, was crowded with officers. Most of them were young fresh-faced subalterns just arrived from training camps; one or two older men had been sent back to the front, having more or less recovered from their wounds. Tom Daly, his old scar livid against his tight jaw muscles, sat at the back of the hut.

Jim Harper had been speaking for some time. One wall was almost hidden by an enormous map. The name 'Ypres' showed up large on the left. Further east, double lines of blue and red showed the present British and German fronts, and the proposed line of advance. The roads and farms had been given English names, and Oxford and Cambridge roads met a few miles east of Ypres. Rotten Row connected Bad Trench and Rotten Trench. Up in the extreme right-hand corner of the map, lay a village which would never have any other name. Passchendaele.

Jim was a good speaker – he had the officers' full attention. 'And so,' he was saying, 'we hope to see the last of Ypres in the coming week. This is a historic battle area, ours is not the first army to leave thousands of dead here. Look at this map – Austerlitz, Marengo, battles every schoolboy has to learn about. Our sons will learn about Ypres and Mons.'

Jim's voice was drowned as he spoke these names by a furious rattle of hail on the tin roof, followed by the swish of rain. He glanced up at the ceiling, and raised his voice. 'I think,' he said, 'that the weather is going to be our worst enemy.' He turned back to the map. 'If the dykes . . . here, and the canal bank . . . here are destroyed by artillery as I believe they will be, we will be fighting in a swamp, all of us.

So we must press on quickly in the hope of smashing the Hindenberg line by mid August. I cannot stress too strongly the need for haste. We face fresh German troops who equally realize that, if they can hold on against us until autumn, the elements will fight on their side.

'Tomorrow, we return to Frezenberg redoubt, where I will establish battalion headquarters. Then, along with the Royal Irish Fusiliers, we attack Zonnebeke.' He indicated the railway junction on the map. 'With the support of the eighth and ninth battalions, I am certain that our attack will succeed. That is all. Dismiss.'

Tom Daly remained when the other men had left the hut. Jim looked at him sharply. 'You don't look so hot, Daly. You haven't got this blasted tummy bug, have you? I'm carrying lime-juice in my water-bottle, and I'd advise you to do the same. There's a rumour that the wells are contaminated.'

'I'm all right, thanks, touch wood. Look, Harper, I wanted to say that if there's any question of establishing a forward post, or of an attack confined to one or two companies, I would be prepared to take part.'

'I know you would, but I can't spare you. Wait for the main attack, and leave the raids to your junior officers. Dash it, if I go, you're in command.'

'I know, but is it fair to our junior officers? Young Bellamy is intelligent and brave, but he's hardly had any experience, Bowles has very little more, and the others none at all. And I've no ties now.'

'Rubbish, Daly. I don't mind telling you that you're a very valuable man and would be missed by all of us as a friend as well as a soldier. Everybody likes and respects you – you lucky devil. So for God's sake don't take unnecessary risks.'

'Spare my blushes.' Tom laughed. They stood in the doorway of the hut. The rain from the corrugated iron had made a pond outside. It had stopped now, and a ground mist was rising.

It was August 2nd, 1917, and the campaign which would be known to millions merely as 'Passchendaele' was two days old. The battalions at the front were being shuffled about incessantly. The Dublins, led by Jim Harper, had been moved up to the fortified trenches near Frezenberg two days before,

and warned that they were going to take part in an all-out
attack. The day had been spent in hurried preparation, and
tempers were short.

By late evening, all the men had been briefed, and a worrying number appointed stretcher-bearers. After a restless night
of waiting, they had been relieved without explanation and
sent back to camp.

Now, after barely twenty-four hours, the regiment was
again ordered up the line to Frezenberg. They made hasty
arrangements to move the following day. The Royal Irish
Fusiliers were in trouble.

Jim Harper, usually calm in any crisis, left the telephone
where he had been engaged in heated conversation for almost
an hour, and went to his quarters. Outside, he saw Tom, and
walked over to speak to him. A month earlier, Tom would
have been on edge, tense, irritated by little things. This was
the man Jim knew and understood; the man who was calmed
and steadied by action. Since his leave, Tom had changed. He
accepted his conflicting orders without comment and carried
them out with no sign of emotion.

Jim was worried about Tom. A pity the poor fellow's love
affair had gone wrong. Jim wondered whether Celia was the
sole cause of Tom's state of mind. Tom had told him almost
nothing about his leave.

Jack padded out of a tent, and came over to Tom. He leaned
against his master's leg, looking up with a question in his eyes.

'Are you taking Jack up the line?' asked Jim.

'I don't want to, but the men are keen. I gather the redoubt
is as safe as most places, and he'd be happier with O'Hara
there than left behind.'

'I am most happy when I am with you, my master.'

Tom stroked the dog's smooth forehead. 'Jack can come
along with the rations,' he said. 'He'll like that. Off you go,
Jack. Go back to O'Hara.'

'As you wish.' Jack gave his master a reproachful glance,
and returned to the tent where Willie was preparing supper.

Tom paced about restlessly when Jim had gone. He was
worried. Not frightened as he used to be when he felt that life
was too sweet to risk and Celia too lovely to lose, but worried

for his battalion. He had served with it for twelve years, and knew all the regulars as individuals. How many were left of the thousand who had been serving in 1914? Fifty? Less. Each time one of these men fell, Tom felt he had lost a personal friend. He felt that his own life was now of less importance to him than theirs.

Although he no longer feared death, the thought of being maimed still frightened Tom. Don't think about it. Thinking brings fear. Not the sweating, trembling, heart-thumping fear which comes in times of danger. No, this was the slow insidious kind, which creeps in, bringing sleepless nights, distrust of enclosed spaces, dislike of having someone behind you. The fear that recurs in nightmares.

Tom gave himself a mental shake. Be careful, he thought. You'll end up like that poor sod who always slept in his boots, and nearly got shot for cowardice. There's only a hair-line between cowardice and broken nerve.

'My master, even now your meal awaits you. Fried bacon, cheese and a hen which I myself caught recently. Will you not come?'

'You're back, are you, Jack? I wonder if O'Hara's conjured up any supper yet. I'll tell you something, old dog. You're better for morale than a week's leave.' Tom followed Jack in the direction of an appetizing smell of frying bacon.

The next day it rained. Jack watched the battalion march out of camp, while his friend Willie O'Hara collected such of their possessions as they were taking with them. The companies left in order. Last went 'D' Company, with Major Tom; Euge and his Lewis gunners bringing up the rear. Some ill-judged and vulgar jokes were made at Willie's expense. Jack was deeply offended, but Willie appeared not to mind. It was their turn at last. They moved off with orderlies and stretcher-bearers, just ahead of a troop of loaded mules.

Given the order to march at ease, they clattered through the familiar ruins of Ypres. Jack trotted along beside Willie, who was talking in an undertone to a grey-haired orderly. 'The old Cloth Hall will fall on somebody one of these days,' he said, and later – 'The Menin Gate again. They should put up a monument to us here. Something like Nelson's Pillar.'

The other man was taciturn. He didn't answer.

Beyond Ypres, there were many holes in the road, all filled with rain water. They left the road and marched four abreast on the verge. It was slow going, and soggy after hours of rain. Ahead was the roar of guns.

Jack could not see where they were going from his position among the men's legs. But, judging by the noise, they were walking straight into a barrage. He tried to close his ears to the crashes, and was thankful that he could not see the shell-bursts. He winced as the ground shivered beneath his paws. The men cursed steadily as they trudged forward.

Soldiers were coming to meet them. Not many. 'It's bloody hot back there,' they said, and 'Good luck.' Some were limping, bloodstained, supporting a wounded comrade or nursing a damaged arm. Their eyes stared. Some had lost their helmets, some their rifles.

Then something occurred that disturbed Jack greatly. They had met several parties of stretcher-bearers. These stood aside with their burdens, making way for the relieving troops. Terrible groans came from the stretchers, and Jack felt his spine prickle. Willie remarked to the silent man at his side, 'I always said those old Jerries must be good for something,' as another party came alongside with a stretcher. But these men who carried the wounded were of Kurt's race. They wore field grey uniforms, and heavy leather boots. They wore no belts or arms, and their tired faces were sullen. Waiting to pass, they set down the stretcher, and one of them, a young boy, stumbled. As he did so, his round cap with its blue band and two buttons fell to the ground.

'Kurt!' But of course it was not Kurt – Kurt was long dead. It was the smell which misled Jack. Hardly knowing why he did it, the dog sidestepped, and picked up the cap in his mouth. He carried it with him, ignoring the mockery of the man behind him. 'Hey Jack, which side are you fighting for?'

'I do not know, my comrade.'

Willie bent down, took the cap from Jack, and stuffed it into his pocket. 'We'll save it for Euge,' he said.

They reached one of those deep ditches with numerous bends, which Jack now knew were called communication trenches. There was some water in it – slimy and evil smelling. They sloshed along it for a short time, then rounded one of the many bends and found their path blocked. The trench had caved in. Rough steps had been cut in the side, and the men climbed up, slipping and swearing.

'If this is what it's like going up to the front, what the hell will it be like when we get there?' they said. Behind them, a hail of shells landed among the luckless mules and their grooms. Carrying provisions and ammunition, they had remained on the surface throughout.

'Come on, Jack lad, we'll stick together.'

'My friend, I fear we will die together.'

Every few yards lay a dead or wounded man, sometimes several together. Stretcher-bearers stumbled through the mud, lifting the wounded. Father Minogue darted here and there, giving absolution.

They found Corporal Sheedy, an admirer of Jack's, a man who liked greyhounds. He and Willie had often talked about fishing from Islandbridge. Sheedy was dead.

They found Fusilier Corry who could play the tin whistle. The stretcher-bearers went to help him. 'Don't bother lads,' he said. 'I'm done.'

They found Sergeant-Major Scanlon, feared by all. He lived, but was bleeding from several wounds.

'Oh Willie, my friend, I am afraid. Let us go back.'

To the horror of shells was added a rain of bullets, coming from fortified emplacements on their flank.

The column broke up into small parties and ran zig-zagging. The whole of the trench they had been following had collapsed. It was no more than a scarred and muddy furrow.

Jack, seeing that there was no turning back, stuck grimly to Willie's side. Somewhere ahead, his master was waiting for him. There were fewer shells now. Had the barrage ended? No, the Germans were shortening the range as the battalion advanced. Two huge fountains of earth and stones only yards ahead erupted into the air. Willie and Jack were showered with lumps of clay and small stones. Willie caught Jack's collar, and tumbled with him into a shellhole. Two men were there already, muddy and scared. They crouched in the hole for over an hour, listening to the frightening din outside, and Jack wedged himself into the smallest possible space.

'What are our bloody guns doing?' demanded Willie angrily.

'I don't know,' said Timmy Coote, one of the men sheltering with him. 'Why don't you go back and ask them?'

'My master, where is he?'

'Quiet now, Jack, don't you start whining,' said Willie. He did not answer Coote's uncivil question.

'Why didn't you leave the dog behind?' Coote asked next.

'Lucky for you that I didn't,' said Willie. 'You're safer with me than anywhere else, because Jack brings luck.'

'I've heard that,' said Coote, but he did not sound convinced.

'It's easing off, I think,' the other man raised his head and looked round cautiously. 'Will we run for it?'

'Might as well,' said Coote. 'One at a time, lads.'

Willie was the last to leave shelter. He hesitated miserably, a man not used to acting alone, frightened and bewildered.

'Come on Jack, old dog, now for it.'

'My friend, I fear we are going to die.'

Willie's lips moved silently. He might have been praying or swearing. Probably praying, for he bowed his head and closed his eyes. He stood up. 'Hurry on, Jack. Up the Old Toughs.' He climbed out of the hole, reaching back to help Jack. The twilit landscape was littered with dead men and some who struggled to rise. They ran past them, keeping their backs to the fading sunset.

'Up the Dubs,' panted Willie. 'That's us, Jack. One poor bloody tailor and his dog.'

'Let us proceed quickly, my friend. We may converse later.'

They ran uphill now. The fortified trench commanded a wide area. The Germans had built it when they had time to choose a site, three years earlier. There were many gaps cut in the barbed wire, and they went through, Jack politely waiting for Willie whose breath rasped in his throat. But when he saw his master, Jack forged ahead.

Major Tom was scanning the countryside with his glasses. He lowered them, and his face was pale and stern.

'My master, I am here unscathed. You may put away your binoculars.'

'Hallo, thought I'd seen the last of you, Jack. So you made it, O'Hara, well done. Anybody else coming up?'

'No sir, I think I'm the last. Sergeant-Major's hit, pretty bad. Sheedy and Corry both bought it.'

'Have you seen Mr Bellamy?'

'No sir, but we were keeping our heads down; he could be out there easy enough.'

'H'm. You'd better go down to the main dugout – it's over there, down those steps. I'll be there shortly.' Major Tom raised his field glasses to his eyes again, staring down the darkening slope. It must be that he was watching for something other than Jack. A blow to one's ego, that.

O'Hara staggered and nearly fell. Tom turned and caught the older man by the arm, supporting him while he regained his balance. Poor little devil, he thought. What with Jack's odds and ends as well as his own pack and equipment, he must have carried eighty or ninety pounds for twelve miles, and the last two under heavy fire. He helped O'Hara down into the trench. 'Sit down here, O'Hara, take it easy.' He shouted for an orderly to help Willie down to the dugout and see that he got a good slug of rum. Willie staggered away down the steps with the burly Tim Coote practically carrying him, and Jack anxiously following.

It was almost dark. Tom knew that he might as well give up looking out for more survivors. The German artillery and machine-guns had taken a ghastly toll.

'Give me a hand somebody.' It was a good healthy shout, and Tom was in time to catch Bellamy as he half climbed, half rolled over the parados. He was bareheaded and his face was smeared with blood, but he grinned at Tom as he scrambled to his feet.

'Bellamy, by God! Thought we'd lost you.'

'The devil looks after his own, sir, so I've heard the men say. I've cut my face a little, and twisted my ankle falling into a shell-hole. Nothing that a fortnight at the seaside won't cure. Any grub going?'

'As much as you can eat. Hadn't you better see the M.O. first?'

'No sir, if you don't mind, I'll eat first. Otherwise I might faint.'

Tom smiled for the first time since they'd left camp. Nineteen-year-old Dick Bellamy had a phenomenal appetite, finishing up whatever food was going, however nasty. Cold porridge and cold stew were welcome when there was no way of heating them.

Tom supported the young man down into the main trench. It was ten feet deep, with solidly timbered fire steps and concrete strong-posts. These fortresses for machine-guns had loopholes on all sides, and were pretty well impervious to shelling. The emplacements were connected by underground passages to bomb-proof ammunition stores and roomy dug-outs. This section of trench was two hundred yards long, and also boasted a bomb-proof dressing station, fitted with bunk beds, and facilities for operating.

Tom helped Bellamy down a dozen concrete steps to a dugout not unlike the one where Hansel had died, but con-siderably larger. A group of twenty N.C.O.s and men were already there. Bellamy limped away in search of food. 'I could eat my own boots boiled,' he said.

O'Hara was drinking rum, and didn't see Tom at the dugout door. Jack spotted him though, left O'Hara's side, and went to him. Willie set down his mug and pulled something out of his pocket. 'Here, Corp, Jack found this for you.' He held out a round cap with the blue band of a Prussian unit to Corporal Boyle.

'No thanks, Willie, they're two a penny. Give it back to the dog. Thanks all the same.'

In a dugout as well built as this one, it hardly mattered that it faced the wrong way. Tom remembered the trenches at Givenchy, the cramped cubby-holes scooped in their sides, supported with planks, roofed with zinc sheets and sandbags. Outside these primitive shelters had dangled shell cases, which a sentry would beat with a rifle butt as a gas warning.

O'Hara was relieved of his duties as a servant tonight, so another man had been detailed to prepare supper, and Tom went off thoughtfully to eat it. Jack made as if to follow, but changed his mind.

A small dugout was occupied by Jim Harper, Tom, and Bellamy, now fed and apparently little the worse. Tom chased him off to the M.O., to have his ankle bandaged. When he had gone, Tom and Jim discussed their situation. Their telephone line was cut, and their dressing station crammed with casualties. There was nothing for it but to sit it out until they were relieved or ordered to retire.

Tom, exhausted though he was, couldn't sleep that night. He got up at last, and went in search of a drink of water. In a small recess off the main dugout, Willie O'Hara lay sound asleep on his mattress. Jack lay stretched out beside him. He opened his eyes when he heard Tom, and thumped his tail, but didn't get up. Tom noticed that the dog's head was pillowed on a small round cap with a blue band.

In the four days that the battalion held the Frezenberg trench, the Germans did no more than harry the Dublins with machine-gun and rifle fire from their forward posts, ensuring that they kept their heads down. The Germans themselves had built the stronghold, and saw no point in wasting ammunition on it unless the Dubs made a sortie. This they were unable to do, lacking the supplies carried by the mules, and having lost so many men on the way up.

Finally they were relieved, and retired under cover of darkness, having achieved nothing.

This time, they were sent to the rest camp at Vlamertinghe, a small town to the north-west of Ypres. The men hated the place, having been gassed and shelled when 'resting' there some time before. Within a week, reinforced by a hundred men barely recovered from wounds, they were moved back to a camp at St Jean, near Ypres, on their way up to relieve the Royal Irish Fusiliers. Reports had been coming back of frightful losses. The Royal Irish, like themselves, had lost half their strength.

In mid August it began to rain in earnest. It poured steadily

for four days and nights. When it seemed as if it couldn't
possibly rain any harder, the heavens opened and poured
down torrents which flooded the camp in minutes, while the
lightning turned night into day. Soon, there was a foot of
water in the tents, and the huts were awash. Cases of food
were ruined, and the men began to complain of stomach pains.
In one day, there were thirty cases of gastro enteritis.

The roads they must follow when they went up the line
turned to rivers carrying every sort of filth, and the bloated
bodies of hundreds of mules.

'Things can't get any worse,' said Tom to Jim Harper, but
he was wrong. The Germans trained long range guns on the
camp, and shelled it night and day. It was impossible to dig in
when every trench they attempted to dig immediately filled
to overflowing with water. Their only protection was sandbags.

On the fourth evening, orders came from G.H.Q. that the
Dublins were to move up the line at midnight and attack
Zonnebeke, while two other battalions supported them to
right and left.

'It'll be drier up there,' said Brian Bowles the optimist.

'If we ever get there,' was the unspoken reply.

Gas had been adding to their misery all day; the yellow cross
'mustard' gas which smelled like a lighted match and burned
and blinded. Willie shut Jack up in the corrugated iron building
which housed the stores.

The battalion had lost twenty-seven officers and 700 other
ranks in a week. Sergeant Duggan assembled the men, now
re-formed into three small companies. 'D' Company had been
added to the shattered 'B' Company. Pat O'Shea and Euge
were the last of the old 'Indestructibles' in the line. They
grumbled bitterly at the demise of their old company. Willie
O'Hara thanked God twenty times a day that he was now a
servant, although he knew he would be called on for other
duties, probably as a stretcher-bearer, before long. As they
prepared to move off in the deluge, Tom said to him, 'O'Hara,
I'm afraid you'll have to go up with 'B' Company. We need
every fit man in the line. I shall be with 'C' Company on your
left. Good luck. Good luck, Jack, old fellow.'

'Luck, my master, what is that?'

So the battalion moved off in the darkness. Jim Harper led 'B' Company in the centre up the road to Frezenberg. Captain Brian Bowles led 'A' Company towards Potsdam Farm on the right. Tom Daly's company struck out to the left. The Bremen redoubt must be rushed before Zonnebeke could fall. Dick Bellamy, their only other officer, was Jim Harper's adjutant, and accompanied him in the centre. The Royal Irish were already dug in at the Frezenberg redoubt, and would be attacking with the Dublins.

As they moved off, the men heard the raucous sound of klaxon horns. Gas again. Gas or not, they had to go.

At two a.m. Tom's party was able to dispense with gas-masks. They had crossed the old trench system, now flooded, where they had fought in 1914, and reached Vampire Farm. This place lay between them and the Bremen redoubt. They had already bypassed Frezenberg by nearly a mile, and there should have been a battle in progress on the right. Instead there was nothing.

It was pitch dark and, for the moment, quiet. They seemed to have come through a solid wall of machine-gun bullets and bursting shells. Now the guns were silent. Tom had started out with forty men, all that remained of 'C' Company. Now there were four – three private soldiers and himself.

Tom had a curious feeling of invulnerability that night. Possibly he was light-headed from too much tough going wearing a respirator. They neared the farm, and suddenly machine-gun bullets zipped by.

'Get down men, don't return fire.' All four dropped flat under cover of a manure heap.

For the first time in two years, Tom had gone up the line without repeating his prayer. Celia had spoiled it for him. But now, as he lay flat in the stinking ooze, he said it over to himself. His own interest in surviving was dulled, but there were three young soldiers with him whom he must do his best to preserve. He didn't know any of them well – they were fresh men. It would be suicide to fire at concealed guns, ignorant of their number. But to go back could be as deadly as to go forward.

Tom knew what they must do. For the time being, they must wait. Four men, armed with rifles and grenades. As soon as there was any light, one of them must creep a little closer, and see if there was any hope of taking the farm and holding it until help came. That man would be – must be – Tom. Unthinkable that he should send a green volunteer.

'Let me not pray to be shielded from dangers . . .'

Jack remembered the fortress with the underground rooms well. He was glad that they were returning there, but oh, how he hated his respirator. However, his friend Willie was wearing one, and also Colonel Jim, so one must make the best of it. Jack also wore his waterproof jacket and the straps chafed his chest.

Jack had not forgotten his last fearful journey eastward; this one was even worse. There was no road, only clinging mud. The darkness was rent by blinding flashes, and each flash was followed by a crack, a bang or a crash, according to what devilish instrument had caused it. It was impossible to hurry. Men staggered and fell. Some screamed. Others, clutching their stomachs and retching, sat down in the mud. Willie kept on going, his lips moving. Sometimes, a huge flash showed a whole group of men thrown about like leaves in an autumn gale. Willie bent so low that he could walk with his hand on Jack's back. They were unable to speak to one another because of their hoods of flannel. They continued their slow, unwilling plod through the mud. Shells were bursting all along the ridge where the fortified trench offered their only hope of shelter.

It seemed to Jack as if a lifetime had passed when finally they reached it. He and Willie lay together in the bottom of the safe trench. Their gas-masks were off, they were alive. When Willie had sufficiently recovered, he crept with Jack down to the main dugout, and the men drank spirits which warmed them and gave them courage. There were fourteen men, and Colonel Jim, and it was he who filled their mugs. Colonel Jim's face, always thin, looked like a skull in the dim lamplight.

Colonel Jim spoke. He said, 'I have received a message from Captain Bowles. Receiving no support, he was obliged to retire from Potsdam Farm with 'A' Company, after coming under heavy fire. The eighth and ninth battalion have also retired to St Jean. My orders are to retire under cover of darkness, as we are unsupported. Major Daly and 'C' Company may or may not have reached Vampire Farm, where, I am told there are at least five enemy machine-guns. I dare not draw attention to his force by signalling. Neither can I retire and leave him and his men to be wiped out. I need a runner, and must ask for a volunteer.'

The men looked at each other. They had not the esprit de corps of the old hands. Willie was the only one of them who had been with the battalion at Messines; Pat O'Shea and Euge lay wounded on stretchers.

Des Mitchell from Walkinstown said, 'I'll go.'

Jack was relieved. He had feared that his friend Willie might volunteer. He rubbed his head against Willie's thigh as the handful of men dispersed to the pill-boxes and fire-steps. They had no leaders save Colonel Jim and Sergeant Duggan. Sergeant Duggan's hand was bound up, and blood seeped through the bandage.

'My friend, how fortunate we are still to be together. Let us remain so, I beg of you.'

Shells were bursting all round the redoubt. The noise was ear splitting. Des Mitchell took the roll of oiled silk containing the message from Colonel Jim. He carried no weapon as he dived over the parapet and, bending low, trotted away lefthanded, his feet sinking deeply in the sticky ground. 'He's clear,' said somebody. A minute passed, and a shell shrieked close. 'He's down!' Sergeant Duggan and two other men dashed out to fetch Des in, the Sergeant clumsy with his bandaged hand. Des was moaning as he was taken away.

'I'll go, sir, when I get my wind,' said Sergeant Duggan.

'No, Sergeant. You've been hit once, and besides you are the most senior man here. It would be up to you to take the men back if anything happened to me.' Jim added under his breath, 'I wish to God I knew if Daly made it or not, and how many men he has.'

'Send Jack, sir,' suggested Sergeant Duggan. 'If the Major's living, he'll find him, and if not, he'll come back to O'Hara.'

Colonel Jim considered for a moment. 'It's the best part of a mile,' he said, 'and he'll need that respirator. I don't know how he could scent anyone out with that on. However, I can't risk a man's life if Jack will go.'

'Send me, sir, don't send Jack.' Willie O'Hara's voice was low and husky.

'Thank you, O'Hara, it's a brave offer, but you would never make it.'

'I'll do my best. I'll go slow and careful. I'll try. Don't send the poor dog, sir. Please don't send him out to get killed.'

'I'm sorry, O'Hara,' said Jim gently, 'but I'm afraid I must try it. Major Daly's safety is involved. Don't let your fondness for Jack blind you to that. And you are the person to explain to Jack what he must do. He understands you.'

Jack had not understood the reason for Des Mitchell's departure. He was uncertain about what was afoot until his friend Willie, having reached safety with so much fear and toil, asked Colonel Jim if he might go out and face death again. Jack concentrated hard. Major Tom must be found, that was it.

Willie and Colonel Jim knelt on either side of Jack. Jim attached a roll of oiled silk to his collar. Willie, whose eyes streamed with tears, put on the loathed gas-mask. They led Jack to a fire-step, and lifted him up. Willie, his voice cracking, said, 'Find the Major, Jack. Find master. Go seek.' A stupid dog could have understood that.

As Jack paused on the sandbagged parapet, overlooked by a concrete pill-box, the sky whitened with sheet lightning. Not so very far away, perhaps one kilometre, down a gentle slope to the left, the broken walls and ragged tree stumps of a farmstead showed for a few moments in stark relief. Willie pointed a shaking finger. 'Go seek, lad, go seek.'

Jack set off fast. He was terrified, and knew that if he did not travel at full speed, his nerve would fail him, and he would return disgraced. In spite of his fear, the little bit of sheepdog in his make-up influenced his actions. He did not gallop straight in the direction which his friend Willie had indicated, but made a wide offing to the left, swinging away so as to approach the farm from the side. Had he run straight, he would probably have been seen.

Behind him, the Lewis guns began firing from the right-hand end of the trench. This manoeuvre, designed to draw attention away from Jack, lent wings to his feet. It also drew shells. They crashed down on his right, some shrieking, some with the dull thud that meant gas.

Jack had been suiting his pace to that of a heavily loaded man all day. Now he galloped where a runner would have sunk to his knees. His paws were hurting him – why should that be? Never mind, soon he would find Major Tom and all would be well. The gas-mask cut off his scenting powers. It was fortunate that he retained his sense of direction, because the mica eye-pieces were soon splashed all over with wet mud. Without them, he thought, he could have seen a little in the gloom; with them, he was running blind. He pressed on in the direction which his instinct told him was the right one, turning in on his objective.

In the darkness, Jack was unobserved. The German machine-gunners were expecting a man, not a dog.

A brilliant star shell curved down behind him, but at that moment, his vision, hearing and scenting powers all reduced by his respirator, Jack raced straight into a shell-hole, filled to the brim with water. If it had been half full, he would have drowned. As it was, he swam across, and climbed out with some difficulty. This thrice accursed coat, thought Jack. This ten times accursed hood of flannel! How much faster and more safely I should travel without them.

The bright light had faded, leaving the night even blacker than before. Jack neared the farm. The water had washed the mud from his eye-pieces, and now he pushed his way through tall rye, waterlogged and battered. Where was Major Tom with his fine company of men? There was no sign of them. Jack hastened through the last of the rye, and fell into another brimming shell-hole with a loud splash. At once a hurricane of bullets came from the ruined farm, sweeping round in a wide arc. They passed harmlessly over Jack's head.

The nose-piece of Jack's gas-mask had been soaked in an unpleasant smelling substance. It was maddening. If only one could rid oneself of unacceptable smells, and perhaps blot them out with something more wholesome. Even through the gauze, Jack could not fail to be aware of a magnificent manure heap. Just the place to shed the alien odour. He would have a quick roll and then, pleasantly scented, resume his search for his master. He rolled and rolled.

Tom, cold, wet and uncomfortable as he was, could have slept. He had lost hope of the other companies moving up to join him, and supposed that, like his, they were too much reduced to go on with the attack. There was no sign of life at Potsdam Farm across the road, away to the right. Somebody was still at the Frezenberg redoubt – there'd been a clatter of machine-gun fire from there five minutes back. He supposed he should try to get back there before it got light. Three o'clock. He'd plenty of time. The Germans were dropping high explosive shells and gas between him and Frezenberg for some reason. Simply plastering the place. He'd have to wait for a lull before attempting to move. The three men with him lay, face down, their heads pillowed on their arms. They might have been asleep, although shells were sending up gouts of muddy water, earth and stones a hundred yards away. Fortunately, the breeze was taking the gas away northward.

The shelling stopped as suddenly as it had begun. The Boches had sent up a star shell, and presumably decided that there was nothing out there to fire at. The sudden silence was broken by a sound of rustling, followed by a loud splash. All four men turned their heads; the noise was behind them, to the left. It was immediately followed by a long burst of machine-gun fire from the farm. Then silence again.

Tom was convinced that somebody was coming towards them. Moving right up to the midden, he stealthily moved into a kneeling position, then, hardly breathing, drew up his right leg, so that he was kneeling on one knee. His limbs were cold and stiff, he wondered whether they would obey him if he had to move quickly. Yes, there *was* something – a faint snuffling and scuffling. It seemed to come from above his head. Tom took a grenade from his belt, and, with infinite caution, raised himself and peered over the edge of the manure heap.

It was a tidy heap, high and solid. A creature which looked

in the gloom like a small earless pig or an overgrown seahorse, was rolling in the muck. Jack in his gas-mask. Tom's heart resumed its normal pace. He returned the grenade to his belt and, reaching up, felt for Jack's collar. The dog saw him, and jumped down.

The gas had drifted away to the north, so Tom pulled the respirator over Jack's head, and put it in his pocket. The dog whined, and began licking his paws. Tom hushed him. The reeking jacket came off next and was discarded. There was a message fastened to Jack's collar, and Tom cut it away with his pocket-knife. The dog must be hurt – he was whining again, faintly. 'Hush, Jack. Quiet.' It was hard to read the message by the light of his fountain-pen sized torch, but he made it out in the end. Jack's message told him what he had guessed, and ordered him to do what he had already decided.

Colonel Harper's information was that there were at least five machine-guns at Vampire Farm. Tom was to retire with his force to Frezenberg and rejoin 'B' Company under cover of darkness with all speed. Tom should split his force up into small parties, and return by different routes. Hysterical laughter rose in Tom's throat and was swallowed . . . three men.

Tom whispered to the men, telling them to discard their equipment. A rifle weighed nine pounds, and even in battle order, the men carried too much weight to make speed through the mud. They crept through rye standing in water. Tom had led them forward; now that they were retiring to comparative safety, he brought up the rear. He noticed that one of the men slid silently through the corn like a fox. That must be the man who said he'd been a tinker before he joined up. He was a yellow-haired youth, good with horses, who never complained about sleeping rough. The other two men scrambled along blindly, and Tom was glad of the cover provided by the manure heap.

Soon they were in the open, going back the way Jack had come. The men floundered through the mud, and every few yards dropped flat as green and yellow flares lighted the sky. Jack lurched along whining. Tom held the dog against his side each time he dropped flat.

There was a pile of bricks, the remains of a house near the spot where Des Mitchell had fallen. The men had almost reached it when a shell buried itself among the bricks. A dud, thank God, but it hurled chips in all directions, knocking down one of the men. He got to his knees, his arm broken. They'd been spotted by their friends, and Jim Harper's voice called out, 'Any more of you?'

'No,' said Tom. Bent double, they ran the last few yards, Jack limping behind.

Jack was in pain. He noticed with annoyance that the man with the broken arm was being taken away to be attended to. His friend Willie was hugging him, and telling all who would listen that Jack was the bravest, the finest, the best dog in the world.

'Very possibly, my friend, but I too am a casualty.' Jack whined loudly and lay down.

'Now then Jack, what's up with you?' said Major Tom. 'We'll take him down to the dugout where we can see.'

It was as much as Jack could do to walk. He stopped at the top of the steps, licked a paw and yelped. Eager hands lifted him and carried him downstairs. Here there was a lamp, and his master examined him. No blood, no broken bones. Then he saw what the trouble was. All four of Jack's paws were burned and blistered by gas.

Jack wondered why the spectacle of his injured paws should make his master swear. Rather, he had expected words of sympathy and comfort. Never had Major Tom sounded so angry, and his face in the flickering lamplight was thin lipped.

'Christ,' he said, 'look at that. One of their gas shells must have landed within yards of Jack. The rotten bastards.' The familiar low-pitched voice trembled with rage. Jack was glad it was not he who was at fault.

Major Tom himself dressed Jack's burns, putting a field dressing under each paw and bandaging it in place. He split the ends of the bandages with his knife, and tied them up neatly.

For the blistered tongue which had licked the paws, he could do nothing.

CHAPTER TWELVE

Twenty-four hours later the Old Toughs marched back to Ypres, en route for rest camp at Poperinghe, the regiment having lost eighty-two officers and 1,550 other ranks in seventeen days, and gained precisely nothing.

The return journey from Frezenberg was difficult because of the state of the ground, but the German guns were silent and there were no further losses.

A long line of stretcher-bearers struggled through the holding mud, four to a stretcher. There was hardly a fit man who wasn't helping to carry a wounded comrade. Behind the last stretcher, walked Willie O'Hara and Timmy Coote, carrying a grey army blanket between them like a hammock. In it lay Jack, his bandaged legs pointing upwards. He was uncomfortable but did not complain. He was a wounded hero – his master had said so. Pride and joy filled his heart, blotting out discomfort. He could not eat properly yet, but it was pleasant to be fed with bread soaked in soup by one's friends, and delightful to be praised and patted by all.

Jack knew he had performed bravely, although scared half out of his wits. One had, however, one's dignity. When being carried over uneven ground upside down, one was at a distinct disadvantage. A dim memory stirred in his mind. Himself a puppy, upside down in a satchel, bobbing on Johann's back. Not since then had he travelled so.

Never would he forget the pain of his burned tongue and paws, and how Willie had smeared his pads with vaseline, and dribbled water into his mouth with a spoon. Jack was improving now, but it would be many weeks before he would be able to march with his comrades.

That dreadful night when he had carried the message to his master had been followed by another day of shelling. As he lay helpless in a dugout, he could hear the thunderous bangs of the big shells, the thudding feet, the shouts — 'Stand to!' 'Get down and lie close!' 'Stretcher-bearers!' Choking fumes of smoke and cordite found their way down to the dugout, in spite of the gas curtain hanging in the doorway.

Then Jack had heard a faint cheer. The sound spread raggedly along the beleaguered trench: they were being relieved. The Argyll and Sutherland Highlanders, who had honoured the Dubs by piping them out of the station when their train reached Arras, were arriving. Jack had learned that the petticoated warriors were to be admired and respected. He knew them as the 'Angry and Suffering Highlanders', for that was what the men called them. They took up their positions, staring curiously as Jack was borne proudly past, upside down in his blanket.

The train from Ypres was delayed by attacks from German aircraft. The men on their stretchers waited five hours on the platform, sheltered by a canvas awning from the sun, if from nothing else. The train, when it finally set off, travelled slowly and jerkily with many stops. Jack's blanket was placed at the end of the row of stretchers next to the one where Pat O'Shea lay. Pat had been slightly gassed and his eyes were covered, but it was thought that his sight could be saved. His arm was strapped to his chest — broken collarbone, not serious. He felt about with his good hand until he found Jack, and stroked the dog's side. Nobody spoke.

At Poperinghe, they were out of range of the German guns, but the constant roar of artillery formed a background to every movement. Jack had come to disregard it. His hearing had been somewhat blunted by the incessant noise during his weeks at the front. He could put up with it.

A fortnight had passed, and the remains of the battalion had been moved to camp at Ervillers to re-form. Pat O'Shea was more or less fit again, and back with his old platoon. He was suffering from depression. Captain Bowles was back too, barely recovered from a bullet through the shoulder. Dick Bellamy no longer joked – he was pale and quiet.

Jack was sitting between Willie and Pat as a dozen of the old sweats gathered round a brazier in their hut. They did not need the warmth of the coals; they were making toast, the pieces of bread speared on their bayonets. Willie dipped pieces of toast in cold tea, and fed them to Jack.

Tom Daly and Dick Bellamy strolled past the door of the hut. 'Look at the brutal and licentious soldiery,' said Tom. He indicated Willie O'Hara and Pat O'Shea, squatting by the brazier, backs turned, Jack's broad back between them. Pat had his arm round the dog while Willie fed him, murmuring endearments.

'Jack's getting fat,' said Bellamy. 'Have you noticed his boots?'

'Noticed them? Of course I have. A dog wearing laced up boots on parade is a noticeable phenomenon. O'Hara's incredibly clever at improvising; one has to turn a blind eye.'

'Why sir?' asked Bellamy. 'Is there any reason why O'Hara shouldn't make Jack some boots? I gather the poor fellow's paws are still very sore.'

'No reason,' said Tom, 'but if you look closely, you'll see that Jack's boots started life as canvas rifle covers.'

Bellamy had been having trouble with his ankle. He'd insisted on marching back to Ypres with the help of a stick, and his leg had become infected. It was still swollen and painful. Tom had developed a stomach ulcer. It would be some time before either was at his best again.

'Blast these games tomorrow,' said Tom. 'I never felt less like judging sports. What job have you got, Bellamy?'

'Organizing team games. I'd enjoy the sports if I could take part, but the prize-giving is beastly boring. Too like speech-day at school for me.' They walked on.

Jack's tongue had healed, he could have managed crusts easily, but when one joins the army, one learns to play the old soldier. Jack accepted the titbits, rolled his eyes, and weakly thumped his tail.

'You are indeed good, my friend. With more of this

excellent treatment, I feel it is likely that I shall make a complete recovery.'

His paws were still tender, but he could walk about, and take his place on parade, wearing his new set of khaki boots, laced up the front.

The men's mood was gloomy. 'They patch us up and throw us back in,' said Pat. 'They have more regard for the horses.'

'I don't know about that,' said Willie. 'The Colonel and the Major are two as decent men as you'll find.'

'Ah, it's not them, it's the brass hats. We've been trained and trained, and bloody well better trained, until we think nothing of ourselves. We don't expect nothing, and that's what we get. We are nothing. Ammo − that's all we are.' He poked the fire savagely.

'You'll catch it if the Sergeant hears you talking like that,' said Willie.

Timmy Coote picked his piece of toast up off the floor, dusted it and spread it with jam. 'That's another thing,' he said. 'Sergeant Larkin's young enough to be your son, Willie. We're getting sergeants and corporals and all, half our age, that knows nothing − only the book. We could tell 'em.'

'We'll never get promotion,' said Williie. 'We don't want it. Who's going to take orders from you or me? Which of us here would make a bloody lance-jack, let alone a sergeant?'

'The C.I.G.S. rose from being a private like us,' said Timmy.

'I wouldn't think he was ever a private like you, Tim Coote.'

'Don't say "private", say "fusilier",' said Pat sternly. 'They should make one of us up to corporal, so they should; the only question is which one.'

'Jack,' said Willie. 'He's officer material, he is. Uses his head, operates on his own. Euge is out of it for the duration − why don't we promote Jack?'

Jack raised his head, and accepted a little more bread. 'What is it that you wish to do to me now, my friend? I trust it will not be painful.'

All the men were talking at once. The idea had caught on.

'Sew a pip on his tunic, Willie.'

'Two pips.'

'Give him some more pay.'

'Let him off fatigue duty.'

'Listen lads,' said Willie. 'If we make an officer of him we've lost him. He can't go in the sergeants' mess no more. No, I'll embroider two stripes on the new tunic I'm making for him and we'll promote him ourselves. From now on, he's Corporal Jack.'

Jack looked suspiciously from one eager face to another. What was all this fuss about? Probably something of no importance. He sighed, and settled down to sleep. He was feeling better. Soon, he would be strong again, but in the meantime he required rest. Rest and loving care.

'My poor boy, you need rest and care – loving care.' The Hon. Melissa Posset-Hunt bent over Tony Greer's chaise longue. This had been dragged out onto the verandah overlooking the Channel. Posset Hall, a huge house of vaguely Tudor architecture, had been converted into a nursing home for officers by its owner, the immensely wealthy widow, Lady Rovehurst. Her daughter Melissa, an ageing heiress with a long neck and pale bulging eyes, dashed about dispensing kind words and cigarettes. She was a good-hearted creature of limited intelligence, and found enormous satisfaction in 'doing her bit'.

The house looked out over the Solent; the aquamarine water, limpidly calm, reflecting the fishing boats near the water's edge. It was a typical English afternoon in late summer by the seaside. The sound of the guns in Flanders might easily have been mistaken for the rumbling of distant traffic.

Tony Greer scowled at the peaceful scene. He hated Melissa, the nurses, Posset Hall, the food – everything. His leg had been amputated at mid calf and he was waiting, like thousands of others, for an artificial one. He felt perfectly well, and yearned to be doing something useful, preferably something violent. He chain-smoked, bit his nails, did crossword puzzles and swatted flies. He was rude to the nurses, curt with Melissa (she forgave him – maddening woman), and he shunned the company of other convalescents because he couldn't bear to see them walking. With his crutches, he hopped and leaped along the parquet corridors, overtaking two-legged patients without a greeting.

He snarled at Celia, when she asked if he'd like to go indoors, 'I'm not *quite* helpless.'

Celia, like Melissa, forgave him because of his leg, but less aggravatingly. She said cheerfully, 'Right then, I needn't bother about you,' and left the verandah.

When she'd gone, Greer wished he'd asked her what her name was. She was desperately pale, she looked ill – but what a stunner! he thought. He hauled himself up, and hopped through the French window into his room. It was bright with flowers, freshly decorated, faced south and was conveniently placed on the ground floor. He loathed it. His whole soul was bent on acquiring and learning to use an artificial leg, and then finding a suitably destructive desk job. The war seemed to be going to last a while longer. He opened his paper and saw the words 'Zonnebeke falls.'

'I see Zonnebeke's fallen.' Curse the woman, why couldn't she knock? Melissa loomed over Greer, smiling archly. 'At this rate, the war will soon be over. Won't that be lovely? Is there anything you want, Mr Greer?' She put up a thin hand, and coyly put back a strand of faded blonde hair, escaped from a wispy bun.

'A new leg,' snapped Greer.

'Oh, but you must wait and be very patient and good, mustn't you? And you mustn't be nasty to the nurses. I don't mind – I understand you too well, but they sometimes complain, poor dears.'

'I'm tired; I'm going to sleep.' (That'll get rid of her.)

'Tired? You've been overdoing it. I knew it. All this rushing up and down. Now you've got to be *very* good and try to rest . . .'

'Oh, for God's sake, go away!'

He was sorry after she'd gone, though not sorry enough to call her back. Poor thing, she was doing her best for the war effort. Oh, but he was irritated beyond bearing. Pent up aggression, like a boil in need of lancing, kept him awake at night.

He hopped out onto the verandah again, and threw himself into the chaise longue. A pretty thing, made of cane and upholstered with rose-patterned chintz, it protested and sagged.

'How are you feeling now, Mr Greer?'

Ah, the beautiful, ghostlike girl, he thought. 'Like a Mills bomb with the pin out,' he said.

'Don't blow up here. Too messy.'

She'd gone. Gone, just like that. Callous bitch! Greer stormed back into his room, crashing his crutches about. He smouldered for a time, and remembered that the voluntary helpers weren't allowed into the patients' rooms except when they were empty. He slammed outside again.

Major Godfrey, grey-faced and silent, who lay on the verandah all day under a tartan rug, muttered, 'I wish you'd settle down, young man. Either in your room or out of it.'

'I'm sorry, sir.' Greer sat down, and waited sulkily for the pale beauty to reappear. He hadn't long to wait, she was carrying a tray with a cup and saucer. She heaved Major Godfrey into a semi-upright position, and supported him; steadying his arm while he drank from the cup. She didn't perform this duty like a ministering angel – more as if she were dosing a bullock, thought Greer. A tall, strongly built girl. Wonder why she's such a dreadful colour.

'I say,' he called to her. 'I've decided against exploding – waste of good material.'

Celia grinned across at him. She tipped Major Godfrey's elbow, so that he got the last of his beef tea in one giant swallow. She came over to Greer. 'I've never seen a sick man look so well,' she remarked.

'I've never seen a well girl look so ill,' he countered.

'I've been ill. I was making munitions at Woolwich and caught diphtheria. They won't have me back for another month at least, so I'm filling in time by making myself useful here.'

'You didn't strike me as a dedicated nurse. Munitions, did you say? Are you keen to go back?'

'As soon as they'll take me.'

When she'd gone, he realized he still didn't know her name. A munitions worker, eh? A girl to be cultivated, he thought. They'd both been working to the same ends.

Lurching restlessly about in his bedroom, he paused to look in the mirror. Yes, he looked perfectly healthy – rather handsome, he considered – and his red hair positively crackled with energy.

The convalescents at Posset Hall didn't wear hospital 'blues' but their own uniform. Greer, who'd been obeying doctor's orders and wearing pyjamas and dressing-gown, decided to dress. It took him some time, but he managed it at last. He thought his empty trouser leg looked rather romantic. Not so the crutches. Impossible to square one's shoulders while using them, so he returned to his seat outside.

It was an hour or more before Celia came back. She strode out onto the verandah with another drink for Major Godfrey.

'Want some?' she called to Greer.

'Beef tea? No thanks.'

'I'll get you some real tea if you like.'

'Please do.'

The next hour flew by. Never had Greer met a girl so knowledgeable about his favourite subject. Major Godfrey raised his weary head and listened in amusement.

'. . . slap three clips in the magazine and bob's your uncle . . . fifteen rounds a minute? Easily . . . Our machine-guns are faster, but theirs are more accurate – we're working on it . . . Marvellous! See that chap fishing out there? These sights would bring him within twelve yards – you couldn't miss. Oh yes, I've won a bit – crack shot? No, not really. Just a hobby.'

Celia made a discovery. 'Why, you're in the Dublins!'

'Yes, I'm from Wicklow, as a matter of fact. Joined up from Trinity.'

'A friend of mine, Tom Daly, is in your regiment. I think he mentioned you in his letters – do you know him?'

'Of course. I was in his company when I was wounded. Nice chap. Years senior to me, but we saw a lot of each other. He had a dog –'

'Yes, I've heard about the dog. I wonder how Tom is.'

'No idea. As I was saying, these new rifles . . .'

'Miss Shane! Come at once. What are you doing out there?'

'Oh goodness, Matron herself. Goodbye.'

Celia fled. What an interesting young man, she thought. I wonder what he got the M.C. for. She hadn't forgotten Tom

by any means, but neither had she changed her mind. Tom
Daly belonged to the past.

Celia had been seriously ill. An unknown wellwisher called
Miss Briggs sent daily enquiries, flowers and fruit. Celia, when
she felt well enough to think at all, thought Miss Briggs must
be one of those elderly ladies who were spending their time
in voluntary hospital work. She was deeply grateful, and when
she was no longer infectious, she asked if Miss Briggs would
call, so that she might thank her in person. Celia was surprised
and amused when Miss Briggs turned out to be a pretty,
bashful young woman with an unfashionable hair style and
countryfied clothes. They'd talked until Celia, still frail, grew
tired, and discovered few interests in common apart from Tom.

Just the girl for Tom, thought Celia. After only two meetings,
Edith couldn't stop talking about him; blushing as she did so.

Tom had written to Celia, friendly letters, concerned with
her illness, and saying nothing about his disastrous leave.
Celia, sitting up in bed, replied in kind, adding, 'I like your
Miss Briggs.' She knew now that she had never truly loved
Tom at all. Her feelings had been a mixture of hero worship
and romantic emotion. The man returned from the front had
been a stranger, a being from another world. Tony Greer on
the other hand, in spite of having been severely wounded
which Tom had not, dismissed his experiences.

'War's a rough game with no rules,' said Tony Greer. 'I was
made for fighting.'

Tom had said, 'War's a disgusting business. Civilized men
hide in holes and ditches, filthy and frightened, waiting to kill
or be killed.'

Celia found Greer easier to understand.

She took Matron's ticking off humbly, but protested, 'I'm
sorry, Matron, but Mr Greer knows nobody here and we have
friends in common. I thought a chat would do him good.'

'I daresay you did, Miss Shane. However, if I consider that
you are spending too much time with one patient, I shall
transfer you to another floor.'

Greer was not the only patient at Posset Hall who had
known Tom. A young gunner, Lieutenant Foster, had been
admitted with shellshock. His yells of 'Help me, Daly!' rang

through the passages as he was taken upstairs. Celia heard, and wondered if it could be the same Daly. She asked whether Foster was in the Dublins, and hearing that he was not, decided he must mean someone else.

Foster was receiving some sort of new treatment, involving talks with a specialist in shellshock cases. It didn't seem to be working. Sometimes he could be seen, drifting about with a hefty young man called Bill. Foster's brown eyes stared, showing the whites, his hands shook. One day, he stopped Celia as she carried a loaded tray across the hall.

'I have broken the most solemn law of God,' he said.

'Come along now,' said Bill. 'Time for a nice cup of tea.'

'Thank you, Philips,' said Foster politely. Bill winked at Celia and led Foster away. Foster shuffled along, head hanging, numb with guilt and misery. Sometimes he would say, 'One day I'm going to shoot you, Philips.' He always called Bill 'Philips'. Bill, a world class middleweight boxer before the war, treated him with thinly veiled contempt and seldom bothered to answer him. He had never been in action, and had little sympathy with the shellshock cases in his care.

When Matron was in her office, safely out of the way, Celia spent a few more minutes with Tony Greer.They went on with their discussion on the rival merits of different kinds of firearm. Foster's voice floated down from the window above. 'They're coming, they're coming! Get down! Leave me alone, Philips, damn and blast you – oh Christ, can't you see?'

'Take it easy,' came Bill's unemotional Cockney voice. 'Nobody coming, see?'

There was a tense pause, a yell and a crash.

'That shellshock case is getting worse,' said Celia. 'He's being moved to a home.'

'A fine excuse,' said Greer. 'Half these shellshock cases are suffering from blue funk and nothing else. Fellows frightened of going back, especially if they've been wounded. Once wounded, twice as windy, as they say.'

'Oh, that's not fair! The poor man's a nervous wreck.'

'That's what I'm telling you,' explained Greer patiently. 'He's so frightened that he's actually made himself ill. The loony bins are full of 'em. Damned shirkers.'

Celia's friendly smile vanished. 'I quite realize,' she said coldly, 'that you have first-hand experience and I haven't, but I think you're talking rot.'

She stalked off, and Greer was left alone to reproach himself, and resolve to censor his remarks in future.

Major Godfrey, motionless under his rug, might have been asleep, or even dead. He turned his shrunken face to Greer and whispered, 'You're a bloody fool, young man, a bloody fool.'

Condemnation on all sides, totally undeserved, thought Greer. He struggled up, hooking one arm round the verandah support, jammed his crutch under his arm and plunged back into his bedroom.

The next day he explained to Celia that inability to get back to the front was spoiling his temper and affecting his judgement. He conceded that some cases of shellshock were genuine.

Celia forgave him and told him her christian name.

That night, Foster tried to hang himself, but was discovered in time by Bill. He was taken away by ambulance.

The following week, Matron was obliged to move Miss Shane to the first floor. She had been noticed assisting Mr Greer in an unnecessarily familiar way.

Dear Tom,

This letter isn't going to be easy to write, especially when you are still out there fighting. You may be hurt by my news, coming so soon after our last meeting, but I feel you should hear it from me rather than somebody else.

Tony Greer and I have fallen in love, and hope to be married soon. As you may know, Tony is still waiting for his artificial leg, but he is wonderfully brave, if not always as patient as he might be!

We won't be well off, and I hope to go back to Woolwich part time. Some married women are employed there. The work won't be well paid, or even interesting, but I'd rather scrub floors than not do my bit, and I'm a frightfully bad nurse.

Tom dear, I hope you don't think I've treated you badly. Honestly I couldn't help it. I think I was dazzled by you when I was very young, and never knew you as a person at all.

Tony sends his regards. He admired you an awful lot, he says.

Thank you for everything,
yours ever,
Celia.

The regimental sports took place at Ervillers in driving rain. Tom was checking the order of the events when Willie O'Hara brought him the post. Jack was with him in his waterproof and boots.

'Thank you, O'Hara. Jack's looking better, isn't he? Eh Jack, old man?'

'Kindly ask my friend Willie to remove this stuffy garment. I do not require it.'

'He's thriving, sir. We'll be leaving off the boots in a few days.'

'Those boots are a work of art. How did you come by the materials?'

'I found them lying about, sir.'

'My boots are made from covers designed for guns, my master. My friend took them from the stores in return for money and cigarettes. Are they not superb?'

Willie fidgeted about instead of leaving.

'What is it, O'Hara? Did you want to ask me something?'

'Yes, sir; it's about Jack. He's been promoted corporal, but of course we don't expect you to post it in the orders for the day.'

Tom's lips twitched. 'Don't you? I'm surprised.'

'No sir. We thought we'd have a small ceremony for him at the sports. Would you do it, sir? Seeing it was you he saved. Say a piece, and put his new tunic on him. I have the stripes sewed on it all ready for him.'

Tom hesitated. Thank God Jim and I are old friends, he thought, as the images of other commanding officers flitted through his mind.

'I don't see why not,' he said. 'It was a very good idea to promote Jack. I need hardly tell you that this is highly unofficial. It might be more suitable to do it after the judging of the team games rather than during the serious prize-giving, but yes, I'll do it.'

'Thank you, sir.'

'My master, I still do not know what you are going to do to me.'

'Find Captain Bellamy, will you, O'Hara. I'd like to see him now.'

Jack approached, and held out a stoutly shod paw. Tom took it and shook it gently. 'How do you do, Corporal Jack,' he said.

'I'd teach him to salute, but he's the wrong shape,' said Willie. 'Come along, Corp, we've work to do.'

Tom was still chuckling as he opened Celia's letter.

The standard of performance at the sports was low. All the battalion's best athletes were wounded or dead. There was some promising material among the newcomers, but they'd had no training, except for one or two newly fledged officers, fresh from university. They ran and jumped to the best of their ability on the slippery ground. In the middle of the programme there were some gymkhana events, including tent-pegging and a bareback race on mules. Tom had decided that these light-hearted competitions would make a suitable introduction to the promotion of a dog.

The sun obligingly came out for the occasion, as Tom walked onto the field, accompanied by Pat O'Shea. He looked round at the expectant faces, seeing only a blur. He read from notes, his voice low, but clearly audible to everybody.

'And now,' he said, 'we have a special ceremony which you will not find in the programme. In all military history, I know of no dog being promoted from the ranks. The nearest I can come to a precedent is the emperor Caligula's horse which was made a consul. I'm sure you all know that Jack, our mascot, gallantly carried a message to me under fire last month. He was severely burned by gas on that occasion. As an appreciation, the men of 'D' Company feel that he should be promoted.'

'What's up with Daly?' muttered Bowles to Bellamy.

'Don't know. He got a letter that upset him.'

'Women!'

Willie came forward and saluted; Jack, booted but without his tunic, at his side. Tom turned to Pat, who handed him a brand new tunic, decorated with brass regimental badges and two gold wound stripes. On each shoulder were stitched two chevrons.

'I present this tunic to Corporal Jack,' said Tom loudly, and handed it back to Pat who buckled Jack into it.

'My master, you are in great distress. Why is this?'

Willie saluted again, and he and Jack marched off to the sound of cheering.

The rest of the proceedings passed Tom by. He spoke, admired, applauded, and took nothing in. When it was over, he went back to the house where he and Jim Harper were billeted. As O'Hara was still his servant, he and Jack lived there too.

Tom went into the dark little parlour, threw his cap in a corner, and sat down. He put his elbows on the green chenille tablecloth and his head in his hands.

She can't, he thought. She mustn't. Not Greer. Hell take it, anybody but Greer.

Rain pattered on the window, gently at first, then streaming down the glass. The door opened, inch by inch. Tom didn't turn his head.

'My master, I do not know what it is that grieves you, but I feel for you deeply and grieve with you.'

Jack's boots were off but he still wore the new tunic. 'I wish to thank you for this beautiful gift.'

'Oh Jack, Jack,' Tom's voice was a whisper. 'Women are the very devil – you've no idea.' He bent to take Jack's paw which the dog was holding out to him, and turned it to examine the scabbed pads and the new skin, still pink and soft. 'You know, Jack,' said Tom in a more normal voice, 'if all of us humans were like you, honest and loyal, there wouldn't be any more wars.'

'Dogs fight, my master; especially when a lady is involved.'

'I wish you could understand, Jack. Perhaps it's as well that you can't.'

Later in the evening, Tom got drunk. Not publicly and uproariously, but alone, except for Jack. Never since his college days had he drunk more than was good for him, but that dark, wet August evening, he returned to the musty parlour with a bottle more than half full of whiskey, and a glass.

This bloody, bloody war! Losing Celia was another thing to blame it for. In peacetime they would have spent more time getting to know one another before committing themselves to an engagement. Then, either the affair would have died a natural death, or blossomed, equally naturally, into marriage. Now Celia was rushing headlong into another engagement.

Tom's mind, sharpened by the first two whiskys, called up memories from his early days in the service. Malta, Egypt, the Sudan, India. Skirmishes and raids. Some bloodshed, but nothing to prepare one for years of butchery.

Happy days in Malta. A subaltern's pay wouldn't stretch to marriage unless he had private means. Tom hadn't, so he played polo, schooling ponies for others in order to afford good animals for himself. In his generous spare time, he had flirted with the prettiest of the hordes of marriageable English girls sent out by hopeful mothers, and known as the 'Fishing Fleet'.

Later, in India, he had played high handicap polo, and had the time of his life. His ponies had been named after regimental battle honours. Plassy, Amboyna, Wandewash and Aden. Then in 1910, he had been going to call a new pony Nundy Droog, but had named him instead Halley's Comet, after the strange phenomenon lighting up the southern sky. Some said it was the star of Bethlehem, others that it heralded the end of the world or a cosmic disaster.

There had been a 'Fishing Fleet' in India too. Tom, now a captain, so infinitely more desirable, had almost been landed by an unscrupulous young lady with a predatory mother at her elbow. This incident had made him cautious. He emptied his glass. India. The trees shedding jet black shadows, and Judith coming towards him, holding up a ribboned parasol and wearing a white dress . . . white dress – Celia. What in Heaven's name had made him think he no longer loved her?

He pictured her in a white dress, walking down the aisle to the falling cadences of Mendelssohn, on the arm of that carrot-haired savage – might he rot in hell! Not even an able-bodied savage, but a mutilated one whom she would have to support. He groaned aloud, but tried not to think of Celia married to Greer, making love, having his children . . .

'My master, is there nothing I can do to comfort you? Shall I perform a trick taught me by my friend Willie, and die for the Dubs? I do not like it, but if it will amuse you I will do it. See! I am dead.'

'What are you doing down there, Jack? I suppose I'd better get a lamp. Might as well kill the bottle first.'

It grew quite dark. Major Tom lay back in his chair and placed his feet on the table. He talked to Jack, and told him many things, most of them incomprehensible. It appeared that he blamed himself for the deaths of his comrades at Vampire Farm.

'I'm a failure, Jack. A contemptible bloody failure. Celia was right.' Jack tentatively placed a paw on his master's knee, and Tom took it in his hand. 'I've tried, Jack. God knows I've tried. And the only hand I can grasp in my failure is a dog's paw. Funny, eh?' He gave a sudden loud shout of laughter.

Colonel Jim looked in. 'You there, Daly? I was wondering where you'd got to. Why didn't you send for a lamp?'

'Come'n have a drink, old boy. My girl's marrying a one-legged hero called Tony Greer. Drink to them, send for another bottle. Drink to their future happiness.'

Jack was grateful to be able to hand his afflicted master over to the capable hands of Colonel Jim. He padded off to find Willie.

CHAPTER THIRTEEN

'Been drinking, have you? Thought you had more sense.' The
M.O. was a peppery little man, not loved by would-
be lead-swingers. He could tell a malingerer a mile away,
and was never inclined to give anyone the benefit of the
doubt.

Sweat stood on Tom's forehead, his face was putty-colour.
'If this is a hangover,' he gasped, 'give me a peaceful grave.'

'It's hangover plus. Whiskey on top of a grumbling ulcer.
Stick to drinking milk. Plenty of good fresh milk, and try not
to miss meals.' He stumped out, an orderly at his heels.

Milk! thought Tom. Regular meals! Silly old fool. He turned
on his face, pressing both hands against his diaphragm and
drawing up his knees.

'Your milk, sir.' The orderly had returned. Perhaps it did
take the edge off the pain for a moment, but tinned, sweetened
condensed milk made Tom vomit. He turned away, groaning.
No position was easy, getting up was impossible. He'd seen
Basil Shine drink twice as much, and be little the worse except
for a bad temper next day. Unfair. Tom had been able to walk
to his room, undress and get into bed. Jim had stayed with
him, but Tom hadn't needed to be 'put to bed', in the sense
that he himself had put Celia's father to bed in London.

There was a tap on the door, and O'Hara came in, carrying
a quart jug and a tumbler. The jug was full of milk. Jack
hesitated in the doorway, unsure of his welcome.

'Milk? Fresh? I don't believe it.' Tom, propped on an elbow,
watched O'Hara pour it, foaming, into the glass. 'Where on
earth did you get it?'

'Found a cow, sir. She was wandering about, in need of

milking, poor thing. Something happened to her calf, I suppose.'

Tom drank the milk gratefully, and the pain eased a little almost at once. He mopped his forehead, and sat up in bed. 'Thank you, O'Hara, that was very welcome. But if a farmer comes to claim that cow, you must return her.' Sitting up in bed had been a bad idea. He lay down again. 'How did you persuade her to wander this way?' he asked.

'Jack persuaded her, sir. You'd have thought he was a cattle dog not a retriever.'

'My master, I persuaded that cow to come to your rescue with the aid of my sharp teeth and many threats. She did not wish to come.' Jack limped over to the bed. 'If you wish for roast veal, I will persuade her calf to come also.'

'What's poor old Jack been up to? He's lame again.'

'He got a little kick on the shoulder. The poor old cow was full of milk, so I suppose she was in bad humour. Then, milking's a thing I was never trained for.'

'Once more, I have been injured in the performance of my duty. Promotion brings fresh risks, no doubt.'

When O'Hara and Jack had gone, Tom, his pain now bearable, dozed for a time, then re-read Celia's letter.Then he read some of her old ones. Reason told him that their temperaments were too unalike for a happy marriage ever to have been possible. He wished, suddenly and desperately, that he already had a wife to go home to. Somebody like Jim Harper's wife. Althea Harper was a kind, uncomplicated woman; motherly, thought Tom. Still, one shouldn't be longing for a motherly wife at his age. His own mother, a vocal campaigner for every fashionable cause in turn, was the least motherly woman he'd ever met. Her second husband, Algy, was a poet, followed in Yeats's wake, but unlikely to leave any ripples of his own. Tom couldn't remember his father. He swallowed some more milk and got up. Please God the cow wouldn't be claimed. The pain had almost gone.

Belfast camp at Ervillers was a busy place all through the first half of September. Intensive training in hand-to-hand fighting, with and without conventional weapons, was necessary to deal with the new delaying tactics being used by the Germans. Picked men were taught how to attack and kill silently, using what were later known as commando tactics. Physical training and instruction in the handling of new types of weapons, went on non-stop from dawn to dusk.

The Old Toughs were still at less than half their early August strength, in spite of the return of a hundred men, recovered from wounds. The sense of urgency pervaded the camp. Time was going on. A wet spring and summer had given way to a glorious spell of weather. Everywhere, grass and flowers sprang up. The men knew that the offensive would not be halted for the winter on the plain overlooked by German positions at every point. The good weather wouldn't last long, and the survivors of August 16th, even the bravest of them, felt a deep reluctance to return to deadlock in the mud.

On a night early in September, Chatham was raided by the new giant German bombers. With a wingspan of nearly forty feet, these huge machines had a range of 300 miles. 132 people were killed in the raid, and hundreds more injured. This was used as an object lesson in the harangues designed to make the men keen – or offensive, as the offical term had it. It worked with the younger men only.

The older men listened to the lectures with dull indifference. They had learned to reckon their dead in thousands. They knew what was coming. Back to the front line and the mud and the stench and the waiting. Waiting for the relieving troops, hoping they would arrive before the order to advance came through – or that bullet with your number on it. In the front line, listlessness would change to stomach-churning fear, and more fear, until sheer weariness allowed fear to be swallowed up in apathy. The men would no longer care what happened. They had all learned that death chose its victims at random. There wasn't a man among them who believed in his own personal luck any more. Even Jack's reputation for bringing good fortune was clouded.

According to rumour, the battalion's next assignment would be a major attack forward along the Menin Road up to the Hindenberg Line. The fortified outposts of the line, scattered all over the plain, had held up all earlier attacks, helped

by the weather. Like most rumours, this one was greatly
exaggerated. The Dublins were considered too reduced to take
part in a major attack. They remained in Ervillers until the
seventeenth, and then returned to the front line, not much
advanced from where their few remnants had left it four weeks
before. They were to capture and hold a sector of trench.
'Straightening out that bit of line,' was the offical euphemism.

Willie O'Hara was the only man in 'D' Company to have
come through three years of war almost without a scratch.
This he put down to Jack's lucky influence.

'He didn't bring luck to the German lad,' said Pat O'Shea.
Willie pretended not to hear.

They were moving up next day, by train as before to Ypres,
and beyond it to St Jean. Jack's boots were discarded, his paws
as good as new, and he had recovered from the cow's kick.
Tom's ulcer, doused with milk six times a day, had ceased to
grumble.

'A pity we couldn't bring the old cow,' said Willie.

Tom had planned to leave Jack with a resting battalion until
their return, but when this seemed likely to provoke a mutiny,
he relented. 'Only as far as the reserve line,' he said. 'I don't
want him mixed up in an attack. Is that clearly understood,
O'Hara?'

The train was packed, and once more the battalion went
out into the wasteland.

There hadn't been the semblance of a road when the battalion had last crossed the plain. Almost a month of fine
weather and no further shelling of the area had changed the
outlook. The great desert of mud and craters, the shelled area,
had sprouted long, coarse grass. Yellowish and tough, it was
of no value as feed, but it masked much of the debris of
war and fringed the shell-holes. This featureless grass-grown
expanse sloped gently away from Frezenberg, then rose to the
Zonnebeke spur. There were no ruins to be seen, because all
the rubble had been carted away and used to rebuild the roads
in the area. Whole villages had disappeared without a trace.
As a result, the battalion marched four abreast on a sound,
metalled road. After a short time it began to rain, then to pour.

Most of the men were too apathetic even to grumble. Rain

was normal. They accepted being constantly wet as a fact of life.

They arrived in the line, and exchanged gossip with the relieved battalion. There had been no action in that sector for several days, and the Germans in their fortified pill-boxes were biding their time.

Ahead of the front line trench, no man's land, overlooked by the Abraham Heights, was known as the devastated area. This was land not yet fought over, but prepared for battle by the retreating Germans. All civilians had been evacuated from their farms, and all buildings and bridges blown up. Trees and hedges were cut, but the land still lay divided into fertile fields, where crops ran to seed and grass matted and rotted. The area was thickly dotted with pill-boxes. Beyond it lay the great Hindenberg Line, a double system of fortified trenches, mostly dug by Russian prisoners. The barbed wire in front of the line was fifty yards deep in places.

Willie O'Hara gratefully struggled out of his pack, and began preparations for a meal. Battalion headquarters had been set up in a damp underground chamber in the reserve trench.

Willie fed Jack first, while getting a meal for his master. Jack gulped down bully beef, a fair sized lump of cheese and a bowl of tea. For Major Tom, Willie prepared an egg-flip. The precious egg was beaten up in some of the last of the milk. Jack ran his tongue round his lips, and watched Willie closely.

'No, Jack. This is the last egg, and I've only enough fresh milk for one more drink.' Willie took Tom his unappetizing meal.

The officers were standing on planks. Water was running down the steps and collecting quickly. Jack slopped across the flooded floor to speak to his master, but Major Tom was concerned with other things. Jack had to be content with the briefest of greetings.

All night it rained, and all of the next day and night. Water poured in. Supplies arrived with painful slowness, the patient mules slipping and sliding on the duckboards. So many horses and mules had been killed that even donkeys were carrying machine-guns, and the sorely needed planks and 'A' frames. These last were wooden triangles for revetting trenches whose banks were subsiding. The men floored the reserve trench with duckboards, and shored it up with 'A' frames. Still the water poured in, and headquarters had to be abandoned for a tin-roofed cave above water level. This slimy cavern was floored with planks which tilted and sent up fountains of mud when trodden on. Tom, looking ill, supervised the sandbagging of the roof.

Jack, sitting on a sodden sandbag outside, thought about the same things as his human friends. Hot dinners, warm water, a dry bed.

Two men trudged past, each a walking pillar of mud, carrying between them a pole on which hung two rolls of wire with wicked inch-long barbs. They set down their load to rest, and at once, bubbling, it began to sink. They swore, and hoisted it up, and plodded on, heads down, until a bend hid them from view.

There was going to be an attack. None of the soldiers knew when or where; they didn't expect to be told anything except at the last moment, if then. 'We attack tomorrow night,' the word went from mouth to mouth, but first tonight had to be endured. The communication trenches were all flooded, and as the water rose, calf deep, the men scraped out resting places for themselves, too wretched even to swear. Plastered with mud, they spent the rest of the night, either on guard duty or propped in angles and crannies, trying to sleep on their sodden feet.

Rats scuttled, splashed and swam, and Jack wondered whether he should attack them. Rats, he felt, were beneath his notice – terrier's work – but when one of them came right up to him it was time to take action.

'Depart, eater of human flesh, or I shall kill you.' The rat turned its head this way and that, watching him. Willie crashed down a rifle butt, breaking its back. Jack's doubts were set aside. In future, all rats should be killed. He was not good at killing rats, he was too slow on his feet, and many dodged him, but he accounted for five that night. He placed them neatly in his master's dugout, and received praise. Their taste revolted him. Not even roasted, he thought, would he eat one.

*

In these days of rapid promotion, Dick Bellamy was now a captain, commanding 'D' Company. Orders had arrived for a major trench raid involving all four companies. This was to be part of what was later known as the battle of the Menin Road, and was intended to divert enemy attention from the advance of Canadian forces to the north.

The officers studied the orders gloomily by candlelight. It was evident that this action had been conceived before the weather broke.

'Bloody night work,' grumbled Captain Bowles. 'It's hard enough to get about in daylight without breaking your neck or drowning. What we need here is the Navy.'

The infantry was held up, waiting for artillery support. The gunners were having an appalling time trying to move their guns up. Whole teams of horses slipped into shell-holes and had to be cut loose and abandoned. Some were shot as they struggled vainly in the morass, others drowned, or were smothered in the mud. Teams of men, floundering thigh deep, dragged the guns into position, only to see them heel over sideways. The gunners had to sleep in the open on soaking straw, rolled in sodden blankets. They lived on bully beef straight from the tin, and army biscuits. Making tea was a major operation, there was no natural cover, and the gun platforms were exposed. Each shell had to be cleaned before it could be fired. Fortunately, the low cloud was grounding the German aircraft.

The Dublins' orders were precise. East Trench was to be captured and consolidated along a front of 350 yards. This would entail capturing an unknown number of German forward posts, and crossing Middle Trench, which might not be as empty as it appeared. The four companies would leave the firing trench at five-minute intervals, and notice-boards would be set up for their guidance. From their rendezvous in no man's land, they would advance in complete silence in parties of twenty-five men. The creeping barrage, starting at zero hour, would be laid down 200 yards ahead. In these conditions, there was no danger that the men would go too fast and be caught by their own guns.

Jim Harper and Tom, directing operations, would go no

further than the assembly lines. They would go back to headquarters, and wait by the telephones, where they would be
informed of the positions of the units on their flanks.

Willie helped to dish out the rum ration, then he retired to
the filthy cave which he called his dugout, to attend to his
feet. After two days and nights of soaking, this was a smelly
but necessary task. Cursing, he unwound his puttees, squeezed
the dirty water out of them, and hung them over a bayonet
speared into the mud wall. Next came the heavy boots, then
the wet, darned khaki socks. Jack watched from his sandbag,
full of sympathy for his friend, as the pulpy feet emerged,
cracked and mottled. Willie doused them with boracic powder,
and rolled on the wet socks again. Rewinding his puttees, he
remarked to Jack, 'Thank God the Major isn't going out. His
stomach isn't the best.'

'My friend, I thank my own personal gods that neither
am I going out.'

The westerly wind was preventing the Germans from laying
gas – Jack's respirator was buckled up in a neat canvas satchel
in Willie's pack. Willie scraped at the wall with his entrenching
tool, making a shelf to rest on. He had already made a small
niche for Jack. A spade was better and quicker, but spades
were at a premium. Willie gouged and grumbled, and water
trickled through the cracks he made. Then a slide of silt
obliterated his work. However, he stuck to it until a narrow,
slimy ledge appeared. On this, he could snatch some sleep in
the daytime, while Jack kept the rats at bay.

The slow day passed – September 19th. Evening came, and
still the rain fell pitilessly.

Except for the occasion of Kurt's death, and the burning of
his own paws, Jack could recall no misery to equal that which
he now suffered. Wet through for days on end, hungry,
verminous; only his friend Willie's affection comforted him a
little. And then Willie developed an affliction of the stomach.
Unable to stand, he was carried away to the rear. Jack knew
not whether he should follow his friend or stay with his
master. Willie was taken to a hut half a mile behind the lines,

Jack following some way behind. There was a new M.O. and new stretcher-bearers.

'Get away, dog; no animals in here.'

'He's the battalion's mascot, sir,' Willie whispered.

'I wish to remain with my friend.'

'I will not have it in here, do I make myself clear? Corporal, take it away and tie it up somewhere.'

It, thought Jack. A fine way to refer to a twice wounded veteran. He evaded the large red hand of the sniggering orderly. 'There is no need to speak in that impolite fashion. I shall return to my master for instructions.'

Jack squelched back to Colonel Jim's filthy lair, and found that the company commanders were listening to their final briefing. He sat down quietly, and nobody paid him any attention.

When it was over, Tom said to Timmy Coote, 'Take Jack right out of the way. What's he doing in here? Where's O'Hara?'

'Sick, sir. Food poisoning.'

'That's bad. You'd better tie Jack up somewhere, and see that he can't get loose. We should have left him at Ervillers.'

Timmy led Jack away to the place where the cooks worked in impossible conditions, where the heating of a tin of pork and beans was a notable achievement. He chained Jack to one of the railway sleepers which supported the corrugated iron roof.

Jack heard the companies moving off, one after another. He felt it rather than knew when Major Tom went out into the open. The rain had ceased. Soon the moon would be up. Jack pointed his nose upward, and prepared to howl his despair. Fusilier Pyle, battalion cook, forestalled him, dealing him a stinging blow with a wooden spoon. It appeared that silence had been ordered. Jack did not yelp – he had seen the blow coming. He leaped sideways, jerking hard; then back and sideways, jerking in the opposite direction. The chain held, but the collar, the old, old collar Kurt had made, parted as its rotten stitches gave way. Jack was free.

Jack paused as soon as he was sure he was not followed. There was no advantage in visiting Willie. He would be driven away again, or worse still, forcibly detained. He determined to find Major Tom and beg him to allow Corporal Jack to accompany him. Thank Heaven he was impeded neither by flannel hood nor waterlogged tunic. He jumped out of the reserve trench, and galloped the 200 yards to the support line. Many soldiers saw him, but they could not stop him because silence was enforced. The support trench was almost deserted. A handful of guards, a few orderlies – Timmy Coote! Jack sprang away as Timmy grabbed at the collar that wasn't there. Jack put a bend in the trench between himself and Timmy before climbing out. At this point, it was a bare fifty yards to the firing trench, and he could see hundreds of men gathering in the gloom on the far side of it. He slid down into the trench, his splash echoed by three separate plops as rats took hastily to the water. He'd no time for them now.

The barrage began. The big guns, hauled with such fearful difficulty to the spur two miles back, sent shells far ahead into no man's land. Mud and water flew up like a shining curtain in the light of the explosions. Jack saw 'D' Company move off as Colonel Jim and Major Tom watched. Hardly had they travelled a dozen yards when the German guns began to answer, and, with a flash and a shriek, one of the light shells known as whizz-bangs landed among the men.

'Stretcher-bearers!' Familiar cry. Major Tom was running. Jack froze in horror. His friends. His dear friends. Pat O'Shea would never bewail his lot again. And there, trying to rise, was young Captain Bellamy; he that Major Tom called Dickie when none was there to hear. Major Tom ran to his side, Jack following. Captain Bellamy looked up and spoke disjointed words. Major Tom knelt and gathered the young man in his arms like a child. He spoke to him in low tones. 'Yes, Dickie, I'll tell her. Of course I will. Good lad – I wish I had your courage. She'd be proud of you, Dickie, we all are.' He laid Captain Bellamy down. Some of the men were hanging back. Sergeant Duff lay, horribly dead. Stretcher-bearers came for Captain Bellamy.

'Dead, I'm afraid,' said Major Tom. 'Take him in. I shall go in his place.' He picked up Sergeant Duff's rifle, and set off. 'Oh for God's sake, Jack, go back. Back, I say.'

'I dare not.'

'Go home, Jack; go home.'

'That, my master, is impossible.'

But Jack stopped. He waited, looking about him, while men overtook him on either side. Lewis gunners set up their clumsy weapon behind a dank tree stump which had put forth a few pathetic leaves. A man had taken the panniers of ammunition from round Pat O'Shea's neck, and soon they were ready for action, firing over the heads of their advancing comrades. The barrage was slow, but too fast for the troops to keep up with. Jack changed his mind. He would follow his master once more.

'D' Company had swung left towards the sector of trench they were to occupy. Jack kept straight on. He overtook parties of men, twenty or thirty together. Some said, 'There's old Jack,' in surprise. Most ignored him. Soon he had passed them by. Where was Major Tom? he wondered. There was a low wall ahead, a few broken tree stumps. He stopped.

What was that once familiar aroma? Why yes. It was the scent of the thin dark cigars smoked by old Helmuth long ago. Cheroots. Was old Helmuth perhaps behind the wall? Eagerly, Jack ran forward and jumped over.

Eight startled Germans grabbed at Jack. They tended a machine-gun on a stand, similar to Euge's Lewis gun. Jack's teeth slashed at the clutching hands. He had made a mistake. He could not know that this was a forward post, waiting for a party of Dublins to come, within unmissable range. The Germans, every bit as surprised as Jack, had orders to keep quiet. In silence, they lunged at him as he dived among their legs; one man tumbled to the ground. Recovering from their first astonishment, the Germans tried to club the dog, rather than catch him. Jack dodged the blows aimed at his head. It was a few moments before it dawned on him that these familiar-smelling men were actually trying to kill him. A thickset sergeant lashed out with the handle of an entrenching tool. This useful article, known to the Dubs as a piggy-stick, could have cracked Jack's skull easily. It came down hard as Jack dived under the gun, and hit the barrel with a dull clang. For priceless seconds, all eight Germans milled about in the dark. 'Thanks be to all the powers there are that my coat is black and the moon is not yet up.'

Jack dodged round the legs of a soldier who had fallen over him, and made his escape. Behind him, a furious commotion broke out. A party of twenty Dubs had rushed the machine-gun post. Vicious fighting with bayonets and hand grenades ensued, and Jack fled from the dreadful sounds. His mind was in a turmoil. Somehow, a brandished club was more frightening than a pointed gun. He did not know where he was going, he had no idea where his master might be. He was running away from his friends' lines, and now there were Germans behind him. He came to a ragged hole in the ground where a great tree had been uprooted, and he dropped, panting, into it. There was water in the hole, but it was shallow and not cold. He lay there, getting his wind and wondering what to do next.

When Tom had stood up, and allowed the stretcher-bearers to carry Bellamy away, his mind for the moment had been a blank. Then rage had filled him, such as he'd never known in his life. The shell that had killed Bellamy and O'Shea had also got Sergeant Duff. 'D' Company was left with eighteen-year-old Second Lieutenant Mullins to lead it. He had joined up at the end of the summer vacation, only days before.

There were hidden machine-gun emplacements every-where. When Tom took Sergeant Duff's rifle and bandolier and led the way forward, he had felt no fear, but only fury. There was no question of a charge. The ground was too holding. A quick walk was the best pace possible. Tom felt lightheaded. He hadn't eaten, and the milk was finished. He felt he could take on the entire German army. Thirty men rallied to him, and together they overran a German pill-box, killing the gunner and taking the other men prisoner. Tom left four men there, with instructions to cover his party with the captured gun; others escorted the prisoners to the rear. In the open again, Tom's group kept doggedly on until their objective, East Trench, was reached.

Except for German corpses, rats, and muddy water, it was empty.

The men set about making the trench habitable, removing the dead, cutting fire-steps facing the German lines, and building a parapet. After a time they were joined by another small party of soldiers.

'Any Dublins here? Any 'D' Company?' They were a bedraggled bunch, unrecognizable in their filthy state. Tom knew young Toby Mullins by his voice and his unusual height. Together, they climbed down into the stagnant mess at the bottom of the trench which had plainly been abandoned days before.

Toby Mullins reported that his party had overcome a German strong-post, captured their gun, and taken six prisoners. 'I don't know why they didn't get us all,' he said. 'We were right on top of them before we realized they were there, and they seemed as surprised as we were.'

A man at the back spoke. 'It was like a dream to me,' he said. 'I thought I saw the dog jump in among the Jerries and attack them – Jack, the lucky dog – and then he was gone. We thought we saw him fighting for us; it put heart in us. You could say he took the post – he kept the Jerries busy until we was in the pill-box.'

Incredible how weary men were heartened by visions, thought Tom. He remembered the Angel of Mons.

Fierce isolated battles were still going on out in the open, where many German pill-boxes were holding out. 'D' Company's orders were to hold and consolidate the trench on a front of 200 yards. There weren't anything like enough men to do this if the enemy counter-attacked. Tom hoped fervently that daylight would bring reinforcements and supplies to his tired and hungry men.

The counter-attack, when it came, was made by artillery. The German infantry remained behind the fortifications of the Hindenberg Line, and in their pill-boxes. Within minutes, East Trench was uninhabitable; within half an hour, it had been obliterated. The Dublins left its dangerous cover, and instead occupied the pill-boxes they had fought for earlier, throwing out the dead Germans, and squeezing themselves inside the concrete forts. Tom was the last to leave the trench. 'Carry on, Mullins,' he said. 'I'll follow you in a minute.'

Tom waited until the footsteps died away. He had thought he heard someone out there in no man's land. It was difficult to be sure while the men were struggling out of the morass which had been a trench. A well-aimed shell could bury twenty of them alive. Let them get back to the pill-boxes.

Yes, thought Tom, there was someone there. As he raised his rifle, a voice cried out, 'About face! Retire to your jumping-off point. On the double!'

The voice was authoritative, the English perfect, but there should be nobody within a mile who could give such an order except Tom himself.

'By whose command?' asked Tom. Then he saw him, the scuttle-like helmet outlined by the rising moon. Tom stood motionless. He thought he heard his own voice saying to Foster, 'I've never shot a man in cold blood – I doubt if I could.'

Tom lifted his rifle and fired.

In the same instant, the German had also fired. He had steadied the heavy Lüger with both hands, and Tom saw it flash as his own rifle bullet caught the German in the throat.

Jack was sure that he was needed. His sixth sense told him so. Half a dozen physical sensations bothered him. He was cold, wet, hungry, itchy, lonely and frightened. I shall attempt to return to my friend Willie, as my master is not to be found, he thought. It seems that the battle has ceased.

For hours the furious guns had made the night hellish with their din. At one time it had ceased, and Jack had crept out of his hole. He had seen nothing but greyness, with fires on the horizon; heard nothing but water desolately dripping; smelled nothing but filth and decay.

Faintly, to his right, where 'A' Company had moved up, he had thought he saw a movement, then coloured flares arose – red . . . green . . . red. S.O.S. The guns had resumed their clamour in reply, and Jack had plunged back into his shelter.

Now the guns had ceased again and Jack was quite certain that he was needed. Not by Willie, but by his master. Where then could he be? And what could Jack do? Two shots broke the silence, not far away. Almost together, the crack of a rifle, and the quite different bang of a pistol. Jack's instinct for survival told him to turn and run towards the west. He knew that some of his comrades were in the German safe place from which he had so narrowly escaped earlier. Sometimes head, heart and instinct are in conflict.

Jack slowly scrambled out of the brackish water, and set off northward, with many pauses, in the direction from which the shots had come. He stopped, listened, stared, sniffed the air. Darkness. Wetness. Silence and decay. He came to East Trench; to the place where it had been. It was a twenty-yard-wide strip of deep churned-up mud. Some weapons lay abandoned. A dead man lay, half in half out of the mire. Jack swung left, avoiding him. Here a copse of young larch trees lay uprooted like a spilled box of matches. Making his way through was slow and tiresome. Again, Jack struck out to the left, skirting the ruined trees.

He came back to the line of the trench, now visible in the misty light of the rising moon. The light glinted on abandoned tins and canteens, glimmered palely on filthy pools, illuminated a dead face. Jack shied like a startled horse and listened again, one paw raised.

Nothing. But he knew that his direction was right, and that he had not much further to go. A crater gaped at his feet. The earth from it now filled the abandoned trench. To the left lay two bodies. Rather than pass them, Jack climbed the hill of wet clay, laboriously. He was now on the wrong side of the trench. He knew he was wrong, but he was unwilling to return. There would be another opportunity to cross.

The moon rose higher. Jack's nostrils were assailed by a strong smell of rum and blood. He stopped. A German soldier lay on his back, his head almost severed from his body. This man was not Jack's concern, and his smell blotted out all others. Jack approached the edge of the trench, here less damaged, intending to cross back to the other side. There, crumpled at the bottom, his master lay, his face half hidden in the mud.

Jack dared not jump down; there was nowhere to land except on the huddled body. He retraced his steps, and slid down the greasy bank on his tail. He knew at once that Major

Tom still breathed, but as he watched, the body sank perhaps a centimetre more. His master's helmet had fallen off, his dark hair stuck in spikes to his face, but there was no blood. There was blood in the water. It came from a dark patch on Major Tom's tunic.

'My master, rouse yourself. Otherwise you will drown, and I will be powerless to save you. You will drown, I say!' Jack willed his master to understand with every fibre of his being. He licked the cold wet face. 'Please, my dear master, endeavour to raise your head.'

Ah, success! Major Tom had heard. He opened the eye visible to Jack. 'Doesn't matter,' he mumbled.

Jack wedged his broad black nose under Major Tom's cheek, and tried to raise his head for him. There was a sucking sound, bubbles broke on the slimy surface, but that was all.

'Please assist me. I cannot lift you. I beseech of you to help.'

'Doesn't matter.'

'Do you not wish to live? Can it be that you prefer to drown in this stinking ditch? You *shall* be saved.' Jack licked away all the mud he could get at. Tom's arm lay limply along his side. Jack burrowed his head under it. Perhaps this expression of love would evoke some response. It did.

His master swore at him. Raised his head and swore. Jack had pressed on a broken rib, and the pain achieved what words of encouragement and devotion had not. Jack's master told him to go away, using a coarse expression not previously heard on his lips. Jack knew that there was hope. He did not go away. He stood over Major Tom, begging him with the utmost eloquence to bestir himself.

Tom thought he was probably dead. Later he wished that he were. Later still he realized that he was very slowly drowning. He raised his head, but his limbs seemed powerless. His brain reeled. He fainted. When he came round, Jack was licking his face. That was comforting. It was sad dying alone in a ditch. But Jack wasn't content to comfort Tom as he died. He tried to raise Tom's head with his own, although in order to get under it, he had to bury his nose in mud. That was brave.

Brave but idle. There was no hope. Nothing mattered. Then the fool dog pressed his head right against the spot . . . Bloody hell! 'Bugger off, Jack. Leave me in peace.'

But Tom had raised his head. Impossible to lay it down again and slowly suffocate. He saw his helmet a few yards away, and painfully moved his hand, pointing at it. 'Fetch it, Jack; good dog.'

Jack, plainly delighted to help, picked up the helmet by its chin-strap, and offered it.

'No, lad – there, under my head.' Clever fellow, you'd think he could understand. Jack pushed the helmet closer and closer. Tom, making a giant effort which hurt him all over, lifted his head high enough for Jack to push his tin hat another six inches. Now, Tom could rest his head on it. A reprieve at least.

Jack watched proudly, his tail swinging. 'Jack, boy, get help, bark or something.' How can I explain to him? thought Tom. He now actively wanted to live. Someone would come soon: they'd have heard the shots, and would have missed him. Tom didn't know that, while he lay unconscious, Mullins, made careless by fear and lack of experience, had come back, looked in horror and sent a runner to headquarters to report Major Daly dead. At that very moment, Jim Harper was hearing the bad news.

Jack must have understood Tom. He was going for help, clever dog. He scrambled up the side of the trench and stood for a moment on the parapet, silhouetted against the pale sky.

A single shot snapped – phtt! Jack's yelp was cut short and he disappeared from view.

CHAPTER FOURTEEN

When the hours of bitter fighting were over, there was the usual clearing up to be done. First the severely wounded were brought in, then the slightly wounded, then the dead. There were still some German snipers about, and the stretcher-bearers' task was even more dangerous than before, for, as the line advanced, they had a greater distance to cover.

Jim Harper found that he couldn't keep still. He paced up and down. Six paces this way, six paces that, in his watery dugout. The telephonist's words still echoed in his head. 'Message from the front, sir. Report from Mr Mullins. Major Daly is dead.'

First Dick Bellamy, now Tom. Jim couldn't take men away from the rescue of the living to attend to the dead; Tom would have to stay where he was for the present. Jim fished in his pocket for fountain pen and writing pad. He'd known the Bellamy family for years – Dick was related to his wife. Jim decided to scribble a quick note to Rosemary Bellamy, that lighthearted, decorative creature who looked too young to be the mother of a grown up son. She'd lost her husband too – on the Somme. Jim imagined her, reading the dreaded telegram. He rested his notepad on a sandbag, and moved the candle nearer.

'My dear Rosemary,' he wrote. 'What can I say? You are in my thoughts, and I am sure you will be hearing from Althea soon . . .'

Jim was supposed to be snatching an hour's sleep. Hopeless. He rubbed his eyes with the back of his hand.

'I am writing in haste to tell you that Dick died in Tom Daly's arms, and I'm pretty sure he gave Tom a message for you. Unfortunately I didn't hear what it was, but I did hear Tom say, 'I'll tell her.' Tom told your son how proud of him you would be, as indeed we all are. I feel sure Dick didn't suffer. He was a general favourite, always cheery and ready to make the best of things. Tragically, Tom has also been killed . . .'

Jim finished off the letter, addressed it, and resumed his pacing. Poor Rosemary. His mind turned to other wives and mothers; those who urged their husbands and sons to go out and fight whether they wanted to or not. Brian Bowles had admitted that he'd joined the army because his mother seemed to think he ought to, although he suffered from asthma. Extraordinary. Soon there won't be any young men left on either side, thought Jim.

He gave the letter to his servant, and went out into the clammy dawn to face the ordeal he dreaded. He himself was going to help to bring Tom's body back for burial. He hoped to God that Tom had fallen to a bullet rather than a shell, and that he had died instantly. So many lay out in no man's land all night, slowly dying; their cries coming more and more faintly to their friends who heard but could not help them. The captured pill-boxes were full of severely wounded men, dragged in by their comrades, who shivered in the open, exposed to the enemy and the weather.

Cruel, futile, degrading . . . Jim made a conscious effort to direct his thoughts in a manner more suitable to a commanding officer. Think of the regiment, he told himself. Think of your own responsibilities. If you cannot, far better try not to think at all.

They were a sad little group. Jim Harper walked in front with the Chaplain, followed by a stretcher party. Toby Mullins brought up the rear. Jim had been at Trinity College with the Reverend Percival Blunt, and knew him to be both brave and sincere. The Chaplain had acted as stretcher-bearer again and again, and had made himself useful in dozens of ways outside his normal duties. He had done the most menial work at the regimental aid post in the front line, and in helping the doctors, was as competent as he was compassionate. By doing these tasks, he had made sure of being at hand if a dying man needed him, while taking some of the load off the overworked orderlies.

Tom Daly and Dick Bellamy were going to be buried in the enormous cemetery near Ypres. The battle of the Menin Road was hailed as a victory, but for the Old Toughs, it was a hollow one. Tom and Dick were popular with everybody, and Jim mourned the loss of a lifelong friend. He wished Percy Blunt would stop talking. A grand chap, one of the very best, but Jim would have preferred to be alone.

They were guided to the spot by a pitiful howling. 'Poor old Jack. He's trying to lead us to his master,' remarked Blunt. 'Wonderfully intelligent dog, that.'

'More likely he's bewailing Daly's death – I don't blame him – I know how he feels.' Jim cleared his throat. 'Sorry, Padre, I didn't mean to speak so sharply.'

'Don't worry, Harper. I thought a lot of Daly myself.'

'He shouldn't have died!' Jim burst out. 'He was ill. He should never have left camp, and he had no part in that raid. When Bellamy was killed, he simply grabbed a gun and rushed off – most unlike him.'

Jack's howls were more urgent now, he had heard them coming. Each howl ended with a sharp yelp. 'It sounds as though Jack has been hit as well,' said Blunt. 'Look, there he is.'

The dog was draped over the lip of the ravaged trench like an old discarded coat. His fur was grey and spiky with dried mud, except for a small patch on his flank where it was matted with blood. His head was propped up on a burst sandbag, and he continued his dismal cries until the men reached him. Then he raised his head to look hopefully at Jim, lifting his ears, and lolling out his tongue. He made no attempt to move.

Jim's hand rested lightly on Jack's head. 'Well done, old fellow,' he said. He told the bearers, 'Lift Jack out of the way – gently now. Get a blanket round him and try not to hurt him.' He kept his hand on Jack's head, and the dog, quiet now, allowed the two soldiers to roll him bodily onto the grey blanket without protest.

Jim and the Chaplain scrambled and slithered down the

side of the trench. The communication trenches were either
blocked or flooded; there was no other way.

Tom lay, half buried in the slime. His head rested on his
steel helmet, and its brim kept him from sinking further. One
arm was thrown out sideways. The mud-caked hand was
trembling violently.

'He's alive!' cried both men together.

Toby Mullins and the stretcher party joined them in the
trench, Toby, red faced, avoiding Jim's scornful eye. Methodi-
cally, working in anxious silence, they set about freeing Tom
from the holding mud. It was a tricky operation, as they
couldn't tell where, or how badly he was hurt. Plainly he had
lost a lot of blood – one side of his tunic was soaked with it.
He was unconscious.

'He's been shot in the side,' said Jim. 'Broken ribs – I don't
think he's been hit anywhere else. He should have a good
chance – in spite of having been left here so long.' He glared
at Toby Mullins who said nervously, 'What about the dog, sir?
His back seems to be broken. Ought we to shoot him?'

'No,' snarled Jim. 'And next time you report a man dead,
make sure.'

Mullins wisely didn't reply except for a muttered, 'Yes, sir.'
He bent to the task of freeing Tom's feet. They used sandbags
to support him from slipping back. They lifted him onto
the stretcher. They hoisted the stretcher out of the trench.
Meanwhile, a runner dashed back to the nearest field telephone.

Jack, trailing his hind legs, dragged himself off the blanket.
He was trying to get to the stretcher, panting and whining.

Tom's eyelids flickered. He mumbled a few words. Jim bent
down, and the Chaplain knelt in the mud.

'Can you understand him, Padre?' asked Jim.

'The only word I caught was "Jack".'

It was light. Even through closed lids, you could tell day from
night. The guns were quiet. Tom had been aware of some sort
of commotion for quite a time. He missed Jack's howls – they'd
had a soothing effect, keeping him company.

Tom knew when he was moved – it hurt – but was powerless

to speak or help. Even opening his eyes seemed like too much trouble. He was on solid ground, and yes, Jack was there still. He could hear him whining.

Tom could picture Jim Harper's long sallow face with its close-clipped moustache. He felt that if Jim were there, being alive might be marginally better than being dead. He thought he might be able to talk – try it anyway.

'Jack sang me to sleep,' said Tom. 'Did you hear him singing? No singing now. Where is he?'

His mind caught at the words of the men at his side. They ought to mean something, but they were jumbled up. 'He's delirious.' That meant something, but what? Tom thought, I must tell them about that German I shot. 'He was called Sigmund,' he said. 'Met him at the Christmas truce. Must tell Foster. Very important.' He opened his eyes; the effort was like lifting heavy weights. 'You here, Padre? Am I as bad as that?'

'You'll be all right, old man, don't you worry.' Blunt kneeling in the mud . . . no cap . . . knees all muddy . . . kind face worried. Tom wanted to tell him to get up, but the words skipped away when he needed them, out of reach. It didn't matter. Why bother? When words came to him, they surprised him by being different from what he expected.

'Let us pray,' said Tom. No, that was wrong – Blunt should have said that. Somebody answered. Harper. But Harper was talking nonsense – double-Dutch.

Tom shut his eyes. '"Let me not beg for the stilling of my pain, but for the heart to conquer it." That's good, isn't it? Appropriate.' What on earth am I saying? thought Tom. He could hear more voices approaching. He sensed that Blunt had got up. What were they saying about him? 'Morphia.' 'Looks bad.' 'Two more stretcher-bearers – quickly!'

An insistent whining in the background . . . 'Jack, where's Jack?'

'Jack's here.' That was Harper speaking. 'Bring him over here – careful, men. Look, Daly, here he is.'

Tom lifted his heavy eyelids, and Jack's face swam mistily into view. Black face, brown eyes, pink tongue, white teeth . . . someone was rolling up Tom's sleeve. Why would they do that?

'Jack, don't go away.' Among the words that were mixed up in the air like a message in code, some letters put themselves together, dancing into place in Tom's brain until they spelled out a sentence.

'I will never leave you.'

Something pricked Tom's arm. He slept.

Jack was bruised and numb. His hind legs would support him, but he could not control their direction. Being carried in a blanket in this unseemly fashion was becoming monotonous. Besides, he could not see out, and those who carried him resented their task. Major Tom was being hurried along at a great rate on his stretcher, borne by eight men. Jack's two, hastening behind, were less careful than they might have been to spare him pain. When they approached one another too closely, Jack's body was bent instead of flat. This was distressing, but must be borne, because he had been rash enough to promise Major Tom that he would remain with him. If only this were allowed.

At all costs, thought Jack, I must live and recover my health. Something had struck him violently behind the ribs. At the time, he had suffered little. His howls had been for Major Tom, whom he believed to be drowning.

They reached yesterday's front line, now behind captured pill-boxes where another regiment had been ensconced. The Dublins had been relieved. The West Yorkshire's M.O. looked Tom over. 'I won't disturb him,' he said. 'Get him back to the main dressing station quick as you can.'

Shortly after this, they reached a settlement of huts and tents, and Jack thought he heard his friend Willie's voice. Major Tom was taken into the largest hut, and Jack, in his blanket, laid down outside. At once, he tried to scramble after his master. The door was shut. Jack howled.

Colonel Jim came out of the hut and consulted with some other men. He said, 'See to Jack, O'Hara; the Major's asking for him. Clean him up as best you can.' And yes, there was his friend Willie, his face ashen; a mule driver called Mahony with a bandaged head, and Timmy Coote. They took Jack to a hut, washed him all over, and called on all the saints to witness that it was a miracle he was alive. A bullet had passed right through Jack's body, and he would probably carry a small scar on either side for the rest of his life. His back was not broken, nor yet his legs. He was bruised, he had suffered, but there was nothing to show but two small holes which with luck would heal in a few days. It was shock and exhaustion which had left him too weak to stand.

Only four months earlier, Jack had been stitched up by an eminent surgeon. Now, his eager friends swabbed his wounds with brown stinging fluid, and Willie, groggy after his bout of dysentery, held him and crooned to him while, like Major Tom, Jack received his anti-tet.

Then, as he was still too weak to walk, burly Tim Coote carried Jack in his arms into the hut where his master lay. Tom was naked; he had just been washed. His body, so stalwart when he and Colonel Jim had bathed Jack, had grown wretchedly thin. The pale skin was stretched over ribs, collar-bones and hips. One side, from chest to groin, was covered with a dressing. There were smells which reminded Jack of his own first wound.

'I have kept my word, but I am, as you see, subject to the whims of my friends.'

Captain Wills, R.A.M.C., covered Major Tom with a sheet. 'Here's your dog come to see you,' he said, in the tones of one who humours a small child. Tim carried Jack to the stretcher, and Tom's eyes opened but did not focus. He whispered Jack's name, also that of the person who no longer wrote to him. She who had caused him so much grief that he had become intoxicated.

Timmy took Jack to an outer room and left him there. He heard the man who tended his master speak of the ambulance which would take him to the casualty clearing station soon.

'Don't really like moving him,' said the doctor, 'but we haven't the facilities here. There'll be a fresh lot in before long.'

'Jack had better travel with Major Daly,' said Colonel Jim.

'I cannot send a dog in an ambulance, sir!' Captain Wills was horrified.

Colonel Jim's voice was like ice. 'I said, send him. Every

time he comes round, Major Daly asks for Jack.' He patted Jack as he left. 'Get well as soon as you can, boy.'

'My Colonel, you are a man of discernment. I am deeply indebted to you.'

A new batch of wounded started to stream in shortly afterwards. The Germans were counter-attacking. Fleets of ambulances, both motor and horse-drawn came and went. Major Tom's, like the others, was packed. Willie O'Hara, still on the sick list, travelled with Jack lying under his bent knees, joggling on the hard floor. It was a dreadful journey of many miles, rocking and plunging over the uneven surface. The men cried out in pain, and some called for their mothers. Major Tom did not cry out, but talked of Ireland, and shooting rabbits, and one called Celia and many other things. Several times, he called Jack's name, and Willie said, 'He's here, sir.'

'I am here but unable to rise. When will we be released from this devilish conveyance?'

The casualty clearing station was twelve miles behind the lines, but there, Tom was put to bed with moderately clean linen and a man to look after him, in a long room, crammed with beds and stretchers. Jack and Willie waited in a little outer room, a scullery. Jack watched Willie with anxious eyes.

'Shall I be permitted to visit my master, friend?'

'Ah, don't whine, Jack. Be easy, will you? We have to wait and see what way the cat jumps.'

'The jumping of cats is a matter of indifference to me. I am concerned only with my master's welfare.'

'Poor Jack. Is your side hurting you?'

Even friends could be obtuse, thought Jack. Nobody came, so Willie settled down philosophically to sleep on the floor. Jack sighed and did the same.

During the night, a worried young doctor came to them and awakened Willie. 'Will you bring the dog in for a minute? Major Daly won't settle down, and I think seeing his dog will help.'

Jack passed by many men laid in rows as he made his way stiffly and slowly to his master's side. Major Tom was reciting in a low voice. Jack had known him to do this before when nobody was there to hear. Willie appeared ashamed when he heard him. 'Here's Jack, sir. Got a bullet clean through him and back on his feet already.'

Tom rolled his head sideways. His eyes were staring. '"Then I entered into the Valley of the Shadow of Death,"' he said, '"And had no light for almost half way through it. I thought I should have been killed there, and the sun rose, and I went through that which was behind with far more ease and quiet."'

'Yes sir. Here's Jack, come to see you.'

'That patient's had a blood transfusion,' said the man in the next bed. 'Takes them all sorts of ways.'

'Did you wish to see me? I cannot stand for long.'

Major Tom's blank eyes turned, and came to life. 'O'Hara.' The voice was stronger and perfectly clear. 'You haven't got that cow with you by any chance? Why Jack, old friend, I thought you were dead.'

'We had to leave the cow after us,' said Willie, 'but I'll get you some fresh milk if I have to go and catch another.'

Tom's eyes closed. 'Bless you both,' he said.

Afterwards, Tom remembered little about his week at the clearing station. Fairly quiet when he arrived, it was packed within a few hours with thousands of casualties. A hideous battle was raging. A boggy half mile had been gained in the face of a deadly fire from fanatical machine-gunners. The losses were frightful, and the newspaper headlines all claimed an important victory. Ambulances arrived with loads of wounded men in an endless procession. Hundreds were left on stretchers on the ground outside the buildings while the drivers returned for another load.

As they passed back from the field dressing stations, the casualties were classified. The obviously dying were left in peace. The walking wounded, which by this time meant any-one who could stand, were bound up, and passed back to base by train. There were several rooms in the building, which had been a farmhouse, and the lucky first arrivals were in beds. By night, the men lay so thick on the floor that there was hardly room to move between them.

The doctors worked all day and all night, operating on one man after another. Apart from surgery, methods of treatment were limited. Wounds were swabbed with iodine or peroxide; the slightly hurt were given aspirin, the others morphia. Every day, trains carried all those fit to travel and many who weren't to base hospitals. Some men died each day, others were sent back into the line. The last group included Willie.

In vain Willie pleaded first that he was still unfit, then that he was Tom's servant and might be of use. No, he was told. He must go back in the next lorry. Willie waylaid a young doctor, and asked him if Jack might be allowed to remain. 'The Major depends on him,' he said.

'No, sorry. Out of the question. Nobody here has time to bother with a dog. Take him back with you.' This meant to camp; the battalion was no longer in the line. Jack still had no collar. Willie had to tie a piece of bandage round his neck and lead him away.

Tom heard Willie's voice through the window. He hadn't seen Jack that day. There simply wasn't room to bring him past the stretchers. Tom called 'O'Hara!' and 'Jack!' There was no reply, and he heard the sound of a lorry starting up. He relapsed into a feverish doze, plagued by nightmares.

Later that day, Dr Gunning, an Irishman who had known Tom for some time, came to see him. He offered a cigarette, but Tom shook his head. Ted Gunning, clearly exhausted, sat down on Tom's bed. He lighted up, and drew deeply on the cigarette. 'I hear we're winning,' he said. 'Today's casualties all say the same thing. There's a hell of a lot of them though. You look better, Daly. We'll get you away to base soon.'

Tom wanted to talk to Gunning. Words were arranged in his brain, waiting to be said. Sensible remarks, but they came out muddled. He tried to explain, and talked earnestly for several minutes.

Gunning looked worriedly at him. 'What do you want, Daly? Try to tell me. Take it slowly.'

Oh God, what had he said? Something about Sigmund was it? Or Foster? As Tom struggled to make his lips form the words, he heard a commotion among the men lying nearest the door. Something was moving among the stretchers. A soldier cried out, 'It's a bleeding dog! Get off!'

Jack picked his way across to Tom's bed. A length of bandage was knotted round his neck and trailed behind him.

'It's Jack – I knew he'd come.'

'That's more like it.' Ted Gunning stood up and grinned down at Tom. 'I saw that dog being loaded into a lorry two hours ago.'

'Leave him here.'

'Sir, I will lie under the bed and disturb no one. Only permit me to stay.'

'Well, Daly, I can see we'll have to send Jack back to the base hospital with you. I wouldn't be you when Matron sees him.'

'Saved my life twice,' said Tom. 'Staying with me. He told me so.'

Gunning smiled indulgently. 'A couple of aspirins for you, Daly, and a night's rest. You'll be talking sense again in a day or two.'

CHAPTER FIFTEEN

Tom lived in a half-crazed dream, populated by ghosts. Occasionally, he came out of his phantom world and into another existence, in which he lay in bed while different ghosts, with busy hands and tired abstracted faces came and went.

Which was real? he wondered. He hoped it was the place of pale, busy ghosts. The other world was a nightmare place, where he found himself in a yard as deep as a well, with dark, towering walls. In the dream, it was always raining, and the walls dripped dismally. An endless, shuffling procession of men trudged round and round like weary prisoners. They were as pale as death itself, and their feet dragged. They made no sound at all, and there was no end to the line. Four abreast, with hanging heads and dangling arms; round and round.

And Tom would run from one to another, calling them by name, catching at a khaki sleeve, peering into a sightless face. Then, in panic, he would screw his eyes tightly shut – let them be gone when I look again – and at once he was sliding into a pit with slippery sides. Drowning. 'I'm drowning, I'm drowning!'

Tom shouted and yelled for help. Was he shouting? He couldn't hear himself, but his own shouts woke him up. He was soaked with sweat, icy cold. The ghosts of the second world were clustered round, he could hear them talking.

'I just can't get his temperature down.'

'When the fever leaves him, he'll either recover or die.'

'Watch out! He can hear us.'

'Not he. The poor devil's out for the count.'

Then a woman's voice – where had he heard it before? thought Tom.

'He seems quieter when Jack's here. I'm sure he hears a certain amount.'

Tom slipped into a more peaceful sleep, and dreamed that he was walking down a country road. There were fields on either side, golden stubble and autumn grass. Tom strolled along, his gun on his arm, his dog at his heels. The early morning sun warmed him, but there was a hint of frost in the air. He dangled his hand, and the dog pressed its broad black head against his palm.

'We will have rare sport, you and I.'

A talking dog? Another dream. Tom was bitterly disappointed. The dream faded and merged into another. He dreamed that Celia was looking down at him, and Sigmund and Dickie. He saw Harper's worried frown, and the Padre kneeling in the mud. He saw soldiers running, falling . . . getting up and running on. Tom couldn't run. His foot was caught in the barbed wire. He watched the silent nightmare ballet, and it grew dark and he was drowning . . .

Tom didn't remember being moved to the base hospital at Boulogne, and he didn't know how long he had been there. Incidents came and went in his mind like lantern slides. He remembered being carried past an artillery post whose guns were being moved forward. The gunners, stripped to the waist, dug the guns out of the holes where the platforms had been. The planks had sunk, and each recoil had buried the guns deeper, until aiming them became impossible. Dead horses all over the place, broken wagons and limbers, stranded and leaning at odd angles. Muddy shell cases. The picture faded and disappeared.

Tom knew in his heart that he was coming back to life. His lucid times were getting longer, his wounds were healing. Sometimes he felt almost normal, conscious of his surroundings, and understanding the doctor's words. He wondered what he said in his nightmares. Although some of his dreams terrified him nearly out of his wits, he was afraid to return to reality – it would hurt. It would be like putting hands numbed with cold into scalding water. He kept his eyes shut most of the time.

The dog came every day. The thin little V.A.D. who insisted

that she knew Tom and that she was Celia's sister, brought
the dog to see him. Tom wanted to tell her not to talk about
Celia. When this girl who said she was Laura Shane appeared,
Tom would pretend to be asleep. But his hand would stray to
the dog's head, and fondle its ears. It looked just like old Jack,
but Jack had been shot by a sniper – Tom had seen him fall.
Ghosts, thought Tom. Even the dog is a ghost.

The V.A.D. called Laura was a wonderful nurse. For a long
time, the voluntary helpers had been barred from all
but unskilled jobs. They had prepared dressings, held basins,
sterilized instruments and made beds. Some of the qualified
nurses resented them. The never-ending flood of casualties
changed all that, and those V.A.D.s who had a natural
aptitude for nursing did nothing else. Laura, with her cool
manner and deft fingers was the best of them all. She
never wasted a movement and was never in a hurry. Tom's
wakening mind told him that he knew her, that she was indeed Celia's sister, that she was doing everything in her
power to help him. His instinct kept him in the half world
of his imaginings.

Few patients were kept in the hospital for long. The new
man in the bed beside Tom's was a Scot. He was so tall that
his legs had to be propped up with pillows under the knees,
otherwise his feet would have been out of bed. He tried to talk
to Tom, but soon gave it up. Donald was not going to recover
and he knew it.

Before lights out, the V.A.D.s went round with Bengers'
Food. Tom thought it was disgusting, but was too tired to resist
being fed with it. Donald refused to take the food when Laura
brought it to him. The following night, the staff nurse on her
rounds caught Laura trying to coax Donald to eat his Bengers'.
'It's foul, I know, but please try a sip. Just a little, come on
now.'

The nurse decided to show this soft young woman how to
deal with a stubborn patient. She forced the cooling beverage
into Donald's mouth, spoonful by spoonful.

Tom lay and watched. 'It's too late. Leave him alone, you
heartless little cow – can't you see he's dying?' Did I really say
that? thought Tom. Apparently not; the girl was spooning the

last of the food into the slack mouth, a satisfied smile on her face.

Donald died that night. Tom woke, moaning with fear – drowning. Two orderlies were taking Donald away, and Laura Shane was making up the empty bed. A patient waited on a stretcher to be lifted into it.

Laura Shane – of course it was Laura! Something had changed, had slipped into place like a lock engaging. Tom was cool and rested. His fears receded. 'It's Laura, isn't it?' he said weakly.

Laura spun round. 'Why Tom, you've come back!' she exclaimed.

'Have I been away?'

'Goodness knows where you've been. You were brought in delirious a week ago, and you've been delirious ever since. Except when we brought your dog into the ward – you seemed to know Jack.'

'Laura, I do believe I'm going to be all right. I thought I was going mad, but perhaps I'm not.'

'Of course you're not.' Laura finished making the bed, and the waiting orderlies lifted an unconscious man into it. 'I must see to this patient,' she said. 'We'll talk when I get the chance.'

Tom watched her, trying to concentrate. The smell of lysol was so strong it made his nose tickle. It helped to mask other smells.

Laura had not undressed for two days and three nights. She felt horrible. Autumn was turning to winter and still the third battle of Ypres dragged on. Still the wreckage of the war passed along the line from battlefield to dressing station to hospital. Most of those who survived a week in Boulogne were shipped to England. It was not a place for prolonged treatment. With casualties coming back at a rate of thousands every day, many by-passed the hospitals on French soil, and were sent straight to England, still in their filthy uniforms and field dressings. There was a limit to the number of men that could be dealt with on the spot.

Unlike many girls of her background, Laura was without squeamishness. No patient ever saw her recoil in horror at the sight of his wounds. She prepared men for surgery, efficiently. She was in demand in the operating theatre, and reticent about what she saw there.

Laura reported that Major Daly's temperature was almost normal, and that he was talking rationally. She had no time to talk to him again until late the following day, and by then he was a new man, propped on his pillows, smoking a cigarette and asking for news of the front.

Laura had asked an orderly to bring in the dog that day, for his daily visit to his master. Jack was the regimental mascot and she wondered if it was the same dog that Celia had resented so much. Laura had thought him a dejected sort of animal. Now, he was like a different dog, grinning at Tom, thrashing his tail in delight, holding up a paw to be shaken.

She knew that Tom would soon be sent to England, now that his fever had gone. He was being treated for a duodenal ulcer, and she had attended an operation to remove splinters of bone from his side.

Tom called her, asking for water. She fetched it, and waited while he drank. She wondered how much Celia had told him about Tony Greer. She wondered how her sister – or any woman – could throw over Tom for Tony.

'When is Celia's wedding to be?' asked Tom carefully.

'I don't know – not for ages. They're a quarrelsome pair. They broke off their engagement once, and made it up again. Tom – I wish you two had made a go of it. I'm sure Celia's making a mistake. She's working at Posset Hall still, perhaps if you were to meet again . . .'

'I think we'd better not. I've no wish to meet Greer, and Celia made it clear that she'd changed her mind.'

'I don't believe those two will ever marry.'

'Possibly not. However, I'd much rather not meet either of them.'

'You'll be sent to London, Tom. Do you know anybody there? If not, what happens to Jack? I'm sure they won't keep him here. Could I make enquiries for you?'

'I don't know a soul in London – not unless Edith Briggs is still there. Celia may have mentioned her to you. Laura – I suppose you never heard anything of Michael?'

Laura's face altered in a subtle way. She answered quite cheerfully. 'I see every man who comes here, and ask everyone I see. No, there's nothing.'

The effort of talking was too much for Tom, Laura could see. She took his empty glass and went away.

Passchendaele had fallen — what there was left of it. Piles of rubble, and a slightly higher pile which was still referred to as the Church. A strongly held German fortified post had fallen, and the Allies had freed some of their own men, captured by the Germans, and employed as labourers and stretcher-bearers. These men were all sick, and the retreating Germans abandoned them, correctly judging that they had served their purpose.

The men were passed along with the current crop of wounded, but most of them died before they reached hospital. One who survived — just — was Mick McCoy, ex officer's servant.

After the battle of Messines, when a shell had demolished battalion headquarters, McCoy had wandered into the German lines in a state of shock. He had run out of the house before the second shell struck it, and the blast had knocked him out. When he had recovered his wits, he was in a German dugout. It was believed by some that he had told the kind German officer who spoke such good English everything he knew. Also that McCoy had things to tell which he had no business to know. Once he ceased to be useful, he had been treated with the contempt he deserved, and set to forced labour, digging latrines, until his health gave way.

In the British camp, rest and better food had restored him, and he was able to walk by the time he reached Boulogne. He plodded in a line of dirty, ragged men to the de-lousing station, waited his turn, drank a mug of ersatz coffee. Then, clean, shaved and dressed in hospital blue, he shuffled with half a dozen others across the hospital courtyard, to be labelled and classified. His hands shook, his head trembled, he was a mass of nervous jerks and twitches.

As the men made their slow way towards the main building, they met an orderly with a black dog. As they passed, the dog turned his head sharply. Then he stopped, growled deep in his throat, and lifted his lip.

'Ah, traitor, I had hoped you were dead.'

McCoy started away, trembling more than ever. 'It's Fritz, the Jerry dog. You hoor, I thought you were killed.' He shambled on. He would be discharged and sent home. His life, to all intents and purposes, was over.

Major Tom was out of bed. He was going to England for a further operation on his side, and for a long sick leave which would give his ulcer a chance to mend. He was promised, as if he might be pleased, that with any luck he would be back in the line soon after Christmas. He was travelling as walking wounded, and taking Jack with him.

Major Tom walked up and down outside, trying to get a little strength back into his legs. It was bitterly cold. Every few minutes, Tom was almost bent double by a cramp in his side. Jack walked with him, stopping when he stopped, going on when Tom did. When Tom sat down heavily on a bench groaning, and pressing both hands to his side, Jack gave him a reassuring nudge with his nose and padded away.

'Courage, my master. Be patient, and I will fetch one of the white-coated ones.' Jack knew where these persons were to be found, and he made haste to the place where tea was drunk at this hour. He stopped the first man he met, a medical orderly as it happened. Jack stood directly in his path.

'Sir, my master is in pain. He is unable to rise. Kindly come this way and assist him.'

'What are you doing out on your own, Jack?' asked the orderly. Jack now had the run of the place, and was known to all, though very few, thought Jack, were capable of interpreting even the simplest message. Jack stared at the man, whining, then set off in the direction from which he had come. The man followed grumbling. On their way, they met some sick men dressed in blue, and Jack recognized the lying servant who had kicked him. He growled in passing, but had no time to waste on traitors. Evidently, the man had received his just deserts.

Major Tom was still clutching his side, still deathly pale.

'You may see for yourself that my master needs assistance.' Jack hung about anxiously as the man helped his master to rise, and supported him back to the ward. Major Tom thanked him, and told him that he was leaving the hospital the following day.

The lady named Laura, she whose heart was broken, was coming along the passage. Jack observed immediately that great joy filled her. Her step was light, her eyes sparkled, she looked younger. She helped Major Tom to his bed, and Jack, escaping notice, remained close by. He was happy for Laura. She, above all others, had cared for his master. She worked hard and ceaselessly, although the light had gone from her life. What had happened? wondered Jack.

'Tom, he's a prisoner! Michael's a prisoner, I've just heard. Oh I think I shall burst! I want to dance, to sing at the top of my voice. Isn't it wonderful? Isn't it marvellous?'

Major Tom rejoiced with Laura; he told her of his delight that this Michael was alive, although a prisoner in German hands.

Jack was extremely perplexed. It appeared that this Michael had a second name which was St John. As if this were not sufficiently strange, he must needs pronounce it Sinjen. This had given rise to confusion, identity discs being lost, with a dead person whose name was Sinden and a missing person whose name was Michael John. Laura's voice was unsteady, she had difficulty in speaking plainly. 'I'm so happy!' she cried, and immediately began to weep.

For a precious moment Jack and Tom's eyes met, and they exchanged a private thought. A small and insignificant one, but a thought, nonetheless. Jack could have died with happiness. If I were a lady, I would weep, he said to himself. He left them to their talk, and trotted away to the kitchen.

Beautiful, delicious Bengers' Food. All that was uneaten was placed in a bowl with fragments of crust, the tails of fishes, and other choice morsels. Jack was popular in the kitchen.

Laura got some long overdue free time to see Tom and Jack off to England next day. Tom had never seen anyone so

transformed. She looked beautiful in her ugly cloak and bonnet; she shone with happiness.

'Laura, don't expect Michael to be the same, will you?'

'Of course he will be. Perhaps not for some time, but he's
the same person. I'm not worried.'

'Laura,' said Tom slowly, 'he won't be the same person. He
can't be. Are you the same person that said goodbye to him
over three years ago? I think you'll survive; you're strong,
and I've seen how you cope with wounded men, but you'll
need a lot of patience. And all your understanding.'

'Bless you, Tom, we'll be all right.' Laura looked at her
watch. 'You must go, and so must I. Goodbye,' she kissed him
lightly. 'Goodbye Jack.'

Laura returned to the hospital feeling pleased and guilty by
turns. How cross Tom was going to be, she thought. He'd think
she'd been match-making as well as interfering when Edith
Briggs met his train. Never mind. Michael was alive, everything was going to be all right.

Tom climbed slowly onto the train. Jack was wearing his best
tunic, and it got him past every barrier. The only questions
asked were about his medal ribbons and corporal's stripes.

Jack had not been at sea since puppyhood, when he had
not liked this form of travel. The boat was packed with
stretchers, and those like Major Tom who were dressed and
able to walk, were crammed into a small saloon. One man
died during the crossing. Jack, making himself small in the
restricted space, remembered crossing the North Sea with Axel
and Hansel. How, he asked himself, can I go for an evening
stroll while travelling? What shall I do? His relief was profound
when the journey ended within two hours, and he and his
master made their way to a waiting train.

Jack feared that his master, whose steps were unsteady,
would lose consciousness; that he would fall to the ground
and be trampled underfoot. He willed his master to have
courage and patience, but his thoughts did not again cross the
frontiers of Major Tom's mind. Luckily, this journey too was
a short one. The train clanked, hissing, into a great glass-roofed
building, and many women and children ran to the doors, and

waited in great anxiety as the wounded men were carried out. Major Tom stepped carefully down onto the platform. Jack jumped down, and looked about him. Perhaps the person called Celia would be there, begging to be forgiven. Someone was hurrying towards them. She was small in stature, with tiny feet in laced black shoes with high heels. There was something familiar . . . Jack looked up at the face, framed with soft, wavy, fair hair. Was it – after all these years – could it be the beautiful, the exquisite Miss Briggs?

The lady bent down to pat him and to admire his tunic, because she wished to conceal from Major Tom that she loved and desired him. She had blushed a deep pink. 'You don't remember me, Jack.'

'Indeed, Fräulein, you are mistaken. I remember you with great clarity. I owe my life to you, as my master owes his to me.'

Jack was disappointed to discover that his master was going to yet another hospital. He had supposed that Miss Briggs had come to take both of them to her residence, where they would all three live in peace and harmony. However, his heart rose as they bade one another farewell in the huge sooty building where Tom was to stay. Jack heard Major Tom say that he looked forward to seeing Miss Briggs the following day, and he thanked her for offering to take care of Jack. Miss Briggs clipped a lead to the cut down leather belt that Jack wore round his neck by way of a collar.

'Will you come with me, Jack? You can't stay here, you know.'

'Willingly, Fräulein. I begin to perceive a bright future for all of us.'

Tom settled into his narrow bed, and slept like a baby. No dreams troubled him. He had been annoyed to find that Laura had taken it upon herself to let Edith Briggs know when he was arriving; now he was glad of it. Edith was an undemanding person, he thought, and Jack had gone off with her without a backward glance. Tom woke with a pleasant feeling of anticipation. Edith was coming in the afternoon. She was still doing voluntary work, living with a married sister in

Blackheath. She could work hours to suit herself, and take a holiday if she wanted to.

So, for a whole month, Edith and Jack went to see Tom every day. Tom had his operation, and was discharged after a short recurrence of his fever. Only once to his knowledge did Edith see him surface from one of his nightmares. She was holding his hand in both of hers, and he found this pleasant and reassuring.

Tom was not passed fit, due to the ulcer which continued to give him bouts of violent pain, so he went to visit his mother in Ireland, and also Dick Bellamy's mother. He came back to London, where he had left Jack in Edith's care, depressed and unwell.

Winter passed and spring came. Tom was passed fit, but not for active service. He was sent to base at Borden, Surrey, and from there to a camp where he took an officers' training course. Every week, batches of cadets left the camp, and Tom, knowing what was in store for them, grew even more depressed.

Late in March, news came of the German offensive in Flanders, and Tom read in stunned horror of the Allied retreats all along the front. Of all the ground, so painfully won, inch by bloody inch, overrun by the Germans in a last, all out effort to win the war. The remains of Passchendaele fell, Wytschaete, Kemmel, Bailleul and Armentières. On Good Friday, the Paris Gun killed eighty-eight people attending Mass in Paris, and wounded many more. Every day the giant gun claimed a few more victims in the city.

Edith had taken Jack home to Devonshire with her at Easter. She took him for country walks, and was amused by his sudden interest in a flock of sheep. Almost as if he were a collie, thought Edith, as Jack crouched low, eyeing the white woolly creatures. He glanced at Edith hopefully. 'No, you silly old dog; leave them alone or the farmer will be cross.' Jack sighed heavily as he turned away.

Two months later, Edith took Jack up to London, and handed him over to Tom. They were going back to the front together.

Tom had been shopping at Garrards. For Jack, he had bought a silver collar, whose heavy links were joined by a plate on which was engraved – CORPORAL JACK.

For Edith, he had bought a string of cultured pearls and a box of crystallized fruits. He had tried to get marrons glacées, but they were unobtainable.

Edith blushed painfully as Tom fastened the pearls round her neck.

'You shouldn't have . . .' she murmured.

'Yes I should. You've been wonderful, Edith. I really don't know what would have become of me without your help. You're a treasure.'

Jack was suitably impressed by the valuable collar presented to him by his master. He attempted to lick Major Tom's face as he adjusted the fastening.

It had not been lost on Jack that his master had also presented Miss Briggs with a collar. His hopes had risen, but now everything was going wrong. Miss Briggs had confided in Jack, many times. Even had she not done so, he would have known her wishes. Miss Briggs yearned for Major Tom with all her heart. She hoped fervently that he would ask her to marry him, so that she could remain with him always. She wished to produce offspring.

Jack climbed sadly on board the train, and witnessed his master's farewells. Major Tom seemed unaware of Miss Briggs's devotion. He grasped her hand, thanked her many times for all she had done, removed his cap and kissed her on the cheek.

Jack in his annoyance could almost have bitten him. 'My master, you are a fool. The beautiful, the desirable Miss Briggs wishes to stay with you for ever, to feed you and care for you and give you children. Now you are about to return to the war, and it is possible that you will be killed. It will then be too late. If I who am only a dog can perceive this, how much more easily should an educated person be able to discern it.'

Jack sulked throughout the journey.

CHAPTER SIXTEEN

When Tom rejoined his battalion in June, battles were raging east of Arras, only a mile or two from the place where Jack had been captured more than a year before.

Jack, who had learned to sleep through most things, dozed on the floor of the railway compartment, his body joggling with the movement of the train, his head resting on Tom's foot. He had forgiven his master for his rejection of Miss Briggs.

Tom stared gloomily through the dust-caked window at the flat fields of northern France; the fertile farmland, the mills and slagheaps. He was utterly disheartened and depression hung over him like a fog. There were eight newly joined subalterns crammed into the carriage with him, and a young captain who had lost an eye, and two fingers from his left hand. Tom pretended to read a paper. He didn't feel like talking.

When he had been wounded, Tom's unit had been attacking. Ground *was* being gained, even though the attack was a weary crawl across open ground in atrocious conditions. The Germans, on higher ground, had sat tight in their concrete pill-boxes until they were forced to abandon them. Now, Tom was returning to an army in retreat, camped among the apple orchards near the pretty village of St Martin Eglise. The tide was on the turn now, the German advance almost halted, but the Allied forces were far behind the Messines Ridge. All their precious ground was lost, and with it, thousands of lives.

During the ten months of Tom's absence, the Old Toughs had at one time been reduced to forty-seven men. They had then been amalgamated with the first battalion, the 'Bluecaps'. Tom found few familiar faces left.

Jim Harper had visited Tom during his own home leave early in the year, so his almost white hair came as no surprise to Tom. Willie O'Hara looked even more bent and frail than before. Jack's boisterous welcome almost knocked him over. The light work of a batman was all that he could manage.

Shortly afterwards, the battalion was moved up to familiar billets, the Doncaster huts at Locre, before going back in to the line.

Jim Harper and Tom strolled about the camp, talking about the campaign, the retreat, the likelihood that the German advance had ended. Jack walked with them. His silver collar, polished by Willie, glinted in the sun. Like Jim, he was going grey, but he had never looked fitter.

'I'm glad you sent Jack home with me,' said Tom. 'He'd have been lucky to survive the rest of the campaign.'

'I agree. Daly, do you remember the sports day last year? When Jack was promoted?'

'I certainly do,' said Tom glumly. 'I'm not likely to forget that day.'

'Oh lord, yes. Sorry. I'd forgotten that was such a bad day for you personally. I've arranged to hold the sports on Saturday, instead of waiting until August. We might not get the opportunity then, and they do cheer the men up.'

'Good idea.' Tom spoke with a total lack of enthusiasm. He still felt unwell.

'I think Jack ought to have a medal. What do you say?'

Tom stared. 'Certainly he ought – an excellent idea. But we can't decorate him officially, can we? The men hung an Iron Cross round his neck once, but I made them take it off.'

Jim laughed. 'No, this will have to be entirely unofficial. I've saved one of the sports medals for him – the swimming prize, we can't give that here – I've had it slightly altered. O'Hara saw to it, but I must admit that I wrote the citation. Here –' He took a flat box out of his pocket and a folded sheet of paper. The medal, in its velvet lined case, was silver. It was mounted on regimental tie ribbon from Tyson's in Grafton Street, Dublin. Narrow strips of emerald divided broader ones of dark blue and dark red. The silver tiger, emblem of the Old

Toughs, stalked with raised forepaw in a circle engraved with the name and motto of the regiment. The clasp on the ribbon which should have read, "Best swimmer. 1918", now read: "Arras. Messines. Ypres."

'What about that?' said Jim.

'Perfect.'

'I've written a short account of your rescue, and of Jack carrying you the message at Frezenberg. I've praised his steadiness under fire, his gallantry, patriotism and devotion to duty —'

'Patriotism?' asked Tom.

'It's usually mentioned,' said Jim.

'All right, but what will the high-ups say? I feel there might be objections to decorating a dog, however patriotic.'

'Damn it, Daly; it isn't the V.C., and this isn't Buckingham Palace. Probably it would be wise to get our most junior officer to read the citation and pin on the medal, then it will pass as a harmless joke if anyone makes a fuss.'

So Corporal Jack was decorated, to the sound of tumultuous applause. Few men there remembered the day when Jack had been found in the trench near Festubert. Willie O'Hara, the last of the Indestructables, proudly held his lead, while Second Lieutenant McManus pinned the medal to the dog's tunic.

The sports were brought to an abrupt end by the Germans, who opened fire with long-range guns that evening. The battalion had to dig in, the huts had not been designed as protection against shells. Willie chiselled out a funk-hole for himself, and as Tom was on the telephone, trying to find out if the Germans were advancing or merely being a nuisance, Jack wedged himself in beside Willie.

It had been a hot July day. The battalion was due to go to Dieppe two days later. The men knew this, and were looking forward to the treat. They hoped desperately that nothing would prevent it. Nothing did. They all marched away on Monday, except for Willie and Jack.

Willie was wearing his cap. His helmet was in his hut, a hundred yards away. Jack snuggled against his friend in the dusty, scooped-out hollow. Two soldiers were burrowing like moles in the open. 'Fair in the middle of the playing field,' muttered Willie. 'Don't know what Sergeant'll say.' Most of the shells landed among the broken stumps in a nearby wood.

Willie cautiously looked out, and ducked again. Jack squeezed himself closer than ever to his friend's side. The blast lifted them both in the air and dropped them again. As the noise hit them, the summer sky was darkened by smoke and fumes. Shrapnel rained down. The splinter was no bigger than a safety-razor blade. It took the top off Willie's ear as cleanly as any razor, pierced Jack's new medal-ribbon, and pinned his tunic to his shoulder.

Jack was as much surprised as hurt. He found he couldn't move his left foreleg, and Willie's ear poured with blood. 'My friend, there is a piece of metal in my shoulder. Pray remove it so that I may fetch help for you.'

If Willie understood, he made no effort to obey. He combed the blood-soaked dust with his fingers, swearing.

There were no more shells. Mr McManus, he who had pinned on Jack's medal, came running with the white cloth off the table where the prizes had been displayed. This he wound expertly round Willie's head, ignoring his curses. Turbaned like one of the Indian warriors whom Jack had observed on other occasions, Willie turned his attention to Jack.

'The bastards. They got Jack again. Look, sir!' Willie drew out the piece of metal from Jack's shoulder, being careful not to break it. Most of the blood that stained Jack's best tunic came from his friend. 'You'd think my throat was cut to see it,' raged Willie, 'And I can't find the top of my ear for a souvenir – I've looked all over. And how in hell will I ever get Jack's tunic clean?'

The M.O. bound up Willie's head and also attended to Jack. The cut was deep enough to be very painful once the shock had worn off. Willie held Jack's muzzle, while the M.O. cleaned the wound, and put one stitch in it.

'Let go of my nose, friend. I know better than to bite the doctor.'

Willie was kept at the dressing station overnight, so he and Jack missed their trip to the seaside.

Jack's shoulder hurt. His friend's severed ear bled, and could not be staunched. His master was elsewhere. Even a meal of eggs and chips and a large bowl of cold tea failed to cheer Jack.

Why were they there? he wondered. He had heard the men singing, 'We're here because we're here because we're here because we're here,' to a tune beloved of the skirted soldiers. Did this make sense?

Jack slept in the store that night. His shoulder stiffened up, and he was unable to account for two rats which sneered at him from a safe distance. He killed a young one which pushed its luck too far, and laid it on a flour bag where he hoped the quartermaster would notice it.

The night passed slowly, and Jack, kept awake by his aching shoulder, wondered whether his master had returned to Miss Briggs, whether his friend Willie had been taken away permanently, and above all, what sort of men could use a cannon to hurt Willie and himself. Not men like Kurt or Hansel, surely?

Jack remembered a black day a year before, when he and Major Tom had been disturbed by the cries of another dog.

'Au secours! Au secours!'

That morning, he had gone with his master to a farm where the dog, the only animal left behind, was tied on a chain. She had no food, and an empty water bucket lay on its side out of reach. Major Tom tried to release her, but she threatened him with her master's vengeance, and with slashing teeth barred his approach. She called him species of pig, despoiler of the poor and other epithets. Major Tom drew his small gun, and shot her dead, having first ordered Jack to remain out of sight. As if that made any difference!

Whatever his master did must be right, thought Jack. He had tried to forget the incident. What was right? What was wrong? He didn't know. What could be the object of this war? Would it ever end? Were the combatants like those dogs trained to fight, which would never cease the battle until one or the other lay dead?

Jack sighed. He could have done with a drink of water. All that tea in wooden boxes. He could smell it, but it was of no use to him. He slept fitfully until morning.

*

The final advance was getting under way, and it was to continue until winter. Tom, returning from Dieppe, found Willie at work with a bandage round his head; Jack limping beside him with a shaved patch on his shoulder where he had been stitched. He ordered Willie to keep himself and Jack under cover and out of trouble. 'I never want to see either of you in action again,' he said. 'Stick to cooking and cleaning, O'Hara, and keep Jack with you.'

'Indeed, there's nothing I'd like better, sir.'

The battalion was in and out of the front line right through the rest of the summer and the autumn. In October, they broke through the main defences, and advanced across unfortified ground. Sometimes there were fierce battles for bridges and fords, mainly due to the fanatical courage of the machine-gunners left behind to cover the German retreat. The Germans, fighting their bitter rearguard actions, never broke through the Allied lines, so Willie and Jack were left in peace.

One late October day, Tom was having a meal with Jim Harper at their billet in Maretz. The regiment had suffered heavy losses at the battle of the Selle, and all the second lieutenants were either wounded or missing.

'It'll soon be over,' said Tom.

'We told each other the same thing in 1914. However, I think you're right this time.' Jim put a saucer of cold tea on the floor for Jack. 'Wonder how old he is,' he said.

'Getting on. The grey's spreading up his face. Getting on for retiring age, aren't you, Jack?'

'I shall retire when you do; no sooner.'

The battalion was in action up to the end of the war, and fought right through the first week of November. Brian Bowles led an attack to take high ground overlooking the Sambre Canal. He was badly wounded, and McManus was killed. Jim's mood became more sombre with every day, although the newspapers screamed success, and the advances were measured in miles rather in yards. Their last action was on November 8th, losing an officer and four men killed, while three officers and fourteen men were wounded. Two days later they crossed the French frontier, and the next day the war was over, almost where it had started, four years before.

Jim Harper read the announcement to the assembled men. The band played. There was some cheering, led by the newest reinforcements. Jack wore his best tunic and his medals.

Afterwards, the men returned to their normal duties. They were in camp outside a village on the Belgian border. There was a profound sense of anti-climax. Some of the men fell asleep; some wept. There were others who flatly refused to believe the news. The remaining regular soldiers were less than the strength of one company, although they were all that remained of two battalions. 'What will they do with us now?' wondered the others.

There was a service of thanksgiving on Sunday in the château grounds at Dourlers. Jack attended it – he was used to church parades. He was unable to identify the strange feeling in the air. If in truth, the killing was at an end, all should have been joy, dancing and singing. Here instead he sensed indifference, disbelief, worry.

'How much longer have you got in the army, O'Hara?' asked Tom.

'Four years, sir. Hope they won't be anything like the last four.'

In the New Year, Tom was put in charge of an officers' training camp in England. He asked whether he might take O'Hara as batman, and whether Jack might accompany them. 'Jack's too old for service overseas,' Tom said when he heard that the second battalion had been posted to Constantinople.

Accordingly, all three went to live in a comfortable little house in a Yorkshire market town.

Tom's health was still a problem. He would be leaving the army in 1922 when the Irish regiments were to be disbanded. Although outwardly he appeared healthy, and he enjoyed hunting with the Zetland and Bedale hounds, he would never be one hundred per cent fit.

Tom asked Willie if he would like a permanent job as manservant in Ireland. 'I've a country house in Co. Galway,' he said, 'with plenty of room for you and your wife; or if you prefer, you could live in the gate lodge.'

'Leave Dublin, sir? I couldn't do that. Not after all the years in foreign parts. And the Missis was never in the country – I doubt she'd settle there. I'm grateful for the offer, sir, but indeed we wouldn't like it, thank you all the same.'

'What will you do in Dublin?'

'There's always work for a tailor, sir. I'll make out. I don't deny I'll miss yourself and Jack though.' It had been agreed that Jack should end his days with Tom in Ireland.

Tom wondered whether, after all, he was really looking forward to settling down at Liscullen. It was his old home, the place where he had been happiest. Since his mother's remarriage, it had been looked after by caretakers. It would be a lonely homecoming. He clicked his fingers at Jack, stretched on the hearth, but got no response. Poor old dog, he was getting deaf. Life, Tom thought, didn't hold much for either of them.

June 1922

By early June 1922, the disbandment of the Irish regiments was almost complete. Each one had been reduced to four officers, twenty non-commissioned officers, clerks, batmen, mess staff and thirty privates. It had been announced that, on June 12th at Windsor Castle, King George V would take the colours of the disbanded regiments into safe-keeping.

The second battalion, Royal Dublin Fusiliers, had arrived at base in Bordon, led by its senior officers on horseback. Major Thomas Daly, who was retiring from the service for reasons of health, was accompanied by the dog known as Corporal Jack. This dog had been the battalion's mascot since April 1917.

At Windsor, the colour parties entered the castle, escorted by the band of the Grenadier Guards. The Royal Dublin Fusiliers were the last of the five regiments to enter, the others being the Royal Irish Regiment, the Connaught Rangers, the Prince of Wales' Leinster Regiment, and the Royal Munster Fusiliers.

The King had written a farewell letter to each of the five regiments, and these were read aloud by an equerry to the detachments drawn up outside the castle. When it was the turn of the Royal Dublin Fusiliers, the flat official voice read '. . . you are the oldest of the British garrisons in India. Your second battalion dates back to the time when Queen Catherine of Braganza brought Bombay as part of her dowry to Charles II . . . to me it is a very mournful task to bid you farewell . . .'

The colour parties emerged from the castle, the band played Auld Lang Syne, and the Royal Dublin Fusiliers ceased to exist.

*

Jim Harper, back from Constantinople, attended the reception at Windsor with his wife, Althea. They were talking to Brian Bowles, who had recovered from his wound of just before the Armistice, and had been transferred to an English regiment. 'This is a sad affair – I wish it was over,' said Brian.

'So do I.' Jim looked round at the other guests. 'There aren't many people left that I know,' he said.

'Major Daly's here, with old Jack – over there, in the corner on his own.' Brian, tall enough to see over most people's heads, looked towards a distant part of the long hall.

'I'd like to talk to him if I can get through this crowd,' said Jim. 'I haven't seen him since the war, and I'm not much of a hand at writing letters. He's never married, has he?'

'No. I think he sees Laura St John quite a bit, but I don't know if they'll make a match of it.'

'Laura? I've been away so long. I thought she'd married her Michael, and they were happy as larks.'

'They were. But Michael was in poor shape when he got back. His health broke down and he died – oh, it must be a year ago. Laura's taken up professional nursing in London.'

'Poor Laura; I'd no idea,' said Althea. 'She never seems to have any luck, and she's worth ten of the sister.'

'Good lord, yes.' Brian laughed. 'Daly had a lucky escape there. Funny really; he was worried sick because he thought Celia'd be scrubbing floors to support Greer, and now I suppose they're rolling in money.'

'Yes,' said Jim. 'Even in Turkey, we heard about the Greer detonator. I daresay there isn't a coalmine anywhere that doesn't use them.'

'I don't think Greer had industry in mind,' said Brian. 'I think he was preparing for a second world war.'

Jim shuddered. 'Don't. I always thought he was a little mad.'

All three made their way through the crowd towards Tom.

Tom wished he could have made an excuse and avoided the reception. He would probably have done so, had Jack not been invited with him. Willie O'Hara had gone home to Dublin, and the old dog, both his hearing and his sight failing, would have been bewildered and unhappy in the charge of someone else.

Tom was thin, and his brown hair was sprinkled with grey, but he had lost the haunted look of four years earlier. A stranger might have taken him for older than his years, but there was no other outward sign of his experiences.

Tom wasn't mixing with the crowd. He gazed up at the carved decoration on the wooden panelling, and thought about Jack. What a shame that the dog had already been past his youth when he was captured. He and Tom could have shared years of retirement. For a long time, Jack had meant more to Tom than any human being.

Tom hadn't wanted to meet Laura again – he'd felt he couldn't cope with more despair and loss, even someone else's. Impossible though, to send a letter of sympathy and leave it at that. Now, their occasional dinners together were an important part of his life, looked forward to for weeks ahead.

Poor Michael. Poor unlucky devil, finding a woman like Laura, and sharing only four years with her. Bloody shame, thought Tom.

Jack sighed. He did not care for this draughty, crowded hall. There was sadness in the air, and his master's sadness was evident. Tea was dispensed in large quantities, but none had as yet been offered to Jack.

Many people spoke to him. 'So this is Corporal Jack.' That was what they said, so far as he could tell. He was getting deaf. In addition to his other decorations, Jack wore the Great War and Victory medals, an extra wound stripe, and two Flanders' poppies on his best tunic.

A stooping man with sparse white hair was approaching, accompanied by a lady. Colonel Jim! Jack bared his yellowed teeth in a grin as he recognized his master's old friend, and received a pat on the head, and kind words.

The lady, who was of middle years, shook Major Tom's hand, and stroked Jack's head. 'So this is Corporal Jack.' She bent low, Jack could hear her words.

'That is correct; but I have now retired.'

The lady was speaking to Major Tom. 'I've always wanted to see him; may I give him a scone? There, you like that, don't you? He must be getting near the end of the road, poor old boy.'

'I have seen thirteen summers, Madam, and hope to see one or two more.' Jack was tired of standing, and of being admired. He wondered when they were going home and what was for supper. He wished his master had taken his advice about Miss Briggs. Jack would not always be there to take care of him. Perhaps the lady with the broken heart? Who knows? he thought. It is impossible to understand the working of a mind so different from one's own.

Jack yawned. He lay down, stiffly. He could feel the reassuring pressure of Major Tom's leg against his neck; he could smell his boot polish, and the clean scent of his hands. Sight and hearing might fail, but not the sense of smell. He could have found his master among a multitude.

Corporal Jack stretched out on his side, and slept.